THE IRON CHRONICLES

Book III: IRON LOTUS

Brad R. Cook

Second Edition

THE IRON CHRONICLES

Book III:

IRON LOTUS

BRAD R. COOK

Second Edition

Book Cover
Designed by Brad R. Cook
Dragonship Illustration by Jennifer Stolzer
Border and other images from Pixabay.com

Interior
Dragonship, Vimana, Sparrowhawk, Milli-train, Iron
Horseman, and Black Knight illustrations by Jennifer
Stolzer
JenniferStolzer.com
Scrolls and frames from pixabay.com
Layout by Brad R. Cook

More of Jennifer's amazing Iron Chronicles art
at bradrcook.com

Iron Lotus, Book III of The Iron Chronicles
was originally published by
Treehouse Publishing Group in 2016

THE IRON CHRONICLES
BOOK III: IRON LOTUS
Second Edition
Brad R. Cook

Copyright 2022 © Brad R. Cook
All Rights Reserved

Published by
Broadsword Books L.L.C.

ISBN: 979-8-9865019-0-1

www.bradrcook.com
@bradrcook

For

My Family

"I am indebted to my father for living,
but to my teacher for living well."

Alexander the Great

Map of the IRON LOTUS Adventure

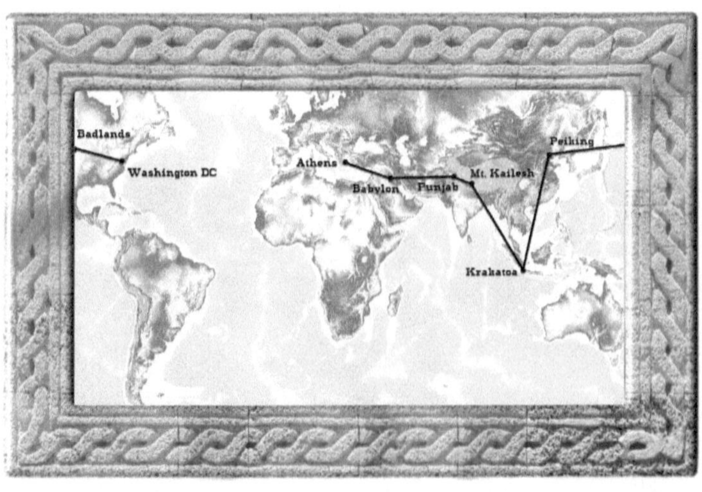

Athens 1883

Third time's a charm. At least that's what I hoped. We'd already chased the demonic Milli-train, after the battle in Zululand, from Cairo and then to Acre, and missed Genevieve and the Knights of the Golden Circle in both cities. Now gliding through the skies on the aero-dirigible, *Sparrowhawk*, we soared into Athens, Greece. I didn't know why Baron Kensington insisted on this city. We were across the Aegean Sea, and on the wrong side of the Ottoman Empire from where I thought the Milli-train would be scurrying around.

I stood on the bridge staring out one of the port windows. Before me lay sights I'd read about my whole life. Perched on the Acropolis, the white marble Parthenon gleamed in the fading sunlight. The ancient temple lay in ruin, but still captivated me with its beauty. Normally, I'd be thrilled to explore it, but Genevieve wasn't here to run through the ruins with me. The baron's daughter was gone. Captured by the Knights of the Golden Circle, held by her mother, a vicious assassin, and the vile

Colonel Hendrix. I'd sworn an oath to find her, but that had been weeks ago, and now, doubt ate away at my confidence. I feared we'd never see her again.

Captain Baldarich leaned one elbow on the arm of his chair and said, "Heinz, bring her about and settle in the airdocks."

"Aye, aye, Captain," the pilot said in his thick German accent as he pushed forward on the wheel.

Baron Kensington stepped onto the bridge and walked up behind the captain. "How long until we touchdown?"

"Not much longer now," the captain said as he spun around in his chair. "But are you really expecting to find anything here? Maybe we should be checking Istanbul instead."

"No, but we must stop none-the-less." The baron pounded his closed fist against the railing surrounding the captain's chair. "We *will* find that infernal monster."

"Will we?" I said under my breath, or so I thought. The entire bridge turned toward me and the lump in my throat dropped to my guts.

The baron gripped his cane. "I assure you; I will find the Milli-train."

"How hard is it to find a giant train with legs?" I spun on my heel, "We were supposed to catch them in Egypt, but they slipped past all the Templars. Then we were waiting for them in the Templar fortress in Acre only to find out they'd already passed us. Now we're here, and she's not!"

The baron's expression hardened. But the feeling of guilt which would normally have cooled my inner fire, faded.

The captain stood up and pointed at me. "Mr.

Knight here has a point. Even I assumed the Templar network would be able to track a giant demonic train walking across Africa."

"It is *my* wife and daughter on that train, remember." The baron inhaled deeply. "I, too, am frustrated, but certain matters here in Athens demand my attention."

I opened my mouth to speak, but the captain cut me off with a sharp look. "Shouldn't you be attending to your duties? Find Mr. Singh and get the *Sparrowhawk* prepped for landing."

I nodded, and forced my response to the baron back down my throat, "Aye, aye, Captain." With several quick steps, I rushed to the deck below. The blue-turbaned young man, Mr. Singh, directed the crewmen holding the thick ropes of the wingsails in place. Wooden yardarms stretched out each side of the aero-dirigible, and patched, white-canvas wingsails billowed in the strong wings. Both needed to be retracted before landing. As I walked up, Mr. Singh pointed to the lashings hanging on one of the inner walls.

"Mr. Knight, prepare to secure the wingsails." The young, bearded-Sikh, commanded the men with a stern tone. Only a year older than me, I considered him one of my closet friends. He was Boatswain of the *Sparrowhawk* and the greatest air-sailor I'd ever known, besides the captain, of course. As the aero-dirigible banked into its final landing position, Mr. Singh waited. He didn't check outside, but closed his eyes and felt when to act. "Prepare to tow the lines" he raised his hand, and the crew reaffirmed their grips on the thick, braided rope.

As ordered, I grabbed several thin ropes off the wall. A second crewman joined me; he took the starboard side of the aero-dirigible, and I stood by the port recess, which ran half the length of the airship. The wind whipped around me through the opening on the side of the hull, so I pulled the goggles hanging around my neck up over my eyes.

I'd served as a crewman on the *Sparrowhawk* for several weeks now. Each day was more tiring than my class work at Eton College, but far more thrilling. After the battle in Zululand, we'd had a number of repairs to make, and they all were accomplished in the air as we chased the Milli-train. I thought of Eton often, usually comparing my life there to my life on the *Sparrowhawk*. I'd given up the structured day of classes for the routine of airship duties, but unlike the noblemen's sons who had been my classmates and treated me like a lowly colonist, the crew of the *Sparrowhawk* had become family.

Ripped from my thoughts by Mr. Singh's gesture, I focused on my duties. As the crew pulled the thick lines hand over hand, I watched the yardarms swivel into the side of the airship. Like the sails of a Chinese Junk, the wingsails of the aero-dirigible had wooden struts running through them for greater stability. The struts lined up and the canvas folded between them as the wingsails retracted. Once settled inside the hull, Mr. Singh ordered the outer hatches closed. I sprang over the railing and lashed the sails together to prevent them from shifting or rattling. With a loud clank and thump, the mooring clamps secured the airship. The vessel lurched slightly as we stopped, but I remained standing having finally found my air-legs.

I finished my last sailor's knot, and climbed back over the railing. Mr. Singh sent the crewmen off and then waved me over.

"Alexander, please do not run off from the *Sparrowhawk* like in Acre."

"I won't," I said, "and I apologize, but I truly thought I saw Genevieve."

"I know." He gripped my shoulder. "We will find her. You must have faith."

I wanted to agree, but we were now on our second continent trying to find Genevieve. I leaned against the railing and exhaled, "With each day, she slips further away."

"She is strong, and I do not believe her mother wishes to hurt her. She had plenty of opportunity on the train. The baroness might be an assassin, but if she'd wanted to hurt Genevieve, she could have."

"I'll try to have faith, but I might be too cynical."

Mr. Singh laughed and walked toward the stairs. "At least you are an honest man."

I shuffled downstairs to the gun deck and entered my room at the bow of the airship. The storage room had served as my bedroom since Genevieve and I had snuck aboard two years ago, and the captain let me remain here instead of joining the crew on the deck above. I hadn't changed anything. The curtain Mr. Singh hung for Genevieve's privacy still split the room, and the coil of rope we'd used for Rodin's bed remained tucked up on the sloping front wall.

Since we'd come aboard, the little bronze dragon, about the size of an eagle, lay curled up inside his usual spot. Rodin lifted his head to acknowledge me, and I walked over to rub under his chin. "I miss her, too."

Swinging out the mechanized arm holding my hammock, I hooked it to a ring on the center beam, and climbed in. As my feet dangled over the sides, I kicked off my boots. Gone were the polished laced shoes, and stiff armored wool of my Eton College uniform. I'd traded them for khaki pants, a grey Henley, and my black vest. I still wore the leather strap that wound around my leg and torso. Holstered on my leg was my Thumper, which had never left my side since I'd joined the crew. I'd never felt more like myself, and yet, happiness without Genevieve came in fleeting moments quickly whisked away by the wind.

"I know I should go up to dinner," I said to Rodin, who'd flown over and curled up with me in my hammock. "I hope the captain won't be too upset." The dragon nudged his head under mine and nuzzled against my chin, poking me with his horns. I reached up and scratched his neck. "I thought we'd track her down before we got to Egypt, but Africa was far larger than I expected, and who knew the Milli-train would be so fast."

My heavy lids kept closing and snapping back open, and when I yawned Rodin did the same. I was glad no one had come down to scold me for not coming to dinner, and as the crew shuffled above preparing for bed, I stretched and relaxed. As I sank into oblivion, heavy boot steps on the gun deck made me pop up. I craned my neck as the captain entered with a plate of sausage and honey drizzled rolls.

"I thought I might find the two of you together." He set the plate down on a barrel, and swiped one of the three rolls. With a smile, he held up the honey drizzled delight. "My compensation for bringing you dinner."

Rodin sprang from the hammock, soared over, snatched the second roll, and flew to his bed. I rolled out of my hammock and grabbed the third before they all disappeared. I popped it in my mouth and swooned, savoring Gustav's delicious baked treat.

"I know you're upset," the captain said, finishing the roll. "But do I look like I'm giving up?"

"No," I mumbled with a mouth filled with bread. "I'm not giving up, either. I won't stop until I find Genevieve."

He chuckled, and clapped his hands. "Now that's the conviction I'm looking for."

I swallowed and sat on the hammock. "Then why waste our time on this side of the Aegean?"

"I don't know. We're here at the baron's request." The captain leaned closer. "He's as torn up as you. He—we all—truly thought we were going to catch them in Acre."

"When we were attacked, I thought we'd found the right place." I grabbed one of the sausages, bit off the end, and pointed the remainder at the captain. "But we missed them."

The captain crossed his arms. "That ambush was annoying, but you held your own. So, tell me, are you keeping up your training with Mr. Singh and Ignatius?"

"I am. Mr. Singh is teaching me saber, Ignatius, pistols, and Hunter's added distance shooting, too."

"Good." He pointed at me. "What about the books your father sent?"

I turned away but the captain's souring expression pulled me back. He raised an eyebrow. "I've read a few pages of the Greek philosophy book, but my duties on the ship—"

"Don't take all day," the captain finished. "I want you reading every day." He chuckled. "You might not be at Eton, but I'll not have you slacking on your studies on my watch."

"Aye, aye, Capt—" I doubled over and grabbed my stomach as it twisted in knots. It wasn't Gustav's cooking, but something far worse.

"Trouble?" The captain's face hardened as he flipped back his long, red leather coat and cranked a small box attached to his belt. Electricity crackled within. A thin-coiled cable ran to the lightning cannon holstered on his hip. "You're better than a trip wire with bells."

I nodded and pulled the Thumper from my belt. I opened the metal baton's breach and inserted a percussion cap. Captain Baldarich drew his lightning pistol as we heard a creaking sound coming from the gun deck. He stepped out first, Rodin landed on my shoulder and we followed.

One man in a long dark coat and bowler hat with brass goggles around the band, stood on the gun deck as a second climbed up through one of the hatches. A third disappeared up the stairs. They looked exactly like Hendrix's henchmen who had attacked my father and me at Eton. I wondered how many were already on board.

The captain fired, an arc of blue electricity zapping one henchman. The man slumped to the deck, his body twitching and blocking the hatch in the floor. The other henchman pivoted toward us and snarled. He lowered his pistol. I pressed the button of my Thumper. The piston on the metal baton roared forward and retracted. The concussive blast knocked the henchman into one of the cannons, and sent his gun skittering away.

Baldarich yelled, "Find the baron," as he ran over to the copper tube poking out of the ceiling. He cried, *"Kampfstationen!"*

Taking the stairs two at a time, I didn't stop at the mid deck even though I heard henchmen scuffling with the crew. I followed the captain's orders, and headed straight to the top deck. The baron's cabin sat next to captain's and the first thing I noticed when I approached was that the door lay slightly ajar. I paused. With my thumb, I slid open the breach of my Thumper. The spent percussion cap popped out and I caught it in my hand before it fell to the deck. Silently, I pulled another from the pouch secured to my leather strap and slipped it into place.

As glass shattered in the cabin, I rushed forward, smashing my foot against the door. The wooden door whipped open and bounced against the wall. Before me, the baron lay pinned to his bed struggling with a man swathed in black, his face covered by a long scarf trailing from a black turban. The assassin tightened his garrote around the baron's neck even as the baron twisted and kicked, trying to free himself, struggling to breathe as his face shifted through shades of blue.

This was no ordinary henchman, nor was it the assassin from last year who masqueraded as a Zulu warrior and terrorized Eton College. But I didn't wait to figure out who it might be. I raised my Thumper and pointed—but then hesitated—from this distance I might strike the baron. I ran toward the end of the bed and jumped. One foot landed on the footboard, the other on the soft mattress. With the Thumper raised above my head, I lunged toward the assailant and swung my weapon like a baton.

Before I could land my blow, the assassin flipped backward and landed on the headboard. The baron was free. Choking, gagging, and struggling to fill his lungs with air, the baron pulled off the knotted sash around his neck and flung it aside. He rolled off the bed grabbing at his cane and pistol hanging on a nearby chair.

The assassin's eyes, dark pupils so wide I couldn't see color, reacted with a warrior's intensity. He pulled two long, curved daggers from the black sash around his waist, and lunged at the baron. I aimed my Thumper and fired. The assassin twirled away from the blast and landed on the floor as the top of the head board exploded, sending shards of wood flying. The baron grabbed his pistol, knocking over the chair in the process, but was able to spin around and fire as I popped open the breach of my Thumper and loaded another cap. The assassin moved with an impossible grace and speed, twisting and contorting to avoid each bullet. Soaring through the door, Rodin roared and flapped wildly, shooting out a column of fire igniting the assassin's turban. A final concussive blast from my Thumper glanced across his left arm, and he slowed.

"Don't move!" the baron rasped; his pistol pointed at the man's heart. The assassin stared down the baron. I lowered my Thumper and stepped forward. The assassin whipped his hand into his sash, pulled out a dart, and in a single motion tossed it at the baron. I gaped as it struck the baron in the shoulder. The assassin launched himself through the porthole as smoothly as an eel slipping back into a dark den.

I rushed to the porthole, barely big enough for me to fit through, and expected to see him splattered on the ground below. But the assassin sprang off the moorings, grabbed a cable with his right hand, and slid to the ground.

I swirled around as the captain rushed into the room.

"Everyone all right?"

"The assassin slid down a cable to the docks!" I pointed out the window.

Baldarich hurried over and peered out. "He's already disappeared into the darkness."

The baron coughed, and in a raspy voice choked out, "I'm alive thanks to Alexander." He pulled the dart from his shoulder and set it on the nightstand.

"But what if that's poisoned?" I asked.

The baron opened a drawer, removed a glass vial, popped the cork and drank the contents. "Four Thieves Potion." He winked at me. "I never leave home without it."

I sighed with relief remembering that Eustache's medieval cure-all would prevent any poison from killing him. Rodin landed on my shoulder, but didn't take his eyes off the baron.

The henchmen have been rounded up," the captain said. "Looks like they were a distraction for the assassin."

BOOK III: IRON LOTUS

The tension shattered with the morning light. Captain Baldarich doubled the guard, and the Greek authorities even sent some troops to protect the docks. I lay in my hammock. Mr. Singh relieved me of duty because of my actions last night. He was trying to be nice, but I would rather have cleaned out the engines than lay around stewing in my thoughts.

Rodin landed on my chest and rooted around my pocket. "Hey, I was going to eat that later." I pulled out some jerky, broke off a piece, and held it out between my fingers. Rodin snatched it up and gulped it down. He nudged my hand with his head, and I looked in his large bronze eyes, which softened as he turned his head. "You are so bad," I said with a smile. "You want the rest? Here you go," I gave him the second half, and with a quick wiggle of his head it disappeared. "I can't resist that face."

"So that's why he stays down here," the baron said as he stepped into my room.

"He's been eating more, lately."

"I'm not here to check up on him." The baron sat down on a barrel beside the pyramid of cannon balls. "I want you to attend a meeting

with me."

I sat up and Rodin slid down into my lap. "Anything to leave this room."

"Good, we leave in an hour." He stood up. "What do you know about the Acropolis and ancient Greece?"

"I've read a ton of books about it, from mythology to historical accounts."

"How well can you read ancient Greek?"

"As good as English. My father made me start when I seven." I shrugged. "He believes you can only understand the philosophers in their original tongue."

"Excellent, then be prepared to hike up there in an hour."

"Yes, sir."

The baron walked out and Rodin flew after him. Probably trying to get more food. I gathered what I might need and made certain to fill my pouch with percussion caps for my Thumper. When Mr. Singh ordered me to go through the pockets of the henchmen, I'd found very little, only weapons like brass knuckles, knives, a revolver, and a couple of Thumpers. But the guys who carried Thumpers had a bunch of percussion caps, and I took them all.

An hour later, I met the baron and Rodin on the gangplank. We walked down, and I waved to Mr. Singh and Ignatius. I thought they might come with us, but only the baron and I departed. Rodin sat on the shoulder of the baron's tailcoat.

We wound through the city from the airdocks toward the towering Acropolis. I couldn't stop staring at the buildings around me. We weren't in ancient Greece, but the old winding streets and buildings cast me back to a world I'd only read about. As we started up the hill, ruins lay all around us. Fallen columns and crumpling walls lined the stone path, and I imagined myself in another world, one in which the gods of the myths and the stories from Herodotus came to life.

The baron looked around as well. We stopped at the ruins of a temple and he ran his hand along the marble column.

"Aristotle used to speak right here," I said.

"He was Alexander the Great's tutor," the baron said as he stepped up into the temple. "Have you read his writings?"

"Every one of them." I smiled remembering fondly those days trapped in my father's office. I was happy to be here out in the world, but those days were now tinged with a nostalgia that made my heart ache. "My father made me read everything he'd ever written. *If it was good enough for Alexander of Macedonia, it is good enough for you,*" I said in the best impression of my father I could manage.

Skipping down a set of marble steps I saw the remnants of a large clay jar. "What is this doing here?" I asked.

"This is supposedly the *pithos*, where Diogenes lived."

"Who?"

Really, you don't about Diogenes? I would have thought you'd know all about him. Alexander famously said, if he couldn't be Alexander the Great, he would want to be Diogenes the Little Dog."

"Are you serious?"

"Of course," the baron said with a playful chuckle. "For a time, Diogenes lived in a jar here beside the temple of Cybele. Plato called him the insane Socrates."

"Wow, I'm pretty certain that's a great compliment.

I've read both Plato and Socrates. It always amazes me that all these great philosophers knew each other."

"An exciting time, for certain."

I stepped into the broken jar, the biggest I'd ever seen, but still too small to live in. "I think there's more room in between the helium sacks on the Sparrowhawk."

"Diogenes was an ascetic; he believed things control us, and that by shedding all possessions he could gain greater wisdom. He destroyed his only bowl after seeing a young boy drink from his hands, and said, 'What a fool I've been carrying this bowl around.'"

As I sat inside staring out on an amazing view of the surrounding temples, I asked, "How did he meet Alexander the Great?"

"Alexander had defeated the city of Thebes, and his army marched on Athens. The city elders, too afraid to meet him, ordered Diogenes to negotiate. They hoped the smartest man in Athens could save the city. After hearing Diogenes had been called the insane Socrates, Alexander rode into the city. He stood in front of the clay barrel looking for the man they called the Little Dog."

Looking around at the ruins atop the Acropolis, I asked, "Did Alexander destroy the city?"

"No, this damage is from earthquakes and war. A terrible explosion in the 1600s damaged the Parthenon and the building was never repaired." The baron stood in front of the barrel, cutting off the morning light. "Alexander stood here and told Diogenes he would grant him whatever he wanted, but would take the equivalent from the people of Athens. The Athenian's concern grew; they treated Diogenes poorly and several feared that Diogenes would take his revenge."

"What did Diogenes request?"

"He asked the great king to take three steps to the left." The baron stepped aside and the sun reappeared, warming the barrel. "Alexander spared Athens, for Diogenes had asked for the sun, and Athens would be like the sun. Its wealth would come, not from its gold or people, but from the ideas it would generate."

"Brilliant."

"Diogenes was a renowned scholar of cynicism." The baron motioned for me to follow as he stepped away. "He was cynical of the world around him. Of money, materialism, and the conventions of society, and so he lived in a barrel."

Cynicism was something I could relate to, as we were sitting on the wrong side of Aegean Sea. Genevieve was in the hands of Colonel Hendrix and the Knights of the Golden Circle. "I don't think I'd want to live in here, but he's fascinating." I sprang out of the barrel and quickened my pace to catch up with the baron.

"I don't think I would, either," he said as we continued across the Acropolis. "Another legend says Diogenes dug through a pile of bones, and when Alexander asked what he was doing, he told him he was looking for the remains of King Philip, Alexander's father. He told the great king that he couldn't tell the difference between kings and commoners."

"So, we're all the same?" I said as I joined the baron.

The baron looked down at me. "A powerful lesson to learn for one who was descended from Achilles."

"Baron, is your blood really a different color?"

"I have bled many times and it's always red."

3
A Secret Meeting

At the top of the Acropolis, the giant temple lay in ruin; yet the marble still gleamed in the morning light. Even though many of the columns had toppled over, and pieces of the roof lay scattered around the ground, this place held a majesty that rivaled the cathedrals of Europe.

"The Parthenon, the temple to Athena, patron goddess of Athens." The baron motioned his cane toward the once gorgeous building.

"Wow, so many of the stories I've read in ancient Greek mentioned this place." Shattered statues lined the ruins with an artistry only rivaled by the great masters of the Renaissance. "When this place was whole, I bet it was stunning."

"Beauty beyond compare." He turned to me and made certain my eyes were fixed with his. "We must preserve the past, even as we strive for the future. It is a sacred task set upon the Templar."

"I thought we fight evil."

"We do, but if we lose everything we stand for, everything that came before us, then we've failed future

generations. Remember, your life is important, but we must also honor those who came before, and, those who will follow in your footsteps."

I nodded, but my mind spun like a gyroscope. The Templars weren't just about war, they wanted to preserve history and honor the past. No wonder my father helped them, why he translated dead languages into words people could understand today. Why he insisted I learn them all.

We left the Parthenon and returned to the city of Athens. Calling the city modern was stretching the term. London was modern, a city bustling with factories and life. Athens, however, remained as it did in the philosopher's tales I was currently reading—a dusty place, relaxed, with one foot still in the past.

Turning north, we crossed a stream that wound between the buildings. The baron leaned in and smiled, "You'll enjoy this. The area we're in is known as the Templar Encampment. After the Crusades, the Order settled in Athens, and we've been here ever since."

My expression shifted from wonderment to puzzlement. "You have a meeting with the Templars. That's why we're in Athens?"

The baron nodded. "You're a bright lad." Our casual stride slowed, then the baron stopped. He pointed his cane at me. "Acre was troubling, and the men who attacked us when we landed confirmed it. Something is afoot."

My head swiveled like a turret cannon. "Were we followed? I wasn't even paying attention."

"I was." The slight upturn of the baron's lip let me know he liked my response. "We are just a couple of tourists taking in the ruins. Our shadow ran off while we were talking about Diogenes."

I kicked myself for not seeing them. I wanted to be a warrior, yet I didn't even realize we'd been watched. Studying every face on the street around us, I wanted to find a spy, but all I found were ordinary Greeks ignoring us as they went about their lives.

The baron led me behind some buildings and stopped on a metal plate underneath a window. The baron pressed his signet ring into a small recess in the wall and turned his wrist. A man appeared in the window and nodded. The steel plate beneath us lurched, and I spread my legs, to steady myself. Of course, the baron stood still as we descended below the alley. Another metal plate closed off the opening above us. The mechanics squealed and whined as we slid down a stone passage. We stopped in front of a large metal door lined with thick, rounded rivets. A small port slid to the side and a pair of eyes with bushy gray eyebrows appeared. A muffled but stern voice said, "Password?"

The baron flipped the lapel of his jacket over, revealing a small pin. "Baphomet. Baron Maximilian Kensington and Master Alexander Armitage here at Grand Master Sinclair's request."

The bushy eyebrows disappeared and the little port slid shut with a *click*. One lock clattered, then a second, and a third. The heavy door slowly opened and we stepped inside. Opulent, white and green marble trimmed with gold surrounded us. Gas lamp sconces lined a long hall, their flickering flames danced across statues of armored knights and tapestries depicting scenes of glory and the symbols of the Templar Order.

"What does *Baffomet* mean?" I asked quietly.

The baron shook his head, as if not wanting me to ask, but softly said, "Baptism of wisdom." We walked along a plush red carpet which dampened the sound of our footsteps. The old man with the bushy eyebrows and a cotton-top led us down the hall. "Have the others assembled?" the baron asked.

"Yes, baron, you are the last to arrive."

"You might want to double the guard. We ran into the Golden Circle last night."

The old man turned, his eyes narrowing, "That is troubling."

"Indeed."

He gestured toward another door and the baron and I continued on. The old man with the bushy hair stepped over to the wall and disappeared behind one of the tapestries.

As we reached the second door, an iron-riveted obstacle slowly opened into a cavernous room which stretched out before us like the interior of a Greek temple. A long rectangular table ran the length of the chamber. Shadows obscured many who sat at the table, but six chairs lined each side, and one chair sat at the head. A lone, empty chair sat next to it on the left side of the table.

The booming Scottish drawl of Grand Master Sinclair called from the end of the table. "Baron, so glad you could join us, and I see you brought the lad. Welcome, Alexander."

The baron bowed his head and I mimicked the gesture. "Thank you, sir," Genevieve's father said in a somber tone. "We would have been here sooner, but I had to make certain we weren't followed."

A French accent from the shadows said, "I object. The boy is not a member of our Order."

The baron smacked his cane against his open palm,

"The *boy* is the Black Knight. He saved London at the Battle of the Thames, and drove the Milli-train from Zululand. Not to mention he saved my life last night. We were attacked by henchmen of the Golden Circle, and an assassin, a *hassassin*. I'm certain of it."

A murmur shattered the stoic silence, and several men at the table said, "Impossible." The Frenchman said, "The old man of the mountain is a myth."

Grand Master Sinclair struck a gavel against the table and the echoing sound silenced the chamber. "How could they have known? This was a secret meeting."

The baron shrugged his shoulders as he walked toward the table, motioning for me to follow. A valet appeared from the shadows along the wall and pulled out the chair for the baron. The valet disappeared and the baron pointed to spot behind him, which I took to be the place where I should stand. Through the shadows, I could make out some of the faces of the people at the table, and I saw that each one wore the same pin as the baron. Across from the baron sat Lord Marbury. He smiled and nodded his head slightly. Eustache sat beside the baron, and raised his goblet with a large grin.

Beside Lord Marbury sat a portly man with dark hair and a long beard. An older woman sat further down. Next to Eustache a man with long hair but no beard, stared at me, his eyes narrowing into a piercing stare, and his chin bore a wicked scar. Six more men sat at the table, but the shadows hid them.

I wanted to wave to Eustache and Lord Marbury, but I knew this was not the time. My father would be proud that I held my excitement in check and behaved as a proper gentleman should.

Grand Master Sinclair motioned and a valet brought

forward a golden tray with several scrolls laying on it. Setting broken sealed parchments down on the table, Sinclair took one and unrolled it. "These are reports from our agents in Africa and the Holy Land about the Milli-train. I also have reports from Europe, America, and elsewhere about the activities of the Knights of the Golden Circle."

"We have too many reports, most must be false," the portly Frenchman said from across the table. "The Golden Circle cannot be so widespread."

"These reports come from trusted sources, and we have no evidence they are false," Lord Marbury said. "We must consider the possibility that they have grown larger than our Order."

"A frightening thought," Eustache said.

"What do we know for certain?" the baron asked.

"The Golden Circle seeks the Crusader Hearts." Grand Master Sinclair's voice dropped low, and held a tinge of fear. "The hearts of the four horsemen—artifacts of pure evil—and as any who have read the accounts will attest, the four from the Crusades were the most powerful in history."

From the shadows, a man with a German accent said, "They already have the ones found on Malta two years ago. Why would they need more?"

"Fantasy at best," another member at the end of the table said. "You try to scare us with these tales. Where is the proof?"

The woman spoke up. "According to the histories, the Crusader Hearts were destroyed."

"Yes, exactly," the portly Frenchman said. "How do we know the Crusader Hearts are real when no one saw them?"

"*I* saw one," I said, stepping closer to the table. I knew my place was to remain silent, but I couldn't let them pretend the events in Zululand didn't happen. "A shattered jade heart, the pieces bound together with a silvery metal. I also saw how it transformed the Milli-train. The reason they need them is because Genevieve Kensington destroyed one of the hearts from Malta at the Battle of the Thames."

All eyes bore through me, and even the baron turned in his chair to glower. I'd been proper, but no more. *I won't let them ignore me,* I told myself. *I faced the Milli-train, the Iron Horsemen, and the Golden Circle. I know what I'm talking about.*

I stood as stoic as a knight as Grand Master Sinclair chuckled, breaking the tension in the chamber. "Alexander Armitage everyone." He gestured my direction. "Our resident expert on all things Horsemen."

"He should learn his place when in the presence of this council," the Frenchman said.

Eustache eyed his countryman. "Or, perhaps you should listen when an Armitage speaks."

"Wait. Did you say *Armitage*?" the woman asked, "Is this the descendent of Armand Armitage, the knight charged with the destruction of the Crusader Hearts? I find this troubling."

My knees wobbled, shattering my stoic stance. Eustache had shown me a book signed by William Armitage, an ancestor of mine. So, I knew my family had served the Order in the past, but I had no idea my ancestor had dealt with the Horsemen. I wanted to know more, but how?

"Alexander is not under suspicion." Grand Master Sinclair grumbled, his Scottish drawl low and fierce. "I do not like the tone of this meeting."

Another member from the end of the table said, "Then let us return to the point."

"Agreed." The baron shifted in his seat and he raked his eyes across everyone seated at the table. "I've come to find out why this Order cannot track the Milli-train with any accuracy."

Several members began to protest, but Grand Master Sinclair pounded his gavel. "Silence everyone!" He turned to the baron. "The answer is simple. We have a mole."

"Amole?" I couldn't believe a Templar would aid the Golden Circle.

Once again, everyone in the room turned to stare at me, but then a murmur ignited like a blaze and everyone around the table began talking at once. Apparently, like me, none of them believed a member of the Order would betray their sacred oaths. Perhaps it was a valet, or a maid, or someone else, but surely not one of their own.

Grand Master Sinclair raised his hands to settle the table. "Lord de Troyes don't you think I've thought of every other possibility? We've confirmed reports from Acre. The minute we showed up, they vanished."

"Last night's attack only confirms it," the baron said. "No one knew I was coming to Athens but the people in this room. Even the captain of the Sparrowhawk didn't know until absolutely necessary. And yet, the Golden Circle was waiting. They tried to kill me, so I wouldn't make this meeting."

"But why?" Eustache asked as his finger traced along his chin.

Sinclair nodded. "I too wondered why it is so important to

kill the baron."

A man in shadows at the end of table said, "His very wife is an assassin, and we are surprised he is a target? Perhaps she sought his death as payment for causing her failure last year."

The baron's knuckles turned white as he clenched his fist, but he said nothing.

Lord Marbury leaned over the table. "We've been digging for information about the possible location of the other Horsemen Hearts."

The baron's stern tone, silenced the murmuring. "Have you found anything?"

"Not yet, but I might join you on the next leg of your journey."

Sinclair pulled his fingers through his white beard. "I'd rather keep you here going through the records, Lord Marbury."

"I must protest. I, more than any of the others at this table, beside maybe the baron, deserve to go after the Golden Circle."

"But we need to search these records."

"May I remind you that it was I who discovered the comet plot, and their search for the hearts on Malta. Kannard tortured me and I escaped to warn the Order. I should be allowed to go after them now."

Lord de Troyes nodded his head, "I agree with Marbury. I can go through the records to find out what Armitage did with the Crusader's Hearts."

I didn't like the tone of his voice. I didn't know what happened back then, and I didn't know my ancestor, but I couldn't believe my family betrayed the Order. Especially since the book Eustache had shown me at his estate in Paris had been written after the Crusades. If my ancestor was a traitor to the Order, I wouldn't expect my family to remain within its membership. I crossed my arms and eyed the portly knight.

"I have a better idea." The baron sat back and relaxed his fingers. "Let's get Professor Armitage to come here. His knowledge of languages will be an asset."

"Better yet," Sinclair pressed his finger against the table, "let's send the records to Eton. Take steps to prevent them from falling into the wrong hands here in Athens."

My father would love to get his hands on all those records. I could see his giddy expression. Thoughts of all the missed dinners made my chest ache as my mind drifted to Eton College. The sun would be rising over the quad soon; my father would be preparing for the sections he taught—unless he hadn't slept—then he'd be running home to get ready. The bustling halls of Eton filled my memory, winter still gripped Britain, which meant a chilling wind would push through the buildings. I certainly didn't miss the weather.

Moments later, with the latent memory of the itchy wool jacket I wore at Eton irritating my neck, the baron stood up and shook hands with Eustache and Grand Master Sinclair. The meeting had ended.

Eustache stepped over to me and grabbed my shoulder as he shook my hand. "It is good to see you."

"It's good to see you, too. I wish we'd had more time in Zululand."

"You fought bravely, and I admire your choice to join the baron."

"Thank you. Too bad it hasn't gone the way I hoped."

His smile grew. "Have faith. I am certain you will

find Miss Genevieve."

I nodded. His confidence was the shot in the arm I needed, and hope filled my heart.

Eustache stepped away to speak with the others, and the baron slid next to me and whispered, "We won't be returning to the ship right away. I want to peak at those records before they are sent to your father." He locked eyes with me. "Think you can translate some Greek?"

"Easily," I nodded. "The books my father sent with me are in Greek. I've been getting a lot of practice."

"Excellent. Don't say a word. Just follow me."

"I understand." I, too, was worried about the mole.

The baron stepped toward the other Templar and a big smile grew on his face as he lit up with a friendly demeanor. I stepped back closer to the valets. I eyed each one. Could they be the mole? But each one looked like me—a young man dreaming of becoming a knight. More likely, it was one of the members of the Order. I studied every face, watching who spoke with whom, and how friendly they acted. Knowing the baron wore a façade, I realized no one here revealed their true selves.

Moments later, I followed the baron out of the hall, and we ascended a set of stairs to the building above. We entered a room with stacks of scrolls and old manuscripts. The smell of dusty parchment transported me back home. My father would love it here.

The baron turned to me, "The historical documents are over here. I don't know exactly what we're looking for, but I'm hoping we'll know it when we see it."

At the back of the room, we found a wall of shelves marked *Istoria ton Stavroforion*. "Here we go," I said. "History of The Crusades."

"We're looking for records from the Second Crusade in the twelfth century."

"Richard the Lionheart and Saladin."

"That's right. After Richard lost Jerusalem, a former Templar created the hearts or took the hearts from the first crusade and tried to use their power to gain victory over Saladin."

"A former Templar? Fascinating." I looked for scrolls and books dated in the 1100s. A set of books without dust stood out amongst the other tomes, a series of books and scrolls recently cleaned made them easy to spot. I pulled them out, and carried them over to a nearby table. The baron took half the books. I took the others and arranged a bookstand in front of me. I even found a thin rod with a small pointer finger on the end. My father would be proud of my set up.

The baron and I read for the next few hours. Most were boring updates, one thousand knights with twenty-four carts of grain; ten chests of gold moved from one city to another, or some other boring accounting of the war. The Templars were known as the first bankers in Europe, and from what I was reading, they had their record-keeping skills well honed. The third book I read was an account of battles fought, which was the most interesting thing I'd read all day.

A valet approached and passed a note to the baron. The nobleman stood and gathered his coat. "I must step off for a moment."

"No problem." I pointed to the manuscript in front of me. "I'll be here reading about troops movements near Krak de Chevaliers.

After finishing that book, I closed it up and set in aside with those I'd already read. As I reached for a scroll case, I yawned and let out a loud sigh. I reached back to stretch and my vision narrowed as darkness closed in. Everything went black and I slipped away.

Light exploded, blinding me. At first, I could only see shapes, which cleared and focused into the undulating movements of the Milli-train. The armored train scurried on its mechanical legs through a barren valley. The demonic inner flames glowed within the iron, and my heart raced as fear clutched me. The Milli-train rushed over a ridge and I tried to follow, but my legs moved as though mired in molasses. I reached out and was flung forward into the Victorian parlor car that we'd stayed in as it dragged Genevieve and me across Africa. The lavish interior looked the same, and the hole I'd blasted in the ceiling had been repaired, but the outline remained.

Colonel Hendrix sat at the table with several soldiers playing cards, each man gripping his hand close to his chest. Everyone, except the colonel—who was half-covered in bronze plates—laughed as one man won the hand and scooped up his winnings. The colonel looked lost in thought, his face painted with his usual scowl.

Genevieve's strength radiated behind me. I turned and saw her on one of the couches. She sat like a proper lady in a beautiful sky-blue dress, but her eyes held the defiance that I had come to know, and love, while on our adventures. I reached out, calling her name, but she didn't react; her contempt for her surroundings etched on her face like carvings on stone.

Rushing to a window, I tried to figure out where

they were, but all I saw was barren rock.

In a flash, the world twisted and melted away until only the darkness remained. Fire ignited around me, and from the flames, the world came back into focus. I saw a lavish room, decorated with silks and statues. Genevieve, resting amidst plush pillows, now wore a red and yellow silk dress, sat, regal as a queen. Gold rings adorned each finger, and bangles ran up her arms.

Beyond a few sculpted pillars, huge gears turned the cogs of a giant machine. Everything shook as if the Earth were being ripped apart. A golden circlet fell around me, and slammed down on the white marble where I stood. The golden walls closed in and I thought I would be crushed. I pushed my arms out to hold the golden walls at bay, as the ground beneath me cracked and pulsed like a heartbeat.

I awoke with the baron and Sinclair standing over me, both calling my name. I sat up, and found myself on the floor. Rubbing my head did little to push away the ache, or the haze.

"Lad, maybe you should lie back down." Sinclair turned to a valet standing at the end of one of the bookshelves. "Get him some water."

"I'll be okay," I said as the baron help me back onto my chair.

"A vision?" Concern etched across the baron's face, but I couldn't answer right away.

Sinclair pushed himself up with his cane to get back to his feet. "Give the lad some breathing room." He took the goblet from the valet and set it before me on the table.

"Yes, I saw the Milli-train in mountains."

The baron tensed, "Do you know which ones?"

"Don't answer that here, Alexander." Grand Master Sinclair smacked his cane against his hand. "Take Alexander back to the *Sparrowhawk*, and find your daughter. But dare not say a word here."

The baron, Lord Marbury, and I rushed back to the airdocks using a carriage provided by Grandmaster Sinclair. The two men spoke quietly, heads together, paying little attention to me. As we roared around a building, I feared an attack from Hendrix's henchmen, but no one appeared, so I forced the air from my lungs hoping it would ease my pounding heart. I knew the assassin was probably still in the city and would be waiting for another chance to strike. Fearing the people gathered on every corner, I clutched at the strap of the leather rucksack secured over my shoulder.

When we reached our berth at the airdocks, I rushed onto the Sparrowhawk. Mr. Singh stood at the top of the gangplank; concern etched on his brow. "Everything all right?" he asked. "You look like you are running from someone."

The baron glanced over his shoulder. "You're not far off, Mr. Singh. We need to depart at once."

Mr. Singh nodded and motioned toward the bridge. The baron

and I ran that way, with the Sikh right behind us. Once inside, I saw the captain leaned over the map table with Ignatius and Hunter at his side. All three snapped up their heads as we burst through the hatch.

"Captain," the baron said, "I'm afraid we need to depart immediately."

Without missing a beat, Captain Baldarich looked at the two crewmen and nodded. Ignatius rushed over to the wall of dials and sat down. The captain grabbed Hunter's shoulder, and said, "Keep an eye on the docks. I want to know if anyone's watching us leave." He then turned to Mr. Singh, "Crew to the wingsails, Mr. Singh! We cast off into the winds at once."

Both answered "Aye, aye, Captain," and rushed off bridge.

The captain motioned us over to the map table. The Mediterranean lay stretched out, pinned at the corners by special brass clasps that looked like a bird of prey's talons. "I had a feeling you'd come running, but the question is, where are we going?"

The baron pointed his thumb at me. "You'll have to talk to this one. He's seen it. A vision."

The captain turned to me; his eyes full of questions. "I'm not sure," I said. "The Milli-train was in the mountains."

"Most of the mountains lie to the East, that's good enough to start."

Lord Marbury raised his gloves and shook them. "But what if the lad refers to the Alps?"

The baron shook his head. "Our latest reports say the Milli-train was last seen heading toward Persia."

As Heinz ran onto the bridge and dropped into the pilot's seat, Baldarich pointed to him. "Nephew, head south until we're out of sight from land. And then," he turned to me, "we head east."

I nodded and the baron smiled at the captain, "Brilliant! Anyone watching won't see which way we intend to go."

"Exactly," the captain said. "Alexander, follow our progress on this map and let me know the way." The captain walked over to his seat and flipped open one of the copper tubes. "Gears, get my bird into the sky."

A raspy voice answered back, "She's ready to fly, Captain."

Baldarich looked over at Ignatius, who checked the dials and nodded. "Heinz, ease her out of here."

With a clatter, the mooring clamps opened and the Sparrowhawk rose into the air as gently as a feather on a breeze. Then Heinz spun the wheel and pulled back causing the nose to pitch skyward. I listened as the wingsails were winched into place and braced myself with one hand on the map table as the wind scooped up the aero-dirigible with a slight lurch. We soared quickly, higher and higher, as Athens shrunk into the distance.

After Heinz leveled us out, Hunter returned to the bridge. He walked over to the captain's chair and leaned on the railing. When Baldarich turned, Hunter said, "One of the dock workers watched us depart and ran off as soon as he saw what direction we headed."

The captain turned to the baron. "They know we're coming."

"Good; let them wonder where we are for a while."

Once the brass arms of the Arial Tracking Dial indicated we were well over the Aegean Sea, the captain called out, "Heinz, port turn ninety degrees and raise the bow by three degrees. Take us into the clouds."

"Aye, aye Uncle—Captain, Sir." Heinz stumbled over his words, but executed the order.

Stepping to the window, I once again marveled at the beauty of the Mediterranean. Homer had called it the "wine-dark sea," and it certainly lived up to its name. A thick layer of clouds above painted the sea below a mysterious midnight blue. No matter how often I experienced the wonder of flight, I never tired of it. And now, waiting for the Sparrowhawk to ease into the clouds above us, I wanted to reach out and slip my fingers through the first wisps of white and grey. As the cloud bank thickened, everything went white. The ethereal vapor enveloped us. I could see nothing beyond, not even the sea.

I adjusted the leather bag slung over my shoulder.

The baron pointed, "What's in your satchel?"

"The manuscripts the Order was going to send to my father."

Lord Marbury eyes bulged. "What have you done? Those are sacred documents!"

I met his gaze. "I can read them, *and* you won't have to risk sending them to England, or wait for a translation from my father."

The baron pinched the bridge of his nose as if warding off a headache. After a moment, he shook his head and a slow smile spread across his face.

Lord Marbury looked to the baron, who turned to Captain Baldarich. "Do you mind if I pull him from his duties?"

Suppressing a laugh, Baldarich clapped his hands. "He needs to study more anyway. But. . ." he said, pointing at me, "I'll expect double duty when you're done, Mr. Knight."

I nodded, and the baron poked the polished handle of his cane at my chest, "Get to work and I'll check on your progress later."

"Aye, aye, I mean, yes sir!"

I rushed off the bridge and hurried down to my room on the gun deck. Once inside, I slid a barrel over to my hammock and set my bag on the floor beside me. Sitting in the middle of my hammock gave me a comfortable seat and I adjusted the barrel until it was right in front of me. Reaching down, I retrieved the first tome. The leather-bound book held thick parchment inside and crackled as I opened it. The illuminated manuscript was decorated with exquisite artwork in the corners and along the edges of the page. A scribe had meticulously formed each letter, all of which were arranged in perfect lines.

This scroll, entitled, *i istoria ton Naitón stavrofries*, or *The History of the Templar Crusades*, sounded way more interesting than the detailed accounting books I'd been reading in the library. I scanned the first paragraph, which was written in Medieval Greek, a language I'd read many times at my father's command. The text started with an edict from Pope Gregory VIII calling for the liberation of the Holy Land, and continued with edicts from several kings.

I reached up and adjusted the knob on the lantern hanging above me, coaxing the flame to brighten the room. My father always said it was important not to strain the eyes when translating texts.

For the rest of the day I read about battles, about honorable deeds, and acts of betrayal. I learned about what I knew as the Second Crusade, but what would turn out to be one of many. The tome read like the end of the world had been thwarted by this war. But veiled between the lines was something besides the war: references to a much darker conflict—the war with four horsemen. They would show up on battlefields and lay waste to whole armies. Sometimes the Templar would ride out expecting to find Saladin's army, only to find them completely destroyed. The answer why was never explained, but I knew.

I read the final page, closed the book, and leaned back in my hammock. The horsemen were most definitely back, resurrected by Kannard, Hendrix, and the Golden Circle. They sought the power to enslave all mankind. The Knights Templar stood against them, and my friends on the *Sparrowhawk* and in Africa stood against the Golden Circle. Would we be enough? I had no idea.

Rodin flew in and landed on my stomach. "*Oof*, you are getting heavy." I scratched under his chin and he closed his eyes. "So, what do you think? Are we going to defeat the Iron Horsemen?"

Rodin's eyes opened and locked with mine. *Yes.*

Of course, he hadn't said anything, but I could swear I sensed his answer. I rubbed my eyes and tried to shake loose the cobwebs of a tired mind. When I focused back on Rodin, I could have sworn the upturned corners of his lips were a smile. I sat up and the dragon curled into my lap. I rubbed the horned nubs on his head as I reached down and grabbed the next book.

This one was smaller, still bound in leather, but was well worn from the centuries. Cracked and faded, I could tell this book hadn't been well cared for, and when I opened it some dirt fell onto the barrel. The handwritten text lacked the scribe's perfection, the letters varied in size, and not a single line was straight. There was a hand-drawn sketch on the first page, but none of the beautiful illuminations of the previous book.

I started to read, this text wasn't in Greek, but Old French. It began with a German inscription scrawled on the blank second page: *The final journal of Armand Armitage, honored knight of the Templar Order. Retrieved from his grave in the great mountains – 1336A.D. His quest fulfilled; he was reburied with honor in consecrated ground.*

I pushed back from the book causing the hammock to swing and Rodin to take flight. I jumped to my feet and shook to shed the weird feeling climbing up my spine. "So creepy! The book was buried with my ancestor." The name repeated in my mind. The dirt that had fallen out was from his … the tingling whipped up and down my spine and I danced around trying to rid myself of the haunting vibrations.

Rodin landed on the barrel and looked at the book as if trying to figure out what had upset me. I walked back over and joined him, staring down at the journal. "How am I supposed to read that, Rodin? It was buried with my ancestor. What if it's haunted? What if it's cursed or something?"

Rodin cocked his head to the side as if contemplating my question.

A thought crept in through the back of my mind, if any book was going to have actual secrets, it would be this one, and not some overly-produced tome. This was the hand-written journal of a knight who had gone on a quest to the great mountains. And, had been discovered after the Templar Order had been destroyed in 1307 A.D. A knight thought it important enough to retrieve not only this journal, but also my ancestor's remains. I shivered and then chastised myself. *Don't be a baby, Alexander. This is important, and it's up to you to translate it.*

I sat back in the hammock and scanned over the third page written in Old French. *The sacred quest of Sir Armand Armitage to hide the Greatest Evil from a world unable to destroy the Hearts of the Horsemen. 1212 A.D.*

"Here goes, Rodin." The little dragon nodded at me as if encouraging me to just get on with it. I reached down and turned the page.

6
The Journal
of Sir Armitage

I write this account for my fellow Knights of the Templar Order should they ever need to know the fate of the four Hearts of the Horsemen. In my fading days, after a life of great victories, horrendous evils, and the saving of my soul, I pen this account as a guide and a warning. We tried to destroy the hearts. I shattered three swords and an ax on the one that looks like liquid metal and left not even a scratch. My older brother was able to shatter the green stone with a blade blessed and anointed with holy water, but it did not break apart. A slivery metal oozed out to seal the cracks and kept it whole. We tried fire. We dropped them off the high walls of the citadel, but nothing could destroy these demonic hearts. Though we were ordered to destroy them, we failed. My brothers and I decided to hide the Hearts and tell everyone they had been destroyed. It is our hope that in doing so, no one will ever seek out their evil.

Three Armitage brothers answered the call and traveled to the Holy Land to fight the evil of the

Four Horsemen. My older brother and one hundred knights were able to rip free the Horsemen's hearts and stop the unholy menace, but my brother and his knights all died. I have been given the honor of this quest. As the oldest remaining brother, the burden was mine to bear. My younger brother will return home to find a wife and, with God's blessing, continue our bloodline.

I tore myself away from the book and wiped a tear that welled in my eye. This account would be heart wrenching to anyone, but knowing the author was related to me, that three brothers had been torn apart by the Horsemen, ripped my soul to shreds.

"It's so sad Rodin, three brothers, one died fighting the horsemen, another died on this quest, and the third returned home to continue the bloodline. I am here because the final brother let his brother go off alone. Wow."

Rodin, sitting in his bed, lifted his head.

"I bet the book I saw at Eustache's estate — *The History of the Order* — was written by a descendant of the youngest brother." I pulled the book onto my chest as I lay back in my hammock.

Rodin lowered his head and curled back into his bed.

I set out on my quest in the year of Our Lord 1149 A.D. with all four hearts. It was good that I traveled alone, for the corrupting draw of their demonic power was stronger than anyone expected. It is only by the grace of our Lord, and my training as a Templar Knight that I did not fall to its evil. Visions have guided me, but I feared they came from the hearts, yet I have come to trust their advice. They have saved me and led me to each of the hiding places. I have traveled across the world, something I may be the first person in history to do. I have placed the hearts so far apart, that it is my sincerest hope that doing so will prevent them from ever being brought back together. Alone they are powerful, but together, they are a force of unnatural, unholy, and unrelenting power.

I laid the journal on my chest. He had visions like me. They guided him as they do me. I wasn't a freak. My brain wasn't weird. My family had visions. I wondered if my father, or my grandfather had visions. No one had ever mentioned this ability before, but here was an ancestor of mine talking about how they guided him. I continued reading.

I made the choice not to hide them with any civilization, nor in any city or village, no matter how large or small. The chance is too great that over time the hearts would be found, or would call to those with darkness coursing in their veins. Instead, I dug four graves, each so deep that erosion will not reveal them. Beyond the reach of any foundation for any building that might be built in the future. By returning them to the embrace of the deepest recesses of our world, it is my greatest hope that they will never see the sun's light again.

"One's already been found; I was there when the jade heart was ripped from the dark African soil." I expelled a breath and dust billowed up from the book. I knew I should be taking notes, writing down the translations, but these words had burned into my brain, and I would never forget them. I turned the page and kept reading, running my finger back and forth over the scrawled words. Translating the Old French wasn't the most difficult thing I'd done, even if it did take several passes to get it all. But I couldn't stop. I had to know.

I will never reveal where the hearts have been buried. Never would I want a disciple of evil to use my words to track them down. It is my belief after years of study that the hearts are evil concentrated into physical form. Evil is not just an emotion, a darkening of the heart. Evil is a force like the air we breathe, or the sunlight that warms our skin. Flowing like a river, it passes through us carrying us deeper into darkness. I do not blame whole peoples for being in league with the Horsemen; rather, now I believe that some men on crusade were drawn into its evil and willing to serve its power.

The room darkened and I reached up to adjust the lantern. Heaviness overtook my eyes and the *Sparrowhawk* faded away.

A knight dressed in a white tunic with a red Templar cross rode atop a brown steed on a seemingly endless ocean of sand. The sun beat down making the horizon as wavy as water. The knight wore a cowl of chainmail, and his eyes were mere slits. A large triangular shield hung on one side of his horse; four large, leather pouches draped the opposite side. He carried a lance, the flag on the end whipping in the strong breeze. I stood on the dune behind him and heard a calm voice bore directly into my mind. I turned and saw the knight beside me. But, rather than the clear image of the young man on the horse, I saw the ghostly image of an older man.

"You're him," I said, pointing to the knight on horseback. "Armand Armitage."

"I am."

"How?"

"My journal. You carry it with you now."

"I am searching for the men who seek the hearts."

He nodded. "That is why I am here. You see, we are bound to the evil contained in those hearts."

"I don't understand."

"Neither did I, at first. It is not a coincidence that your father translated the texts and found the first hearts. It is destiny. Once again, an Armitage stands ready to defend the world. First, I rode south crossing the great desert of the Nubian Continent. Past the largest lake I'd ever seen. In the far south, I met dark-skinned warriors with an honor I easily recognized. Not within their village, yet near them, I placed the green stone atop a hill beside the winding river."

Then, I saw him diving into the shimmering water fully clothed. As the water rippled out my vision mirrored the lake's surface until it cleared revealing a village. I didn't recognize the people, but I knew the Zulu village would sit on this hilltop eventually. The knight dug in the dirt, his spear planted in the ground beside him. He placed the jade heart within the hole and started to replace the earth.

"My hope was that the remote and dangerous terrain, along with the deterrent of these noble warriors would keep the heart safe."

My vision shifted, as if I'd turned too fast, and I saw the knight back atop his steed. Behind him, several lions stalked through the tall grass. As they charged, the horse kicked and made the most frightful noises. His hoof connected with one of the large cats, forcing it back.

"The great cats would have defeated me if not for

my steed, who gave his life for mine. Every step I took was fraught with danger. The hearts did not want to be separated, and once I made my intentions clear, they vexed my mind and spirit, and called forth all the evils on my path."

"For a week I walked without water. Mind you, I was not afraid to die; I was afraid to fail. But as I was about to collapse, a young shepherd boy discovered me and tried to give me shelter. In the shadow of a long-forgotten pyramid, we were besieged by a band of brigands. They killed the boy, and, I, weak and without hope, drew strength from the injustice, and my determination was reignited. I defeated them and watched as their blood drained into the rocky soil. I tried to compensate his family, but they would not accept anything, and citing the law of hospitality, they insisted I remain and thanked me for vanquishing the brigands. I however, could not stay."

The image shifted through waves of desert heat, and I saw another crumbling pyramid standing alone amidst a vast sea of sand. I assumed we stood in Egypt. I watched as Armand buried the quartz pyramid, the second unholy heart, at its base.

"I must confess it was at this moment that I had my greatest crisis of conscience. So close to home, I could have traveled to Alexandria and returned to my brother in France, but my quest wasn't finished, and the dishonor would have been too great to bear. I could not live with such a mark, so, I said goodbye to the world I knew and traveled east. From the Gnostics in Egypt, I was able to resupply and get new horses."

"That must have been such a difficult decision." My excitement tempered by the sadness of his tale left me torn inside, but I couldn't wait to hear more of his story. "Where did you go next?"

"For three years I crossed into the lands of Russia. I had to avoid the land occupied by Saladin and his allies."

I watched Armand struggle through a forest thick with trees so tall they blocked the sun. Once, one of his pack horses stumbled and fell. My eyes widened as I realized they were traveling on icy, packed snow that was as deep as his horses' withers. "I searched for a place to bury the hearts, but could not dig through the frozen ground. Eventually, I found my way into China." Surrounded by soldiers, I watched as he was led into a large palace decorated with dragons. "I feared my quest was at an end. They had a rule forbidding foreigners, and I feared they would seize the hearts. But tragedy followed in my wake."

Smoke rose, and as it cleared, I saw the sick and dying filling the rooms of the palace. Fires burned night and day trying to incinerate the foul air they feared was the cause.

"After three seasons, the emperor called me before him. I was declared the reason for the tragedies, they wanted to execute me, but I asked to speak. When they refused, I took a stand in the center of the room and made my impassioned plea. I told the Emperor about the hearts, explained that they, not I, were the reason for their blight. I told him how we'd tried to destroy them, of our failure to accomplish this feat, and of my quest. Several times, I feared his guards would strike me down where I stood, but the Emperor waved them off each time."

The Emperor sat on his throne, stroked his long beard. Soldiers brought Armand's belongings to the chamber and he was escorted to one of the Emperor's ships. Once at sea, the biggest storm I'd ever seen carried the ship across the great ocean. Battered for weeks, many of the crew died at the hands of the Hearts. Armand washed up alone on a sandy beach.

"My despair turned to joy when I realized how far I was from the Holy Land. I traveled inland, searching for the perfect place to bury the third heart. Months passed before I reached towering mountains, and from their heights I saw a great plain, a grassy sea that stretched to the horizon. On this plain, I met another group of noble warriors, and there, on a barren scar of land, I buried another heart, in four towers of rock that resembled the gnarled fingers of a battle-scarred hand. Then I left, hoping this land was so far from those searching for the hearts that no one would ever find it."

"The final heart I carried with me." The ghostly figure bowed his head. His face strained and he closed his eyes unable to look at me. "I could not let it go. Its power had entered my own heart and stitched itself to my soul. I had not lost a single battle. Every enemy I encountered, whether man or beast, fell to my blade. I returned to the shore, forced the natives to build me a boat, which they fashioned from the trunk of an enormous tree. I took several men to sail with me back across the great expanse of water. Eventually, after much struggle, I reached the southern shore of China. I followed the coast, through jungle and war-torn lands, and, there were times …" He shook his head sadly. "I'm not proud of my actions." Armand was older now, with dark circles beneath his eyes. A series of images flashed before me. All were of Armand in battle. Brutal attacks, some against unarmed farmers and townsfolk. Blood dripped from his blade.

Armand's voice lightened. "In India, I met a guru

who sensed my pain, my burden. He sent me north into the tallest mountains I'd ever seen. To a spiritual oasis, where the river cascaded down the mountain before connecting with a wide river. There, in the temple at the top of the mountain, I found myself again."

This mountain paradise was spectacular. Colorful temples perched on forested, rocky terraces, with clouds gathering below them. Bald men wrapped in orange robes sat motionless, meditating, or moved noiselessly around the temple. Armand sat among them writing in a journal.

"With these mystics, I buried the last heart, the one I could hardly bear to part with. I then committed my quest to parchment."

"The journal," I said, suddenly aware of the weight of the book resting against my chest. "I don't know what to say."

"Finish what I started. It's up to you …"

The image faded into darkness.

Then out of the pitch black an explosion of color and movement. Blurry images flashed past, nearly blinding me with their intensity. I was tossed this way and that with dizzying speed, whirling and twirling in endless circles so that my head ached and my stomach roiled. I heard picks clattering against stone, hammers pinging against metal. Anguished moans rose up only to be silenced by the crack of a whip. As the vision finally came into focus, I saw a jagged mountain peak capped in snow and dotted with a cluster of exotic buildings tucked against its side. A crystal-clear stream tumbled down the rocky slope until joining a river topped with white-capped waves racing through the valley below. The ground shook, and the mountainside was ripped apart by a force beyond imagining. And then I saw it—a shimmering heart made of silvery molten stone burst forth as if cast out by the gods themselves. In the distance, a dragon's deafening roar rolled over the mountain like thunder.

7
Babylon

I awoke, my arms flailing like a scared chicken. The journal fell to the floor kicking up a cloud of dust and I followed shortly with a *thud*. Rodin beat his wings and rose out of the hammock as the dust whipped around, and I could swear he was laughing as he hovered above me.

I sat up rubbing my head and brushing the dirt and dust from my back. My heart pounded and my temples throbbed, but with each breath the sensation eased. Rodin landed on my shoulder, and rubbed his head against mine.

"That was an intense dream," I said. Rodin cocked his head and held my gaze. "Not an ordinary dream. I think I saw where the hearts are hidden. And I have a very bad feeling, Rodin. I need to tell the baron."

I pulled myself to my feet as Rodin flew off my shoulder, out of my compartment and toward the stairs. Once on the gun deck, I rubbed my eyes against the bright light streaming through the ports. I waved to Mr. Singh and darted up the stairs after Rodin. When I arrived at the hatch to the bridge I paused, collected myself, and turned the handle. Before I could enter,

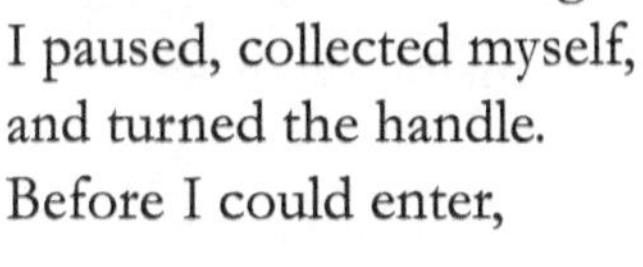

the door swung open and Ignatius rushed past me. I jumped back out of the way. From the look on his face, I knew there was trouble.

Stepping onto the bridge, I saw Lord Marbury and the baron standing behind the captain. Tension hung thick in the air, like moisture on a hot, humid day. I looked around the room. Hunter sat at the wall of dials monitoring the *Sparrowhawk's* controls.

Baldarich turned to Hunter and in a stern and sober tone, asked, "Is the pressure holding steady?"

"No Captain, still rising."

"Not good." He flipped open one of the copper tubes and leaned closer. "Gears, tell me you can fix this."

"Sorry, Captain. The engines are burning up, but I still can't figure out why."

Baldarich slammed his fist on the armrest of his chair, then spun around and locked eyes with the baron. Then he turned back to the tube, and took a deep breath before he spoke in a coarse whisper. "This is no ordinary engine problem, Gears. If your goal was to sabotage us, make us drop out of the sky without ever tipping your hand, how would you do it?"

There was silence on the other end, and then Gears spoke. "I've got a few ideas, Captain. I'm on it."

Baldarich flipped the cover back down and grabbed his chin. Then the three men turned and eyed me. I must have had an odd expression on my face, because each of them stared at me as if I had the answer. I opened my mouth to blurt out my vision, but if this was more sabotage, I feared the wrong person might overhear. Instead, I asked softly, "Can I help?"

"We don't even know what the problem is yet. I sent Ignatius to help Gears." The captain turned to

Heinz. "Bring us down out of the clouds. If we get into trouble, I want to be closer to the ground."

Lord Marbury returned to staring at the dials, but the baron's eyes narrowed as he looked at me and Rodin. "Everything all right?"

"Yep." I nodded, hoping I looked convincing.

I stepped to the window to avoid the baron's piercing eyes. As the clouds parted revealing the desert below, I saw an ancient city, one of the largest I'd ever seen, with stone ruins covering everything below. "Where are we?"

Lord Marbury stepped to the map table, but the baron joined me by the window. "Impressive," Baron Kensington said quietly. "My guess, only one city out here could be that big. Babylon."

"Babylon!" I pressed my face against the window to see as much as possible. "One of the largest cities of the ancient world, and the place where Alexander the Great died."

"That's right," the baron said. "You certainly know your Alexander the Great history."

"My father has always used his death as a cautionary tale."

"Because he pushed himself too far, too quickly?"

"Partly, but the end of his life is filled with mystery. He became seriously ill on the return from India. Some say he was poisoned. Some say his doctors killed him trying to treat him. Some say he'd given too much of himself. No matter the reason, here is where he passed into legend."

The baron tapped his cane on the deck. "You're a wise man, Master Armitage. Beware doctor's meddling, beware ambitious men, and beware the wrath of God."

I thought about this betrayal. It was said that some of his men feared Alexander's ambition, that he really wanted to conquer the world. They'd followed him from Greece across the entirety of the known world. They were tired and just wanted to go home. So someone poisoned him. Now, we had betrayers in our midst. I was certain of it. The ruins of Babylon passing below me seemed to be a warning.

The *Sparrowhawk* lurched and the starboard side dropped. I grabbed hold of the window to prevent myself from slipping. We turned as the captain flipped open one of the copper tubes. "Gears! What are you doing to my ship?"

A raspy voice echoed back. "I have cascading failures, Captain. We have to set down."

The captain smashed his fist against the railing and cursed under his breath. "Heinz, set us down on the edge of the ruins." He turned to the baron, "Looks like we'll be a little delayed."

"Captain, I fear this isn't a coincidence. We should prepare for unwanted visitors."

"Agreed. Hunter, after we land, I want you on the top deck. Shoot anything that moves."

"Aye, aye, Captain."

I locked eyes with the baron. "Maybe I am a student of Diogenes, because I don't think this is destiny, either."

The baron smiled. "Cynicism is healthy; it will keep you alive."

Captain Baldarich's eyes burned and his face darkened. "When I find the man who did this, I'll make him walk the plank at five thousand feet." He pointed over his shoulder, "Go help Gears, Mr. Knight."

As I passed the captain, Lord Marbury asked, "Why

does he call you that?"

"A nickname I earned in Zululand," I said with a slight nod and smirk. "The Order may not be ready to make me a knight, but that doesn't mean I don't have the heart of a knight."

"Well said," the baron added.

I bowed toward him, and then ran off the bridge to find Gears.

I heard yelling before I even reached the engine room. Gear's thick accent didn't echo so much as it slammed through the corridors. He was speaking in German, which was never a good sign, and his grease monkeys were running from the engines to the boilers like frightened mice. Ignatius stormed out ripping his Stetson off and smacking the hat against his thigh.

He saw me and waved his Stetson. "Come on kid, you're with me. We have to check the helium cells."

I nodded, relieved I didn't have to ask Gears any questions.

We ran up the stairs to the small hatches behind the deck gun hoist. I hadn't been back here since the captain, Genevieve, and I hid amongst the helium cells to avoid Zerelda, the Sky-Witch. Those memories could've taken place a lifetime ago. I was a completely different person back then, a scared kid, overwhelmed by the world. Not a crewman on a mission.

"Check each cell; Gears swears we're venting helium." Ignatius said in his continental accent with a cowboy twist. He'd been born in

the wrong country, Southern Germany, not the Wild West. "And here, take this patch." He handed me a large swatch of treated canvas and a small bottle of sealant.

"Will do, Mr. Peacemaker." I climbed inside, crawled along the metal grating, and through bulging gas cells. Heat rose from the engine room. I passed over a beam of light shooting up through a missing rivet. Memories of Genevieve, the captain, and me huddled around the small hole looking down into the engine room as Zerelda tortured the crew flooded my mind. Baldarich said he hadn't fixed it because it had come in so handy. Now the thought made me chuckle.

The third cell rippled and lacked the bulging seams as it deflated. "This must the one," I said in a squeaky high-pitched voice. "We're definitely venting."

I tried to yell to Ignatius, but my voice wouldn't carry. I sounded so funny and felt funnier. I couldn't help but say whatever came to mind. "I sound so weird. *Oooooh. I am the Black Knight!*" I laughed.

Sliding around the gas sack, I found a six-inch gash on the back side. I looked around for a metal barb, or broken brace that might have caused the tear, but found nothing. I pulled out the patching material and the bottle of sealant. Sticking my fingers inside the rip, I ran them along the sliced edge of another tear on the inner bag. Each large sack was filled with internal cells, so if one ruptured, the whole sack didn't deflate. I didn't have enough material to do both. I'd have to seal the outer bag for now, and make a better repair once in port.

As I put the patch along the tear, I noticed the smooth edges. This hadn't been torn, but cut with something sharp like a knife. Not good. That meant someone had sabotaged the *Sparrowhawk*. Someone on board. I applied the sealant to the back of the canvas, and laid it over the hole. Then I spread more around the edges to ensure everything was air tight.

When I was satisfied it would hold, I crawled back to the hatch and climbed out. Ignatius stood with the captain. Both men had their hands on their hips.

"Well?" Baldarich asked, as he pushed back his long red coat.

"The third helium bag had a six-inch gash that ruptured both the inner and outer containers." I tried to be serious but my squeaky voice cracked. "I sealed it, but it needs a more permanent fix."

Both men laughed at me. Ignatius tipped his Stetson back, and Captain Baldarich slapped me on the back, "Good job, Mr. Knight. Now say it again."

"Captain, this is serious," but both men continued to laugh hysterically. "Captain, the bag was sliced open. A clean cut. Nothing around it could have done the damage." My voice was lowering back to normal, but still sounded strange.

Baldarich forced himself to stop laughing and nodded. He hit Ignatius' shoulder which caused him to stop. "Round up the three new guys we picked up in Egypt, but quiet like. Let's not tip our hand."

Ignatius nodded, "Aye, aye, Captain."

Baldarich put his hand on my shoulder. "Did you get it patched?"

"The outer bag. The inner one had already deflated and I didn't have enough material."

"Good work. Now go tell the baron that I'm rounding up the crew." I started to head off, but he stopped me. "Don't say anything if the crew is on the bridge. Pull the baron aside. He'll want to be present for the questioning."

I saluted, and with my normal voice said, "Aye, aye, Captain."

Before I could dart off, Gears walked up holding a broken hunk of metal. "Captain, we have a problem."

"Tell me something I don't know, Gears."

"We can't lift off without something to replace this strut."

"That's not what I want to hear. What do we have that can replace it?"

"We don't have anything on board. I need something a foot long that is strong enough to take the weight." Gears wiped his hand across his brow leaving a long black smudge. "I thought about cutting up one of the wrenches but it's not wide enough."

I raised my finger to cut into the conversation. "Would a piece of stone work?"

Gears looked at me. "It might, but where are we going to get cut stone?"

"Babylon. We're surrounded by stone. All we have to do is find a piece the right size."

Captain Baldarich slapped my back. "I like the way you think. Change of plans. Tell the baron about the stone, and once off the ship, tell him the other thing."

I smiled. "Will do."

9
Fixing the
Sparrowhawk

As the baron and I walked down the gangplank, I told him about the gash in the helium cells, the stone piece we needed to find, and the crewmembers who were being rounded up for questioning. Then, as soon as my foot touched the dirt, I rushed forward toward the ruins and heard his trailing voice say, "Alexander, wait."

I couldn't restrain myself. Alexander the Great had ruled this city. He'd died here. His tomb might be lost somewhere in Alexandria, Egypt, but this was where he'd lived before heading off to India. Babylon had more history than any other city I'd stepped in. I walked up the main causeway lined with reliefs depicting ancient Babylonians, and now my footsteps fell into theirs.

The baron rushed to catch up with me. "Alexander, don't get too far away."

"Do you know where the ruins of the Tower of Babel might be? I thought there'd be more." I'd been expecting the ruins of a tower. The legends said the tower had been built so high it approached God.

"No, why do you ask."

"It's the reason I had to learn so many

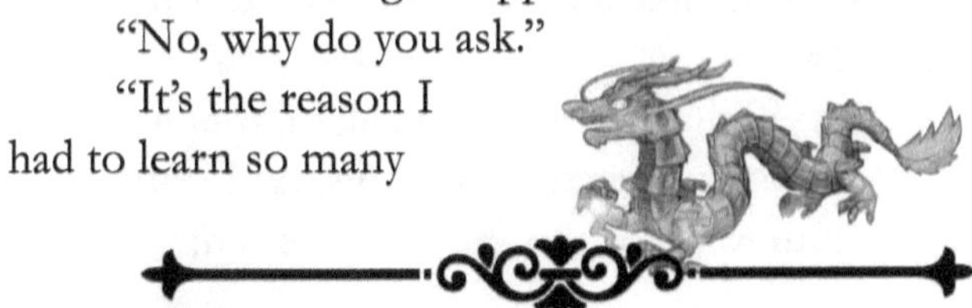

languages."

"I never thought of it like that before, I was actually hoping more of the ruins of the Hanging Gardens would be visible. I suppose they're buried."

"The Hanging Gardens, I forgot about them." I jumped onto a toppled column and scanned the city. "You'd think a giant garden created by the king for his homesick wife would stand out."

"They're the only one of the Seven Wonders of the World that hasn't been located."

"I know and I have so many questions. What did they look like? It's said they were based off the mountains which were her home, but then how did he get all the water to the highest tiers? How and why would anyone destroy them?"

"All good questions."

I pointed at the only thing that stood out. "There's a blue gate over there."

"The Ishtar Gate." The baron motioned with his hand. "Come on, let's find this stone, and get back to the *Sparrowhawk*. We shouldn't wander too far," he said. "I wouldn't be surprised if we had unwelcome company."

I jumped down and we searched through a pile of stones until we'd identified several candidates. I put three of them in my leather shoulder bag and we started back toward the airship.

As the sun rose higher, the heat increased. I wiped the sweat from my brow, and turned to see if the baron was ready to pass out like me. Not a drop of sweat marred his brow.

As we passed through a ruined hall of toppled columns, my stomach twisted up in knots. As I doubled over, the baron drew his saber, and sure enough, henchmen in long black coats and bowler hats with goggles around the band emerged on all sides.

Snarling, one said, "Well, lookie here boys, we don't even have to sneak on the airship. They sent 'em out for us."

"How nice of 'em," said another as he smacked his baton against his palm.

The baron stepped closer to me. "I'll deal with this scum. Get the Sparrowhawk out of here."

My fingers curled around the handle of my Thumper. Before we'd landed, I'd made sure I had it strapped to my leg and put my extra ammunition in my pouch. "I'm not leaving you."

One man in black cracked his knuckles. "Yeah, let the kid stay; we're here for him, too."

All the henchmen charged at once as the baron stood his ground. One tried to punch me, but I dove into the dirt and tumbled past him. I popped up and fired my Thumper. The concussive blast smacked into the henchman's back and knocked him into a stone column. The man collapsed onto the ground.

I glanced at the baron who fought off three men with his saber, slicing one as he kicked another. Two others headed toward me, and I turned and ran. Unlike the first time I faced down the henchmen in my father's office, I wasn't paralyzed. Fear wound its icy grip around me, but I was battle-tested, and my heart quickened but didn't pound against my chest. I ran only because I needed time to reload.

Popping the percussion cap out of the baton, I slipped in another and sprinted behind a column. As the two men closed in on me, I spun around and fired. The blast ripped between them spinning them both like tops.

Darting behind another stone, I popped the breach open sending the cap into the sand. As I slipped the next one in, a henchman came around the stone, looming over me with a snarling expression.

Startled, I reacted and kicked his knee. He looked down, more annoyed than hurt, and I saw the top of his hat. I smacked him hard with the metal baton, my Thumper. He pitched sideways. His Thumper rolled out his hand and I scooped it up. As I popped up, I saw the baron still fighting multiple opponents. Creeping out from behind a stone directly behind him, an assassin, dressed all in black, face covered by a black scarf drew two curved knives from his belt.

I fired my Thumper, and without even looking my direction, the assassin bent backward away from the blast until his head almost touched the ground. He rose back to his feet and continued stalking the baron. With both batons in hand, I ran after him. I swung my Thumpers one after the other, but the *hassassin* blocked my attacks with his knives, never even looking at me. His eyes, like the assassin in Greece, had pupils so large all I saw was black. He moved like a trained warrior, as skilled as the baron, or Genevieve.

Finally, the assassin turned his haunting expression toward me, and a chill ran up my spine. He had dodged my attacks, and now his vacant eyes focused on me. He slashed at me with his blades. I blocked his attacks with both Thumpers, but he swung faster, and I had trouble keeping him away. I stepped back once, and then again, as one of the curved daggers whipped past my stomach. I remained barely out of reach, and the clinking of our weapons rang in my ears.

"Baron!" I yelled, knowing that I was about to

falter. I only hoped the blades weren't poisoned.

His knives moved faster than my eyes could track, and because I was busy blocking every attack with my Thumpers, I couldn't fire. I hadn't even checked to see if the henchman's Thumper was loaded. I steeled myself for the strike, knowing that when his blade finally struck home, I'd have only a split second to blast him. Only a split second to save Genevieve's father.

My arms were heavy, my muscles growing tired as the assassin effortlessly pushed my baton away one last time, opening my core to his other blade. I flinched and prepared myself to feel cold steel on my hot skin when the man's head disappeared and a mist of pink and white engulfed me. Then I heard the crack of Hunter's elephant rifle.

I exhaled, forcing the breath from my lungs, as the assassin's body crumpled to the ground. I looked at the headless body. When I realized I was covered with what remained of the man's skull and brains, I heaved the contents of my stomach into the stand.

I wiped my face with the back of my sleeve as a crack of lightning drew my attention toward Captain Baldarich. In the distance, a henchmen fell backward, twitching against a fallen pillar. Ignatius ran alongside the captain with Peacemakers in each hand. He shot one henchman attacking the baron, and pivoted to shoot another rushing to attack the captain.

Another assassin rushed out from behind the stones. He charged the baron with a clay jar dangling a lit fuse. I heard a zinging sound as one of Mr. Singh's Chakrams whipped past and sliced through the jar. Black powder spilled everywhere as I lowered the second Thumper and fired. The concussive blast smashed into the assassin and sent him sprawling.

The baron rushed forward and pressed his saber against the assassin's neck. "Who sent you?"

The assassin pulled out a small glass vile and popped the stopper with his thumb. Before the baron could stop him, he poured the liquid in his mouth. The assassin contorted, shaking violently before he collapsed. Dead.

The baron dropped to his knee and rooted through the assassin's clothes. The captain stepped up beside him and said, "Baron, we need to return to the *Sparrowhawk* and get out of here. I doubt he'll have much to tell."

"They are professional assassins, and I think I know who hired them." The baron stood up, apparently not finding anything he considered useful. "I agree, Captain. We should depart as quickly as possible."

"I found some stones that might work to replace the strut," I patted my leather bag.

"Excellent!" the captain said with a grim smile. "Maybe we won't be grounded for long after all."

Running toward the aero-dirigible, I gripped my new Thumper, now scratched from all the knife strikes. It—and Hunter—had saved my life.

We rushed onboard and I hurried to the engine room. I set the stones in front of Gears who inspected each one as I stripped off my shirt and threw it to the ground in a heap. He picked each stone up, examined it, chipped at one with his wrench, and licked another, before settling on the third stone.

"This one will do." He handed the stone to me. "Get this set."

"Right away."

I ran over to the central propeller shaft. The support had been broken, and without it secured, we wouldn't be able to use that engine for long. Before I placed the stone, I had to cut away the damaged section of the brace. One edge had been cut and bent out of place. I was staring at an obvious work of sabotage, and anger swelled within me. Who would do this to our airship? Who even had the opportunity?

With the cut in the helium cell, and now this, someone was really trying to keep us from continuing on

our journey. We must be on the right track. I scanned the engine room staring at each crewman. Most I'd known since Genevieve and I stowed away on the Sparrowhawk. I couldn't believe that after two years they were now turning to evil. It couldn't be one of them I told myself. It had to be one of the crew picked up in Egypt to replace the men killed during the battle in Zululand.

I cut the strut just below the bend, and wedged the stone into the cavity. Gears walked by and checked my work. He smiled "Excellent." He put weight on the shaft to see if the stone shifted. "She'll hold. At least until we can fix her properly in an airdock."

"Who did this?"

Anger flared across Gear's smudged face. "I don't know but when I find them, I'm shoving this wrench down his throat. Hurting my girl,"—he looked around lovingly at the airship—"I'll smear them with grease and lock 'em in the boiler." He leaned closer. "Captain's on it. I bet he dangles a few outside when we're up in the clouds. Nothing gets the truth like staring at a three-thousand-foot drop."

A couple of years ago, I might have bristled at the comment, but a part of me hoped the captain would really do it. Saboteurs deserved nothing less.

"Anything else need fixing?"

"Oh yeah, I have a list." He pointed to the engines. "Let me get her up in the air since captain wants to get out of here. Then we'll get to the repairs." Gears looked at me sideways, noting the shirt wadded up on the engine room floor.

Before I could tell him I'd been covered with brains, Baldarich's voice echoed from the copper tube jutting out of the wall, "Gears, is she ready yet?"

Gears walked over and yelled, "We've repaired enough to get out of here."

"Good. Prepare to depart."

I grabbed my shirt and left the engine room so I wouldn't be in the way. Heading down to the gun deck, I saw Mr. Singh stood in the center with crewmen manning the cannon and Gatling guns. With his focus aimed outside looking for more henchmen or assassins, I let him be. I leaned down by one of the ports and tossed my shirt out. I wanted no part in cleaning it. As we lifted off the ground, I stared at the ruins of Babylon. I was happy to be leaving. Not only did it mean we were leaving the henchmen and assassins behind, but we were back on Genevieve's trail.

I only hoped these delays didn't mean we'd lost the Milli-train one more time.

Mr. Singh ordered the cannon stowed and plugged once we were away from the ruins. I remained at the open gun port. Below lay a beige world of desert and rock, but above lay a bright blue sky spotted with puffy clouds. Up in the heavens, the troubles below never seemed to matter, as if the sky allowed us to soar above our problems.

I sighed, closed the port, and returned to the engine room to see what Gears had for me to do. As I climbed the stairs to the mid-deck, I saw Mr. Singh and two crewmen heading up to the top deck fully armed. Mr. Singh didn't usually walk around with all his weapons. Were they keeping an eye out for saboteurs? I wanted to ask, but I had to get to the engine room.

I waved as I entered. "What else needs repairing, Gears?"

He poked his head out from behind engine three. "I

have just the job for you, but thank goodness your father isn't here. He would not approve."

I brightened. "Sounds like I'm going to like it."

"You may not when I tell you the details." Gears ducked under the spinning shaft and pulled off his thick work gloves. "One of the wingsail bindings has loosened or broken off, and I need someone to go out and fix it. If I remember right, you like climbing around airships."

Excitement rippled through me as I thought of being outside. "I *might* have walked around the *Storm Vulture*."

"And you fought the Sky Witch Zerelda on top of the *Sparrowhawk*."

"Don't forget crash landing onto the *Sparrowhawk*, too."

Gears chuckled, "I almost forgot about that. See, you're my guy." He pointed to a pouch of tools. "That's everything you'll need, and Hunter agreed to spot you."

"I'll get it fixed at once." I scooped up the bag and ran off. First, I stopped by my room for a new shirt and sweater, and to grab my goggles. Then I darted up to the top deck.

Hunter waited, leaning on the ladder to the conning tower. I saluted as I reached the top of the stairs. He returned the gesture.

"Are you here to make sure I don't fall off?"

"Something like that. I'm making certain no saboteurs cut your line."

I hadn't thought about that. This would be the perfect time for a traitor to get rid of me. One snip and I'd fall, or with a locked hatch I'd be stuck outside.

I must have an odd expression because Hunter said, "I wouldn't worry. The captain is rounding up the possible suspects right now."

"That explains why Mr. Singh was fully armed." I grabbed hold of the ladder and stepped on the first rung. "Thanks for keeping an eye on me."

"Of course," Hunter said with a nod. "It's what I do."

I climbed up and opened the hatch. The wind whipped around me, pushing my hair into my face, but with the goggles, it didn't matter. Once on top, I clipped my lifeline to the rail that ran the length of the airship. At full speed, the air rushing over the *Sparrowhawk* pushed against me, but crouching a bit and keeping my feet wide apart helped me moved with ease.

Hunter exited behind me and clipped his line onto the rail as well. Together we slipped to the back of the ship. Below, I saw one of the winglets, a small stabilizing wingsail, fluttering in the wind. Before we reached the two humps on the back of the airship that housed the helium cells, I stopped and checked for the best way down.

"Here I go." I slid along the canvas-covered metal ribbing. Every so often along the side of the airship short metal rails poked out, some acted as rope guides, others redirected lighting, and some were mounted for the reason I was here—to walk along the hull.

I shimmied along the rail to the small winglet in the back. My whole body pressed against the canvas. Without hand holds or a firm place for my feet, the risk of slipping rose with every gust of wind.

"Stick like tar." I exhaled and repeated, "Stick like tar."

The winglet pounded against the air like a drum, never relenting, almost nerve shattering. I tried to push the unrelenting, almost nerve shattering, annoyance away and focus on what I had to do. A broken iron ring and a bent bearing on the hull was the cause, an easy fix in an any air dock, but here, in the sky, near impossible.

I kept telling myself not to look down, but the winglet was below me. Every time I tried to figure how to make the repair, the ground far below called like one of the sirens luring sailors to their death.

I focused on the winglet, until a scream cut through the raging wind. Raising my head, I feared Hunter had slipped, but instead saw one of the crew dangling upside down. A rope tied around his legs tethered him to the airship. The captain and Mr. Singh leaned out the cargo door.

They must have discovered the saboteur.

It gave me an idea. I double-knotted my lifeline around the rail and let go. I fell under the winglet right next to the bent bearing and broken ring. Reaching into my bag of tools, I pulled out a wrench bound to the bag by a leather tie, and hooked the bearing. Locking my feet against one of the metal ribs under the canvas hull, I pulled with all my might and bent it back into place. A few strikes on top worked it back into place. I snagged the broken ring with my fingers, pulling the winglet toward me. Working the broken iron through the grommet, I retrieved a replacement from the bag and slid it through the winglet.

As I grabbed the pinchers from my bag, I slipped away from the airship. Spinning on the end of my tether, the wind forced me up and down and side to side. I pushed off the hull with my feet and hooked the ring with my fingers. Pulling myself toward the winglet, I hooked my foot on the yardarm and brought the pinchers forward. Upside down, with the bag hanging over my head, I had great access to the winglet. With the pinchers in one hand, I secured the tool around the two sides of the ring. Then with one last grunt, I clamped the handles, bringing the two ends together.

Pulling the pinchers away, I yanked the winglet taught and hooked the ring around the bearing. With a few strikes from the handle of the pinchers, the bearing wrapped around the ring, and though it wasn't perfect, it was repaired. Hopefully, it would hold until we could get to an airdock.

Now I had to get back inside. Releasing my foot, I swung into the air. I pulled myself hand over hand until I could grasp the railing. I untied the double knot, freeing the rope, which was still connected to the top of the airship. The rope went taut and tugged me off the railing. I looked up to find Hunter hoisting me up. I used the metal ribbing poking through the canvas hull to help guide me past the obstacles on the side of the Sparrowhawk.

When I reached the top, Hunter extended his hand and yanked me up. I lay down and exhaled. Hunter leaned over me. "Are the repairs done?"

I nodded and held up my thumb.

Hunter smiled, "Come on, let's get inside."

Again, I held up my thumb. The enormity of what I'd just done was sinking in and I feared my voice would betray me. I could still feel the emptiness between me and the ground as I'd hung upside down. Hunter pulled me to my feet and my knees wobbled beneath me.

"That was some trick," he said, steadying me. "Can't wait to tell the captain."

BOOK III: IRON LOTUS

11
Milli-Train
Tracks

After three ambushes, Captain Baldarich wasn't taking any more chances and we zigzagged toward the mountains. They told me we were looking for the Milli-train, but I overhead him talking to the baron about preventing anyone on the ground from knowing where we traveled. I didn't like it. All I could think of was that another week had passed, and the Milli-train was getting further away as we crossed the steppe.

The steppe was what the baron and the others kept calling the land before the top of the world. The mountains in the distance looked like a wall of stone that stretched from one end of the horizon to the other.

The closer we flew to the Himalayas, the more impressed I became. Snow-capped peaks rose above us and pierced the clouds. The mountains looked impossible to pass. I'd never seen the *Sparrowhawk* fly high enough to go over them, and with the peaks jammed next to one another, I didn't see a way through. Not a single pass cracked the horizon.

"Welcome to the rooftop of the world." Baron Kensington walked up behind

me as I peered out the window on the bridge.

"I've never seen anything so massive." I remained pressed against the glass, each exhale fogging it up even more.

"Thousands of miles of mountains. They stretch to the north and to the east. It's so high you'll have trouble breathing."

"Fascinating. I take it you've been here before."

"When I was stationed in India, we chased bandits up through the Punjab and into Tibet."

"That's where you helped Mr. Singh."

"Yes, I found him defending his parent's bodies in the Punjab."

I looked back toward the hatch. "I haven't talked to him since they discovered the saboteur. I should check on him."

"You're a good man, Alexander."

Captain Baldarich shouted, "There!" and shattered the moment between the baron and me.

We spun around and found him vaulting out of his chair and pointing at the ground.

"Ten degrees starboard, Heinz." The captain stepped up beside the pilot.

Heinz nodded and adjusted the wheel. The baron and I walked over. I tried to see what had excited the captain, but all I saw was barren ground, rocks, and two parallel lines of churned up earth. Then I realized, I'd seen those lines before. In Africa. The tracks of the Milli-train.

I rushed forward. The tracks led over a ridge and into a mountain pass. From here I could see where each leg of the train had poked the ground, tearing up the soil as it pulled forward, and then the next leg striking right behind the original hole. The tracks wove back and forth, just like the Milli-train had done when it crossed Africa.

I pumped my fist in the air. "We've found them."

"Not yet," the captain reminded me. He pointed toward the pass. "Take us in Heinz, but watch the mountains, I don't want to lose a wingsail."

"Aye, aye, Captain. Can we go higher?"

"The helium isn't going to lift us much more." Captain Baldarich walked back to the copper tubes, flipped all four open and leaned closer. "Hunter, I need your eyes on the bridge."

Within moments Hunter appeared and joined me by the windows. "Eyes on, Captain."

"Don't lose those tracks."

I pointed as the Milli-train's trail climbed over a high mountain pass.

"Captain," Hunter said, "course adjustment to port twenty degrees. Take us over that ridge."

Baldarich clapped his hands. "Heinz, you heard the man, get us over that ridge."

Heinz turned the wheel. "Bearing to port, twenty degrees."

Hunter pointed over my head. "Get ready for a sharp starboard turn after the ridge."

"How do you know that?" I asked staring at the ground trying to see what he was able to read.

"See how the tracks are curving at the ridgeline, and then the back slope of this mountain over here. They had to turn right."

"Fascinating," I said, and as Hunter explained, when we crested the ridge. The tracks led through the valley and then tore straight across a village perched on the side of a mountain. Several buildings of the tiered city had damage.

Hunter turned to the captain. "A village sir."

The baron looked up from the map table and said, "Captain, can we land? They'll be able to tell how long ago the Milli-train passed through."

"My thoughts exactly, Your Grace." He cracked his knuckles. "Heinz, take us down."

"Where? I don't see any docks or even a strip of land big enough."

"Hunter?"

"The top plateau should be big enough, barely, but we won't have to worry about getting tangled in those flags."

Baldarich stepped over beside us. He surveyed the spot and nodded. "Heinz set her down gently. The winds will be wicked so close to the mountain." He then turned to me. "Tell Mr. Singh to fold the wingsails in early. We won't be able to get close enough if he doesn't."

I nodded and ran off. I found Mr. Singh on the middeck. "We're about to land and the captain wants you to close the wingsails early or we won't have room to land."

Mr. Singh nodded and cupped a hand to his mouth. His voice rose over the noise. "Prepare for landing. Crewmen to the wingsails."

Several crewmen ran onto the deck and lined up along the ropes. Mr. Singh walked over to the hull and pulled a lever, opening the doors to allow the wingsail to retract. He then marched to the other side of the airship and flipped a similar lever.

I crossed the way and asked Mr. Singh, "Do you need me to tie up the wingsails?"

He counted the men who had gathered and shook his head. "No. But I want you to go down to the gun deck and watch the landing strut. If they aren't on firm ground, come and tell me."

I nodded. "Right away."

Traversing the stairs two at a time, I ran down to the gun deck and pulled open the hatches in the floor. The rocky ground drew closer and I leaned out to check the landing struts. In an airdock it didn't matter, the moorings held the airship in place, but landing on the ground, the *Sparrowhawk* rested on two landing struts and the wooden underbelly of the gun deck.

I heard the grinding and clatter of the wingsails being retracted and kept my eye on the front struts to make sure they were secure. The one was close to the edge and looked like it was about to slip off. I was about to run up to the bridge, but the *Sparrowhawk* pivoted and the strut landed on firm ground. I breathed a sigh of relief and closed the hatches.

Rushing into my room, I got everything I might need, including a coat, and dropped out of the hatch. I wasn't certain if they were going to ask me to go or not, but if joined them it would be harder to say no.

The baron, with Rodin on his shoulder, the captain, and Ignatius strode down the gangplank. I met them at the bottom. The baron smiled, but the captain gave me a look. He didn't say anything; he just motioned for me to follow.

Tiers were cut into the mountainside, each one supporting brightly colored buildings constructed from brick and stacked stones. The houses weren't one or two colors but several. Reds, yellows, blues, and greens. The bright colors brought a vibrant glow to the whole village. Ropes strung between the tiled roofs held colored flags with writing on them. Everyone watched us and I got the feeling airships didn't land that often.

The people we passed were dressed in fabrics as colorful as the buildings. A woman passed by with a coat of beautiful embroidery. She smiled but scurried off.

We approached a house partially destroyed by the Milli-train. An older man, with deep wrinkles on his face, was lifting stones to rebuild the corner of his home. The baron approached and said something in a language I didn't know. The man shook his head and placed the brick. The baron thanked him, turned to the captain, and shrugged. Together they looked around at the village, and the captain pointed toward another building that had been damaged. I watched as the old man labored to pick up the next stone.

After he set the stone and wiped his brow, he took several labored breaths. I moved forward. I couldn't stand here and watch him struggle any longer. I picked up a stone and pointed toward the wall. The old man smiled, and nodded, then showed me where he wanted it to go. After I placed the third stone, the old man took a drink of water. I kept rebuilding the wall while the old man walked over to the baron. He pointed off toward the east. The baron thanked the old man who then walked back over to me, he said several things, I had no idea what, but from the look in his eyes I thought he appreciated my effort. The walls were done. He only had to fix the roof.

The baron came up and Rodin jumped onto my shoulder. "That was very noble of you to help rebuild this man's house."

"I couldn't watch him struggle."

"Well, it made him want to talk to us. The Milli-train passed by here a couple of days ago."

"How close are we?"

"I'm not sure."

The captain joined us, "In this terrain we should be able to catch up to them."

We all rushed back to the *Sparrowhawk*. As we ran up the gangplank, Lord Marbury waited at the top. "Did you get answers?"

The baron nodded. I remained to retract the gangplank and close the cargo door as the others ran to the bridge. Once the *Sparrowhawk* was sealed up, I walked down to my room with Rodin. I pulled out some jerky I had in my bag and tore off a bit for the dragon and shoved the rest in my mouth. Rodin curled up in his bed and I jumped into my hammock.

The *Sparrowhawk* lifted off, and I exhaled slowly. I heard Rodin do the same.

"We're close Rodin, I can feel it. I just hope she's okay." I put my hands behind my head. I wanted to believe I was days away from seeing Genevieve, but something in the back of my mind screamed it wouldn't be that easy.

BOOK III: IRON LOTUS

<h1>12
The Lady
and the Owl</h1>

eavy eyes and thoughts of Genevieve sent me spiraling from the belly of the *Sparrowhawk* into the darkness.

Torchlight flickered against blackened walls of a large room and flames danced atop candles on the heavy tables. I ran through tables and chairs, tossing them aside as if Genevieve lay under one, and I, desperate to find her, had only to discover the right one. The room was full of dark, heavily bearded men and I ran up to them, demanding they tell me where she was, but from their blank stares I knew they didn't know. The sound of wings flapping, a heavy pounding against the air, drowned out all other sounds. The doors to this place blew open and the wind rushed in with a terrifying thunder. I was hurled across the room, tumbling end over end until I landed at the tiny feet of a young woman. She leaned over, her short black hair covering most of her face. On her arm sat a large owl with feathery horns above its

eyes. She reached down but I fell away and slammed against something hard.

I sat up, on the floor, below my hammock. I rubbed my head and looked up at Rodin who stared down at me from his bed. He cocked his head to the side as if to say, "Again?"

"What, you've never fallen out of bed before?"

He shook his head.

I stood up, rubbed my back, and then sat on the barrel. "I wonder what that meant. Who is the lady with the owl?"

Rodin curled back up and ignored me. I guess he figured I was okay and so he wasn't interested in my dream. *Or was it another vision?*

Even here in my room it was cold. I could see my breath with each exhale. I figured the snow-capped mountains would be colder, but winter was supposed to giving way to spring. At least in the rest of the world it was spring.

I stood up and patted my shoulder. Rodin stretched and then flew over and landed. I left my room and slowly walked up the stairs to the bridge. The captain spun in his chair as I stepped through the hatch. He smiled and waved me over.

"What do you think of the roof of the world?"

I leaned against the railing around his chair. "It amazes me people live here."

"I've almost been around the whole world, and you want to know something? From the highest mountain, to farthest island, I've found people. We're all over the place."

I smiled. The baron came up and stood beside me. "These mountains were home to some of the first cosmopolitan people. Traders from the east and the west traveled the Silk Road, the first trade route, and met here in the high plateaus."

"Fascinating." I looked out at the vista surrounding us. "They are majestic."

The baron tapped his cane on the deck, "The Buddhists and the Hindus both claim them as their own. There are more sacred places in this range, than cathedrals in Europe."

"I feel like we're getting close to Genevieve."

"I pray that we are." The baron looked at me. I could see the pain in his eyes, even if his face remained as stoic as always.

Hunter, who still stood by the window, turned and said, "Captain, the Milli-train's trail ends in that village."

"Heinz, find a place to set her down and let's ask some questions."

"Aye, aye, Captain." Heinz pushed forward on the wheel, and slowed our speed.

The captain smiled, flipped open the copper tubes, and in a booming voice, said, "Attention, prepare for a landing."

The baron nudged me with his cane. "Get your things together, and bring Rodin with you."

I nodded and rushed off the bridge. I had a feeling this was the place I'd learn about Genevieve. Hopefully, I'd find the lady with the owl from my vision, and she would know the way. It was a longshot, but my visions had been right about my father's kidnapping and the village in Zululand. I had to trust they were right about

Genevieve, too."

I loaded my bag with some rope, my dad's monoscope, a powder charge from one of the canons, a couple of pieces of fruit, and the extra Thumper. I slipped my bowie knife and my Thumper in the leather strap that wound up my leg, around my body, and down one arm. I pulled a long, wrapped bundle from a hidden space tucked up behind a pipe and tied it to my back. Lastly, I hooked the pouch of percussion caps on my hip and pulled on the heavy coat with a fur collar. I patted my shoulder for Rodin and he flew over and took his place. "Don't worry," I told him, "I brought plenty of jerky for you."

Together we walked up to the gangplank as the airship gently settled on a mountain ledge. The crew threw open the doors and slid the ramp out. The captain, Ignatius, and the baron came down the hall with Hunter carrying Gretel, his elephant gun.

The captain turned to Hunter, "Perch yourself on top of the *Sparrowhawk* and keep an eye out for trouble." He then walked over to Mr. Singh. "You're coming, too. Get your gear and weapons and meet us outside."

He smiled and bowed ever so slightly. "Yes, sir!"

As we walked down the gangplank, I surveyed the town for the building from my vision. Like the last village, this one was built on tiers cut into the mountainside. Some of the buildings had multiple stories, and all were made of stone or brick. Again, bright vibrant colors burst forth from each one. This village was bigger than the last, and it was difficult to see all the buildings. I was eager to rush off, but we waited for Mr. Singh. Finally, we followed the path into the village with the baron and the captain leading the way and me sandwiched between them.

The captain walked with his usual wide smile and pirate swagger, but his eyes darted from one person to the next. I watched how he assessed each new section of the town. The baron strode on the other side of me. He, too, had an ease to his step, but an intense look in his eyes. The others were less subtle, Ignatius kept his hands on two of his pistols, and Mr. Singh had one hand on his sword, and the other on his Katar dagger.

I wasn't certain how to walk because what I wanted was to run. This processional took forever, but I had to stay with my crew. It would be foolish to run off. I could be ambushed—or worse—miss a clue that could lead us to Genevieve.

As we came to the center of town, the doors of one large building swung open. I stopped. Inside flicker flames rose from torches on the wall. It looked big enough to be the right room, and an uneasy feeling rippled through my core. Everyone stopped and looked at me.

The captain leaned in. "What is it, lad?"

"This is the place. We'll find answers here." The captain and the baron exchanged glances.

"Then lead the way," the baron said.

I walked up the few wooden steps to the doors. The aroma of food and a warm breeze enveloped me. I exhaled, letting some of the tensions slip away, and stepped inside. The others followed.

Inside, tables and chairs were scattered about the main room. Small groups of people filled the room. They all turned as we entered. In the dim light, I saw four swarthy guys sitting at the center table drinking, another couple eating by the fire, and a group of foreigners, like us, sitting around two tables on the far side. A woman rushed from the back and welcomed us in a language I didn't know. The baron answered her, and she motioned us over to a table where we arranged our chairs so we could watch the other patrons.

It was so odd to hear a language I knew absolutely nothing about. Besides Africa, everywhere I traveled, I knew all the languages, or at least enough of them to understand the gist of what was being said. But here, every word spoken was unusual and completely foreign to me. I kind of liked it, though, and I realized that besides Zulu, I had a lot of them left to learn.

The baron spoke to the woman and held up five fingers. She scurried off. He leaned closer to me, "So now what?"

Ignatius motioned his head toward the four swarthy men, "I say we kick over some tables and start demanding these varmints tell us where that train is."

I shook my head. "No, I'm looking for someone."

They all turned toward me. They knew I wasn't telling them everything, and the baron looked annoyed by my vague answer, but the captain smiled.

I noticed Rodin hadn't moved, he sat on my shoulder but I could feel him staring at a ratty blue curtain hanging over a doorway at the back of the room. "I'll be back," I said. "You stay here in case some of these guys are protecting her."

"Who?" The baron asked, but I stood up without a word and walked through the tables. I heard the baron ask, "Do you know what he's talking about?"

The curtain hadn't been pulled all the way over, leaving a slight gap. As I drew closer, I peered through trying to see anything inside. A man appeared before me, he filled the whole doorway, and passed through, throwing the curtain aside. I stepped aside and he brushed past me and disappeared into the kitchen across the room. I could smell the cloud of spices, alcohol, and tang of smoke that swirled around him. I started to follow him when I heard the hoot of an owl.

I spun around and stepped through the curtain. A thin strand of smoke trailed up from a long pipe with a bulb on the end. The pipe rested on a cushion, one of several back here but tucked in the far corner, perched on a stool sat a young woman. Short, black hair covered her face, and she wore a long, flowing silk garment with pants peeking out from underneath. The color, once a beautiful red that had faded over time. She wore tiny embroidered shoes, just like my vision. If I needed even more evidence, sitting on her arm, which was propped up by a cane, was an owl with clockwork wings.

I gasped. I wanted to say something, but the piercing eyes of the owl mesmerized me. Two feathered tufts above the large golden orbs looked like horns, and her tawny feathers dotted with specs of white, were accented by brass gears and pneumatics that made up her wings.

Rodin shifted on my shoulder and dug his claws in. The pain snapped me out of my trance, and I realized the two animals were sizing each other up. Neither made an aggressive move, but the owl shifted back and forth on his talons as Rodin puffed out his chest.

I knew I had to say something, I was bordering on the verge of rudeness. I wanted to speak with her before the man returned.

Without moving anything but her head, she lifted her gaze, only one eye stared at me. The other was covered by her silky black hair, but I stepped back from her intense, icy stare.

I had to speak now. I placed my foot back where it had been, and held my palms out in sign of peace. "Pardon my intrusion, but I think you know where my friend might be. I was wondering if I could ask you some questions?" I smiled, hoping she understood English. I quickly flipped through the various languages I knew, wondering which would be best known in these parts. Alexander the Great hadn't traveled this far, but I thought I'd try Greek, just in case. "*Synchorisi eisvoli mou—*"

"The boy with dragon," she said in English. "But you are only a dream."

"Whoa—" Not only did she speak English, but she'd seen *me* in a dream. A flood of questions rushed through my mind, but I forced them away to focus on Genevieve. I didn't know how much time we had. "I had a vision you'd help me find my friend."

"The girl with the sword,"

"Yes!" I nodded. My heart soared. If anyone could describe Genevieve in five words, those were spot on. I stepped toward her. "Do you know where she is?"

"On the train with legs."

"Yes!" My excitement boiled over. This woman knew exactly who I was talking about. "How long ago did it pass through here?"

"The monk told me you couldn't be real."

"I am," I said. "My name is Alexander."

"The invader's name." Her head lifted higher and with her free hand, she pushed back her hair. She was stunning in a way I had seen few times in my travels. With her soft features, dark eyes, and smooth intensity, this woman stood out among all those I'd met. She cocked her head to the side. "In my vision, you freed me and guided me to my destiny."

"You're not . . . free?"

She pulled back her sleeve and it folded over the owl's talons. An iron manacle encircled her bruised wrist, as a thin chain dangled below. "I am the bound falconer of the Spice Master."

"What is your name?"

"He calls me Ershou Long." Her smile lit up the dreary room as she motioned to the owl. "This is Kō'ilā."

"This is Rodin; and we'll do whatever we can to free you."

13
A Fight for Freedom

I looked at the chain and manacle holding her to this stool. She eyed me and Rodin.

"Your dragon is not a machine?"

"No, and I see your owl isn't, either." I didn't have a lock pick and I debated if my Thumper would be too loud. I was more worried about hurting her. "Where is the key?"

"The Spice Master wears it around his neck." She motioned to the chain. "The chains are iron, forged in China. They are unbreakable."

"I wouldn't be so sure." I pulled my Thumper from its holster. "Cover your ears." I glanced at the dragon on my shoulder. Rodin, "Go to the baron. You might want to send the owl off, too."

She let a leather strap tied around the owl's leg slip through her fingers, and motioned with her other hand. The owl flew off and landed on the other side of the room. I folded the chain in a loop and hooked it on the end of the baton.

"Turn your head." I pointed the Thumper away from us and pressed the button. The piston slid

forward, and the shockwave obliterated the chain in a thunderous blast that shook the walls of this building. The manacle still surrounded her wrist with seven links dangling below, but the rest fell to the dirt floor.

She jumped up, grabbed her cane, and thrust her arm out. The owl flew back and landed on her sleeve. She walked over and sat on a mechanical spider, a seat with eight articulated legs. As she pressed forward on a handle on the arm rest, the seat came to life. We turned to leave, but there filling the doorway was a thin spindle of a man, eyes burning with anger and lips curled into an ugly snarl. I glanced at Ershou. Her eyes were on fire. This must be the Spice Master.

The man started screaming in Chinese; Ershou yelled in return. She didn't act like a timid slave, but had the same fire I'd seen in Genevieve. I had no idea what they were saying, but as he reached into his coat, I raised my Thumper. Before I could strike him, Ershou lifted her arm, and Kō'ilā's feathers bristled.

"Attack!" She pointed, and the owl took to the air.

The Spice Master threw up his arms to shield his head and tried to run out of the room, howling in pain as the owl's talons clawed at his back and beat his head with her powerful wings.

Ershou threw open a chest and pulled out a silk sash with four bone-handled knives dangling in embroidered sheaths. She tied them around her waist and drew one of the knives, spinning it in her palm. She and I bolted into the main room, past the flailing Spice Master, but she stopped, the walker rose up on its legs and lifted her up to the Spice Master. She pressed the blade against his chin. "Never again."

I didn't say anything but motioned for her to head

straight toward the captain and the baron. As we ran, she held up her arm and the owl flew to her.

The Spice Master whipped around, drew out a silk pouch from the folds of his clothes and threw it on the table where the four swarthy men were watching the events unfold. The men eyed each other as the pouch landed with the heavy clunk of coins.

"Whoever retrieves my property will get this payment—and more."

The four swarthy men kicked back their chairs and stood, reaching for their blades, but before they could take one step toward Ershou, Captain Baldarich drew his lightning cannon and fired. The blue electricity zapped the closest man in the chest and sent him crumbling to the floor with a thud. Before the man's companions realized what was happening, Ignatius had drawn two pistols from the holsters on his hips, and fired, wounding two others in the leg, which sent them tumbling sideways as they grasped tables or chairs—or thin air—for support. In a blur, Mr. Singh vaulted over the table, pulled his Katar dagger with flintlock barrels on each side, from the sheath on his chest. As he confronted the fourth man, he spun, and in one swipe, knocked the man's legs, which were thick as tree trunks, right out from under him. He, too, crashed to the floor and Mr. Singh stood over him daring him to move.

The Spice Master screeched in plain English, "Ershou! You *belong* to me!"

"I am no one's property," she hissed, spinning the blade in her hand, she threw it at the Spice Master. The knife sank into the wooden wall just over his shoulder. She turned away from him. The baron glanced at me and then to Ershou. "You are safe with us," he said, as he motioned her toward the door with me leading the way. Behind us, the men of the *Sparrowhawk* formed a wall separating Ershou from the Spice Master.

Mr. Singh grabbed the money pouch from the table, emptied the coins into his palm, and dropped the empty pouch on the fourth man's chest. With a bright smile he nodded and joined the captain.

The Spice Master moaned and yelled as if in terrible pain. As we reached the door, he rushed forward, but Ignatius fired again, the bullets impacting around the Spice Master's feet, and the man jumped back, eyes wide as if he couldn't conceive of what was happening to him.

I shoved the door open and stopped on the threshold, stunned to see a group of soldiers standing at the base of the stairs. They carried rifles, and the man in front carried a revolver. I didn't see a flag patch, or any other markings to indicate where they were from.

I raised my hands, trying to think of something to say. The soldiers stunned by my action, looked to each other, everyone except the man with the revolver. In English he said, "Come with me or die!"

"This is just a misunderstanding," the captain said behind me.

"No misunderstanding. You are coming with me."

"Under whose authority?" the baron demanded.

I glanced at Rodin, and found him looking at me. We shared an unspoken moment, and when the dragon winked at me, I knew he had a plan stirring in his mind.

He screeched, a piercing sound that sent searing pain through my ears. Startled, the soldiers gripped their heads. Rodin lifted off my shoulder and unleashed a column of fire on the soldiers, who dove and ran to avoid the flames.

Pointing his lightning pistol at the soldiers, Captain Baldarich fired. Electricity arced from one soldier to another creating a chain of twitching men who collapsed into the dirt even as more soldiers appeared in the distance. "Follow me," I whispered, as I jumped down to the narrow decking that ran along the front of the building.

We leapt off a large stone next building and then slid down to the street. I ran started to run toward the Sparrowhawk but she grabbed my arm. "No! This way. They are this way."

I nodded and followed. Rodin fluttered in the air behind us, and as I looked back, I saw the others rushing toward the *Sparrowhawk* as the soldiers fired on them. Gunshots cracked like thunder and echoed off the mountains. I heard shouting in the distance. More soldiers gathering together to charge toward my friends.

Ershou and I ducked behind a house and froze, standing as still as the mountains. The soldiers filed past the front of the building. I risked a look around the corner and saw the captain and Ignatius holding the soldiers back with gunfire, while the baron and Mr. Singh rushed toward the *Sparrowhawk*. One of the rocks the soldiers were using for cover shattered as a thunderous gunshot echoed through the whole valley. The soldiers retreated as a second shot ripped through a wooden cart.

"Hunter will make them think twice with Gretel."

Ershou stared at me with a puzzled expression, but I didn't want to take the time to explain.

"Who are these soldiers?" I asked.

"I do not know. They arrived at the same time as the train with legs."

"Hendrix's soldiers. The troops he had with him in Africa." My fist tightened into a ball. "We need to get back to the *Sparrowhawk*."

"No, this way," Ershou used the handle of her cane to point toward the mountain. "The train with legs is this way."

I paused. I should return to the ship, but Genevieve was on the Milli-train. I knew the baron, the captain, Mr. Singh, and the rest of the crew would be angry if I ran off again, but if I didn't follow her, Genevieve might be lost.

I peeked around the corner again. More soldiers poured out of the buildings and rushed up the path toward the ship. I told myself, Ershou was the woman from my vision, and was destined to help me find Genevieve. I exhaled heavily, nodded, then followed her as she slipped behind into an alleyway. Now I only needed to leave markers for the captain and baron to find.

We climbed a path along the side of the mountain, staying behind buildings, and hiding, when possible, behind boulders. I wondered where she was leading me. How could the Milli-train disappear? Where could it go? There weren't any tents or buildings big enough to conceal a giant train. I started to ask her, but she put her finger to her lips and motioned me to stay low.

The walker, which looked like it had metal spider legs, made little noise as it moved, no more than a bird chirping with a slight clicking as the legs tapped on the ground.

Finally, she stopped, and she and the walker crouched behind a boulder, she looked down on the village. No soldiers followed us, but gunfire still rang out in the distance.

"What powers your chair?"

She looked at me and then pointed at a solenoid on the back of the walker. "My walker runs on electricity which recharges as I walk."

"Fascinating, but I have to contact my friends." I dug through my pouch until I found the percussion cap with the red cover. "The captain gave me this after Acre, in case I got into trouble." I tore off the paper cover and slipped the brass cap into my Thumper. I held it out away from the mountain. "I bet we're about to run into trouble." I fired and a red flare exploded out the end and soared off. We ducked down, and I hoped only friends saw the signal.

Satisfied we were safe, she took my hand and led me toward a large expanse of rock on the other side of the path. Letting go she motioned to the rock wall. I shrugged, uncertain what she was trying to show me.

"Here." She motioned to the wall.

"Where?"

She reached out and touched the wall; it rippled like cloth. I stepped up and touched what I thought was rock, but I felt heavy canvas under my fingers. Looking more closely, I recognized paint, bits of stone, and thick canvas like the hull of the *Sparrowhawk*. It was like a backdrop at a theater. A cloth painted to look like the side of a mountain. *Ingenious.*

"A false wall," I said, pulling my hand away. "What's behind it?"

"A tunnel." She pushed the curtain aside.

"Wait, I have to mark this." I unsheathed my knife and scratched the rock beside her, creating a chevron pointing toward the tunnel. "Like the labyrinth on Malta." Finding the edge, I pulled the tarp back from actual stone.

Only darkness lay ahead. A faint, dank odor offended my nose. I held my breath and slipped inside. Ershou followed.

14
A Secret Palace

Endless darkness led to a point of light at the far end, like a beacon, calling us forward. I slid my hand along the cool stone wall as we made our way through the cavernous tunnel.

"How do you know about this place?" I whispered.

"We all saw them arrive, but the Spice Master deals with them."

"Does that mean he's going to run and tell them we're coming?"

"No, they don't like him."

"Why?"

"He's Mongolian."

I started to ask why that would matter, but I already knew. To the men seeking the Hearts, only certain races and cultures were accepted. The rest, deemed unworthy, were destined only to be slaves and servants. The thought burned me inside.

We walked in silence, the light growing brighter as we approached the other side of the mountain. A heavy tarp also covered this opening but one corner had been pulled back creating the beacon

that guided us through. I was worried we hadn't run into any soldiers and feared they were standing outside waiting for us. But everything was quiet. I crawled up to the opening and peered out. Nothing but snow and barren rock. I pushed it open and we stepped out onto a wide ledge. We'd gone straight through the mountain and the tracks of the Milli-train continued on.

Ershou motioned for me to follow, pulling my attention away from the giant tunnel.

The wind howled as we reached the top of the ridge. Though it was early spring, the chill bit into my skin like the coldest London winters. I pulled my fur lined hood up and cinched it tight. Ershou pointed. I followed her finger to a point in the distance and squinted, but couldn't see anything. Then tucked into a notch on the mountain across the river, I saw a tiered palace. The majestic building boasted several levels, all with tiled roofs, brightly decorated walls, and elaborate columns featuring exotic animal designs.

"What is that place?"

"A hidden palace of a long-forgotten kingdom." Ershou kept moving, and her head darted back and forth carefully examining the path before us. I suspected she didn't like being exposed on this ridge. "Come."

I stared down at the river thousands of feet below, a thin ribbon with tiny flecks of roiling rapids. The Milli-train tracks led across the valley toward the palace on the other side.

"How do we get there?"

She pointed straight down, but I couldn't see a path. Then I realized she was gesturing to the river below. "We can't swim that. The rapids are too swift."

She pointed again. "Not the river. The rope."

I squinted until I saw a thin line spanning the valley. My heart dropped.

"Follow me," she said as she scrambled down the rocky trail.

"Doesn't this country have bridges?"

She cocked her head, considering me for a moment, and then gestured toward the rope stretched taut above the river valley and anchored around a heavy boulder with prayer flags fluttering on the end. "This is faster. You're not afraid, are you?"

"No." I puffed up my chest and stormed up to the edge. The river raged below, churning like a boiling cauldron. "No problem."

She ignored me and handed me a looped rope with a small pulley wheel on top. "Tie this around your chest, under your arms. Hook this part over the rope." She walked over to the rope, the front two and back two legs of her walker rose up and hooked onto the fibrous braid. She hooked the pulley around the rope. "It's easy, just push off and when you stop, pull yourself the rest of the way. Wait until I'm on the other side before you go."

As she shoved off the edge, she bounced a couple of times as she sped over the river. Her owl flew right beside her, its bronze and feathered wings spread in majestic grace. I secured the rope and waited until I saw her walker climb off the line on the other side. I took a deep breath, but as I was about to leap, a hand grabbed my shoulder. I drew my Thumper and spun around. Mr. Singh stood in front of me with a large smile beaming under his thick beard.

"I was sent after you, and found your mark at the tunnel." Mr. Singh looked at the rope across the valley. "Where is she leading you?"

"Ershou knows where the Milli-train is. Where Genevieve is." I pointed across the valley to the palace built into the rock. "She says they are there. The Spice Master sold them goods."

He eyed the girl crouched on the opposite side. "Are you sure this isn't a trap?"

I paused. I could understand his thoughts, but I knew she was right. Mr. Singh was one of my best friends, I could trust him. "I saw her in a vision. Besides, if she leads me to Genevieve, it's a risk I'm willing to take."

"Alexander. That is not wise. We should wait for the others."

"Can't," I handed him a rope to tie around himself. "If you're coming, great, if you want to wait, you know where I'll be."

Mr. Singh shook his head and wrapped the rope under his arms. I shoved off the edge and slid along the rope, the wheel rattled as I raced across. Rodin flew beside me, darting from side to side. Dangling over the churning white water below my pulse quickened, but the sensation was like flying and I couldn't help but smile. When I landed on the other side, Ershou was crouched behind a boulder staring up at the palace, watching something intently.

"Is someone watching?" I tried to see as I untied myself.

"Not at the moment, but had you gone sooner, he would have spotted you."

"My friend is coming over, too." I pointed as Mr. Singh leapt off and zipped across the river.

"He had better be quick about it."

Mr. Singh arrived and planted his feet on the stone, stopping easily. I helped him out of the rope and we dropped beside Ershou. She and Mr. Singh locked eyes, and he nodded, but she turned away. With a wave of her hand, she said, "Follow me."

She ran off, skimming the rock wall as she hurried up the trail. I slapped Mr. Singh's shoulder, "See, come on. Let's go get Genevieve."

He hesitated. "Alexander, we should be more cautious."

I heard him, but didn't listen. I didn't just trust her; I trusted my intuition. I ran up behind Ershou and pressed myself against the rocks. Mr. Singh joined us. He was about to say something, but she held a finger to her lips.

Above us I heard voices, two men speaking in English.

"See anything?" the first man asked.

They must be guards. I glanced back at Mr. Singh who nodded as if he read my thoughts.

"Nothing," the second man said. "Too cold, I guess. Haven't even seen a rat to use as target practice."

I rubbed Rodin's head as he sat on my shoulder. "Stay close," I whispered. He pressed his head against my cheek.

Ershou motioned for us to follow. We crept along the trail until she stopped by a small opening in the rock face.

"This is the drainage for the palace," Ershou whispered. "I saw it when the Spice Master and I came here. I don't know where it leads once inside, but the only other option is to climb the mountain." She pointed to the sheer rock face. There was no way we could climb it—there were barely any handholds—and we'd be exposed the whole time.

The opening angled up toward the palace but was only big enough to squeeze through. We couldn't continue up the trail, which led to where the guards stood. Besides, if this led into the palace, it was the perfect way inside.

I turned to Mr. Singh, "You wait out here. If I'm not back by nightfall, then go get the cavalry."

"No, I must go with you."

"Then we might both get caught." I gripped his shoulder. "Ershou doesn't know the crew or the captain. You do. I'm going to be careful."

Mr. Singh cocked his head to the side, and raised his eyebrow. "Really?"

"Yes. I will be. I promise." I smiled. "I'm trying to free Genevieve, not join her."

Mr. Singh sighed and then nodded in resignation. He didn't like my plan, but he knew I was right. Someone had to stay outside in case I was captured.

I turned to Ershou. "You have my eternal thanks for your help. Please, stay with Mr. Singh, once back with our allies, I can properly reward you." I took off my coat and wrapped it around her. "Here, this will keep you warm while you wait."

"Thank you. We will give you until nightfall."

"In and out, no worries." I pulled Rodin off my shoulder and placed him in the drain. "You first." I squeezed in behind him, the opening was barely wider than my shoulder. A trickle of water ran down the sloping sluice as I began to climb.

The rough rock quickly turned into a segmented clay pipe that I could easily climb, while Rodin used his talons to scale the sides and kept his wings tucked in. It was slow going, but I moved at a steady pace. A faint light lay above me, and drew me ever higher. The fear of falling crept into my mind.

Why did you look down? I chastised myself. *Haven't you learned anything from flying on the Sparrowhawk?* I slid my arms up to grab the next segment of pipe and kept my feet firmly pressed against the sides. I looked up and saw Rodin perched on an edge, his tail swinging back and forth. *Just a little farther.*

Reaching the edge, I found myself staring at Rodin's cute little dragon butt. I pressed against the sides, but my hand and foot hit a slick patch and I slipped. My fingers clung to the edge and I pushed my feet out to stabilize myself. I slammed against the side and my lips pressed into the trickle of water running down the pipe. It tasted like bile. I spit repeatedly and wiped my mouth on my shirt. Straining, I pulled myself back up. Rodin turned around and rubbed my face as I hooked my elbows on the ledge and lifted myself up over the edge. Once secured, I breathed out a long sigh. Before me the pipe widened, and a set of vertical iron bars separated me from a dark stone room lit only by a single flickering torch.

"I'd better be able to fit through here," I said to Rodin. "I sure don't want to climb back down."

The bars were just wide enough that my head slipped through, twisting my shoulders and feet, I squeezed between the gap. If I were any bigger, like the captain or baron, I wouldn't have fit. Once inside the room, with a raised center, the edges acting as a drain that flowed to the pipe. In the center of the room chains lay on the floor. I realized I was in a dungeon.

Thank goodness Genevieve wasn't here.

In the distance, voices beyond the door made me

plaster myself against the wall next to the wooden door. I tapped my shoulder and Rodin landed. Neither one of us made a sound.

The voices grew louder, passing the door just inches from where I stood, and then trailing off in the distance. I let out a long breath and Rodin rubbed my head. As quietly as possible, I pulled on the large iron ring and opened the door. Thankfully, it didn't creak. I double-checked my Thumpers were loaded, and stepped out into the hall.

Like the dungeon I'd climbed into, there were several other rooms cut from the rock. Rodin flew forward, in and out of each empty room, and landed back on my shoulder.

"She's not being kept in the dungeons, so where is she?" I turned my head toward the dragon. "I guess we head upstairs now. Stay close."

Rodin secured his grip on my shoulder, digging his claws into my shirt. Together we slipped up a curving, rock-hewn staircase. I paused at the top and peered into a hallway. I stepped out and slowly navigated a series of corridors lit only by torches. Faded paint on the walls depicted mountain scenes of farming and hunting, along with unusual animals and frightening demons. The once glorious decorations had faded with age. The palace must have been a luxurious place at one time. *The Knights of the Golden Circle only bring decay*, I thought.

I stopped at two crossing passages as angry voices rose in the distance. An argument. "Sounds like the

Golden Circle."

Keeping my back pressed against the wall, I slid toward the heated discussion. This hallway led to large room, so I veered down a side passage until I came across a wall cut in a lattice design. Through the wall, I could see into the room and hear everything without being seen.

I hunkered down next to a column hoping no one would pass through this hallway. On the other side, several people sat surrounded by lavish pillows. I didn't recognize anyone at first, but then I heard a voice that sent a chill through my body. Fear dug itself out of the depths of my memory and sunk its teeth into my heart. The southern drawl was something I would never forget, something I could not scrape from my soul—Colonel Hendrix.

Hendrix was the shadow that loomed over my life for the past two years. The nightmare that haunted my dreams. My heart pounded, and blood raced through my throbbing temples.

A man with a German accent said, "*General* Hendrix, you need to calm down. Everything is on schedule. The Templar will take weeks to discover us, and by the time they do, it will be too late."

"Do not try to placate me. The Templar are *here*; I feel those righteous bastards in my bones."

I held my breath.

With a Chinese accent, another man said, "You still have not explained what happened to Lord Kannard."

"All you need know is that *I* am in charge now!"

"The inner circle runs this organization, not you," a third man with a strange accent said with a sneer.

"Perhaps at one time, Lord Xerxes, but the world has changed." Hendrix's southern drawl reverberated in low tones. *I am* the one who retrieved both the ancient hearts and the Crusader hearts. *I am* the Horseman of War! *I am* the inner circle."

"No one can deny your greatness," the Chinese accented voice remained calm. "But we have worked on this much longer than you."

"And you failed. But that was Kannard's fault, and he paid for that misfortune. *I am* the one who provided the gold. I am the one who will provide more. *I am* the one who holds the power, and *I am* the one who controls the Iron Horsemen."

A woman, with a smooth, sultry voice, silenced the rhetoric. "Gentlemen, your dueling egos are sucking the air from this room."

The baroness! I drew back, realizing the woman's voice belonged to Genevieve's mother. The assassin who had struck fear at Eton, blamed my friend the Zulu for her crimes, and caused us to chase her across the African continent. I was in the right place, but I had been foolish in not waiting for the others. Mr. Singh was right. I turned to Rodin, who had crouched low on my shoulder, his teeth bared as a low growl escaped his belly.

"General Hendrix is our leader now," the baroness continued. "He has seized control, and not a one of you can take it back. However, your contribution to the cause is still significant. Why fight amongst ourselves when we can all share in the glory? Soon the world will be encased in the Golden Circle. And when that happens, we will all be emperors, or in my case, an empress."

"Wise words," the German said.

"Indeed," General Hendrix said as he raised a golden goblet. "A toast to the baroness for recognizing exactly where things stand." He took a drink and slammed the cup back on the tray.

I'd found the inner circle. Kannard and Hendrix had fought over control on the Milli-train as we crossed the savannas. And I knew the fate of Kannard. Hendrix had run him through with his sword, I used to think their fight was about the gold Kannard had wasted, but now I understood. It had been about control. Hendrix would have remained a colonel under Kannard, but now he was a general who had seized control of the Knights of the Golden Circle.

Hendrix's southern drawl pulled me back to the lattice wall. "So where are we on the plan? Are the machine's ready?"

Another man, one I hadn't heard before said, "Soon."

I leaned in hoping they would tell me their plans, but heavy boots stomped down the hall. The sound drew closer and I knew they would soon spot me. Then Rodin sniffed the air, and flew off. I reached out and tried to stop him but he was gone.

I couldn't remain here, so I rushed after the little dragon. He turned down another passage and I ran after him, trying to be as quiet as possible. As Rodin soared up a set of stairs, I whispered, "No, Rodin, get back here."

I slowly made my way up the stairs, hugging the wall, and taking each step with caution, looking behind me again and again. I didn't hear any alarms or guards yelling, so Rodin hadn't been discovered, but I still feared being discovered.

Once I'd reached the doorway, I peered around and didn't see anyone, including Rodin. Instinct guided me, I walked down a hallway. My heart pounded; my breathing shallowed. My stomach lurched and twisted as footsteps, two pair, walked in unison. I had to hide. I opened the first door I found and slipped inside.

I pressed my ear against the door and waited for them to pass, but then from behind me I heard a voice.

"Alexander!"

Genevieve.

I spun around and found Genevieve sitting on a low bench surrounded by silk cushions. She was dressed in a light blue sari and adorned with gold jewelry on her wrists, neck, ankles, and fingers. Strands of gold chain were even woven through her hair. She held the little bronze dragon in her lap, clutching him close. I stopped. Unable to breathe. Unable to think. I knew I had to say something to answer her question, but I was frozen.

A smile spread across her lips. I finally shook my head freeing myself from the stupor, and managed to croak out, "I'm here to rescue you."

BOOK III: IRON LOTUS

**16
Genevieve**

"I don't *need* rescuing." Genevieve's brow hardened and one eyebrow rose. "Is my father about to come crashing through the window to save me, like a damsel in distress?"

"No, but he is here." I stumbled over my words, confusion pulling my mind in so many directions. "Well, he's not here, at this palace, but he is nearby, on the Sparrowhawk." My hands went to my hips. "But, you . . . were . . . kidnapped. I'm here to save you from Hendrix."

"I was *not* kidnapped." She rubbed Rodin's head. "My mother bested me in the sword fight on top of the Milli-train, outside the Zulu village. She disarmed me with a move she'd taught me when I was younger. That's when I knew she was my *real* mother." Rodin rolled over on his back and she scratched his belly. "She told me my father had lied to me, that the Templars were trying to control me, and she demanded I go with her so she could prove it. I needed to know the truth, Alexander. So, I went. We climbed into the Milli-train and she showed me proof . . . in the Templar's own words."

"The Knights of the Golden Circle aren't keeping you

hostage?"

"No. I am their *guest*. My door isn't even locked."

"Oh, I didn't know … I mean I did, I just opened it, but—" I knelt down in front of her. "I found your sword; I thought they had taken you. We've been searching everywhere for you."

"I had a feeling you would."

"We chased you across Africa, and I thought we'd catch up with you in Egypt but we missed. Then we waited in Acre, but again, you slipped past us. It wasn't until we came to these mountains that we finally found your trail, which led us—me—here."

I pulled off a long bundle wrapped in cloth slung across my back and set it before her. "Your saber. I even sharpened it."

Her hands caressed the package and she looked into my eyes. "Thank you." She unwrapped the cloth, revealing the silver hilt with an oval-shaped piece of lapis lazuli in the pommel. "I am so pleased you've returned it to me."

I nodded. "Are you sure you're okay?"

"My mother's explained everything to me. My father and the Templars haven't been completely honest with us. Not that the Golden Circle is always right, but what they did to her—the Templars—the choices they forced her to make … it broke my heart."

My mind swirled, my thoughts became a jumbled mess. I tried to speak, but the words jammed up before I could utter them. Hendrix had been trying to tell me the same thing on the train. He insisted I wasn't a prisoner, but a guest, and he'd told me how evil the Templar were, but I didn't believe him. Now, Genevieve's mother told her the same thing. I could see how it would be easy to believe. I didn't know what to think, or who to trust. Genevieve wasn't easily fooled. More than anyone else in the world, she had my complete confidence. I pushed the pillows aside and sat next to her on the bench.

"Mr. Singh and Ershou are waiting outside. We can get you to safety."

Her face softened for a moment at the mention of Indihar, but then she shook her head. "I have no idea who Ershou is, but I am not leaving. Nor am I going back to England to be put into a gilded cage with the Duke's son!"

I cringed at the mention of Richard, Genevieve's betrothed. I certainly didn't want her marrying him, but how could she stay with the Golden Circle?

"Did you know it was the Templars who set up my marriage? Against my mother's wishes. My father went along with the plan, but—" She stopped and took a breath, then locked eyes with me and shuddered. "Alexander, the Templars want power, a leader with royal blood on both sides. I'm to be a broodmare, with no other destiny than to bear Richard a son who will be groomed to be the future Grand Master of the Order."

The idea of Genevieve and Richard enraged me. But knowing the Duke and Richard, it sounded like one of their dastardly ideas. Her disgust radiated like heat, and I shared her anger.

"But I can't leave you here."

"It's not up to you whether I stay or go." She reached over and touched my cheek, her fingertips electrifying my skin, like I'd been zapped by the captain's lightning cannon. "*You*, however, have to leave. Hendrix still wants you to become a Horseman."

"I *can't* leave you with the Golden Circle. What if

we take your mother along, too?"

"My mother?" She laughed, and her smile ignited a fire within me. Then she shook her head again. "My mother would never go with us. As much as I am glad to see you, you have to leave before anyone—including my mother—realizes you are here."

I took her hands in mine and looked into her eyes. "But I just found you. I don't want us to be separated anymore. Not one minute longer."

"Hendrix is obsessed with you. He claims you are the key to the hearts." She slid closer to me, and I wrapped my arm around her without even thinking about it. Like it was the most natural action. Something I'd done countless times before. She rested her head against my shoulder. "I never want to be apart, either, but I am afraid fate has other plans."

"But . . ." Words failed me, I'd come to rescue her and she didn't want to be rescued. "You look amazing," I mumbled. "I like your dress. It's very pretty, especially with all the gold. You look like a princess."

"Thank you," she said and nuzzled closer. Her fragrance, a mix of roses, and exotic spices I couldn't name, drew me ever nearer. I could stay in this moment forever. I had to admit I no longer wanted to leave. "It is really good to see you, Alexander. In truth, I have missed you."

I lifted her chin, staring into her eyes, they dazzled like starlight. Time, the world, and all my troubles disappeared. I tried to think, but all my mind would focus on was her. I leaned in and kissed her. Her touch and the soft caress of her lips zapped me again, sending a buzz of electricity through me.

Time ticked onward, but we remained in an endless

moment I never wanted to end. Genevieve finally pulled back and rested her head against my shoulder. She ran her fingers along my shirt, and intertwined them with the leather strap wrapped around me.

She looked up at me. "You should be back at Eton, making a future for yourself."

"Well . . ." I smiled, "after the battle at the Zulu village, I sort of told my father I wouldn't be going back. I joined the crew of the Sparrowhawk."

"You joined the crew. Wow. How did your father take it?"

"Better than I thought he would, but he understood why." I cleared my throat. "He understood I was doing it for you, to find you. Of course, I've got a room full of books. '*Searching for Genevieve is no excuse to slack off on your studies*,'" I said with a chuckle, mimicking my father.

"I wish I had been there to see that." She touched my cheek and I looked down at her. "I do apologize for making you worry," she said. "There simply wasn't time. I had to make a decision, and so I went with my mother to find the truth."

She kissed me again. Flying high above the clouds was the only sensation I could compare to having Genevieve in my arms, her lips pressing against mine. Suddenly my stomach twisted and lurched. I pulled back from her, my eyes wide.

The door swung open and a voice shattered our tranquility. "Hello, Alexander. I see you finally found my daughter."

I turned and saw Baroness Kensington standing in the doorway with her hands on her hips. Her hair was longer, and she was dressed like Genevieve, but her sari was a deep purple.

Panic shot through every muscle in my body, and I slid away from Genevieve and Rodin. "We . . . I came here to rescue Genevieve."

"Haven't you learned yet that Kensington women don't need rescuing?"

"I have now."

Baroness Kensington, turned her head, and I heard heavy footsteps in the hall. A southern drawl echoed into the room. "What'd I tell you, I knew that boy couldn't stay away." Hendrix. A chill shot through me. I'd never forget that voice.

The baroness reached into a silken sash tied around her waist and removed a small metal pneumatic blow-dart gun. She pressed the button and a tiny wooden twig plunged into my neck. I pulled it out and briefly wondered if I'd suffer the same fate as the murdered professors at Eton. Then the room began to spin and it seemed as I was pitching up and down on the high seas. I tried to focus, but I couldn't keep my eyes open. Hendrix pushed into the room, and the last thing I saw was his face, half-covered in bronze plates.

<h1>17
Captured</h1>

"Alexander . . ."

I heard a soft voice, a man's, but I couldn't open my eyes. I didn't think I was dreaming, but I couldn't move.

Someone pressed fingers into my skin and gently shook my shoulders, but still I couldn't react, in fact, it felt like my body lay miles away.

"He's breathing," the voice said. "That's a good sign."

I kept willing my body to move, and eventually my fingers tapped against something hard, and then I forced open an eye. I was on the floor looking up at a blurry, blue turban looming over me. I tasted bile in the back of my throat and my face was wet. As Mr. Singh came into focus, I sat up and wiped the drool from my cheek.

"Careful you are coming out from under the effects of the potion." Mr. Singh helped me sit back against the wall. "You've been out for quite some time."

"How long?"

"Almost three hours."

"My head feels like it was shot out a cannon."

Another voice,

Ershou's, said, "They used a sleeping potion on you. It will pass."

"Ershou? What are you both doing here?"

"They captured us on the path. They knew we were here."

"Yeah, Hendrix and the baroness found me with Genevieve."

"No, Alexander, we were captured right after you disappeared into the drain. They were expecting us."

"They even knew that it was just the two of us." Ershou's eyes burned.

"The mole." I clenched my fists until my knuckles ached. "The mole on the Sparrowhawk must have found a way to contact them."

"He would have had to send a message as soon as I left the ship," Mr. Singh said.

I looked down and felt for my Thumper, but the holster was empty. Mr. Singh shook his head. "They took our weapons."

"What about Genevieve?" I sat up but my head spun and I laid back against the wall.

Mr. Singh rested his hand on my shoulder. "Take it easy. I have not seen her. We were brought here after Hendrix gloated, and then they brought you in. Did you talk to Genevieve?"

"I did, but she doesn't want to be rescued."

Ershou shook her head. "Wait, if you had explained we were taking someone against their will, I never would have agreed to help you."

"No, it's not like that," I said. "I thought she was in trouble, but now, I think she's working another angle." Mr. Singh eyed me, I'm not sure he believed me, but he said nothing. I eased up, and said, "She was brought here by her mother, who has been filling her mind with the evils her father and the other Templar have committed. Plus, she doesn't want to be forced to marry the Duke's son. I think she's confused—or, she has a plan."

"I will not take anyone by force." Ershou crossed her arms.

For the first time, I looked around the cell. Though we weren't in the dungeons I'd explored earlier, the door's small window was covered with iron bars, same as the window. I stood and looked out the window. We were perched on the sheer side of the mountain, with a drop that didn't stop until it reached the river far below.

Mr. Singh walked over to Ershou and sat beside her. "Were you taken by force from your home?"

Her head dropped, and slid closer to her. "I would not marry, so I ran away."

"Were you betrothed to an evil man?" I asked.

"The man I loved was killed and his murderer assumed the betrothal."

"No wonder you ran," Mr. Singh said.

"But in doing so, I dishonored my family, and was banished."

"I am sorry, Ershou," I said and pointed to Mr. Singh. "Indihar here had to leave India when he was young. Like you, Genevieve is betrothed to a man she doesn't want to marry, and I have an over-bearing father who tries to run my life. You're in good company."

She studied both of us, but said nothing.

Mr. Singh bowed his head. "How did you come by your owl?"

"Kō'ilā was my first friend after I fled. I rescued her from a snare set outside a coal mine." Ershou stood up and slowly stepped over to the window. "I nursed her back to health, and she has been a good friend ever since."

"How did you end up with the Spice Master?"

"He picked me up because he wanted the prestige of an eagle hunter within his caravan."

"Falconry? Where did you learn that?" I asked.

"From my father. He served a noble house." Her eyes focused on the far wall of the canyon, as if staring into a memory. "I was trained in music, art, calligraphy, but falconry was my favorite. My father hoped my beauty would bring our family a noble rank."

"I'm sorry you are separated from them," Mr. Singh said, his head bowed. "I understand the difficulties you faced. After my family was killed, Baron Kensington found me. If he hadn't helped me, I'm not sure where'd I be. Eventually, I made my way to the Mediterranean, where I was able to join the *Sparrowhawk's* crew."

Heavy footsteps, the clatter of a door being opened and then slamming shut, silenced us. I heard Hendrix bark at the guards, "Get that door open, and be quick about it."

I tensed. The Confederate colonel, who had apparently promoted himself to general, always made me uneasy. The embodiment of evil, I'd never forgotten that he'd kidnapped my father, or that he'd pierced Eustache through the heart. Yet, he'd also offered me the chance to be a horseman. He'd offered me great power, and although I knew he was evil, we agreed about the nobles, that a man's worth was in his actions, not his birthright. Genevieve said he was obsessed with me. That he wanted me at his side. But why?

The door swung open and Hendrix stepped inside with several soldiers right behind him. They wore thick wool winter uniforms and carried long rifles. Hendrix stared at me with his one good eye. The other, a bronze aperture with electricity sparking behind a crystal lens, turned as it zoomed in. It unsettled most people, but I'd stared into this man's heart, and his mechanical eye didn't scare me. I held his gaze. I didn't falter or recoil. My eyes narrowed, and he smiled.

"There's that fire." Hendrix hit the palm of his mechanical hand. "The Inner Circle wants to torture you and your friends here for information, but I done told them, it ain't gonna work. Alexander's tough as nails."

"My friends don't know anything."

"But you do, don't yah?"

"I don't know what you mean." I said, kicking myself for not having included me in my statement. He was right though; I knew way more than anyone else.

"Oh, I bet you do, I can see your mind working." Hendrix pointed his mechanical finger at me. "You've seen that I treated the lass right." His crooked smile made me burn. "I treated her and her ma right. I want you to remember that."

"Thank you, but you know if you hadn't, I wouldn't rest until I avenged them."

"See that's what I like. You're in my jail, cut off from your allies, not one of them infernal armors anywhere in sight, and yet you're defiant and ready for battle." He chuckled and it rattled my nerves. "We're more alike than you'll admit."

I remained silent. I didn't want to give him the satisfaction of agreeing with him, or the joy of my defiance.

"You'll stay here for now, so get comfortable. You and your friends will be with us for some time. And I wouldn't worry about the *Sparrowhawk* coming to your rescue. They are chasing the Milli-train on a little jaunt to the south. By the time they figure out you're not on the train, we'll have moved on." He tipped back his Stetson and stood upright. "You see, I thought of everything. That imbecile Kannard ain't in charge anymore."

"You can let the girl go. She doesn't know anything. All she did was show me how to cross the river."

"No, I think she'll stay right here, that is, until we sell her back to the Spice Master."

Ershou cringed and I saw a burning rage seething in her eyes. She didn't say anything. She just eyed Hendrix through narrow slits.

Hendrix turned, and along with the soldiers, walked out of the cell, his bronze plated leg thumping, giving him his distinctive gate, that faded into the distance.

Mr. Singh turned to me. "I do not believe him. I think they will torture us to get you to talk."

"I agree. But I'm not sure how to get out of here or what to do once we do escape."

"The *Sparrowhawk* didn't know about this place. They were focused on the Milli-train. That part of his story rang true."

I nodded. "We might be stuck here for a while."

Two soldiers stepped up to the window in the door and looked inside. One sneered and said, "The Inner Circle wants the one in the turban first." He looked at the other soldier. "You get the manacles, and I'll find out where we're to take him. Meet you back here." Their footsteps clattered down the hallway.

I tensed and saw Mr. Singh do the same. "Hendrix lied," I said.

"The Inner Circle might be fighting with him," Mr.

Singh said.

"Or they're evil, and hurting people is what they do." Ershou said with a huff.

I heard a *pssst*, coming from the window. I rushed over and saw Genevieve, dangling from a rope, like she was scaling the side of the fortress. "What are you doing?"

"I'm here to rescue you."

18
Escape into
the Mountains

Mr. Singh and Ershou joined me at the window. I gripped the bars as I stared out at Genevieve, who now wore brown pants and a blue jacket. Another rope was looped over one shoulder. "Am I glad to see you!"

"Of course you are." She winked, swung closer on her rope, and grabbed a bar. "We have to get you out of here, though."

"You're coming with us, right?"

"I can't leave yet." She looked at the bars and then at the window frame.

"I'm not leaving without you."

"You have to. They're going to torture you, and Mr. Singh." She motioned her hand and Rodin flew down and landed on the window sill. "Rodin, I need your fire." She pointed at the wooden frame.

The dragon wiggled his tail, stretched out his neck, and unleashed a column of fire. The wood charred, blackened, and turned to ash. Rodin inspected the frame, and with a quick flap of his wings I could tell he was pleased. Genevieve tested the edge of the sill, which

crumbled at her touch. She wrapped a cord around three of the bars. She took the other end and slid down on her rope. Leaning against the bars I watched as she tied the cord around a stone. Genevieve pushed the stone away from the palace. The cord pulled on the three bars and ripped them from the frame. The bars and stone tumbled to the river below.

Genevieve climbed up her rope to the open window and climbed in.

"That was impressive," I said.

Mr. Singh bowed to Genevieve, and she hugged him. "It is good to see you, Indihar."

"I am pleased to see you are well."

Genevieve extended her hand to Ershou. "Hello, pleasure to meet you."

"They call me Ershou."

Genevieve paused, let her hand fall, and then turned to me. "There is a ledge below us. Climb down and you'll be able to get away."

"But we can't leave without you." I wanted to grab her and run, but she was so defiant, so assured. I was back to being a school boy.

"Alexander, no. I'm not finished here yet."

"Finished with what?"

Mr. Singh and Ershou moved to the window. Genevieve pulled off the rope slung over her shoulder and gave it to Mr. Singh who tied it to the remaining bars and tugged to make sure the whole rig would hold.

Genevieve ran her hand along the side of my face. "Hendrix and the Inner Circle have been talking for weeks. Soon they'll be heading to some sort of secret lab or factory. They have a grand plan to seize control of the world and destroy anyone who gets in their way. They are searching for more Horsemen Hearts. They've even found one. My mother is taking me there soon. Then I'll know for certain."

"I know where the hearts are. I found a journal written by my ancestor, the one who hid them. From there, well . . . it gets complicated."

Her eyes pleaded with me. "Then you *have* to go, now. Finding the hearts is an obsession around here. If they knew you had the information they seek, they'd kill us all to force you to reveal the locations."

"I don't like this plan." I took her hand, intertwining my fingers with hers. "Come with us. We'll rejoin the Sparrowhawk and find this place and the hearts together."

"We may never find this place on our own. All I know is that it is hidden in the mountains, and it is big. Big enough to drain much of their resources."

"But if we can't find the factory, how will we find you?"

"I don't know, Alexander. I don't have all the answers." She looked at the door and turned back to me. "Rodin and I have been linked since birth. He'll be able to find me; he always can. Follow Rodin and he'll bring us back together. But now, you have to hurry."

I pulled her close and whispered in her ear. "I will be back in two to three weeks. No longer." I locked eyes with her, and almost lost myself. "And if you're not here, I will find you."

She kissed me and then ran over to Mr. Singh. After she hugged him, she climbed back out the window. Still connected by her rope, she swung out and scrambled up to the balcony above us with Rodin flying beside her. Mr. Singh and Ershou climbed down to the ledge. I climbed out and sat on the window sill. I didn't want to leave. I never wanted Genevieve out of my sight again, but I'd seen that determined look before. The same as when we set out to rescue our fathers. She couldn't be stopped, and she was right. She was in the perfect place to learn their plan. As Ershou landed on the ledge, I grabbed the rope and slid down. Mr. Singh helped me find my footing and we scurried on to more secure ground.

Genevieve lowered the walker down and Mr. Singh eased it onto the ledge.

Rodin flew down carrying the straps of our bags in his talons. He dropped them at our feet and landed on my shoulder. He looked sad, and kept turning back to look at the palace, just as I did. I rubbed his head. "Looks like you're coming with me, but that's good. Together, we'll find her again."

Mr. Singh took his belongings, and Ershou slung her bag diagonally across her chest and sat on her walker. I grabbed my leather bag and checked to see what was inside. All of my gear, including the Thumpers were within. I took one last look at the palace hidden on the side of the mountain. I will be back.

The little dragon rubbed against my head and we hurried to catch up with Mr. Singh and Ershou.

"Which way do we go?" I asked. "Back to the village?"

Mr. Singh shook his head. "The baron wanted to head south to the Punjab, for reinforcements."

I looked around trying to get my bearings but with the towering mountains all around, the horizon was hard to find. "Which way is south?"

Ershou held out her arm. Kō'ilā, the owl, swooped down and landed on her glove. Kō'ilā folded her bronze and feather wings back and settled. "This way."

19
The Lotus

We followed Ershou down a narrow trail that clung to the mountain's edge. I kept expecting riders or airships to come looking for us, but we never saw them. I wondered why, but Mr. Singh said, "They probably thought we went to the village."

After a couple of hours, the path merged into a wider road. Although there were wheel ruts and it was flatter and easier to walk on, I noticed Ershou was slowing her pace, wincing in pain. She used her feet to control the walker, like the Black Knight she pressed one pedal to move a direction and both to go forward or back. She tried not to show it, but I could see her ache with every step.

I walked alongside her and Kō'ilā, "Why don't we rest for a second? I could use a break."

She eyed me, but nodded.

Mr. Singh pointed. "Those rocks will provide us with some cover."

We sat in the shadow of a pile of rocks that had tumbled down the mountainside and blocked half the path. Rodin and

Kō'ilā flew off to hunt, and I sat back as Mr. Singh removed a pomegranate from his pack and cut it up for us. Ershou rubbed her feet, but wouldn't remove her tiny shoes.

"You have the smallest feet of anyone I've ever known," I said.

Mr. Singh got an odd look on his face and tried to dismiss my comment with a wave. Ershou eyed me with narrow slits as if I'd said something wrong.

"Apologies if it's a sore subject, I think they're fine. Not everyone has big ol' feet like me."

Mr. Singh smacked his forehead. But Ershou laughed.

"This is your first time to Asia, I assume."

I nodded. "It is, but I've always wanted to come."

"To make me more desirable," Ershou said, a hint of sadness in her voice, "my family gave me lotus feet. They bound my feet as a child so I could fit into these shoes."

Mr. Singh said, "Before I went to Europe, I traveled to China, and the lady of the house where I stayed had the same thing done to her. It can be painful to walk. Binding the feet of girls means they will grow up to live a life of pampering in a good house." He handed Ershou some of the pomegranate. She bowed her head and accepted it.

"I didn't know. I'm sorry."

"Do not pity me. I do not. Chinese men desire women with feet like mine. British women wear corsets that reshape their bodies. It is no different."

I'd never thought of it like that, but Ershou was right. I'd seen some women with waists so small I could wrap my hand around them.

"Thank you, Ershou, for educating me. I still think they're cute."

She cringed as I said her name, but quickly recovered and forced a smile as she said, "You wouldn't if you saw them un-bandaged."

"I'm sorry if I've offended you, I only want to know you more." I leaned over and grabbed some fruit. "The Spice Master called you Ershou, and I assumed it was your name, but I've notice you recoil whenever I say it."

"Ershou is the name he gave me." She bit a piece of the pomegranate and let her short hair fall over her face.

"What does it mean?" I asked.

A soft voice replied, "Second hand."

Mr. Singh snapped his head up and my hand went to my chest. I thought I'd been using her name, when in truth I'd been insulting her.

"Forgive me, please! I thought it sounded interesting, but please tell us your real name."

"My name is Lianhua; it means lotus, but I'm not her anymore."

"Well, you certainly aren't second hand either." Rodin returned and landed on my shoulder. He crawled down into my lap and circled until he found the right spot. "Besides, Lianhua is a very nice name."

Mr. Singh nodded. "Yes, the lotus is a beautiful flower."

She pushed the hair from her face and finished off her fruit. "Tell me about your dragon."

"You know about dragons?"

"I have heard many stories."

"Really? I'd love to hear them sometime." I rubbed Rodin's head. "He's actually Genevieve's. They were born on the same day."

Kō'ilā flew down and landed beside Lianhua. The tail of a rodent hung from her beak, and she tilted back her head to suck the last bit inside.

"That is a special bond," she said, petting her owl. "She is all I have now."

"After we find our friends, I think you should join us."

"Join you? What do you mean?"

"We're trying to save the world." I smiled and held out my arms as if to encompass the entire globe, "I know, it sounds corny, but it's true. The Knights of the Golden Circle want to enslave everyone and are searching for the power to do so. They want to unleash the Four Horsemen, to bring everyone under their control—and kill everyone who resists. They've tried before, but we," I pointed to Mr. Singh and myself, "stopped them, with Genevieve."

"The people in the palace."

"That's right," Mr. Singh said. "General Hendrix, the one half-covered in bronze, he is the Horseman of War."

"He's their leader," I added. "Now they seek more power and even greater machines to threaten the world."

"How will you stop them?" Lianhua stroked Kō'ilā's head feathers.

"They seek powerful stones called the Hearts of the Horsemen, but they don't know where they are. We must find them first, and then we'll destroy their machines with our Iron Armors."

"Iron Armors?" Lianhua asked.

"Our knights," I replied.

"But we didn't bring the Black Knight and the Iron

Templar with us" Mr. Singh looked at me and his brow rose.

"No, but they're on a war zeppelin that is with the Templar Aircorps."

Lianhua's eyes passed back and forth between us. I knew she had more questions, but with the traitor on the Sparrowhawk still unidentified I didn't want to give away any information. I trusted both of them, more than any others we traveled with, but if they knew too much, they could be in danger.

Rodin and Kō'ilā popped their heads up and turned toward the east. Mr. Singh raised his hand to silence us. "Did you hear that?"

I listened, and in the distance, I heard a repetitive scraping on the rock. We stood up and peered down the road. A cart with a man and a single horse rolled toward us.

"I think I know how we're going to get out of here." I turned to Lianhua. "Can you ask him if he'll take us south into the Punjab. We can pay him."

She nodded and stepped out to stop the man. They spoke for several moments. Then she waved us over. Mr. Singh and I approached slowly; the old man welcomed us with a large grin on his face.

Lianhua bowed to him and turned to me, "He is heading south and will take us. But he wants to know how we will pay him."

I reached into my bag and pulled out a gold bracelet, one of several I'd noticed earlier that definitely weren't there before. "I think Genevieve slipped us a few trinkets to help us out." I handed one over to the old man and he lit up with excitement, bobbing his head and waving to the back of his cart.

The two of us jumped in as Lianhua's walker climbed on. The legs folded under to make a seat. The cart lurched forward and continued down the bumpy mountain trail. Luckily our ride was cushioned from the uneven road by the mound of colorful textiles beneath us and the burlap sacks of grain we leaned against. As Mr. Singh and Lianhua talked, I stared at the scenery behind us. I'd found Genevieve only to lose her again, but I knew with every drop of blood in my veins that it wouldn't be for long. Soon, we'd be together again.

Still, I worried about her. She remained with the Knights of the Golden Circle. I hoped they wouldn't find out she helped us escape, that they'd assume we broke out on our own. I trusted Genevieve's mother not to harm her, and I knew Hendrix wanted her as a pawn to use against me. But all I could do was hope the rest of Inner Circle wouldn't overrule them.

For the next hour or so, I thought over my plan. Find the baron and the captain. Tell them what we found. Discover the mole. Race back to the hidden palace, and track Genevieve's new location from there. I rubbed under Rodin's chin. "Don't worry we'll see her soon."

The terrain transformed from towering mountains with snow-capped peaks, to tall, thin trees in an undulating land. Soon the trees turned to farmland, but the land never truly flattened out.

With the sun sinking toward the horizon on the second day, we approached a wide river with thin islands poking up between the two banks. A modern bridge spanned the two sides, and the old man turned to us. He said something and Lianhua answered. I leaned forward as she turned to us.

"We will cross the river and stop in Buchepela this evening. He says we will be able to find another merchant to take us on to Lahore. He'll be heading back to the mountains tomorrow."

"Thank him for bringing us this far," I said.

"I did."

I thought about what we could use for currency. I still had some bracelets, but wasn't certain if I should spend them all getting to the capital city, Lahore. How much farther

would we need to travel? From here ... Buchepela ... the word hit me like a gust of wind.

"This is Buchepela ... Ask the gentleman if this is the Hydaspes River."

She tapped the man on the shoulder. They spoke for a moment and then she turned back to me. "He says, once it was called that. Long ago."

"I can't believe it." I stood up, causing the cart to wobble. Lianhua grabbed the sides.

She looked at Mr. Singh and he shrugged. "The Battle of Hydaspes was fought on this river's shores," I gestured to the land. "This is where Alexander the Great barely defeated King Porus." I looked around half expecting to see a forest of pikes from the great battle fought so long ago. Finally, as we crossed the river and entered the village on the other side, I sat back down. "Sadly, this village is named after Bucephalus, Alexander's beloved horse. Alexander had ridden that horse since he was just a boy and they survived countless battles together. Until the Battle of Hydaspes. Bucephalus died defending him and afterward, Alexander founded this village in honor of his great steed."

Mr. Singh looked around. "His empire was so large. We are far from where I first met you and found out about your namesake."

"One of the largest empires in history."

"Not bigger than Genghis Khan's," Lianhua shook her head. "His horde scorched the earth. From China to your Europe."

I nodded. "You're right. I suppose these lands have always known conquerors."

"Too many."

We said goodbye to the old man and found an

inn for the night, which was simply a waystation for traveling merchants. I sat by a window, thinking of the battleground—and of Genevieve. "She has never needed anyone else to protect her," I told myself. "She has her saber back, yes; but still, she's in the clutches of the Knights of the Golden Circle. She'll never be safe with them."

Rodin curled up in my lap and I found myself stroking the ridge of his spine, like a cat. He didn't mind, and nudged my hand when I stopped.

"We'll see her again soon," Mr. Singh said, "but first, we have to find the baron and the *Sparrowhawk*."

The next morning, we found a caravan heading to Lahore and they let us ride along. We didn't even have to pay. I watched the land around me. Yet again, I traveled over the same ground as Alexander the Great. He'd led his army—now a mixed force of Greeks, Persians, and warriors from other tribes and conquered lands—through this very forest. I thought about what it must have been like, a column of soldiers stretching for miles. Our caravan was only ten carts, two elephants, and a couple dozen men and horses. The two images melded in my mind, and I took a deep breath.

With Eton more than half a world away, my time there felt more like another lifetime. The Hindu believed in reincarnation—that the soul returned to this world over and over again. Being here, being in such a different place, no fathers, no rules, no Eton uniform, I was a new person, and could easily believe in reincarnation.

We snaked through the countryside, across rivers, around hilltop villages, and through endless farm fields. Unlike the large estates of England or America, farmers tended thin strips of land. I was amazed at the endless diversity of people we passed. Here at the top of the world, I'd seen so many cultures, like in New York or London, but the people had been this way for many more centuries than anyplace I'd visited before. As we neared Lahore, I started to see more people, more densely populated areas. I didn't know much more about the city, other than the British had established themselves there, and the baron said he'd travel this way if he needed reinforcements.

After we entered the city and said goodbye to the merchants, we headed to the airdocks to search for the Sparrowhawk.

Mr. Singh watched everyone. Several wore turbans in the same fashion that Mr. Singh did. I realized they were other Sikhs. I notice Mr. Singh walked taller. He even bowed to several men and they returned the gesture.

I nudged Mr. Singh after the Sikhs moved on. "Well, aren't you quite the respected man."

His bright eyes and large smile beamed. "I haven't been back in so many years. I'd forgotten what it was like to be among my people."

The thought had never occurred to me. I was having a quite the adventure away from London, but for Mr. Singh, he usually lived far from his homeland.

"I wish there was more time for you to visit."

"I don't."

I paused in street.

Mr. Singh gripped my shoulder. "My home is on the *Sparrowhawk*. My parents, most of my family were killed years ago." He looked around. "The memories I want to keep are of the captain, the baron, you, and Genevieve."

Before he could react, I pulled him in for a big hug. "The crew of the *Sparrowhawk* is like a family, and you,

Indihar … well, you're like a brother to me."

Rodin pushed in between us, wanting attention, and to be part of our show of affection. Kō'ilā hooted and it drew our attention to Lianhua who stared at us and then looked around at the people on the street.

I pushed back from Mr. Singh, cleared my throat, and said, "The airdocks are over there."

Mr. Singh nodded, and took off, leading the way through the crowd, darting through a mass of merchants, food vendors, and others maneuvering around the city. Lahore brimmed with people, more than I'd ever seen in one place. More than London on a busy day. The airdocks weren't far, and we were relieved to see the *Sparrowhawk* sitting in one of the few mooring clamps available. A merchant blimp sat in another berth, but the two remaining spaces were empty. In London, airships jockeyed for any opening, but the Punjab must not get the same amount of air traffic.

We ran to the gangplank, where Mr. Singh and I started to rush on board, but Lianhua paused. I turned around and motioned her forward. "It's okay. This is our ship. You'll be safe here. Besides, we owe you for your help." I motioned to the aero-dirigible. "Good food, friendly people, and I'd really like to pay you, too."

Her hand went to her chest, and then she nodded, and the three of us walked up the gangplank together.

Hunter walked past the open cargo door and stopped. He turned toward us and his face lit up. He rushed over and grabbed Mr. Singh by his shoulders. "Indihar!" He slapped me on the back. "Alexander!" He shook his head. "I can't believe it. You're back!"

"Hunter!" My spirit lifted as words escaped me. Warmth filled me, and I realized how much this airship had become home. "It's good to see you."

"How did you . . . nevermind." He motioned us onboard. "We've got to get you on the bridge." He led us to the hatch, and gestured for us to enter. "I'll be right back."

I stepped through the metal doorway and the familiar aroma of wood, grease, and Gustav's mouth-watering food knocked my senses over. I'd never had the experience of going home. I'd always lived at a university or at Eton, places I never felt I belonged. But the *Sparrowhawk* was different. I'd missed this place, this smell, these people, and hadn't realized how much.

The captain sat in his chair, holding his chin with his arm propped up on the armrest of his chair. As we stepped closer, he turned his head slightly, then spun around. "Alexander! Mr. Singh!" He leapt out of the seat and scooped both of us up in a big bear hug. "How the devil did you get here?"

"We hitched a ride through the mountains."

"I told the baron and Ignatius here, that if anyone would get out and find this airship, it'd be the two of you." He craned his neck over us and stared at Lianhua. "You're the girl with the Spice Master." He looked back at me. Last I saw you, the two of you were running around the side of a building. What happened, and where is Genevieve?"

Mr. Singh and I exchanged a glance. I blew out a long breath, then said, "This is Lianhua, she helped us find Genevieve, and then helped us get away. Genevieve refused to come. She has a plan, but I have no idea what it is."

Captain Baldarich studied all three of us as if we were on inspection. Finally, he nodded, and looked at

Lianhua. "You must be a very brave and resourceful girl to have helped Alexander and Mr. Singh find Genevieve, and then to help them get here to Lahore." He pushed past me and took Lianhua's hand in his. "You have my thanks. Welcome to the *Sparrowhawk*."

21
The Sikh

Ignatius and Heinz shook our hands as everyone crowded around, happy to see Mr. Singh, especially, back safe and sound. The captain punched my shoulder and pulled me in by wrapping his arm around my shoulder.

"I don't want you running off anymore. I don't want to have to keep sending Mr. Singh off to find you."

"I'll try. I left clues and fired off the flare so someone could follow, but since you were fighting off the soldiers and Lianhua knew where the Milli-train was, I couldn't wait. Besides, I didn't think we get captured."

"Captured?!"

I cringed. I should have said that with a bit more layering so it didn't sound so bad. "Lianhua led me through a secret tunnel, and we found the Milli-train in a hidden palace on the other side of the river. Mr. Singh caught up with us and I snuck in and found Genevieve. Then Genevieve helped us escape, and we traveled back here with the help of some merchants."

Baldarich and I turned as we heard the hatch open. The baron and Lord Marbury

stepped onto the bridge, and all the joy that had built up inside me drained out, and I crashed like a plummeting airship. The baron scanned the bridge, looking for his daughter, but then he settled on me, hope fading from his eyes. Ever the nobleman, he collected himself quickly and stepped up to Mr. Singh.

"Indihar, it is good to see you." He extended his hand and Mr. Singh grabbed it with both of his. The baron then turned to me. "Alexander. I don't know what to say. I want to yell at you for running off, but having made your way back to us is remarkable. I can't wait to hear your tale."

I stepped away from the captain and hugged the baron. He stiffened, but then embraced me and as I pressed against him. I whispered, "I found her. We talked. She's fine. Full of fire. But she said she's not done yet, and wouldn't escape with us."

He gripped me tightly. He didn't say anything but the force of his embrace said it all. After several moments he let me go, slapped my back twice, and said, "Thank you."

Lord Marbury turned from Mr. Singh to me. "We were so worried. It is wonderful to have you back."

We introduced Lianhua, and shared more of our adventure, but I didn't tell anyone about what the Inner Circle had said or General Hendrix's plans for me. There was a mole on the *Sparrowhawk*. I didn't know who, but I wouldn't be the one to spill what I knew.

The captain pointed at me. "You and Mr. Singh have lost a pound or two I can tell, and this girl who aided you deserves a good meal." He walked over to the copper tubes and flipped all four open. "Attention! If you hadn't already heard, because gossip spreads faster on this ship than fire, Mr. Singh and Alexander have returned. Gustav, fire up the ovens! These boys need to eat!"

After we'd filled our bellies and laughed with the crew, the baron stood up and said, "I should be going if I want to make my meeting. Mr. Singh, I'd appreciate if you'd come along." Mr. Singh nodded, and left the table. "I'd like you to come as well, Alexander."

I nodded and pointed to Lianhua, "May she come as well? She knows all about the mountains and speaks several languages."

"Certainly. Perhaps she will prove useful."

I shifted to Lianhua "Do you mind coming with us?"

She drew back and her eyes nervously darted to the crewmen. I realized she didn't trust them and I smiled trying to put her at ease. After being held against her will by the Spice Master, I understood she wasn't used to trusting anyone, much less an airship full of strange men.

I motioned for her to follow. She and Kō'ilā joined me. I grabbed my gear and filled my leather bag with some supplies we might need, and one of the small pouches of black powder.

"I don't know what this meeting is about, but I don't think it would be good to leave you here. There is a traitor on board."

"I would rather travel with you and Mr. Singh."

I nodded.

"I'm glad you're coming," Mr. Singh said as he stepped into the doorway. She and I pivoted as Rodin flapped his wings. Mr. Singh was loaded with gear like we'd be traveling for days not running out for a meeting. Much like me. He pointed to the stairs. "The baron is ready to depart."

Hunter stood just inside the cargo door, watching the airdocks. We rushed to the gangplank and followed the baron down. A carriage waited for us at the bottom. Finely crafted and trimmed with gold, the vehicle stood out among the common merchant carts. Then I saw Britain's imperial seal on the side of the door.

"Who are we going to see?" I asked the baron.

"A guest of the Punjab Governor." Baron Kensington waited for us to step in, and then he motioned to the driver we were ready. He took his seat beside Mr. Singh. A footman closed the door. The baron waited a moment until the rattle of the wheels and cantering of the horses covered up all the ambient noise. "I am attempting to get reinforcements, and once we have them, we'll head back to that palace."

"How long will that take?" I asked.

"Depends on where the troops are and how many can be reassigned. Perhaps as long as a month."

"We don't have that kind of time. I told Genevieve we'd be back in two to three weeks."

"They have too many soldiers. Without additional forces, we'll never stop the Golden Circle."

Mr. Singh adjusted his Katar dagger. "He's right Alexander. We need soldiers to breach and take that palace."

I didn't like it, but I knew they were right. I brooded as we rolled through Lahore, but eventually noticed the baron studying Lianhua. I glanced at her, but her gaze was fixed on the baron, too. Finally, the baron turned his attention to her owl, who had trained her large eyes on the nobleman.

"A fine bird you have there."

Her short hair fell over her face but her piercing

stare never wavered. "He is."

"I am—"

"The girl's father. I see the resemblance." Lianhua spoke softly, but her words cut like a blade.

"Yes. Genevieve is my daughter."

"Do you control her?"

Mr. Singh shifted nervously, and I pulled my collar away from neck. Tension in the carriage thickened until it became hard to breathe. It was as if all the air had been sucked out by her question. I knew the real answer. Yes. Or at least he tried. I stared at the baron, though I wanted to turn away. He sat there, silent, as if absorbing her question, and thinking about his response. But like a typical nobleman, he remained cooler than the snow-capped mountains we'd left behind.

"I only want what's best for her." The baron said in a matter-of-fact manner. "But she very much has a mind of her own."

"She is very brave."

"Yes." He relaxed his shoulders ever so slightly. His eyes flickered to Lianhua's feet and then back to her face. "I see you were raised by a fine family."

"Until my father demanded I marry a horrible man . . . for the sake of my 'fine family'."

I held my breath. The baron, too, was making Genevieve marry the Duke's son, even though he was everything she hated. The baron stiffened and shifted in his seat. I'd seen him face henchmen, nobles, royalty, and even death, but this girl made him squirm. I stared at Mr. Singh and we had a conversation with our eyes. He couldn't believe she made the baron uncomfortable either.

The carriage stopped and the footman opened the door releasing the tension like an open valve. The baron gestured for us to step out. Mr. Singh went first, and Lianhua followed as her walker unfolded and exited. I hopped down and Rodin flew out, circled above us, and landed on the baron's shoulder after he exited the carriage. Two soldiers in British uniforms snapped to attention, saluted the baron, then motioned for us to follow.

Above the door of the district office, several flags whipped in the cool breeze. One was the crossed bars of the Union Jack, but the other was a lion atop a shield with a sun over the wavy lines of water. We entered the double doors and the soldiers led us down the hall to a lavishly decorated waiting room.

A man with a twisted mustached rose from his seat and bowed. "Baron Kensington, a pleasure to see you again."

"Fitzwater, how are you?" The two shook hands.

"Well as can be in this insect-plagued quagmire." The two chuckled. "The governor will be with us in a moment, and I have word Mr. Shah is on his way."

"Excellent." The baron removed his gloves. "It will be good to see Sir Egerton again."

"You didn't hear? As of a year ago, we have a new governor, Sir Charles Aitchison."

"Really? They appointed Aitchison?" The baron's brow popped up. "Do you think he will help me?"

"It won't be like Egerton, who would have given you whatever assistance you needed." He leaned closer to the baron. "The Governor will want authorization from New Dehli."

"That is time I don't have." The baron pinched his chin, as he rested his elbow in his palm. "My hopes rest with Mr. Shah then."

A soldier walked in and nodded to Mr. Fitzwater who motioned with his fingers. The soldier saluted, spun on his heel and left the room. A moment later a man with an oversized turban walked in. A silver trident was wrapped within the center of his turban. He wore a blue tunic and his thick white beard came to a point. A smile adorned his face but his bright eyes pierced everyone in the room. Until his attention fell on Mr. Singh, then he cocked one eyebrow.

Mr. Fitzwater stepped forward. "Thank you for joining us, Mr. Shah."

"I am here for the baron. I remember when he aided my people near twenty years ago."

Baron Kensington walked over and bowed before Mr. Shah. The Sikh returned the gesture and the two men shook hands. "I thank you for agreeing to hear my plea."

"Will the governor be joining us?"

Mr. Fitzwater nodded. "He is supposed to, but his schedule is very busy today. We may want to get started."

Mr. Shah shrugged. "Let us continue with the introductions." He stepped around the baron and walked to Mr. Singh.

The baron was quick to follow. He extended his arm. "This is Mr. Singh. He serves as boatswain on the aero-dirigible the Sparrowhawk."

Mr. Singh bowed and when he righted himself, stood as tall and rigid as one of the landing struts of the Sparrowhawk. I could tell he was trying to appear impressive, but he couldn't stop staring at the large turban or the trident within its folds.

Mr. Shah looked my friend up and down. He studied his hands, his stance, his Katar, and Kirpan. Mr. Singh's weapons and adornments were not as elaborate or immaculate as the Sikh before him, but Mr. Shah nodded his head slightly.

He moved on to Lianhua, and bowed to her, he pointed to her owl. "A stunning animal. Fearsome, with the demeanor of a warrior."

She didn't respond. Like her bird, she, too, had an almost disturbingly calm appearance.

Mr. Shah turned to me and I didn't wait for the baron to introduce me. I bowed and said, "It is a pleasure to meet you, Mr. Shah. My name is Alexander Armitage, and I'm here to fight a great, tyrannical evil that remains hidden in the mountains to the north."

I paused, thinking I would have to explain myself. But he knew.

"The strange noises and kidnappings. Yes, I know of what you speak."

"They are preparing to enslave—or destroy—us all."

22
Marbury and
the Governor

The baron and Mr. Shah spoke for the next twenty minutes. Mr. Singh hung on their every word, but my attention kept shifting to the window, to the mountains sitting on the horizon. A couple of days had already passed. It would take several more to get back into the snow-capped peaks. If we didn't leave soon the Golden Circle might have already left the hidden palace. Then how would we find Genevieve? What if she was counting on me?

Rodin sat on my shoulder, rubbing his head against mine. I was glad he was with me and hopeful that his connection to Genevieve would be strong enough to help locate her. But it struck me that Genevieve had another motive for sending Rodin with me. She knew the Inner Circle planned to torture Mr. Singh to get me to talk. Perhaps she thought they'd hurt her prized dragon in order to make her do their bidding. The thought of her in Hendrix's clutches, surrounded by all that evil, made my blood boil. I kicked myself for leaving her behind. I should have sent Mr. Singh and Lianhua off and remained with her.

"I'd appreciate any

information you can tell us about the Golden Circle," the baron said.

"My men no longer wander the mountains," the Sikh said with a frown. "Not since the metal millipede showed up."

"The Milli-train," the baron said. "We fought it in Africa."

"The mountains were dangerous before, but now an entire village has disappeared. Vanished. No bodies were found. Rumors are that more than one village has been emptied."

"That's horrible," the baron said, his brows knit in worry.

"Sounds like they kidnapped them," I said, giving voice to the thought that popped into my head. I didn't mean to say it aloud.

The Sikh turned and stroked his beard. "What makes you say that? We assumed they saw something they shouldn't have and were eliminated."

I shifted in my chair. "The Golden Circle wants to enslave the world. They're planning something big, and they'll need workers. They're building something. It's big, it's a weapon, and it's meant to defeat us. They have secret lab or factory somewhere in the mountains." I didn't want to say that Genevieve had given me that information. "The villagers were probably taken as slaves."

"How confident are you that they live?" Mr. Shah's bushy eyebrow rose until it touched his large turban.

"Very," I leaned forward, now convinced my gut instinct was right. "In London, they had a house full of slaves building the electromagnet. In France, they had a castle full of slaves, and most were put on the train. It only makes sense that if they are building some new wonder weapon, they're using enslaved people as labor."

"That is an offense to our very way of life. The British might have seized our land, but they leave us in relative peace."

"Alexander speaks the truth," the baron said, ignoring the last bit about the British. "Plus, he was recently in their palace."

"Thank you for your candor."

"Of course. Mr. Singh has told me much about the Sikhs. I would never lie or mislead you. I find your beliefs quite honorable."

"You speak very highly of my people." He bowed to me and then nodded toward Mr. Singh.

The door opened and several soldiers stepped in, followed by Lord Marbury and a man dressed in a fine suit. The baron and Mr. Shah stood up to greet the men properly, and I hopped out of my chair. Mr. Singh rose and once we were all standing, Lianhua got up.

I was surprised to see Lord Marbury here, the baron hadn't mentioned that he was coming, but from the friendly demeanor between him and the man in the suit, they were obviously friends. The baron stepped forward and extended his hand, "Governor Aitchison. Baron Kensington. A pleasure to meet you again. Congratulations on your appointment."

So, this was the governor. I should have known from his arrogant attitude. He eyed Mr. Singh and Lianhua, but ignored them and shifted his focus to Mr. Shah. They barely shook hands. The governor looked like he was going through the motions, but only out of a sense of decorum. Tension filled the space between the two men, and the baron stepped forward and motioned to a chair. "Sit, please."

The governor waved the request aside. "I'm afraid I cannot remain long, but I am here to listen to your request."

"Thank you, Governor." The baron twisted his hands around his cane, in seething frustration. "We are here to request the aid of Her Majesty's army to fight the Golden Circle in the mountains."

"Yes, Lord Marbury and I have been discussing this."

The baron tried to hide his surprise, but I could see the concern in his eyes.

Lord Marbury said, "I'm afraid I may not have been completely convincing."

"I need troops to put down the rebels here in India. Besides, the Himalayas are beyond my mandate." The governor turned to Lord Marbury. "However, I have agreed to send a formal request to New Delhi. Perhaps in a few weeks I can get authorization."

"But we need them now!" Everyone turned, and I realized I'd done it again. If my father were here he'd scold me for speaking out of turn, but now that I'd captured their attention, I wasn't going to waste it. "In a few weeks the Golden Circle will have finalized their plans. In a few weeks, it will be too late to stop them, and their tyranny will flow over the world like a great flood. In a few weeks who knows what will happen to the baron's daughter who is at this moment being held prisoner. Forgive me sir, but we need troops now. The Golden Circle almost destroyed London. They cut a wide swath of destruction across Africa, and have terrorized the mountains, kidnapping whole villages. The time to act is now. Alexander the Great knew to look for the precise moment to strike, and we must do the same. Gentlemen, that time is now—before it's too late."

The baron smiled and Mr. Shah continued to stroke his beard, but the governor and Lord Marbury scowled. The governor shook his head and pointed at me. "And who might this be?"

The baron aimed his cane at me, "I would like to introduce Alexander Armitage, savior of London, defender of Africa, and scourge to the Golden Circle. An American, his father has been aiding us as a linguistics expert."

"The fact that he is an American is obvious." The governor shook his head and I could tell he didn't like me. He reminded me of the Duke. He pinched the bridge of his nose and said, "Despite your impertinence, I cannot send the army off without authorization." He motioned toward Lord Marbury. "As I was telling his Lordship, I haven't heard any of these reports. I've never heard of this Golden Circle. I find your accounts preposterous."

Mr. Shah snorted. "I myself have stood in this very room with you discussing the strange happenings in the mountains. I've told you of the scourge of the metal millipede and of villages emptied of their inhabitants."

Lord Marbury raised his hands. "What has transpired in the past is not what brings us here today." He turned to the governor. "I thank you for submitting our request. We shall wait in Lahore for word."

Mr. Shah shook his head causing all his adornments to jingle. "Baron, I pledge my warriors to you. This young man who stands with a Sikh has convinced me your cause is a noble one." He looked from me to Indihar and back. "I shall send one thousand Sikh warriors."

Lord Marbury's face contorted, and the governor raised his hand to speak, but the baron cut him off.

"Thank you, Mr. Shah. I truly appreciate your generous offer."

"I cannot allow that," the governor said. "Those warriors are not recognized by my authority."

Mr. Shah squared his shoulders. "Precisely, Governor. As you just said, the mountains are beyond your authority. Therefore, I do not need your… authorization. Indeed, with my men's attention focused elsewhere, you can inform New Delhi that your troops won't have much to keep them busy. Perhaps, they would even have the time to aid the baron in this worthy cause—that is if you are brave enough."

The governor's eye's widened and he opened his mouth to speak, but then shut it. He turned to Baron Kensington. "Baron, you are a man of the crown and your exploits in the Punjab are the reason I agreed to this meeting, but I implore you to reconsider. Wait for word from the crown."

"As Alexander said, we don't have time. My daughter's life is at stake. *Everything* we cherish is at stake." He tapped his cane against his palm and then set the end down and leaned on it. "I will accept the help offered by the Sikhs, and hope Her Majesty's army can join us soon."

The governor turned on his heel and stormed off without even saying goodbye. Lord Marbury stepped over to the baron. "Maximillian, we need the British army to face the Golden Circle. A thousand Sikhs may not be enough. Let us go talk to the governor without the others. Maybe in a day or so we can get him to change his mind."

"I agree with Alexander. We must move now, before it is too late."

Lord Marbury nodded. "But we must do this the proper way."

"Why did you speak with the governor without me?" the baron asked. "I had hoped my service here would sway him."

"I thought my station would aid us, but he is tied up fighting the rebels of this wild province." Lord Marbury stared at Mr. Shah and then pulled the baron to the side of the room where they spoke in whispers.

I stepped over to Mr. Singh and Lianhua, but before I could speak, Mr. Shah interrupted, "It is Mr. Singh, correct?"

"Yes, Indihar Singh, sir."

"Who is your father?"

"My parents were killed years ago, sir."

"Where are you from?"

"A village near Shimla."

"Balkar Singh wouldn't be your father, would he?"

Mr. Singh nodded and a large smile crossed his face. "Yes, that was his name."

"Tragic what happened, but your father was a brave warrior." Mr. Shah extended his hand and grasped Mr. Singh's palm. "It is a pleasure to meet his son. I knew him well."

I'd known Indihar for a couple of years, and he rarely talked about his family. They'd been killed by bandits when he was young. The baron had rescued the young boy who tried to fight them off. Indihar only knew a little about his family, and I saw his face light up as Mr. Shah spoke.

I raised my finger to interject. "Mr. Singh helped save London from the four Iron Horsemen. He is a very brave warrior."

"The Iron Horsemen?"

"The unholy warriors of the Golden Circle," I said.

"Four evil warriors, atop demonic iron steeds."

"I must hear more of this battle." Mr. Shah squeezed Mr. Singh's hand. "Your family would have been proud to see you stand up to such tyrants."

Lord Marbury left the room, and the baron came over to us. Mr. Shah dropped Mr. Singh's hand and embraced the baron. "We are ready to stand with you, Iskender, and the son of Balkar Singh."

He'd used the name Alexander the Great's enemies used for him. I clenched my teeth together and tried not to show the wide smile attempting to break out from within.

The baron clapped a hand on the Sikh's shoulder. "Thank you, Mr. Shah. I look forward to fighting at the side of the Sikhs once again."

D ays. Mr. Shah told the baron he'd be ready in a week. That meant we'd barely make it back to the palace within the time frame I'd told Genevieve. If there were any delays, we'd miss my target date and she might already be gone.

The baron insisted on remaining at the governor's office to speak with Marbury further, and sent Mr. Singh, Lianhua, and I in the carriage back to the *Sparrowhawk*.

As the carriage came to a stop, waiting for a herd of cattle and goats being lead through the streets, I turned to Mr. Singh and Lianhua. "I think we should go . . . before the others."

"The captain will not like that, and neither will the baron." Mr. Singh stroked his beard.

Lianhua pointed at me. "I am with Alexander. He will miss his deadline if we wait for these people. Besides, I do not trust any of them."

We both looked at her. I couldn't argue with her, but wondered why she didn't trust any of my friends.

"I trust the baron,"
Mr. Singh said. "But the
saboteur could interfere,
and with that many people,

there will be delays. They'll have to get supplies, too, and what if the governor puts up restrictions on our movement?"

"Then it's settled. We rush back to the *Sparrowhawk*, get what supplies we'll need and depart."

"Wait. It won't be that simple." Mr. Singh raised his hand. "We cannot run from the captain again. Plus, we will need more than we can carry. We must be smart about this."

"Then what do we do? If we tell the captain, he'll tell the baron and we'll never get away."

"Tell your captain we are going ahead to scout the palace." Lianhua brushed the feathers of her owl. "Then we're helping and not running away."

Mr. Singh and I turned toward each other. "Brilliant!" we said in unison.

"If we send Rodin back to the *Sparrowhawk*," I said, "they'll be able to find us faster, and we really would be scouts."

"The captain might go for it," Mr. Singh said with a nod.

"Let's try."

When we arrived at the airdocks, we jumped out of the carriage and rushed up the gangplank to the *Sparrowhawk*. Hunter gave us a slight wave of his hand, and I asked, "Is the captain on the bridge."

He shook his head, "In his cabin."

I said a quick, "Thanks," and we ran down the hall to his door. I knocked.

A voice within said, "Come in, but it better be worth disturbing me."

Mr. Singh put a hand on my arm to stop me, but I opened the door and stepped in. Mr. Singh and Lianhua followed.

"Captain, its Alexander."

I crossed the small cabin, with a bed built into the wall on one side and a desk on the other. Trophies like wheels, name plates, and flags hung on the walls showing battles he'd won, or airships he conquered. A tattered German flag dangled over one side of the porthole, while the union jack draped the other side like curtains.

Captain Baldarich sat on a bench below the large porthole. He stared out on Lahore, but turned as we entered.

"I thought you were at that meeting with the baron and governor?' the captain grumbled.

"We were," I said. "But they're still talking and we wanted to see you."

"Really?" He stroked his mustache and eyed the three of us. "Something's up. I can smell it."

"We have an idea, Captain," Mr. Singh said, shaking like a thin tree on a windy day. "But we won't do it if you disagree."

I glanced at him, wishing he hadn't said that, but I understood Mr. Singh didn't fear anything—except the captain.

I turned back to the captain. "We have to get back or we'll miss the date I told Genevieve."

The captain nodded as if he knew why we stood in front of him. "I see."

"We want to scout ahead." I tried to bolster my confidence with a Baldarich like swagger. "We'll head into the mountains. Find the KGC, and see what they're up too. Then we'll send word back to the *Sparrowhawk* and to the troops telling you where we are and what to expect. We can use Rodin and Kō'ilā as couriers." I paused to see if he was about to have an explosive reaction, then added, "This isn't about taking them on ourselves, Captain. We just want to get back to Genevieve in case she needs us. Plus, you'll know what they're doing and where they are so you won't have to search for them . . . or us.

The captain didn't say anything at first, he just stared at the three of us, and then at the owl and Rodin. I started to fidget, trying to think of a thousand reasons why my plan wasn't foolhardy, but he sat there letting his fingers smooth his mustache and sideburns.

Mr. Singh took a step back, and I feared he might bolt for the door, but I held my ground. The captain stood up. "So . . . the baron got his army. Good."

"The governor is sending a request to New Delhi; he refuses to help without authorization, but the Sikhs are going to join us. It will take them at least a week before they're ready, and even longer to get word from the British."

"So you want to go find Genevieve and send us word about what you find?"

"Exactly," I said. "You'll know what you're facing before you even get there."

"And what if something happens to Rodin or the owl? How would you let us know where you are?" Before we could answer, Baldarich walked over to his desk, opened a drawer, and pulled out a box about the size of a book. It had brass trimmings on the corners and a circular metal rod emerging from the top. He tossed it to me.

"Put this in your bag," the captain said. "There's a switch embedded in the side. Switch it on when you find them and I'll get your signal."

The three of us lit up. I couldn't believe he was going along with our plan! "Thank you, Captain." I flipped the device over and saw a switch in a small indentation on the side. "What is it?"

"Another of the Tinkerer's inventions. He calls it a radio transmitter." The captain pointed at the device. "It works with the Arial Tacking Dial. He says I could put this on a ship and always know where it was, or give it to someone to locate them. Perhaps he knew you all too well, Mr. Knight," the captain said with a chuckle.

I slipped the transmitter into the leather bag slung over my shoulder. "We should get going."

"Wait. Before I give you the go ahead, I want to know your plans."

I glanced at Mr. Singh and Lianhua. "We'll return the same way we got here. We'll travel with a merchant heading back into the mountains, and then once we're close to the hidden palace, Rodin will make contact with Genevieve, and we'll signal you."

The captain studied Mr. Singh and Lianhua, and then stood for a moment staring at me. He was quiet for a long time, then he shook his head and said, "Alexander, you're either bravest man I've ever met, or the craziest." He put his hand on my shoulder. "Either way, get out of here. Go find Genevieve."

I pumped my fist. "Thank you, Captain. You won't regret this."

"Oh yes I will, but go anyway. And Mr. Singh," he reached out to shake his crewman's hand, "you're in charge of making sure Alexander doesn't do anything *too* foolish. And don't forget to signal me."

"Aye, aye, sir."

We ran out of the captain's cabin eager to get everything we'd need for the journey. Mr. Singh headed off to check his weapons and gather his things, and I took

Lianhua to the galley. Gustav helped us pack our food, and even slipped a few honey-drizzled rolls into a bag. He even gave us each one to eat before we left.

We met Mr. Singh at the gangplank and Hunter, still on watch, said, "The captain is letting you go?"

"How did you know?" I looked around as if there were spies everywhere.

"I know you, Alexander. You aren't one to wait around for someone else to ride to Genevieve's rescue." He looked us up and down and then laughed and slapped me on the back. "But you forget I've seen that girl wield a sword, and I'm not sure she needs the likes of you two to save her."

"She doesn't. I already tried," I said with a chuckle. "I'm glad she and I are on the same side."

"We're going to scout ahead," Mr. Singh said.

"Well, I'm impressed. I didn't think the captain'd go for it." Hunter motioned toward the second floor of a nearby building. "Wait before you leave."

"Why?" I asked.

"We have a little birdie watching us. He's been there since we landed."

"Is the Golden Circle everywhere?"

"Perhaps." Hunter stepped back from the cargo door. He motioned for us to do the same. "Don't get a ride from anyone in town, and take a different route into the mountain. The road you came in is watched."

"Then how do we get out of here?" Mr. Singh asked.

"I have an idea." He pulled a smoke grenade from his pocket. "I was going to use this when the captain wanted to head out, but this seems like a good time. Exit through the gun deck, and don't worry. The birdie's attention will be elsewhere." He pulled the pin and rolled the smoke grenade toward the conning tower's ladder.

We rushed down the stairs as smoke started to fill the *Sparrowhawk*. As we arrived on the gun deck, I heard several crewmen screaming, "Fire!" I opened one of the hatches on the floor and we dropped down to ground. The three of us ran the opposite direction ensuring the *Sparrowhawk* was between us and the spy.

Once we were several blocks away, I stopped and looked around. "I don't think we're being followed. Now what?"

Lainhua pointed toward the northeast. "Now we do what your friend said. We get out of the city, find transportation, and then we head to Shimla. It still leads into the mountains. From there we follow the river north to the palace."

I nodded. "Good plan."

Mr. Singh remained silent. A haunted look washed over his face. I realized I recognized the name of the city. Shimla. Where he'd been born. Where tragedy had struck. Where his life completely changed.

I put my hand on his shoulder. "We're with you, Indihar. But we don't have to go to that way."

"No, I will be fine. There aren't many ways into the mountains, and Lianhua is right, Shimla is an excellent choice."

BOOK III: IRON LOTUS

24
Going Beyond Alexander the Great

Two days later we were bouncing along the rough trail on burlap bags riding in the back of a grain cart. We were still navigating the foothills, but anywhere else in the world, they would have called these mountains. Shimla would be our next stop, this afternoon, and with each passing mile, Mr. Singh grew quieter and more withdrawn.

I wanted to say something, but I didn't know what. I never wanted to return to Princeton, where my mother had died from the flu. So, I understood. His whole family had been killed in this city. Their lives snuffed out to send a message to those who resisted.

Lianhua talked to him. Not about his family, but about the mountains. She could pull him out of himself for a time. I stroked Rodin, who had curled up in my lap, and thought about Genevieve. I grew more anxious, and with each turn of the wheel, my heart soared higher. The weight of worry eased. I knew in my gut we'd make it back to her. Only this time, I wouldn't get caught.

Shimla was a beautiful town perched atop a small mountain surrounded by snow-capped towering peaks. The city bustled with traders and we easily slipped through the streets. Though we watched everyone, looking for spies.

Lianhua asked Mr. Singh. "Where was your home? Would you want to stop and visit?"

"That way." He motioned down the ridge, and looked around at the city. "Some parts feel familiar, but too many years have passed." He pointed north. "We should really focus on finding Genevieve."

"We have to stay for the night to avoid the treacherous mountain passes. If you want, we can look around."

"Sadly, I don't know, but even if I did . . . it might be . . . too much."

"I understand, my friend."

Lianhua nodded and we had the merchant drop us off in front of an inn at the town's highest point.

As we entered our room, Mr. Singh said, "Shimla is one of the major centers of the Punjab."

"Good; we need a place we can get lost in." I patted his back. "And I have to say, it's a fascinating place, your homeland. I'm glad I got to see it."

"I am too."

We stayed in the room that night to avoid any unwanted attention. The next morning, we found a trader returning to the mountains and paid him for the journey. This time, Mr. Singh brought money, which was a good idea, because, besides Genevieve's bracelets, we didn't have much to trade.

As we drifted further away from Shimla, Mr. Singh relaxed. I was glad to see him smile again. He'd come from a stunning town, but it held pain for him, and I understood why he hadn't returned. We stayed in the merchant's carts that night on the outskirts of a tiny village. The next day, we crested over a ridge and found a wide river cutting through the mountains.

The merchant turned and spoke to Lianhua. She asked a question back, and the man nodded. I asked, "What did he say?"

"He said we've reached the Hyphasis River, and I had never heard of that. He corrected himself, and said it was now the Baes River." Lianhua pointed north. "He said we're on the right track and we'll follow this river into the mountains."

My brain seized on the familiar word, and raced to find the memory. I knew this place—but how? I jumped off the cart, causing Rodin to take flight. I rushed to the edge and stared at the ground. Then scooped up a handful of dirt,

"Alexander. What is it?" Mr. Singh asked.

The cart ground to halt behind me and the yaks snorted in protest.

"We're here, we're really here." I stared at the river, the opposite shore, and took in the mountains around me. This was it. The furthest Alexander the Great had traveled. "This is where Alexander the Great's army forced him to turn back." I splayed my hand on my chest and paused. "He went no further than this spot."

Mr. Singh jumped down and stood beside me. "We have traveled further than he ever did. You started in London, further west than he ever went. We traveled across Africa, where he only went to Egypt. Now we will travel beyond him on the eastern front. I think maybe we will have to call you 'The Great'."

I smiled, turned, and shook my head. "Ha! Those are kind words, Indihar, but I don't lead an army, and I'm not conqueror anything, or leaving my mark everywhere we go."

"Oh, but you do lead an army, and your friends will follow you far beyond this spot," Mr. Singh said. "And, Alexander, I believe this world will remember you, too."

He was right about one thing: I'd traveled further in every direction than my namesake. I hadn't thought about my journeys as paralleling his, but they had. Now, as soon as we crossed this river, I'd no longer be stepping in Alexander the Great's footsteps, but by making my own.

We climbed back into the cart and forged the river through the shallows. Once on the other bank, we continued up into the mountains. Looking back. I could almost see the ghosts of a Greek army lead by a king, who would soon pass into legend. Alexander the Great had seen the east as something more to be conquered. His men after years of war, just wanted to return home. I looked east, and knew I had more to do, more to see, more to stand against. I would conquer the land *for* Alexander the Great. Okay, maybe I wouldn't conquer it, but I would never stop. I'd chase the Golden Circle to ends of the earth if needed. I put my arm around Mr. Singh. It brought comfort to know that my friends would follow me to the end as well.

It took two more days to find the hidden palace again, but soon, the three of us stood in the valley staring at the masterpiece of ancient engineering.

I scanned the castle perched on the rock. "Something's different."

"Fewer guards," Mr. Singh said. "I only spot two. Last time I counted, thirty-six."

"That's not a good sign."

Lianhua shook her head and sent her owl off. "If no one is watching over this place, there is nothing left to guard."

Mr. Singh agreed, but I kept my eyes on the two soldiers. "If everyone's gone then why is anyone guarding this place?"

"There must be someone, or something, they left behind." Mr. Singh placed his hand over his eyes and studied the palace. "We should be able to get closer, maybe climb up to the lower tier and avoid the guards."

Lianhua pointed to her owl circling on one side of the

palace. "There is something or someone over on that side."

"Genevieve's room." I turned to Rodin who sat on my shoulder. "Go see if she's there." With a quick nod he leapt off and soared up toward the owl.

The guards noticed the two winged-creatures, but when they flew beyond sight around the palace, the soldiers returned to talking.

We slipped along the rock face to the lowest tier where we could climb up the side of the building to a balcony above us. If there were guards everywhere, like before, we'd never make it without being seen, but with only two by the main door, it was relatively easy.

Mr. Singh held out his hand. "Give me your rope and I'll tie it off once I'm up there." He scaled the wall, using the sculptures on the column as a ladder. Once over the edge, we couldn't see him. The rope flew over the side and uncoiled on the way down. I wrapped my leg around the end and climbed up. Mr. Singh extended his hand out and pulled me onto the ledge. Lianhua grabbed the rope and we pulled her up.

The three of us snuck through the palace. With most of the people gone, we had little trouble. No one sat in the great room, and we slipped up to the upper floors with ease.

I found Genevieve's door, and listened. When I heard her fawning over Rodin, I pushed opened the door. She was alone, but we stayed quiet. Her eyes lit up and she clutched the dragon. She looked up and smiled. Kō'ilā perched on the window sill behind Genevieve.

"You came back." she said with the subtle hint of a smile.

"I told you I would. We're even on time."

She kissed Rodin's head. "Unfortunately, the Inner Circle—everyone except my mother—has already left."

"We figured that part out." I knelt down beside her. "Get your things together and we'll go after them."

"The guards come every fifteen minutes to check on me. We have to find a way around them, plus, my mother is still here. We're to join the others in a few weeks, once they are certain neither I, nor anyone else, can alter their plans."

"Then there is still time to stop them. What are you supposed to be doing today?"

"Remain in my room until tonight. I have dinner with my mother every night, and then I go to bed."

"I have a plan. I think." I turned to Mr. Singh and Lianhua. "You two sneak back out, and wait on the eastern footpath we used to get here. Stay out of sight, and we'll meet you later."

"How will we get out of the palace in a quarter of an hour?" Genevieve face held a look of concern.

"I'm not sure yet."

She poked me. "After dinner. When it's dark." She brushed her hands over the fine silk dress she wore. "I can change after dinner, and then be hidden under the covers when they come to check. That will give use the maximum amount of time to get away."

"Brilliant. Sounds like you've done this before."

"I might have snuck past Mrs. Henderson once or twice." Her coy smile lit up her face.

"It's a plan," I said with a nod.

We heard heavy footsteps outside in the hall. Genevieve motioned for us to hide. Lianhua grabbed her owl and ran into the adjoining room. Mr. Singh followed her. I grabbed Rodin, who didn't want to leave Genevieve and clung to her dress. Genevieve plucked off his claws and handed him to me. The door opened and it was too late to run into the next room. I dove under her bed. I barely fit between the bed frame and the floor. I sucked in a deeply. I could see a little from under here, and clutched Rodin close.

The two soldiers walked in, their boots thudding against the wooden floor. Genevieve said, "Hello, *again*. Is this really necessary?"

"General Hendrix's orders, Miss." The soldiers said in a southern American accent.

Without another word or an extensive search, they left. As their footsteps faded into the distance, I scooted out from under the bed with Rodin. He immediately flew up and landed back in Genevieve's lap.

Mr. Singh and Lianhua came back into the room and quickly said their goodbye's and snuck back out of the palace. I sat down beside Genevieve and took her hand. "We have fifteen minutes until they come back."

"We should work on our plan."

"We will." I intertwined my fingers with hers. "It's good to see you again."

"Yes." She leaned in, resting her head against my chest. "Is the *Sparrowhawk* nearby?"

"They're on their way, and I can signal them; but it will be a few days."

"Hendrix didn't trust me after your escape. They went on to wherever they're building their machines and left us here."

"Don't worry, we'll find them, and when we do, we'll call in the *Sparrowhawk* and an army of Sikhs."

"An army?"

"What can I say? Mr. Singh and I are very

convincing."

"Yes, you are." She squeezed my hand.

"I have rope. We'll use it to scale down the side of the palace."

"Better yet, there is a zipline in another room. If you could get it during dinner, we could use it to get away."

"A zipline? An excellent idea." I brushed her hair out of her face. "See, the team's back together, and destiny is just laying the answers before us."

She chuckled, and I soared inside seeing her light up.

"What did I miss?" she asked. "Anything good?"

"We passed over the spot where Alexander the Great turned back. So, I've gone further than he ever did."

She chuckled again and shook her head. "That is wonderful. What about my father?"

"He's on the *Sparrowhawk*."

We sat against each other for a few minutes I told her about my journey and she told me about the Milli-train. I loved sitting with her, and could have stayed there all night, but she had to get ready for dinner.

Genevieve stood and pointed to the other room. "I have to prepare for dinner. When they come for me, you go for the zipline. Last I saw, they had it stored three doors down. On the left."

"Will do," I gave her a thumbs-up. "When you get done with dinner we'll get out of here." I rushed into the next room and Rodin landed beside me. My stomach growled and I realized I hadn't eaten in a while. I knocked lightly on Genevieve's door.

"What is it?" She whispered.

I stepped into her room and froze. Genevieve stood wrapped in a red silk sari with small flowers made from what shone like real gold thread. My mouth fell open, and all the words that I'd wanted to say evaporated into thin air. Her hair lay over one shoulder in a long braid. Every finger held a gold ring, and a series of bangles ran up both arms. She was more beautiful than I'd ever seen her.

"What?"

"I . . . you look . . . *are* beautiful."

She smiled. "Thank you. The Inner Circle insisted we all dress for dinner, every night, and my mother—who loves the formal traditions more than I remember—insisted we continue even after they left."

"Stunning. You look like royalty," I stammered. "I mean you are royalty, and you always look great, but now you really look like a princess."

She bit her red lip and a shudder ran through me. She shook her head. "You have to get back in that room. They will be here any minute."

I quickly blurted out, "Try and get something to eat for Rodin and me."

She motioned to me as a noise from the hall made me run. The door whipped open and Genevieve's mother, said, "Everything all right?"

"Everything is fine. For some reason, I am starving."

26
Escape

As Genevieve stepped out of her room, her mother paused. She turned toward the door I hid behind. I watched through a crack, but pulled away as she studied the room.

Genevieve said, "Is something wrong?"

The baroness shook her head, and left the room, "No. Come, I hear dinner will be wonderful tonight. You look lovely."

They walked down the hall, and eventually their voices trailed off. I ran out of her room and searched for the zipline gun. I found the device right where she said it would be, and I maneuvered it into position by the window. Turning the knobs, I adjusted the two axis until the brass sight was lined up with the mountain pass outside. I checked the coiled line and the large spearhead hook making certain nothing was broken or worn.

I didn't fire yet. The guards might see. We'd launch the line when we were ready to leave. After everything was set, I slipped back to Genevieve's room to wait for her.

An hour later, Genevieve was escorted back to her room by

two soldiers. She entered with her head lowered, as if defeated. I hid behind her bed. The moment the door shut she snapped up with a fire burning in her eyes. I popped up and she smiled.

"Are you ready?" I asked.

"I am. I gave my mother a chance to turn away. Begged her to leave the Golden Circle, but she is heading to their secret location in two weeks."

"That means we have time to find them. Good."

"She refuses to give up on the dream . . . of having all that power. Now she is a member of the Inner Circle, and a Horseman." Her fists were clenched tight, but after a moment, she relaxed them and covered her face with her hands. "I was not important enough to change her mind."

I rushed over. "You can't blame yourself. I've been reading about the corrupting influence of the Horsemen's Hearts. It can be difficult to give up such intoxicating power."

She leaned into me. The smell of rose petals enveloped me, and I wrapped my arms around her. I didn't want to let go. I wanted to take her pain into me, but I knew I couldn't. I could be here for her. Comfort her when she needed it, but I couldn't bear her pain for her. But together, we could stop the Golden Circle. Whatever devious plan they'd concocted, we would be there to thwart it—together.

"Thank you, Alexander." She squeezed me tighter. "Knowing you're here and that we're going after them makes it easier to deal with her."

"Always."

"I need to get changed. This is not a good outfit to travel through the mountains."

I chuckled. "Too bad. You look amazing." No words passed between us. We just remained in each other's arms. Then I said, "You have to let me go."

"I don't want to."

"Neither do I." I exhaled. "But we can't stay here."

She nodded and pulled back, but when I saw her eyes, my hands tightened around her waist. She leaned in and lightly kissed me. I melted and she was able to slip out of my arms. I stepped back toward the room adjoining hers, and leaned against the wall. I could hear her moving around, opening a chest in her room.

"Is everything ready?"

"Yes, zipline is prepped. Mr. Singh and Lianhua are waiting for us in the pass. Your father and an army of Sikhs are on their way."

"Excellent." I heard some shuffling, and then she asked, "Where have you been reading about the power of the hearts?"

"I found a journal written by one of my ancestors. That led to a vision of my ancestor. He hid the Hearts all over the world."

"Really, that is fascinating."

"It is, but he succumbed to its power and found it hard to give up the last heart."

"That is so sad," her voice trembled. "Alexander, can you help me with this corset."

"Of course," I rushed in "Is everything ready?"

"That will work." She picked up her long blue coat and slipped it on. She grabbed her silver-hilted saber with the belt wrapped around the sheath. "I'm ready."

"Let's go."

"Not yet," she paused and pointed to a clock. "They'll be checking on me soon. We'll wait until they've come and then flee."

I nodded. She climbed into the bed and pulled the covers over herself. I blew out some of the candles to dim the lights and then slipped into the next room. I sat on the floor with my back against the wall and waited. Within a few minutes two soldiers opened Genevieve's door.

They stepped in, and one said to the other, "You check that room, I'll check sleeping beauty."

The door beside me opened. I sat behind it, but if the door went too far, it would hit my foot. My fingers slipped over my Thumper and I held my breath so I wouldn't make a sound. I could see the barrel of his rifle, but he never stepped inside. I heard him say, "Nothing," and I quietly exhaled, relieved I hadn't been spotted.

"She's asleep, let's go."

They left and I stood up. When I entered her room, she had popped out from under her covers and was wrapping her sword belt around her waist. I opened the door to the hall slowly and checked both directions.

"They're gone." I turned around and saw her standing defiant with Rodin on her shoulder. "Good to have you back."

She nodded. "I feel right again."

"Come on, I set the zipline up just down the hall." We slipped out into the hall and moved by hugging the walls. Once at the correct room, we entered and I made last minute checks that the zipline gun was still on target. "It's all set."

"Fire at will, Mr. Armitage," she said with a coy smile.

"Right away, milady." I paused, listening for anyone coming and then pulled the string. It released the valve and burst of air vented out of the cylinder as the spearhead grappler shot out unfurling the coiled cable. It arched across the open expanse and sank deep into the rock. I bowed. "Ladies first."

Genevieve took one of the metal handles already secured to the cable and gave Rodin a scritch behind his horned nubs. "Follow me, Rodin." The little dragon nodded and she leapt off the balcony.

I ran to the edge and watched as she sped down the line. She moved with perfect grace, as if she'd made the run a hundred times. At the end she dropped off, landing on her feet, and without even a second step. I grabbed the next handle and jumped off. I swung back and forth, whipped about by the wind. My hand slipped, and I gripped the lower half of the handle even tighter. Thoughts of falling raced through my mind, and would mean certain death. But I held tight as my knuckled turned white. At the end, I let go and slammed into the rocks, tumbling until I hit a small boulder.

"Are you okay?" she asked.

"We can't all have your grace." I rubbed my back and stood up. "But I'm not eager to repeat that landing."

Genevieve drew her saber and cut the cable. It whipped back toward the palace and dangled against the rock. I motioned for her to follow and we walked up the mountain pass.

I heard the hoot of an owl, and saw Mr. Singh and Lianhua perched on a rock. They hopped down and Mr. Singh hugged Genevieve.

"It is good to see you free," Mr. Singh said.

"Thank you, Indihar." Genevieve said with a large smile. "I'm thrilled to be back."

Lianhua looked at Genevieve and said, "I am now

known by my real name, Lianhua."

Genevieve glanced at me and Indihar and then back and Lianhua. She stuck out her hand and Lianhua took it. "I am very glad to meet you."

"Now," Lianhua said, pointing at the pass ahead of us. "We should be moving."

"Yes, of course," Genevieve said as Rodin landed on her shoulder. "Let's get far from here before my absence is noticed."

We traveled throughout the night without stopping. If they'd discovered Genevieve's absence, we saw no signs of it. Not one airship, horse, or soldier entered the pass. We'd rescued Genevieve successfully. Still . . . I wondered why it had been so easy. I thought of a hundred different reasons, but as the sun rose through the mountain peaks I said, "We did it. We got away."

Mr. Singh nodded. "Yes, but I fear the reason."

"My mother isn't worried," Genevieve said. "She knows where we're going. That she'll see me again."

Lianhua gestured toward Genevieve, "Yes, it was too easy. They let us go."

"How could they know?" I stopped.

"She told me last night at dinner. She knew you'd come back, granted, she expected the *Sparrowhawk*."

I kicked myself for not thinking of this possibility. We continued on, moving deeper into the mountains. Eventually we found a road, and merchants moving along the mountain trails.

Once again, Lianhua was able to get us passage. We climbed into two

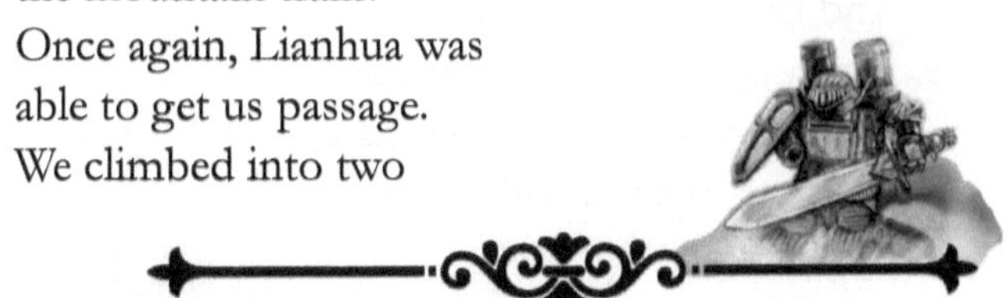

different carts, Genevieve and I sat on bolts of fabric, while Lianhua and Mr. Singh rested on burlap sacks of grain.

"I'm worried about seeing my father again," Genevieve said after a long period of comfortable silence. "I'm certain he'll be angry."

"No, he's worried about you, but he knew you were with your mother. He believed she would protect you from the worst of the Golden Circle. I scolded him for not telling us more."

"You did?" She sat up and turned toward me.

"He should have told us his wife had been an assassin. Not just a noblewoman."

"She is . . . interesting."

"Of course; she's your mother."

Genevieve leaned back against me. "I don't know how I feel, even now. It's all so confusing."

"She disappeared for years. You thought she was dead, only to reappear and murder those Eton professors."

"I am so torn. She is nice to me, but she is not the best person. She is under the influence of—even controlled by— Hendrix and the Inner Circle. They have something on her. I know they are manipulating her."

I sighed. "Our next meeting with them is going to be complicated."

"Definitely," she wrapped her fingers around mine. "They want you to be a horseman. My mother is a horseman. And we must stop them."

The cart stopped and we looked around. A huge four-sided pyramid-shaped mountain rose up before us. Snow-capped at the top, but with perfect horizontal-lined ridges marking the sides. If I didn't know better, I'd swear I was staring at a pyramid in Egypt. The driver said something to us, but I couldn't understand him. He and the others jumped off and walked away.

We climbed out and joined Lianhua and Mr. Singh. "What's going on?" I asked.

"They are going no further," Lianhua said. She pointed at the mountain. "They will be worshiping here for several days."

"Where are we?" Genevieve asked.

"The center of the world." Lianhua cocked her head as she looked at the three of us. "This is Mount Kailash." She looked stunned when we shrugged our shoulders. "*Gangs Rin-po-che*, or *Kangri Rinpoche*?"

"The name sounds familiar." My mind flipped over the spellings until it locked on the hand-written word. "The journal! This is where Armand Armitage was able to regain control over his life."

"This is the mountain of four rivers. From its peak, the four most sacred rivers in Asia flow. The Hindu God Shiva lives on this mountain." She stroked the feathers of her owl. "When Kō'ilā and I fled China, this is where we came."

The merchants joined a long precession of people prostrating themselves on the ground. "What are they doing?" I asked.

"Praying. To show their faith in the gods, they must circle the mountain while performing this ritual."

I watched as men and women slid forward on their hands and knees until flat on the ground and then shuffled forward to perform the ritual again. "They go around the whole mountain like this?"

"Several times."

"Whoa." I'd never seen such devotion to a religion

before. "And I thought listening to the priest every Sunday was hard enough."

Genevieve looked back toward the palace. "I do not think we have the time to wait."

"No. We must get moving, but we should honor this place." We followed Lianhua to a shrine on the path. We knelt and prayed, each in our own way. I even made the sign of the cross over my chest.

I don't know what the others asked for, but I prayed for success. Not money, or glory, or power, but to save this world from the Horsemen's evil. After taking a moment to say thank you for reuniting me with Genevieve, I stood and brushed off my pants. The others finished and we continued on to the southwest.

We soon encountered two large lakes. Walking along the shoreline, we passed several shrines. All were lovingly cared for, but some looked older than the ruins I'd seen in Greece. For the rest of the day Mount Kailash was ever present, always just a glance over my shoulder. Smaller peaks stacked up in front of it the further we traveled, but the holy mountain remained like a beacon in this land.

In the fading light, we traveled into a valley on a trail that looked as if it had been untraveled for many years. We'd intentionally turned off the main path to head on a more western course, but now we found ourselves alone. I heard a rumble, like thunder in the distance, or rocks sliding in another valley. I assumed it was nothing to worry about, but Rodin lifted off of Genevieve's shoulder and flitted around us, darting from one direction to the next.

Then Kō'ilā hunkered down and tucked in closer to Lianhua. I didn't double over, but an ache deep in the pit of my stomach told me something wasn't right. We carried on; each step taken with more caution.

Rodin landed on Genevieve's back, his head poking out above her shoulder.

Suddenly, a thunderous *whoosh* swept down the valley, and a huge shadow blocked out the setting sun. We spun around and all I saw were large leathery wings. An immense dragon, bigger than an airship, soared into the valley, and landed in front of us. Dust and rocks kicked up, the sound of shattering rock split my ears as its claws dug deep into the ground. Reddish-brown scales the size of shields covered its body, and fangs as thick as my leg and just as long filled its mouth. With horns taller and thicker than I was curling off the top of its head, and claws extending from each of the bony joints in its wings, I was overcome with both awe and fear. The dragon lowered its head and stared straight at me. Every inch of me trembled as I tried to look away, but couldn't break the dragon's gaze.

"What are you doing in my valley?" the dragon roared, and waves of wind and sound reverberated in my chest. Then the dragon noticed Rodin. Its great head turned and large eyes focused on Genevieve.

The immense dragon leaned down. Genevieve tried to remain brave, but even her stoic stance shifted. The dragon exhaled sharply blowing her hair back. Rodin stood on her shoulder and flapped his wings. He made a series of vocalizations, chirps, and small roars that would have been adorable if not for his much larger counterpart.

I started to speak, but before I could utter a word, the dragon snapped its eye toward me again. With a shake of its head, it returned to Rodin. I took a deep breath and hoped a column of fire wasn't in our future.

The dragon sat back and folded its immense wings down. "Very interesting," the voice rumbled deep within the dragon's throat. "I see."

I realized it was talking with Rodin. I knew Rodin understood a lot of what I said, he'd often react appropriately, but he and this creature were having an actual conversation. Genevieve looked at Rodin and then smiled at the large dragon.

"We come in peace," I said.

"Rodin says you search for evil men."

"Yes. That's right."

I couldn't stop talking. I was trying, but words kept spilling out. "We're looking for the Golden Circle."

The dragon's neck curled down and eyed each of us. The creature settled down in front of Genevieve. "Rodin tells me you are his soul sister."

"We were born on the same day." She bowed, and Rodin did as well while clinging to her shoulder. "You are magnificent," Genevieve said.

"You are not like the humans I usually see."

"My name is Genevieve, daughter of Baron Maximillian Kensington. My father found Rodin's egg. When he hatched, he became part of our family. This is Alexander Armitage," she said pointing to me.

"Armitage." The dragon cocked his head toward me. "I know that name. It once belonged to the only knight, who, unlike all those who came before or after, did not try to smite me. Are you related to him?"

I nodded. "Yes, Armand Armitage. He traveled these mountains seven hundred years ago."

"In my younger days." The dragon stared at Lianhua and Kō'ilā. "Who are you, and what did you do to this creature?"

She pulled Kō'ilā back and said, "My name is Lianhua, and I fixed his broken wings."

The dragon turned toward Mr. Singh, who blurted out, "I'm Indihar Singh, a Sikh, a soldier and a traveler, born here in these mountains, in Shimla."

The dragon nodded and then said, "I am *Āgō āmdhī*," It bowed deeply, its head almost touching the ground. "I welcome the friends of a dragon to my valley."

"Thank you," Genevieve said. "I didn't know other dragons existed. I've never met any beside Rodin."

"Once we were numerous. Now we are few. I

haven't seen a young one in many, many years."

"Will he get as big as you?"

"In time, but our lives are not like yours. A hundred years is nothing more than a trip around the sun." *Āgō āmdhī's* lip curled up in a smile. "Our growth is tied to age but more to ourselves, to where and how we devote our power."

"You must be very powerful," I said.

Āgō āmdhī chuckled, a deep reverberating laugh that shook the ground. "I am."

"Have you seen a long metal serpent with legs?" I asked.

"What are you doing?" Genevieve asked. "We shouldn't insult the dragon with mundane questions."

"These mountains are his home. He knew Armand Armitage. He might know about the Hearts or where the Knights of the Golden Circle are hiding."

Āgō āmdhī moved its head so that it was right in front of me and though I tried to be brave, I couldn't help but take a step back. "Why do you want to know about the Hearts?"

"We seek—"

"The little dragon already said that! I want to know what you plan to do with such evil."

"Nothing."

"Lies!" the dragon roared. "All humans seek the power of the Hearts."

"We want to prevent their power from being unleashed in our world. We've fought them in London and Africa, and now we are here to stop them." A lump formed in my throat and my knees wobbled. "I do not lie. The power of being a Horseman was offered to me, but I said no. We want to find the men who seek to wield their power and stop them from spreading the evil of the Hearts."

The dragon pointed one of its claws at me. "I hear the truth of your heart." *Āgō āmdhī* gestured toward the east. "I do know where the evil men hide. In a valley not far from here. They pound metal day and night. They poison the water and kill off my food. Their evil grows since they found the heart hidden in these mountains."

My heart skipped a beat and I lowered my head. "They've found a second heart." They must have found the one Armand hid near his grave. I wonder if they have the third one that was in Egypt."

Genevieve asked, "If we can find them, they will leave these mountains and you won't have to deal with their evil anymore."

"Good. I tire of their noise and the horrors they commit. They killed the monks who guarded the Heart. I would visit the monks at night and we would talk about the universe. They were among the few humans I could tolerate, and I miss their curiosity, their desire for . . . wisdom."

"Thank you, *Āgō āmdhī*," Genevieve said as she reached out and touched the dragon's face. "We truly appreciate your wisdom, and may I say it is an honor to meet another dragon."

"We will avenge the monks and villagers they have killed or enslaved." I slammed my fist against my palm. "I, too, tire of the suffering these evil men bring."

"You have an inner fire, like a dragon. I have not seen it in humans for some time."

"Thank you," I managed, eyes wide and in complete awe that not only were we talking to a dragon, but that it compared my resolve, my "inner fire," to a dragon's! My father would never believe it.

"Rest now," *Āgō āmdhī*, said. "The next series of mountain passes are treacherous, especially in the darkness." It turned and unleashed a torrent of fire on some nearby boulders. The rocks glowed red and their warmth chased the cold night air away. "This will keep you warm tonight.

"We are honored," Genevieve said, bowing deeply.

We settled next to the heated boulders. The dragon remained near us and Rodin flew around the creature, chattering away in their dragon tongue. Lianhua sent Kō'ilā off and she returned awhile later with a rabbit for us to eat.

The next morning, I opened my eyes and found the dragon stretched out beside us, his body a barrier between the path and the steep drop-off at the edge of the mountain. I sat up and *Āgō āmdhī* stirred. The fear I'd felt yesterday rose within me, but I knew the dragon wasn't going to hurt me. I walked toward him.

"Thank you, again. We might have walked for days, or even right by them."

"Destiny envelops you. Like the knight."

"I'm still shocked you knew my ancestor. What was he like?"

"An honorable warrior."

"But he succumbed to the evil of the Hearts."

"Honor doesn't mean you are always good. It is about understanding thyself and those around you. Honor is about making the right choices—or at least attempting to make the right choices—no matter the consequences. Yes, your ancestor succumbed, for the evil of the Hearts is immensely powerful, but"—the dragon lifted a talon and lightly tapped me on the chest—"the goodness of your heart is even more powerful."

I nodded and

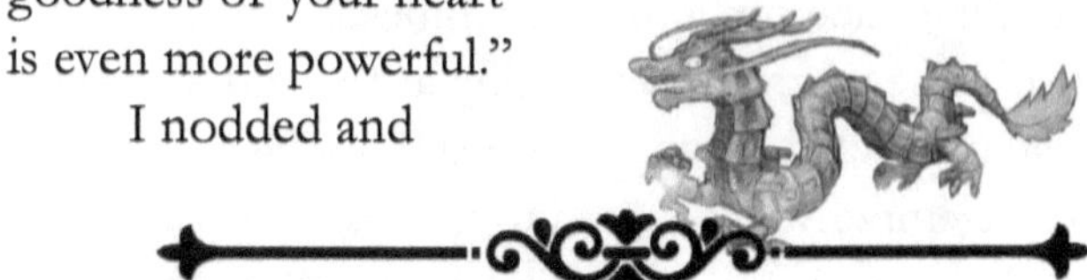

hoped this creature was right. This dragon knew more about life and wisdom than anyone I'd known before. I wanted to ask more questions, but the others were waking and we needed to start moving.

Āgō āmdhī pointed toward a mountain pass leaving the valley. "Follow that trail for two days. From the top of the ridge, you will see the valley where the machines are built."

Genevieve nodded. "Thank you. Is there anything we can do for you?"

Āgō āmdhī chuckled. "Take care of Rodin. He gives me hope that my kind will continue." The dragon stood and flexed its wings. Gasping, we crowded together as it leapt off the mountainside and soared out of the valley.

Rodin unleashed a little roar, and *Āgō āmdhī* answered with a thunderous roar that shook the entire valley causing a rockslide at the other end. Within moments it had disappeared behind the mountains.

Rodin and Kō'ilā flew above us as we tread carefully on the narrow, rocky path the dragon had pointed out. Surrounded by towering peaks, the sun only shone upon us when it was directly above, but most of the day was spent in shadow. Toward evening, the path drew near a mountain stream and then turned and followed the fast-moving water. Finally, we made camp as it got too dark to go on.

"I still can't believe we saw a dragon," I said to Genevieve.

"As if pulled right out of a storybook," she said.

Lianhua pulled out a bronze Chinese coin, a rectangular piece of metal with a ring at the end. A snake-like dragon undulated down one side. "I always wondered. The Chinese emperors were said to be descended from dragons. Now, I think I believe them.”

“I’m thrilled to know Rodin isn’t the last one.” Genevieve rubbed his horned numbs. “I do, however, think we will have to build him a bigger bed.”

“Not yet, but eventually,” I said as I sat beside her.

Mr. Singh kept looking to where we’d come from, as if still trying to see the dragon, then to our path forward. “I’m wondering where the *Sparrowhawk* is?”

“Me too, but don’t worry, we still have a way of calling them.” I patted my bag. “Once we find the Knights of the Golden Circle, we’ll signal them.”

At first light we continued on. By late afternoon, the path narrowed and became more treacherous, until it was nothing more than a game trail. We traveled on loose rock and unsteady ground, which made it difficult for Lianhua and her bound feet. At one point we had to turn sideways on the ever-narrowing path. I heard a rumble above and my stomach twisted into knots. Pebbles pelted us from above, followed by a river of rock sliding down the mountainside. We moved as fast as we could, one foot in front of the other on the narrow ledge. I shoved Genevieve forward and leapt out of the way of a large boulder.

However, Mr. Singh and Lianhua were knocked off and tumbled with the rocks down the sloping mountain face. Once the rock slide had stopped, I leaned over the edge with Genevieve. Kō’ilā landed on a spot a few meters down and I saw Mr. Singh’s blue turban.

“Indihar! Lianhua! Are you all right?” Genevieve shouted.

I pulled the rope out of my bag and tied one end to large boulder. I tossed the other end toward our companions. Mr. Singh sat up, and I saw Lianhua wave her arm.

We sighed in relief as Mr. Singh crawled over to Lianhua. He looked up at me and said, "She's injured. We'll need help getting up."

"Coming." I grabbed the rope and used it to help me down the rocky slope, trying not to dislodge any loose stones. I slid in beside Lianhua and Mr. Singh. "Are you injured?" I asked him, as I saw a few cuts and bruises

"Some pain in my arm"—he rotated his elbow— "but everything works."

I put my fingers to my own forehead and nodded toward his "You have a cut on your head."

He reached up, and then pulled his fingers back streaked with blood. "It's not deep. I'm fine."

He knelt beside Lianhua and I crouched beside him. "Where are you hurt?"

"My leg," she said. "And I lost my cane." Her walker lay beside her, one of the legs was bent at an odd angle.

"I checked her over," Mr. Singh said, "and I don't believe it is broken. But her cut is bleeding a lot. She needs a tourniquet."

Mr. Singh pulled the sash off his waist and tied it around her leg. He and I lifted her, then wrapped the rope under her arms and tied a secure knot. I climbed back up using the rope, and once back on the trail, Genevieve and I pulled Lianhua up while Mr. Singh guided her over the rocks. Once back on the trail, we all rested in the shadow of the boulder.

The hidden valley had to be near, but neither Mr. Singh or Lianhua were in any condition to take on the Golden Circle now. I rested my head back against the rock face and closed my eyes. And then, a pinging in the distance.

"Do you hear that?" I cupped my ear to hear more. "Too repetitive and constant to be natural."

Genevieve nodded, "Sounds like workmen." She pushed herself to her feet. "We've got to be close!"

I reached into my leather bag. "Why don't you two stay here and wait for the Sparrowhawk?"

"We'll scout ahead and see what exactly is going on," Genevieve said. "Don't worry we'll try really hard not to get caught."

Mr. Singh started to protest, but I whipped out the radio transmitter. "Take this. Flip the switch on the side once we've left. The *Sparrowhawk* will find you. Then you can all come after the two of us."

Mr. Singh shook his head. "I do not like your plan."

"We'll be fine, and this way, if we do get captured, they won't be able to destroy the transmitter."

Genevieve patted her shoulder and Rodin landed. "We should get going before it's too dark."

Mr. Singh looked from me to Genevieve and then to Lianhua, and I realized he was worried about our safety. "It's the best way," I said, motioning to the transmitter. "Flip the switch and then send a message with Kō'ilā to the captain."

"I don't like it, but I agree it is best." He pulled a notebook from his pack and looked up at me. "I'll pass along what Genevieve said when we left the palace. The captain needs to be prepared for whatever we might find."

I nodded in agreement and we departed leaving them alone on the rock-strewn path as Genevieve and I continued to pick our way carefully along the narrow ledge. An hour later, as we neared an abrupt curve around the mountainside, we stopped. The pinging of hammers echoed off the mountains. The trail narrowed even further, and I didn't want to risk turning the corner without scouting ahead.

"Rodin, see what you can find beyond this corner," Genevieve said. The little dragon leapt off her shoulder and flew along the side of the frozen mountain. Darkness enveloped us as the sun disappeared. A cold wind whipped up reminding me that late spring at the top of the world wasn't at all like back home.

The little dragon was gone just a few moments and then came back and landed ahead of us. He flapped his wings and hopped forward, guiding us along the treacherous path. We stepped carefully behind him, and, as we rounded the corner, we stopped at the ridgeline of the secluded valley.

"This is it," Genevieve whispered.

The sound of hammers, engines, and other industrial noises mixed with the anguish of moaning men, and the hardened commands of soldiers. We'd definitely found the right place. Three-fourths of the valley was made of metal and brick. A huge factory spewed smoke from its three stacks, and several barracks lined the high mountain walls. A fleet of airships were moored to the airdocks nestled in the valley, including a couple of War Zeppelins, and the biggest airship I'd ever seen. The black, rigid airship had a large red Z with a crown perched on top painted on the side.

However, on the far side of the valley sat two bizarre buildings, one was a palace in the shape of a coiled serpent. Trimmed with a golden spine, a balcony lay in the open cobra's jaw. The other dominated the valley floor. Made of metal, it looked like a pyramid-shaped castle with four towers sticking up, one out of each side. The towers held giant propeller blades.

"What is that weird building with the propellers?" Genevieve asked.

"I don't know, but it looks like a Vimana." I pulled my father's telescope out of my bag. I wrapped the two lenses in the leather case and secured it with the brass toggle.

"What is a Vimana?"

"I read about them in the Mahabharata. A sacred Hindu book that is thousands of years old, kind of like the Hindu Bible." I peered through the telescope. "They were conical flying palaces used during a war at the beginning of time."

"Do I even need to ask why you read a Hindu holy scripture?"

I shrugged. "My father. He thought learning about other religions would be a good way to spend the summer."

"Why would there be one of these flying palaces here?"

"I don't know." I pulled my eye back. "But we're definitely in the right place." I handed her the telescope and pointed toward the snake palace. "Look at the mouth. Recognize anyone?"

She raised the lenses to her eyes and said, "Hendrix."

BOOK III: IRON LOTUS

30
The Factory

Genevieve put her hand on my arm. "Should we wait for the *Sparrowhawk*?" She handed me the telescope.

I shook my head. "And waste this opportunity to learn more?"

"Excellent; I was hoping you'd say that."

"The question is where do we go first?" I said, pointing toward each spot in the valley. "The factory? The airships? The Vimana, or the Snake Palace?"

Genevieve studied the valley. "I'm not sure, but I have a feeling it's going to be a question of where we go without getting caught."

"There are thousands of pairs of eyes down there." I smiled. "I say let's do a little lurking at the Snake Palace."

"If we take that path," Genevieve motioned toward a trail, "it will take us by the factory, and we can see what they're making. That will take us past the Vimana, too." She looked to me to see if she'd pronounced it right,

and I nodded. "Then up to the creepy palace."

"Sounds like a plan." I smiled.

Rodin nodded. "He agrees," she said, patting him on the head. "Always a good sign when the dragon approves."

We slipped down the trail, moving slowly so we didn't attract attention. We snuck up to the immense brick factory, like something right out of London. I peered in a window and saw a huge foundry pouring orange glowing molten metal. Genevieve tapped my shoulder and pointed at two guards heading our way. We slipped inside, through a loading dock, and stayed along the edge. Genevieve stopped and covered her mouth to silence a gasp. I came around the large water tank, and saw an assembly line of large metal armors stretching to the other end of the factory.

"I thought they were making parts for the Vimana, but what is all this?"

"It's an army of Iron Armors." She turned to me. "Those are meant to fight the Black Knight and the Bronze Knight."

I nodded. "They have the same tread-foot design, but these are smaller than our armors. I bet that's why they need the Vimana, to carry all these armors."

"Frightening," she said.

"You can say that again."

We slipped past the armors, careful to avoid the workers being forced to assemble them. Guards stood watch with whips ready. Seeing these people, I could only assume they were the missing villagers. My blood boiled. We passed through empty villages on our way here, and now I knew why—to feed a huge industrial complex that would soon be the scourge of the world.

We left the factory behind us, and used the stacked crates outside to hide. I wanted to climb inside the Vimana that dominated the valley, but every entrance had several guards. Genevieve pointed at some exhaust vents we could use to get inside, but several soldiers walked the perimeter.

"I don't want to get caught just yet. We should move on."

"I agree," Genevieve said, "Besides you already know what it is, but how are we going to destroy something so big?"

"I have no idea." I was looking at thick armor plating, a structure bigger than anything I'd seen in the sky, and yet from the propellers and other design elements it looked like this building was meant to fly. "I think a cannon ball would bounce off."

As we moved around to the other side, we saw workmen installing cannon and other guns on several of the tiers. Three rows of ten cannon lined the bottom tiers, and five cannons on the three above that. I counted five machine gun nests and three Gatling guns on each tier. My mouth dropped open. Genevieve grabbed my arm and pulled me behind one of the train cars that ran from the factory to the Vimana. We crouched down as two soldiers passed where we'd been standing.

"The Vimana is armed to the teeth," I whispered. "I bet every side has that many guns."

Genevieve nodded. "We will need an armada just to get close to this monstrosity."

I had seriously misjudged the Knights of the Golden Circle, and so had the Templars. I'd been so focused on the Horsemen; I'd forgotten about the horrors that our modern world had created. "The

Templar Knights, they aren't expecting anything like this."

Genevieve's eyes grew wide. "Now I understand what my mother meant when she called them foolish old men without a clue of what was coming. It was a phrase she often used, but I didn't think she was serious."

I tapped her shoulder and pointed toward a trail moving up the side of the valley floor. "Come on, this leads up to the 'creepy' palace."

We snuck over to the side of the valley and started up the trail. We passed behind the airdocks, and I stared at the huge black Zeppelin. A large, odd-shaped hatch dominated the back of the dirigible, and the gondola was lined with gun ports. Genevieve pulled me along as sky pirates walked out onto the airdock's catwalks.

Soon we stood at the base of the giant coiled snake palace. Deep grooves cut into the stone gave the appearance of scales, and a golden ridge on the back made for a fearsome roof- line. The tip of the tail curled up and over itself creating a gateway inside. Six coils led up to the head, its mouth open as if about to strike, but the lower jaw appeared to be a balcony.

I pointed to the door lying just beyond the curled gate. "I don't think that's our way in."

"Too guarded," she said. "We should check the back side for a secret way."

"Excellent idea." I pointed to a window on the next coil up, "We might even be able to get through one of those windows."

We squeezed around the back of the palace, and, thankfully, the carved scales continued even into the parts that could not be seen. I grabbed the cut groove and secured the tip of my boot in another. I climbed the side of the snake palace, and once on top of the first tier, I turned around as Genevieve hurried up the scales behind me.

We moved to an open window and I peered inside. "An empty room without decorations, only a twin bed and a chest."

"Rooms for the Inner Circle's attendants."

We jumped through and pressed against the door. I couldn't hear anything in the hall. I opened the door just a crack, and when I didn't see anything, we slipped into corridor. The inner half of the structure was a continuous hallway that sloped upward, with rooms dotting the outer side.

"This is an odd place," I whispered.

"It is, but strategically it makes sense. I bet there are heavy doors every so often that can seal off this corridor, making it harder for an enemy to get to the top. Only one way in and out, means you only have one hall to guard."

We moved cautiously but quickly. Genevieve was right, within a single turn we ran into three doors, one right after the other. Then on the next level we ran into three more. When we heard voices in front of us we slipped into a room. Spears and crossbows lined the walls and in the center of the room, rifles stood in a teepee like structure. Two soldiers passed by, but they weren't on patrol or duty. The lack of people in the palace worried me. Had we missed them? With everyone in the valley, I thought for certain they'd be here. I expected more people, though, like the hidden palace I'd snuck into before.

"Why aren't there more people?" I whispered.

She shrugged. "I assume they're in the valley, or up in the highest tiers."

"That's where we saw Hendrix."

"They don't need a lot of guards. They aren't expecting anyone to sneak in. I bet they're expecting a big attack, and those barracks in the valley are full of soldiers."

I nodded. "Good theory." I motioned toward the door. "We can go. I don't hear them anymore. I was thinking about something . . . the inner corridor doesn't have windows. I bet there is a secret way up on the other side of the wall."

"Why do you say that?"

"The defenders would need a way to sneak past a force and get behind them. Or you couldn't move without everyone in the hall seeing you."

"Good theory," she said with a smile and the bump of her hip against mine.

"Let's go." I opened the door and we snuck through the hallway. I looked for any kind of secret door, or opening. I even tried a dozen sconces in a row.

Then I noticed the pattern at the base of the outer wall. A coiled serpent, small enough to fit on a single block. Most were well worn, meaning they were original and there was only one in each section. I stopped at the next symbol, but instead of going to the outer wall where there was no room for a secret passage, I went to the inner wall. I found a stone poking out a little further than the rest. I pushed on it. Nothing happened. Genevieve tapped my shoulder and pointed up the hall. People were coming, the footsteps grew louder. I pulled on the stone and the wall beside it slid back. We stepped into the secret passage and I saw a stone handle on the same stone I had pulled. I grabbed it and tugged. The wall slid into place. Genevieve exhaled, and I wiped my brow.

Dust covered the floor, and spider webs draped the

passage. I pushed them aside and kept moving. There were windows on the inner walls of the passage, but we couldn't see into the darkness. I could tell there was a ceiling, a room, above the central core. We heard voices, specifically, Hendrix's southern drawl, and stopped. We ended up outside a room in the very center of the palace. Genevieve pointed to a beam of light piercing the dark passage and we found a thin slit in the wall. We knelt down and peered through. The Inner Circle sat in high-backed chairs—thrones, really—equally spaced in the circular room. Stairs led up the sloping curve of one wall. We couldn't see where, but we were high enough that it could only be the head of the snake.

One chair was empty; I guessed it was for the baroness, though I couldn't be certain. I saw the Pirate Queen Zerelda relaxing in another chair. Seven chairs in all.

Hendrix pounded his fist against the arm of his chair. "If I didn't know better, I'd say you were stalling."

"I am not. These machines are siphoning off too many men," A bald man said, his distinctive Persian accent lowered an octave. "I need more diggers to search for the Horsemen relics."

"Those *machines* are what's gonna deliver the world into our hands, not your mysticism." Hendrix snarled.

"We have almost completed the armors and machines." The Chinese man I'd seen at the mountain palace said. "After that, I'm sure we can dedicate more men to hunting the Hearts."

Another man leaned forward, and put his elbows on the armrests. His short-trimmed brown hair and olive skin looked Mediterranean. "Those ugly things are nothing compared to slaves. With an army of a hundred thousand slaves, I could do anything. Seize this world in my hand, build any bridge, or castle in days. Your factory has taken months to do what my slaves could do in no time."

Hendrix stood up and drawled, "Well you only got a thousand slaves."

"I was only allowed to clear a few villages, none of the towns, and you keep working them to death!"

Hendrix grabbed a goblet from a servant holding a tray and up ended the cup. Much of the liquid splashed over his cheeks and then he threw the golden goblet to the ground.

The bald man held his hand up and my stomach twisted into knots. "My mysticism," he said with pointed sarcasm, "tells me that someone is here. There." He pointed directly at us. "Hiding in the wall."

I clutched my stomach and doubled over. Genevieve gripped my shoulders, and tried to hold me up, but I slumped to my knees. The wall opened and Hendrix looked down at us. Beside him, the bald man held one of the Hearts in the palm of his hand.

"Welcome, Mr. Armitage, Lady Kensington." General Hendrix stepped to the side and gestured with his hand. "I knew you'd find us."

My stomach still wrenched, twisted into knots, but as bald man stepped back, taking the Heart with him, my insides unwound themselves, and I could stand up straight again. I realized then it was the Heart that set me off; not Hendrix.

Genevieve stepped out of the hidden passage and I followed. The Inner Circle looked surprised, with several staring at us with stunned expressions. However, Queen Zerelda stood up and put her hands on her hips. Her leg stuck out the high slit of her skirt and she still wore all black with golden skulls on her corset. "Well, look who's decided to join us, Hendrix's pet and the girl who thinks she's a swordswoman."

Genevieve's eyes narrowed, "You need to stop running away from our duels, so we can finally decide who the better swordswoman is."

The German chuckled and Zerelda snapped him a look that could have sliced him in two.

"You two never disappoint," Hendrix said motioning to the servants to place two chairs from the side of the room beside his throne. Sit. I insist."

I nodded and sat. but Genevieve didn't move. She stared down Zerelda until the pirate queen stepped back to her throne. Only then did Genevieve sit beside me.

"You might have escaped before but not this time. By the time I'm done you'll want to join me." Hendrix smiled and tipped his hat. "Thank you for delivering Alexander, Genevieve."

"That's not true! How dare you." Genevieve turned to me. "Alexander, I swear I did not lead you here."

I didn't think she had. We'd rescued her, after all.

Hendrix clapped his real hand against his bronze appendage. "Didn't you? I left you at the hidden palace to be rescued. I knew you'd follow us here. I even dropped clues while you were my guest. You did exactly what I wanted."

Genevieve started to protest again, but I put my hand on her arm and gave her a soft squeeze of reassurance. "We came to stop you." I turned to face Hendrix. "I know about the Hearts. They're too powerful to be controlled. They'll corrupt your minds."

"They corrupt *lesser* minds," Hendrix said with a chuckle. "I bet you saw my machines."

The bald man stared at the Heart in his hand. "Those soulless hunks of metal will do nothing. The boy is right. It is the Hearts that have the real power. It is the Hearts that will deliver the world to me."

"To us, don't you mean?" Zerelda said with venom in her voice.

"Alexander, allow me to introduce the future rulers of our world." Hendrix made a grand gesture. "You already know Zerelda the Pirate Queen. I believe she and Genevieve can't go five minutes without a sword fight. Then we have Shangguan Bo, descendant of Shangguan Jie who usurped Emperor Wu all those years ago. Antiochus is an Italian, descended from Roman Senators." He pointed to the German man, "This is Wilhelm, he's not one of the Triumvirate like the others, but he is my liaison to the Kaiser, and personally led his troops at the Battle of the Thames. Wilhelm, here's the kid who stopped you." Hendrix chuckled, but the German man's eyes narrowed. "Lastly, we have Xerxes. You might recognize the name; he's Persian, descended from the great kings of old. Oh, and he hates Alexander the Great. All the western conquerors. What do you call him? That Macedonian Brat. Meet his namesake— Alexander Armitage."

Xerxes grumbled, and I saw the hatred in his eyes. But he was holding the Hearts that looked like shiny liquid metal. He clutched it close to his chest as if someone around the table planned to snatch it from him.

I looked at each of them. These were the people who had made my life miserable over the last two years. Kidnapped my father, tried to kill the baron, murdered my professors at Eton, and chased me across half the world. Only Hendrix was a commoner like me.

Genevieve looked lost in her thoughts. I wanted to console her; tell her I didn't believe a word of what Hendrix was saying. But I wasn't certain what Hendrix was trying to do, other than divide us.

Hendrix pointed at me. "Alexander has been a thorn in our side since Eton. He rescued his father, saved the baron, discovered our plans, and drove the Black Knight to victory. He solved the mystery of the assassinations at

Eton, tracked us to Zululand—" He counted each point out with his mechanical fingers.

Zerelda stood up. "Don't forget, trashing my first airship and blowing up my place in Zanzibar. I won't forget what you and your little friends have done."

"I shall never forget what you did to the crew of the *Sparrowhawk*." Genevieve's hand slid to the hilt of her saber.

Hendrix laughed. "Ladies, enough or I will have you duel for my pleasure." He turned to me. "You know how to pick'em kid. I still need a fourth rider, and you're the one destiny has chosen. There's a reason you're a thorn in my side."

"I'm here to stop you, not join you. An Armitage will always stop the Horsemen."

Hendrix leaned in and his mechanical sparked with electricity. "You're going to be a Horseman. Either by choice, the nice way, or by force—trust me you don't want me to use force. You have friends you don't want to lose and a pretty girlfriend here you don't want hurt."

I tried to bury my fear deep within me, but inside I trembled, my hands were sweaty, and I worried he might be right. What if I did have to join him?

"This is ridiculous," Xerxes said staring at the Heart in his hands. "Quit your complaining. I am a Horseman, the Heart calls to me."

"That Heart is going with Shangguan to the Dragonship."

"No!" Xerxes jumped up, clutching the heart close to his chest. "This one is mine. I will use it to unlock the magical power of the Horsemen."

The smile faded from Hendrix's face. He stood and faced the Persian. "That's not the plan, and you know it. We need the Hearts to power the machines. Once we have all four, then the Horsemen will bring about the resurrection of Emperor Burr's vision of the world!"

"We are enacting Darius the Great's imperial dreams!" Xerxes' snarled and stepped close to Hendrix. "An army of a million slaves lead by the Four Horsemen will lay waste to this world. We're here to control men, not machines! You will not destroy a plan set in place generations ago."

"The Horsemen are the key—" Hendrix started as Xerxes to another step forward. Shimmering energy swirled around Xerxes' arm in waves of purple, moving down to his hand as he shoved Hendrix. The magic slammed into Hendrix's shoulder knocking the big man off his feet.

"See!" Xerxes held up the Heart and stepped into the center of the room. "Mysticism over machines. The ultimate power is mine."

"If you're going to try and kill a man, you best succeed." Hendrix pulled himself up and walked back to his throne. The gears of his right arm whirred as his hand slid into his sleeve and was replaced by a tree clawed grappler. With a whoosh of air, the claw fired off and snagged the Heart right out of Xerxes' hand. Hendrix slammed his real fist against a button on the armrest causing the floor to fall out from under where Xerxes stood. With a scream of protest, the bald man disappeared as if he'd never been there, and Hendrix retracted the claw. The cable zipped back into his sleeve until Hendrix held the Heart.

Hendrix released the armrest and the floor returned. Shangguan and Antiochus turned and stared at Hendrix as Zerelda sat back and smiled. The German eyed everyone in the chamber, as Genevieve covered her mouth and stared at the floor. I kept my eye on the Heart, and noticed I'd stopped trembling.

Hendrix stared at each one of us. "Anyone else have a problem with *my* plan?"

I raised my hand. "I do."

Fire erupted in Hendrix's good eye, and his other sparked with electricity. "Let me guess; you're going to stop me."

I met his gaze. "Yes, as a matter of fact, I am."

He snorted loudly—like a raging bull—and then shook his head. "I know you're gonna try, boy. That's why I like you!" He leaned toward me and growled, "But mark my words, you ain't gonna succeed."

"Calm down, General," a velvety voice with a soft French accent glided in from the hall, followed shortly by the baroness who stepped into the chamber. "He's just trying to get you to do something rash, like hurt him. Remember, you can catch more flies with honey than vinegar."

"Mother," Genevieve didn't sound surprised only annoyed.

"Thank you for bringing Alexander here, darling." She sat on Xerxes throne. "Now, we have to go. The Templar are coming."

"How do you know?" Hendrix snarled.

"I met a friend on my way here." She motioned toward the door as Lord Marbury stepped into the chamber.

"The *Sparrowhawk* leads an army of Sikhs and they're headed our way," Lord Marbury said.

My mouth dropped open, but a fire raged within me. "Lord Marbury, you're the mole!"

Hendrix turned to me. "Marbury's been with us since the beginning." He chuckled. "He was the first operative the Templars sent to see what we were up to. He was easy to capture and after just the tiniest bit of torture, he turned to the Golden Circle. He's been ever so helpful."

"Why are you telling him this?" Lord Marbury said to Hendrix. "Besides, they're supposed to be locked away as security against the Templar. That was the plan,"

I remembered the first time I met Lord Marbury, the fear he showed for the Knights of the Golden Circle. Sinclair, and the baron wouldn't talk about it, but they put the fear of the KGC in me. I couldn't believe he'd betray his vows to the order. Then I remembered the murders at Eton, one of them had taken place in his house. My stomach churned and I felt sick inside. He knew the *Sparrowhawk's* flight plan and when we'd landed in Athens. He knew everything. Which meant the Golden Circle knew everything. Well, not everything. I hadn't told him about the visions or what I'd learned about the Hearts. Now, I was glad I'd kept my mouth shut.

"How can you go against the Order? They're your brothers." Pain ripped through my voice.

Betrayed by those I called friends, I wanted to spit venom at Marbury, the Templars, and the Golden Circle. They'd wronged me, all of them, and they all deserved to be cursed with every searing word trapped inside me. I wanted chaos to rain upon their houses. But as the words formed in my mind, it was thoughts of Armand that poured water over my vengeance and kept my hand from my weapons. Now I had to find a way to carry on, to bear the weight of their betrayal. For they carried none of it. To let vengeance overtake me was to wallow in the mud beside them, not soar beyond them. My racing heartbeat slowed, my vengeance waned, and I let the clenched breath out. A friend's betrayal was the greatest of crimes, but I had learned one lesson—they were never my friends—and the fault was mine for failing to see the blackness of their hearts.

"You couldn't understand," Marbury turned to Hendrix. "Get them out of here."

"Afraid not, *Lord* Marbury." Hendrix sinister smile curled one side of his lip. The other was bound to the leather plate and couldn't move. "That kid's got more sway in this room than you. He's the fourth horseman. He's already agreed to it; he just hasn't said it out loud yet."

"What? You promised me power, a kingdom of my own!" Lord Marbury's eyes flared and he threw open his coat as he placed his hands on his hips. "Why did I betray the Order for you if not to gain power for myself?"

Hendrix pointed his thumb at his own chest. "Because *I* told you to. Because *I* stopped torturing you. But don't worry, Marbury, you're still going to get your land." He turned away from the nobleman and said, "After I decide whether or not to scorch it first."

"Then who are the Horsemen?" Shangguan Bo asked. "I'll be laying waste from within my Dragonship."

"I am the Horseman of War!" Hendrix held his arms stretched out; the hematite Heart still clutched in his claw. "Zerelda has proven herself and will continue as the Horseman of Famine." He spun on his heel and pointed at the Genevieve's mother. "The baroness showed she can handle her own in Africa, and will be the Horseman of Pestilence." Genevieve's mouth was set in a stern line as she turned to her mother who nodded to Hendrix with a cold, steely expression.

"How can you be a Horseman?" Genevieve demanded. "You told me we had to get away from these madmen."

The baroness sighed and waved Genevieve's concerns away. "The Templar will never leave us alone. They haven't stopped hunting me for over a decade. After they are destroyed, we will leave the Golden Circle behind us."

Genevieve shook her head in disbelief. She lowered her voice and said, "I cannot believe I ever listened to you. Everything you say is a half-truth with conditions attached."

I watched as her mother's head bowed slightly, but no one else was paying attention. They were all focused on Hendrix. He held the Heart high above him and then turned to me. He pointed the hematite Heart at me, thrusting it like a sword. "Lastly, our fourth, the Horseman of Death—Alexander Armitage."

"But the boy has refused," Antiochus said. "How will he be Death?"

"Antiochus, I don't need dissention; I need team players. The Armitages are connected to the Hearts. What Kannard didn't understand is that we need them, not just to find the damn things, but also to win the war. With an Armitage on our side, we will not—cannot—fail. And Death, not only does it mean he will hold the sword that cuts the lifelines of those who stand against us, but his entire line of ancestors will be standing behind him."

"But what about me," Antiochus said. "I was to be—"

"Don't you fret, my friend. You'll lay waste to our enemies from the Vimana."

Antiochus nodded and my heart sank. Hendrix's argument made perfect sense. My family was connected to the Hearts. Armand spent years traveling across many lands to hide them after the crusades. My father translated the ancient texts that led to their rediscovery. And I had fought against them. Those were just the ones I knew about. What other relatives had interacted with the Hearts of the Horsemen? Had they been riders before?

I didn't deny or push back against Hendrix, and everyone noticed. Hendrix smiled and continued. "He understands what we're fighting for. The Templars represent the real evil. A bunch of landed noblemen who've done nothing to merit their wealth and power other than to be born into the right family and inherit the right title. Desperate to hold on to the decaying remnants of their old-world order, they are no match for the Knights of the Golden Circle. We will reshape the world. And Alexander here knows it's the truth."

All eyes turned to me. Genevieve even cocked her head as if waiting for me to say something, anything. I averted my eyes, staring at the spot on the floor where

Xerxes had been standing just moments before.

Hendrix walked over to Lord Marbury, his bronze leg striking the floor with a thud while the regular one glided in silence. He switched the Heart to his real hand, and grabbed Marbury's shoulder with his claw. "Come, we have to prepare for the *Sparrowhawk* and this Sikh army of Baron Kensington's."

"Yes, they will be here soon." Lord Marbury turned away with Hendrix's hand guiding him.

Genevieve's mother followed, but Zerelda stood up and stared at me. "Hendrix might think you are a Horseman, but I still haven't paid you back for nearly destroying the *Storm Vulture*, and blowing up my place in Zanzibar." She leaned closer. "I'll never forget our meeting atop the *Sparrowhawk*."

"Neither will I. I know you could have easily killed me, but you had to run and save your ship." I forced a defiant look on my face and wouldn't let it slip.

Antiochus jumped off his throne. "I know Hendirx is trying to resurrect the American Empire, but I say we take both of these meddling children outside and put them before the firing squad."

"Now there is a good idea." Zerelda said.

Antiochus took a step toward me and Rodin blew a column of fire between us. "Oh God!" He stumbled back. "That thing is real!"

"Yep, and I'll skin the little lizard alive." Zerelda thrust her hand out to snatch Rodin, but he leapt off. Genevieve shoved the pirate back then sprang to her feet and drew her silver-hilted saber. Zerelda drew her wickedly-curved cutlass, the black hilt decorated with skulls and bones.

"Genevieve. Don't. Please." I raised my hands and

stood.

Antiochus motioned to the guards and several soldiers raised their rifles. "If the little wench, moves shoot her."

"Fly, Rodin, get out of here!" Genevieve said and Rodin flew up the stairs and out the mouth of the snake palace.

Shangguan watched Rodin soar off and then turned to Antiochus "Don't shoot them here. Hendrix and her mother will not be pleased, and we will have an ugly fight on our hands. If you must kill them, take them to the fang balcony and be done with it."

Antiochus and Zerelda glanced at each other and nodded. "An excellent idea. Move," he said, "or I'll shoot you in the kneecap and drag you up there." Antiochus raised his hand as if about to give the order.

I touched Genevieve's shoulder. She turned toward me and we locked eyes. She nodded slightly, lowered her sword, and we walked toward the stairs leading up to the balcony. With everyone behind us, I reached down and slid the scratched Thumper from its leather strap. I tucked the baton under my sleeve and Genevieve smiled.

We entered the serpent's head. The rose-colored glass eyes acted as windows. The open mouth was a perfect balcony. The large curved stone fangs formed a railing. We walked to the edge and looked out over the valley below. Soldiers and workers ran around, many loading onto the Vimana. Some ran for the airships, including Zerelda's huge black War Zeppelin. Then I saw the Milli-train crawl out of a tunnel and up the side of the mountain.

"This does not look good," Genevieve said. "We have a firing squad behind us and a valley full of enemies in front of us."

"And yet, with you at my side, I'm not worried."

She bit her lip.

"That's far enough," Antiochus ordered.

Zerelda laughed wildly. "The destruction of your world and everything you've worked so hard for over the last two years will be the last thing you see."

The soldiers cocked their rifles, and I reaffirmed my grip on the Thumper tucked up my sleeve. I would spin around and fire, signaling Genevieve to strike. My muscles tensed. I drew in a breath, and then the palace shook and a deafening roar filled the air followed by a torrent of fire cascading down to envelope the Milli-train. *Āgō āmdhī*. The huge dragon broke through the clouds as the train burst into flames. From the balcony, I could see the armor plating glow in the intense heat. Another blast of dragon fire rocked the train side-to-side and I watched, mesmerized, as it tumbled off the side of the mountain, crashing into the valley as a series of explosions ripped it apart. The dragon swooped down and blasted the valley floor, igniting the factory and part of the airdocks.

I heard one soldier behind us drop his rifle and cry out. Turning, I saw the rest retreating inside as *Āgō āmdhī* roared again, unleashing yet another inferno on the buildings below us.

"Look!" Genevieve said, pointing. The *Sparrowhawk* appeared in the mountain pass with two other airships close behind it.

Another explosion ripped through the air as one of the Knights of the Golden Circle airships moored in the airdocks exploded. Zerelda screamed, "Damn you, brats, I'll not lose my ship again!" She shoved us aside and drew a grappling crossbow from her back. She shot a line to the ground, secured the end on the balcony, and sheathing her cutlass, turned to us. "This isn't over." She slung the sheath of her cutlass over the line and slid down.

I spun around, letting my Thumper slip into my hand. The only one left on the balcony was Antiochus. I pointed the Thumper at his chest and pulled the trigger, knocking him backward just as the dragon landed on the snake, his claws clutching at stone. Its head was bigger than the whole balcony.

"Jump on!" *Āgō āmdhī* said.

I looked at Genevieve and climbed onto its head. She followed and sat behind the large horns. "Watch out," she yelled. I turned to see Antiochus scramble to his feet, grab one of the dropped rifles, and run to the edge.

"Get down!" I yelled as *Āgō āmdhī* took flight. Ducking my head, I ventured a look and saw Antiochus taking aim. I heard the crack of a rifle and turned to Genevieve. She was safe. Antiochus had missed. Then I heard him cursing and looked back to see him holding a bleeding hand to his chest and swearing at something in the distance. I turned and saw Hunter leaning out of the *Sparrowhawk*, his long rifle still pointed at us. I pumped my fist in the air, and he raised one of his long rifles in salute.

The dragon banked and slowed to land on a wide ledge overlooking the valley. It lowered its massive head and we jumped off. "Thank you, *Āgō āmdhī*," I said. "You saved us."

"Rodin called to me." The dragon said as its little counterpart soared up and landed on Genevieve.

She bowed. "Perfect timing and you did more damage than any army could hope to do."

Below us, the Sikhs slid down repelling lines from the airships behind the Sparrowhawk and, led by the baron, freed the workers and attacked the soldiers around the Vimana and burning factories. In retaliation, gun installations around the valley and on the Vimana took aim and began firing on the dragon and on the airships. A volley crashed into the mountainside near us and Genevieve and I ducked and held our arms over our heads to protect from falling rock.

Small arms fired peppered the rocks around us and bounced off the scales of the dragon. A round from one of the deck guns of the Vimana slammed into its side charring the scales, and tearing a small bit of its wing.

"*Āgō āmdhī*, they're targeting you!" Genevieve exclaimed.

"Those big guns might pierce your hide!" I pointed toward the clouds. "You need to get out of here. We'd feel horrible if you were injured saving us."

"I'm happy to be able to repay them for what they've done to my mountains." The dragon said as it spread its wings. "For now, I leave the humans to battle amongst themselves. If you need me, have Rodin call. A blessed journey to you both!" *Āgō āmdhī*, leapt off the ledge and blasted a couple of the cannon in the valley before soaring over the mountain to disappear.

A thunderous noise mixed with the sound of a whirling wind as the giant propellers on the four towers of the Vimana spun to life. Slowly, the large iron castle lifted off the ground. A cloud of dust kicked up around the Vimana, and I saw that a bunch of armors and soldiers were left on the valley floor. The Vimana rose out of the thick black smoke and orange glow of the flames and rose into the sky.

"They're fleeing!" Genevieve said pointing at the Vimana.

"And they hadn't finished loading all their equipment." Relief washed over me, this battle wasn't over, but we'd dealt them a significant blow.

The *Queen Z's Revenge* lifted out of the moorings and soared out of the valley bearing south. The *Sparrowhawk* followed, and flew straight toward us. Mr. Singh stuck his head out of the gun deck and dropped a rope ladder. I looked at Genevieve and she smiled. As the ladder whipped by, together, we grabbed hold and were whisked into the sky.

33
Chasing Z

Genevieve climbed up the ladder first and I followed. Once inside we were greeted by Mr. Singh and Lianhua. I smiled. "Am I glad to see both of you!"

"The transmitter worked perfectly." Mr. Singh held out his hand and helped Genevieve to her feet. "As soon as they picked us up, we pointed them to the valley." He reached out for me and pulled me to my feet. "We weren't expecting the dragon to help."

"That was Rodin's doing," Genevieve said, scratching the little dragon under his chin. "He called *Āgō āmdhī.*"

"And a good thing too, I don't know that we would have done as well with only the *Sparrowhawk* and the Sikhs." I pointed to Genevieve and myself. "They were about to execute us."

Mr. Singh's eyes bulged, but we all turned as Hunter came down the stairs. "Everyone all right?"

I stuck my hand out to shake Hunter's. "Great shot, my friend. You saved our lives."

"It was a tricky, but

I couldn't let him shoot you in the back."

"I can't believe you hit him from that distance," I said.

He nodded. "It was one of the longest I've ever made, easily a thousand yards.

"Wow," I said.

Genevieve looked around and turned to Mr. Singh. "Where is my father?"

"He led the Sikhs during the attack."

Genevieve ran to one of the gun ports. She looked out, scanning the ground, until she pointed. "There he is."

I joined her and saw the baron leading a small group of warriors as they attacked the last open door of the Vimana. They fought their way inside, cutting down soldiers as they went.

The *Sparrowhawk* shook as a shell exploded outside. We all jumped as shrapnel hit the wooden hull of the gun deck. A reminder that the battle wasn't over yet. Genevieve said, "Come we must get to the bridge."

We ran up the stairs to the bridge and found Captain Baldarich on his feet, gripping the railing in front of him as he barked orders at the pilot and into one of the copper tubes. "Three degrees starboard and up five degrees," he said pointing at the windows, then he leaned over to the messaging tube. "Gears! Give me everything you've got and then give more." He spun around and big smile crossed his face. "You're back! And you brought Genevieve! Glad to have you aboard! You're just in time to help me get that sky witch!"

Gear's voice echoed up through the tube, "More power coming your way!"

"Get us alongside them, Heinz, Now!" Baldarich slammed his fist against the railing. "That's a big blimp, but she moves like an airskiff. What kind of engines do they have?"

Genevieve pointed at the Vimana as it rose into the air and headed east at a much slower pace. "Captain, we need to follow that… flying city."

"A Vimana," I said. "Looks like they took the design right out of the *Mahabharata*."

Mr. Singh turned to me, with surprise on his face. "It does." I looked at him puzzled. He was a Sikh, not a Hindu. He smiled and said, "I've seen paintings."

The captain smoothed out his moustache and sideburns with his fingers, "That thing is too big and too heavily armed. We'd never get close enough. Plus, she moves like a walrus on land. Better to take Zerelda down first."

Genevieve rushed to the window. She pressed her hand against the glass as the Vimana soared away. I put my hand on her shoulder and she took a deep breath. "I'll see him again."

I nodded. "You know you will." I squeezed her shoulder. "I agree with the captain, with all those guns I don't think the *Sparrowhawk* can take it on, but we haven't given up."

She turned toward me, "Then let's bring Zerelda down."

On the other side of the *Sparrowhawk*, the *Queen Z's Revenge* flew through a mountain pass. I noticed black wisps trailed from the fins and main body. The gondola beneath the dirigible morphed into a more organic and wicked shape. The smooth lines of the shaped wood contorted and looked like a gnarled tree. Gun ports popped open on the sides and aft section of the airship. Demon-headed cannon emerged from the ports and belched fire and lead our direction.

"Rise! Three degrees up angle and bank starboard!" Captain Baldarich ducked as the cannon balls whizzed past. "How do her guns have a greater range than mine?"

"Zerelda's Horsemen's Heart." I turned to Genevieve and she nodded. "You can tell by the way it's morphing, just like the Iron Horsemen and the Milli-train."

Baldarich spun around, "Zerelda put one of those infernal hearts in her airship!"

"See the black wisps trailing from the fins. The Iron Horsemen do the same thing."

"That's not fighting fair!" Baldarich slammed his fist against the railing. "but I should expect nothing less from the treacherous sky-witch."

"Captain," Hunter pointed out the window at the *Queen Z's Revenge*. "A large hatch opened on the underside of the aft section."

I stared out at the *Queen Z's Revenge* but we were rising above the airship and I couldn't see the airship's belly.

The captain said, "Heinz drop us down while they're reloading."

The *Sparrowhawk* tipped its nose down and soon we saw the bottom of the *Queen Z's Revenge*. A small aircraft lowered out the large hatch by a crane. The aircraft had a wooden frame around the balloon with four wingsails and a propeller on the back. The aircraft detached, dropped for a moment, but then the propeller whirled to life and they banked toward us. Two jagged iron spikes on the front and a crossbow mounted in front of the pilot made it clear what this mini-airship was designed to do.

"He's going to attack," I said.

Captain Baldarich flipped open all four copper tubes in front of him. He leaned down and yelled, "Battlestations! Prepare to defend against multiple targets!"

"Zerelda's airship is carrying attack craft!" Genevieve pointed. "A second one is lowering out of her hold."

Hunter nodded. "She's right, captain. There's another one."

"Those are Hornets, but I've never seen them launched from a zep. That's a neat trick." Baldarich pushed his coat back and scanned the sky as he paced back and forth. "Heinz, ten degrees up, and ten degrees to port. Hunter, get on the deck gun, use your rifle, I don't care how you do it, but take out those aircraft." He stopped in front of me. "Alexander, go with him and reload."

"Aye, aye captain," I saluted and darted after Hunter who was already running off the bridge.

The *Sparrowhawk* went into a steep bank, both to the side and tilting up. I had to grab the railing running down the hall to keep from sliding around. I finally reached the conning tower ladder, but didn't see Hunter. I held on as the cannons two decks below roared. Knowing the captain said to use the top deck gun, I decided to get it ready. Behind the ladder the long-barreled deck gun sat within the airship. I pulled the lever down opening the hatch in the ceiling. Next to the lever was the crank to winch the deck gun into place. I turned the handle and the platform with the gun mounted on it, started to lift up the tracks.

"Good work, Mr. Knight," Hunter said as he came up the stairs from the deck below. He cradled his three long rifles, Hansel and Gretel, the two Kentucky long rifles, and his elephant gun. "Get that deck gun in place and then load the hopper with shells. Once I'm on top I'll pass down the rifles to be reloaded."

I saluted but kept cranking the handle. Once the deck gun locked in place, I grabbed shells from a box and loaded them into a hopper on the wall. The shells fed into a conveyer that lifted them to the top deck. I then ran to the ladder to take his rifles if he handed them down.

My nerves rippled and my foot began tapping the last rung of the ladder. I couldn't see the battle, but knew that cannon balls could rip through the hull at any moment. The deck gun fired, sending thick black smoke into the compartment where I stood. The wind whisked away through the open hatches, and the empty casing fell to the deck in front of me.

I didn't hear Hunter celebrate, not that I ever did. He was more the quiet, subdued type. The cannons two decks below continued to fire, shaking the *Sparrowhawk's* metal framing. I looked up as the barrel of Hunter's rifle passed over the hatch. A puff of smoke shot out the end, and Hunter passed the rifle to me. One of the long rifles. I grabbed it by the stock and pulled down. I sat beside Hunter's bag, which he'd left inside the *Sparrowhawk*. An old muzzle loader, I had to pour the powder, fit the cloth wadding, and then ram the miniball down the barrel.

Hunter yelled, "Alexander get up here!"

I slung his Kentucky long rifle across my back and scurried up the ladder. As I reached the top, I paused and pulled my goggles over my eyes. I climbed onto the roof, stepping out of the conning tower. Hunter rotated the two wheels on the deck gun to elevate and turn the gun.

He saw me and pointed at the deck gun, "Take over

the deck gun! Either hit those Hornets or force them to turn."

"Will do!" I ran to the platform and saw the Hornet almost in the large ring sight.

Hunter grabbed his elephant gun and turned the other direction. I glanced over my shoulder and saw the other Hornet. The cannons below fired and shook the *Sparrowhawk*. They threw off my aim and Hunter waited to fire.

Hunter's gun spit fire and smoke, but I couldn't check his shot. I kept turning the wheels until the crosshairs lined up on the Hornet.

"Permission to fire?" I asked. I wasn't certain if I supposed to or not, but Mr. Singh would make me swab the deck if I fired a cannon without an order.

"You don't need me. Just get that buzzard out of the sky!"

"Will do!" I stepped on the pedal to fire the gun. Smoke and fire shot out the barrel, as it slid back and expelled the shell. The round passed only a foot from the wingsails. "I missed." However, the only reason I missed was because the Hornet turned away.

"Don't give up, keep the pressure on."

The Hornet came around for another attack run. Hunter ran up beside me and and pulled the long rifle from my back. The other aircraft appeared from under the *Sparrowhawk*. I quickly loaded another shell into the deck gun. The one Hunter had been chasing drifted into my sights as I closed the breach. I hit the pedal and fired. The shell tore through the balloon and ignited the hydrogen within. The Hornet exploded in a fireball that plunged out of the sky.

Hunter turned his attention to the other hornet

and fired. He punctured a hole in the wingsail and the craft veered off once again. The Gatling gun below rained shells up at the aircraft and the pilot turned back toward the *Queen Z's Revenge*. Hunter raised his rifles and I pumped my fist.

Hunter quickly pointed at the deck gun, "Get this stowed below. This isn't over yet."

34
The Chase

I cranked the deck gun down into place and pulled the lever to seal the hatch above. Hunter and I went to the bridge to see what was happening. As we stepped through the hatch, the captain barked at Heinz and Ignatius. "Get us moving. Zerelda got behind us while we were fighting those little Hornets."

"Which way?" Heinz asked.

"Keep running southwest. If we turn those guns of hers will shred us to pieces." The captain stepped back to the map table with Genevieve. "We have to find a place to fight her." Baldarich pulled a scroll from the cubby holes beside the table and unrolled a map of southern India. I helped him secure the corners with brass talons. He leaned over the table and began running his finger over the parchment.

"What are you looking for?" Genevieve asked.

"We need favorable winds." Baldarich kept checking the terrain. "Darkness or a storm would help."

Ignatius said from the wall of dials, "I can't push anymore speed out of the engines, and Mr. Singh says they're still gaining."

"We need to lighten the load. Have Mr. Singh bring me a list of heavy cargo to dump."

"Aye, aye, Captain." Ignatius tipped his Stetson and ran off the bridge.

"And tell Gears, no, we cannot dump Gustav!"

"Why don't we turn and fight?" I asked.

"I'd love nothing else, but they have at least twice the cannon power we do, and she's still lobbing lead further than I can. She'd shred us before we were in range."

"I'm ready to fight whenever we can," I said patting my Thumper.

"Me too, Alexander."

Genevieve pointed at the map. "We will be passing over southern India. The winds will pick up the closer we get to the coast."

"I'm counting on it."

I watched as they followed the markings over the Bay of Bengal. The Indian Ocean wasn't too much further away. I understood he was trying to outrun them until dark.

Ignatius came back and handed the captain a list. "I'd suggest the crates, and Mr. Singh thinks, and I agree, we can put parachutes on them and maybe hit the *Queen Z's Revenge.*"

"An excellent idea," the captain nodded with a devious smile. "Get them ready. Alexander, go with him." He turned to Genevieve, "You might want to get below. In case Zerelda takes aim on the bridge."

"Yes, sir," we said in unison.

Ignatius and I ran down to the gun deck. There were several crates secured with ropes in the center of the room. I cut the lines as Mr. Singh and Ignatius pulled them over by a large hatch in the floor. Mr. Singh tied silken sheets from fabric bolts in the cargo to each of the crates. Within a few minutes we were ready.

Mr. Singh stood under the copper tube here on the gun deck and yelled, "Captain. We are ready."

A voice echoed back through the tube. "On my order, Mr. Singh."

Mr. Singh turned to me and said, "Open one of the aft hatches and tell me if these crates get close to the *Queen Z's Revenge*."

I ran to the back of the gun deck and flipped open a hatch. The large black airship lay behind us, and a chill ran up my spine as I stared at the wisps trailing off its edges. The *Sparrowhawk* pitched upward and I had to hold on to keep from slipping. We rose above the *Queen Z's Revenge* and then I heard the captain's voice echo through the tube. "Release the crates!"

Ignatius and Mr. Singh shoved the crates out the hatch. The wooden boxes fell until the chutes billowed above them. Then they drifted toward the War Zeppelin.

"On target," I yelled.

Mr. Singh held up his thumb and they pushed two more crates into the sky.

The demon-headed cannon of the *Queen Z's Revenge* belched smoke and fire, they hit the first create which exploded in a torrent of grain. The second crate exploded and a cloud of spices sprayed the front of the large war zeppelin. They pushed two more crates.

The *Queen Z's Revenge* smashed through the last of the crates as spices exploded across its hull. I hoped I'd see a tear or any damage but it looked like a bug being smashed upon a carriage window. I closed the hatch, and turned to Mr. Singh, "No damage."

He nodded. "Worth a try, but we are much lighter, sadly poorer." He looked at Ignatius. "Those spices would have fetched a good price."

"We'll just have to take something of Zerelda's." Ignatius tipped his hat and walked up the steps, his spurs clinking as he walked.

I walked into my room, the front storage room, and found Genevieve and Lianhua sitting in hammocks on her side of the curtain. Genevieve came up and hugged me, and I wrapped my arms around her. The smell of exotic spices in her hair made me take a deep breath, and I clutched her a little tighter.

"What is going on up there?" I could hear the concern in her voice.

"We're trying to find the right spot to turn and fight Zerelda."

"We." She smiled. "Being a crewmember of the *Sparrowhawk* suits you."

I smiled. "Joining the crew was the only way anyone was going to let me track you down." I loosened my stance trying to be manly. "When Sinclair and my father returned to England with the Duke, I refused to go. And here I am. With you."

"Wait," She cocked her head. "The Duke and Richard returned to England?"

I nodded. "They wanted to get back, but your father, the crew, and I we chased the Milli-train all the way up to Acre. We just missed you, though."

"No, you did not, we knew where you were the whole time." Pain entered her eyes. "Hendrix was tipped off every time."

"Lord Marbury!" we said in unison.

"I'm sorry. I should not have gone off with my

mother."

I touched her cheek. "You needed to give your mother a chance to explain, a chance to change." I pushed her hair out of her face. "You had to get to know her."

"In the end she still chose the Golden Circle over me."

"It's not the end yet."

"Your optimism is appreciated. My world's been shattered, and you're the only thing, along with Rodin that still makes sense."

I smiled, but shook my head. "I'm so unsure of everything. For some reason the only Templar Knight who trusts me is your father. And … I'm running out of arguments against Hendrix. He's right I am connected to the Hearts. My family—"

She squeezed me tight and pulled me against her. "You are the most honorable man I have ever known."

"You're too kind." I pulled back and seeing Lianhua watching us with a large smile, I suddenly felt out of place, and stepped back. "We're gaining ground on Zerelda's airship, but we'll probably fight them this evening."

Genevieve motioned toward Lianhua, "We have been getting to know each other."

Lianhua nodded. "We seem to have much in common."

I sat down with the two of them. Lianhua and I told Genevieve about our trip through the mountains, and Genevieve told us about life in the Hidden Palace and traveling on the Milli-train. Her tale sounded like a lonely one. She might have lived in lavish splendor, but she did not have the freedom she'd known with her father.

Mr. Singh came by with food awhile later. "Here, eat

this. I doubt we'll be having dinner tonight."

"So, the captain is going on the offensive at night fall?" I asked taking a piece of bread and some sliced sausage.

Mr. Singh nodded. "I fear it will not be easy."

"Maybe we can help," Genevieve said.

"We'll all be on the guns later."

"I have been thinking . . . what if we board them?" Genevieve said. "Take the fight to them. Do we still have the Kite Sailer we used over France?"

Mr. Singh shook his head. "Yes, but it's in no shape to fly."

"Wait!" I said, "Genevieve's a genius. I just watched the crates drift over to the airship. If we used the kitesail or something similar, we could drift over to the *Queen Z's Revenge*. Just like the cargo, only we'll use the cover of night."

She nodded. "I was hoping for an airskiff of some kind, but that would work. I need to settle this duel with Zerelda once and for all, and we need to take her out of the fight."

Mr. Singh stroked his beard as we all waited for him to respond. He finally tapped his finger on his chin, and wound it though his beard. "It could work. But we'd be on their airship while the *Sparrowhawk* is blasting it with cannon. And how do we get off the *Queen Z's Revenge?*"

Genevieve smiled. "We steal one of the aircraft that attacked us earlier."

"See? She is a genius." I raised a finger for each point. "We get over there. We delay their guns from firing. We sabotage their engines. And we get out."

"It's a solid plan," Genevieve said. "We will sell it to the captain. Mr. Singh, see if we have more cloth for the

kites."
    Lianhua said, "I'll help Indihar."

BOOK III: IRON LOTUS

35
Boarding Party

"You *both* are crazy!" Captain Baldarich said with a shake of his head. "It's good to have you back on board."

Genevieve smiled. "Then you will let us go?"

"Absolutely not." The captain looked over at Ignatius who simply shrugged. "I am not sending you over to that demon ship."

"But they outgun us," I said. "What if the *Sparrowhawk* gets damaged trying to close the distance?"

"You need to have faith . . . " the captain said, but his words trailed off as the *Queen Z's Revenge* fired. "And a lot of luck."

I crossed my arms. "Captain, no one is better at causing chaos than we are, and we need to get back to find the baron and those infernal machines."

"You're right about that," the captain said with a chuckle. He looked at me and then to Genevieve. "If we're going to do this, then we'd better get ready."

"Wait, you're coming with us?"

"Do you think

I'm going to let you face those sky pirates without me?" Baldarich threw back his coat and put his hands on his hips. "I can't let you have all the fun!"

"Let's do it!" I pumped my fist.

"Hunter!" Captain Baldarich spun on his heel as Hunter stepped on the bridge. "You have one job— keep the *Sparrowhawk* out of range of their guns. Then when you see chaos break out over there, turn and fire." Baldarich grabbed him by the shoulder. "Give them everything, that's an order."

"I will, Captain."

"Good; now you two come with me." The captain pointed at Genevieve and me. "Ignatius you too." We stepped off the bridge and the captain stopped at the cargo doors. "You two get anything you'll need, wear several layers, and tell Mr. Singh to bring everything up here."

"Aye, aye," Genevieve and I said in unison. We rushed down to the gun deck and as she entered our room, I said, "Mr. Singh, we're a go. Get ready, and I'll help you take anything you need to the cargo doors."

He nodded and I entered the front storage room. Genevieve and Lianhua were layering on clothes. I grabbed my coat and put it on, slung my leather bag over my shoulder, and checked my Thumpers and my knife. Genevieve secured her sheath on her side and Lianhua checked on all her knives. We joined Mr. Singh on the gun deck, where he was outfitted for war with his Katar, sword, and chakrams. We helped him take the silk cloths and canvas tarps up to the cargo door where the captain and Ignatius waited.

We crafted something between a kitesail and a parachute. Four ropes tied to the corners of the cloth.

The four ends were connected, forming a harness.

Mr. Singh grabbed the ropes. "Fit this around you, and hold right here, just below where they're connected. You want to go right, pull on the right rope. Left, pull on the left rope. But do it subtly or you'll turn too far."

We all nodded. The captain pointed to Genevieve and me. "Since she's going after Zerelda whether I tell her to or not, you and I will go with her spreading chaos. Mr. Singh and Ignatius will seek out the engine room."

"What about me?" Lianhua asked.

"You're not going."

"Yes, I am."

Baldarich drew in a breath and eyed Mr. Singh and me. Then he exhaled and said, "Then go with Mr. Singh and Ignatius."

"We will not fail." Lianhua held out her arm, resting it on the new walker Mr. Singh had fixed with a brass strut and some dark hardwoods, old parts of the *Sparrowhawk*. Kō'ilā landed and her mechanical and feather wings folded against her sides.

"Get onto the airship, mess up what you can, and then get out." He looked each one of us in the eye. "We'll go out the conning tower, then run to the back and let the wind carry you off. Got it?"

We all nodded.

"I can't believe I let you talk me into this." The captain shook his head. "Be safe everybody."

Captain Baldarich went first. He secured the harness around his waist, and carried the canvas tarp up the ladder. Genevieve went next, followed by Mr. Singh and Lianhua. Then it was my turn. I wrapped the harness around my waist and between my legs. I carried the folded-up silk sail and ropes up the ladder. I climbed onto the top and found myself surrounded by white clouds. The sky burned with an orange glow as the sun set. The moisture whipped across my face and I wiped the droplets off my goggles.

Lianhua's mechanical legs tapped quickly as she rushed along the top of the *Sparrowhawk* until the wind lifted her off and she disappeared into the clouds. I knew it was my turn. I took one more deep breath and let the silk fall from my hands. The wind whipped it up and the silk square billowed out before me. Pulled along, I struggled to keep up until the wind finally whisked me off the *Sparrowhawk* and I soared into the clouds. I could barely make out the shapes of the others, but tried to stay near them.

I drifted along using the ropes to adjust my course, but relying on a sense that the *Queen Z's Revenge* was behind us to make my mark. I would have waited for total darkness, but the captain made the call to go at dusk. I heard the cannon roar. They sounded close and there were too many shots to be the *Sparrowhawk*. It had to be Zerelda. I was close. The sound came from below, and I worried I would pass right over. A large dark black shape lay below me. I broke free of the clouds, and saw I was on an arcing path down to the airship.

Below me, the captain landed on top of the airship and cut his kitesail free. He helped catch the others, but strong wind whipped me past them and carried me further down the airship. If I didn't act soon, I fly past the *Queen Z's Revenge*, I reached down and pulled my dagger from its sheath.

In one wide arching swing, I sliced through the ropes. I dropped like a stone and tumbled across the top of the black canvas. I grabbed hold of a guide cable, one of many holding the huge beast together, and laid there for a moment to catch my breath. The captain came over, bent down beside me, and thumped my chest. "Nice landing; let's go."

I sprang up, and we ran to one of the hatches. Baldarich pointed to Mr. Singh, Lianhua, and Ignatius. "You three head aft. You should find the engine room that way, just head for the sound." He turned to Genevieve and me. "Ready to face the Sky Pirate Queen?"

I nodded and Genevieve drew her saber. "Let's finish this!"

Captain Baldarich chuckled, and we rushed through the hatch. If we'd been spotted, I was expecting to find the entire crew here, and I even grabbed my Thumper from its holster, but the corridor was empty. We'd made it onboard without being seen.

Lianhua launched Kō'ilā and she, Mr. Singh, and Ignatius followed. The captain, Genevieve, Rodin, and I made our way down the stairs. We had to cross the entire height of this airship to get to the gondola underneath, where the bridge would be.

After descending two flights of the metal stairs, we enter a giant chasm filled with hydrogen cells. The huge gas bags sat one after the other and ran the entire length of this airship.

"That mad woman is using hydrogen. Watch your aim, if we ignite one of those, this whole War Zeppelin is going to erupt in a fireball." The captain motioned and we kept moving, especially now that we were in the open. "That's why I use helium. She's probably cutting corners, hydrogen is cheaper."

I kept looking for anyone, and pointed at two crewmen walking far below us. They inspected the hydrogen cells. The captain held up his hand and we paused. Once they'd moved out of sight behind some gas bags, we continued.

Running down the metal stairs, I thought we sounded like a herd of elephants and would be caught quickly, but the churning of the engines, the continuous whine of the wind beyond the hull, and a mix of noises I couldn't identify, meant it was hard to hear each other. I could barely hear my own thoughts.

Halfway through the hydrogen cells, we encountered another catwalk. It ran the length of the airship right down the center. We had arrived at a junction because two more catwalks ran perpendicular to the main corridor and stretched to the hull on either side. I was starting to get an idea of how this ship was structured with long walkways running both the length and breadth of this airship.

I saw two crewmen coming this way, but they were talking and not looking ahead. I tapped the captain and gestured toward them. They weren't the uniformed soldiers of the Knights of the Golden Circle, but swarthy sky pirates, with cutlasses on their hips and pistols stuffed into their belts.

Baldarich pulled us off the stairs and onto one of the side catwalks. He drew his lightning cannon, and I raised my Thumper. Genevieve patted her shoulder and Rodin landed, but she kept her saber at the ready.

The sky pirates passed and headed up the stairs. I took my knife and stabbed the hydrogen cell beside the catwalk. I dragged the knife forward making a long cut. The captain turned and stared at me. I shrugged. From the expression on his face, I wasn't certain if I should have cut that, but we were here to cause a little chaos.

"Did you not hear what I said about the hydrogen?"

"I did, but . . . chaos?"

He shrugged. "Just don't cause any sparks."

Genevieve stabbed the cell on the other side. Captain Baldarich threw up his arms. "I just said to him—" He pointed to me.

"He does not get to have all the fun. I have always wanted to cut these things open." She looked at Rodin. "No fire in here." Rodin nodded and closed his mouth.

We rushed off as the smell of rotten eggs started to overpower me. At the bottom of the stairs, we found two decks with hallways full of doors. We didn't stop to search them, as we wanted to get to the gondola before word arrived of trouble in the engine room. The gondola was down the next set of stairs. I took a deep breath, knowing the bridge was filled with sky pirates and Queen Zerelda.

We rushed down the last few steps and charged onto the bridge. We were toward the front of the airship, so we ran right in front of the pirate, Queen Zerelda. She sat on a large high-backed, black leather-clad throne with elaborately decorated wrought-iron armrests. The twisted metal shaped like a scorpion was the most terrifying captain's chair I'd ever seen. A spiked stinger hung over her head, and looked like the chair could come to life at any moment and attack us.

"Well, look who was foolish enough to come into my den." Zerelda laughed, but her crew jumped up and drew their swords and pistols. "Captain Baldarich, so good to see you, and Genevieve, come to taste my steel again?"

"I am here to finish what you keep running away from." Genevieve stood stoic with Rodin perched on her shoulder.

"Daddy isn't here to stop us. Neither is mommy. Are you sure you're ready for me?"

"They were absent from our other duels as well. Quit gabbing and raise your sword."

"Why are you talking so much?" Baldarich asked. "I assumed we'd be fighting already, but you're stalling. Why?"

Zerelda smiled, a wicked little grin that made my skin crawl. She was up to something. I looked around, at the bridge. An easy thing to do when no one was paying attention to me. Then my eyes passed over the pilot's station. Unlike everyone else in the gondola, he was not focused on us, but on the *Sparrowhawk*. The four throttle levers were pushed all the way forward and beside them sat a dial. The *Queen Z's Revenge* was marked in the center with a red line arcing around it, and an 'X' marked in grease pen just ahead of the line. The distance was closing between the line and the mark. Then it hit me like a cannon blast that mark was the *Sparrowhawk*. The line probably represented the range of the guns. The Pirate Queen was stalling, waiting to blow my home out of the sky.

"Captain she's about to fire on the *Sparrowhawk*!"

Zerelda threw her head back and cackled. "Kill them!" She jumped up and grabbed the cutlass leaning against her throne. "Ready, little princess? It's time to die."

36
The Duel

The Pirate Queen Zerelda stood with her hip cocked and her leg jutting out of the slit of her skirt. Her long dark curly hair fell about her face, covering her eyes which locked on Genevieve. With a snarl crossing her lips and tension hardening her jaw, her expression remained evil with a hint of the demonic wisps that infected this airship.

Genevieve looked like a stoic knight, her stance that of a warrior about to strike. She had a bounce to her step so she remained light on her feet. She turned so her sword arm aimed at Zerelda's heart, and kept her other arm behind her on her hip, for balance. Her eyes were focused and intense.

The captain raised his lightning cannon and fired as the crew raised their pistols and swords. I lifted my Thumper and fired as well. Several fell to the deck, but I heard more storming down the stairs.

Zerelda spun her wicked-curved cutlass as she took a step toward Genevieve who stepped forward and thrust her saber. Rodin lifted off her shoulder and blasted some of the crew with fireballs.

The two blades clashed and their duel began. They moved back and forth, their blades slicing past each other as the captain and I kept the rest of the pirates away.

Captain Baldarich fired his lightning cannon hitting the metal stairs at the back of the gondola, arching the bolt from one crewman to the next. I fired my second Thumper and knocked several crewmen to the deck. Genevieve pushed Zerelda back with a flurry of strikes. Zerelda spun and almost sliced through Genevieve's jacket. Zerelda slipped behind her throne as Genevieve thrust her saber. She spun the chair, knocking Genevieve's saber to the side. Zerelda kicked her back, but Genevieve quickly recovered and thrust forward to force the pirate queen away.

The gondola shook, as the guns fired. I spun on my heel and looked at the dial. The 'X' marking the *Sparrowhawk* had crossed the red line. I looked up and saw the aero-dirigible turning as Captain Baldarich had ordered. The guns of the *Queen Z's Revenge* fired repeatedly. I didn't know what to do, but I had to act. I reloaded my Thumper, aimed it at the pilot's station, and fired. The concussive blast smashed the controls, and the pirate at the wheel was knocked out of his chair, slammed against the controls he fell to the deck. Smoke rose from the controls and Zerelda turned to me.

"What the hell have you done, boy?" She drew a pistol from her waistband with her left hand, "That's twice you've ruined my airship." I dove as she fired, and as I hit the deck and rolled, I heard one window shatter. The wind rushed in, howling so loudly, Zerelda's screams were carried away.

Genevieve knocked Zerelda's blade aside and brought hers down on the pistol, smacking it from the pirate queen's hand. The gun slid across the deck as Zerelda swung her cutlass trying to slice Genevieve who dodged and blocked with her saber.

Zerelda locked swords with Genevieve and pulled her closer. She leaned up to the blades and nearly spat in Genevieve's face. "I'm going to gut you and then your boyfriend, princess." Then she grabbed Genevieve's corset, yanked her closer, and head-butted her.

Genevieve fell back with a thud and Zerelda pressed forward; her cutlass pointed straight at Genevieve's heart. I fired my Thumper, but Zerelda twisted out of the way and my concussive blast ripped off her throne's scorpion's tail. Genevieve jumped up and swung her sword in large arcs to push Zerelda back. She pressed her attack with a series of thrusts, but Zerelda danced out of her way and then lunged again. Genevieve parried the blade, and drove the point of her saber through Zerelda's black corset.

"First blood is mine!" Genevieve said, as she pulled her blade free and stepped back to regain her warrior's stance.

Zerelda stood up, and I noticed a black wisp, just as I'd seen on the ship coming from her wound. She ignored the pain, reaffirmed her grip on her cutlass and smiled wickedly. She stared at Genevieve, who held her ground. Zerelda screeched an ear-splitting demonic scream and rushed forward, thrusting her sword through Genevieve's coat. "No!" I gasped, thinking she'd been stabbed, but Genevieve pulled away, slicing open her coat. The blade had run along her corset. Then Genevieve spun her blade tightly around Zerelda's sword, and with a flick of her wrist, Genevieve pushed Zerelda's blade away almost sending it from her hand. As Zerelda was trying to regain control, Genevieve punched the pirate queen with her left hand, and knocked her back with a kick to her midsection.

Boots on the stairs behind me made me spin around. Reinforcements. I unleashed both my Thumpers in their direction and the concussive blast mangled the stairs sending the first few men crashing to the deck.

Flashing lights on the control panels caught my attention. I quickly looked over them and saw that pressure was building in one of the engines and had fallen in another. Mr. Singh, Ignatius, and Lianhua must have reached the engine room. I turned and saw the captain fighting pirates at the back of the gondola. I searched for the *Sparrowhawk* through the windows and found it dodging cannon fire as it drew closer. A cannon ball ripped into the bridge of the *Sparrowhawk* and I saw smoke. My heart dropped. I hoped everyone was okay, but how could they be? If the shell was an explosive one, then everyone standing there would be obliterated.

"Captain!" I pointed out the window. "The *Sparrowhawk* took direct hit."

Zerelda cackled.

Captain Baldarich yelled, "Clear the deck! Let's get out of here!"

I nodded. "Aye, aye captain, but we'll have to use the back stairs."

"I'm not leaving until she's dead." Genevieve said.

"You can't kill me. I am a Horseman!" Zerelda smacked Genevieve away and tried to slice me as I passed. "I'll kill you for what you've done to my ship, boy!"

Genevieve screamed, "No!" and blocked her blade. Rodin landed on her shoulder and blasted the pirate queen with fire. Genevieve beat the blade back and thrust her saber into Zerelda. She pulled her sword from the wound, and Zerelda stepped back, but didn't fall over.

"You can't kill me! I'm the Horseman of Plagues!" Zerelda stood up, black wisps seeped from both wounds. Her pupils grew larger until all I saw was black.

I loaded a percussion cap into my Thumper and aimed it at Zerelda. I pushed the button, and the blast sent her tumbling to the front of the gondola. "And I'm the Black Knight!" I grabbed Genevieve's arm, "We have to get out of here."

"I can defeat her." Genevieve said.

"But at what cost?" I locked eyes with her. "Genevieve, please, we have to get out of here."

She stared at me with pain blazing in her eyes. She looked at Zerelda, and then me. She nodded, and we ran toward Captain Baldarich. He cleared the stairs with his lightning cannon and we rushed up to the deck above. Gun decks lay on either side. They continued to spit lead at the *Sparrowhawk*. I reached into my leather bag and pulled out the powder charge I'd been carrying through the mountains. I shoved a wick inside and called for Rodin. "I need fire!"

The little dragon flew over and landed on my shoulder. Without another word, he blew a flame onto the wick. I tossed the powder bag toward the cannons that were firing and ran after Genevieve and the captain. A moment later, I heard a small boom, followed by a bigger explosion. The whole airship shook and we were tossed against the wall.

The captain led us back toward the aft section of the *Queen Z's Revenge*. We passed a door marked Engine Room and Mr. Singh burst through. He raised his Katar dagger, until he recognized the captain. Then a large smile crossed his face. Lianhua rushed out with the owl right behind her. I heard Ignatius' revolvers firing inside the engine room.

"We have to get out of here, captain," Mr. Singh said lowering his Katar. "They flanked us on the port side."

"Keep moving aft, Mr. Singh. That's where the hanger bay has to be," the captain pointed with his lightning pistol. "And take these three with you." The captain stepped up to the door as Ignatius ran through and he fired his lightning cannon into the engine room.

Mr. Singh led the way and we all followed until we climbed through a hatch and entered into a large open area.

"Look at this!" I couldn't believe it. Hornets, like the ones that attacked the Sparrowhawk hung by hooks on a cable system.

"Get in," Mr. Singh ordered. "Two to a ship."

Genevieve and I jumped in one. She settled into the pilot's seat and I aimed my Thumpers at the hatch. Rodin curled up in my lap. Mr. Singh pulled a lever which opened the hanger door on the underside of the airship and spun the wheel to move us into position. A hook lowered and snagged our craft. It dropped us out the ship, Genevieve started the propeller and the hook released. We dropped but the wingsails billowed, and we started moving forward.

Genevieve flew us along the side of the *Queen Z's Revenge* and I saw a large hole on the gun deck.

I kept an eye on the underside, a moment later Mr. Singh and Lianhua dropped out of the hanger with the owl following behind them. I leaned closer to Genevieve, "We need to go back to make sure the captain and

Ignatius make it out." She nodded and banked us back toward aft section.

I saw the captain and Ignatius being lowered out on the hook, but Ignatius was still firing into the hanger bay. I leaned in and said, "Get us closer."

She flew up underneath the *Queen Z's Revenge* and I noticed the hook holding their craft was being retracted into the War Zeppelin. As we passed them, I raised my thumpers and fired. The blasts hit the hook, and obliterated it. The captain and Ignatius dropped and as the propeller spun to life, we both flew off toward the *Sparrowhawk*.

37
Krakatoa

Mr. Singh and Lianhua demonstrated how to get back on the *Sparrowhawk*. He flew over the top of the aero-dirigible and they jumped off. The Hornet continued on and arced toward the ground.

I turned around expecting to tell Genevieve which direction to dodge the incoming cannon fire. Instead, I found the *Queen Z's Revenge* turning south. Zerelda was running. I wondered why, but had to assume we'd damaged the war zeppelin more than I thought.

The captain and Ignatius jumped onto the top of the Sparrowhawk. Their Hornet sailed off and Ignatius shot it full of holes. Genevieve angled us toward the Sparrowhawk. We lined up behind the airship and she pushed the propeller to full speed. As we neared the conning tower in the center of the aero-dirigible, I untied myself and Genevieve did the same. Rodin flew off. I tapped Genevieve on the shoulder. "Ready?"

She put her thumb up and we leapt off. We dropped onto the *Sparrowhawk* and ran for the conning tower. The captain slapped each of us on the back, and then we all climbed down the ladder into airship.

We rushed to the

bridge to see what damage the shell had done. Bent metal and shredded canvas on each side of the nose brought the wind whipping in. Shattered glass and splinters of wood stuck in every surface. Including Heinz. He sat at the controls with bandages wrapped around his arms, and side. He looked pale but remained at his station.

Hunter stood in front of the captain's chair. He had cuts and scrapes, but nothing as bad as Heinz. Hunter turned and nodded. "Glad you're back captain. Apologies for not returning her in the best of shape."

"I'm just glad you both are okay." He turned to me and Genevieve. "Alexander, help Heinz down to his bunk and tend to his wounds. Get Gustav to help you. Milady, I wonder if you'd do me the honor of piloting this wounded bird."

I nodded and walked over to Heinz. Genevieve sat down as I helped him up. He was weak and leaned on me.

"Hunter, go with them and get yourself checked out," the captain said as he brushed off his chair.

Hunter helped me with Heinz and as we passed the captain, he stopped us. "You did well, nephew."

Heinz smiled, and Baldarich sat down. We limped off the bridge. Hunter and I helped Heinz to his bunk and I ran to get Gustav.

I saw Lianhua in the corridor and she turned to me. "Is everyone okay? Mr. Singh was worried about the men."

"Heinz, the pilot, is injured. I'm looking for Gustav to help heal him."

"I can help," she said.

"Thanks, we'll take whatever we can get." I pointed down the corridor toward the crew quarters. Then I ran into the galley. "Gustav. Heinz needs you."

The cook emerged from the kitchen, "I was boiling up something to help and getting some new bandages."

"He's in his bunk." I pointed over my shoulder. "I'm going to get Mr. Singh and see about patching up the nose of the bridge." I ran off to find Mr. Singh.

Soon, he and I were back on the bridge with canvas and wood to make some quick repairs. The captain looked surprised to see us, but he smiled and we got to work. We cut away some of the twisted metal and braced it with wood.

I looked out and saw we were chasing the *Queen Z's Revenge*. I turned to Genevieve, "She's running away?"

"More like limping, but they're still dangerous."

Baldarich leaned on his elbow. "Looks like we took out one of her engines, and damaged another, but she's still roaring over the ocean. However, I think her steering is messed up because she's flying in a curved line."

"I did smash the pilot's station with my Thumper."

Baldarich chuckled. "We can't get too close or she fires on us, but I'll not let her go. Like a hunter with a wounded animal. I will follow until we can knock her out of the sky."

"Shouldn't we be heading back into the mountains?" I asked. "The baron— " I stopped speaking as I looked at Genevieve. "I think General Hendrix is on his way to America. He wants to resurrect Emperor Burr's vision of my country. I think he means Aaron Burr, and it's not a pretty vision."

Baldarich shook his head. "If we let her go, she'll come back with all the power of the Horsemen. She's already corrupted to the core. I worry what she'll be like if we let that kind of power fester."

I couldn't argue with him. She'd taken two stab

wounds and it barely affected her. I knew about the effects of the Hearts, and she was one of the original bearers. *What did that mean for Hendrix?*

I turned back and began helping Mr. Singh fix the hull. Once we had a structure that would hold, we wrapped the outside in canvas. I nailed the treated material to the structure we'd created. Then we did the same thing to the other side.

I turned to Genevieve. Opening her eyes fully after squinting for so long into the open air, she rubbed tears away with her sleeve. Several of the windows were gone, but with the nose made up of many smaller panes, her vision wasn't too hindered.

We followed the *Queen Z's Revenge* for hours. Nothing but the dark ocean shimmering in the moonlight lay below us. As the sun rose, Captain Baldarich called me to the bridge. "Alexander, take over for Genevieve so she can get some rest."

"Captain, I'm fine. I can keep going." Genevieve said, even as she stretched her neck to relieve the tension.

"Rest. That's a request." He smiled. "I'd never presume to order you, milady. I don't need that sword fight."

She laughed and nodded. "I will but just for a short time."

I walked over and slipped into the pilot's chair. I was finally going to get to fly the *Sparrowhawk*. I'd dreamed of this day, and as I gripped the wheel my heart soared. As if nothing stood between me and the clouds.

Genevieve leaned in, "She's favoring to port. Not sure why, and don't force her past three quarter speed, the engines are running hot."

I looked up and said, "Thanks, I'll remember that."

For hours, I stayed on the tail of the *Queen Z's Revenge*, but out of the reach of her guns. The ideas I had about flying, dashing maneuvers needing quick second reflects, were the dreams of someone who'd never flown. All I did was make course corrections as Zerelda drifted offline and adjusted the throttle whenever Ignatius told me the engines were acting up.

In the distance, I could make out an archipelago of islands. The captain stepped over to the map table. He drew a few lines, and made some calculations. "She's heading to southern Sumatra. I think her plan is to get lost in the pirate bays scattered amongst the islands." The captain came over and stood by me. "In order to lose us she'll have to attack. If I had to guess she's used this time to repair the guns."

"Agreed."

He looked down at me, and smiled. "Get ready to follow orders. Do everything I command."

"Of course, Captain."

Baldarich studied the *Queen Z's Revenge*. His fingers traced his beard, and he even leaned in as if those couple extra inches would make the scene clearer. I watched him in awe and looked at the airship, trying to see what he saw. Then I noticed the propellers slowing down, I could see the individual blades. Seeing the captain's expression change I knew he saw it, too.

He pointed. "This is it!" He stepped back to his chair and sat down. "Up angle three degrees. Speed to full. Yaw, three degrees starboard and rotate us twenty degrees."

"Aye, aye captain." I pulled back the wheel until the one dial matched, then rolled the airship on its side to aim the cannons down on the *Queen Z's Revenge*. As the captain predicted, Zerelda's war zeppelin had slowed to draw us in. Now we were climbing above her, and she was trying to turn. "Course corrections made, sir."

"Level out our assent but keep us rolled on our side." The captain hit his armrest. "I need those guns pointed down."

"Yes sir." We all had to hold on as the Sparrowhawk tilted so far to one side. With the port side angled down. We were slowly losing altitude.

The guns of the *Queen Z's Revenge* began to fire but couldn't tilt as far as we could and we remained above their guns. The captain waited. He flipped open the brass tubes and paused. We were still out of the range of our guns, and I thought he would wait longer, but he slammed his fist on the railing surrounding his chair and said, "Fire!"

All three guns and the Gatling gun erupted, raining lead down upon the *Queen Z's Revenge*. The cannon balls slammed into the roof of the War Zeppelin as the rounds from the Gatling gun shredded through the canvas. Being above the airship meant our cannon's range was extended. We couldn't miss.

"That's brilliant!" I smiled, but held the wheel tight so we wouldn't slip, and I had to maintain the tilt. "Captain, you're a genius."

"She might be a queen, but I am king of the skies," Baldarich leaned back to the copper tube. "Fire!"

A moment later, the second round of cannon fired roared. The lead ripped through the ship. As the center section deflated, I saw an orange glow within the war zeppelin. The Queen Z's Revenge burst into flames.

"Hard to port and level us out!" The captain shouted. "Get us away from her in case she explodes!"

I turned the wheel and hit the foot pedals to make the turn. The *Sparrowhawk* already wanted to go that way so it wasn't hard. Ignatius and the captain stood to get a good look. I peered out the window as well. The entire aft section was engulfed in bright orange flames. The *Queen Z's Revenge* drifted forward as she began to drop out of the sky.

The fiery wreck plummeted toward a mountainous island, but I could tell they still had some steering capability left. The fiery wreck veered into the volcano's smoldering crater. Suddenly, the captain yelled, "Get us out of here!"

"What's wrong?" I asked, but before anyone could answer, my stomach twisted in knots and I doubled over the wheel. I fought the pain to remain in control of the *Sparrowhawk*, but I knew I hadn't felt anything as severe since I'd first run into the Iron Horsemen.

BOOK III: IRON LOTUS

"What's happening?" I said, my hands gripping the wheel.

"Krakatoa is erupting."

"The volcano?" My heart lurched in my chest and I nosed the ship north and started to climb, but the captain said, "No take us down we'll need the speed." The earth rumbled and roared, making the most frightening sounds I'd ever heard. An explosion ripped through the sky and rattled the bones of the *Sparrowhawk*. A ringing filled my ears, and everything was muffled and distant. Chunks of the island, billowing ash, smoke, flaming magma, and heated gases blew thousands of feet into the sky. Far above the *Sparrowhawk*. A concussive blast, like a Thumper hooked up to a Heart of the Horsemen, smashed against the *Sparrowhawk*. The aero-dirigible bounced about in the sky. We tumbled and spun, losing over a hundred feet of altitude.

The wheel ripped free and whipped back and forth. I grabbed hold and forced it to center. I strained all my muscled to right the *Sparrowhawk* and stop the spinning. A flaming hunk of stone smashed into the hull

above us, burned through the canvas and slammed into the deck behind the captain. Baldarich and Ignatius smothered the flames. The eruption blocked out the sun, bringing darkness to the world around us. A bright orange glow forced me to look up and I saw a flaming boulder the size of a house coming our way. I spun wheel and pressed the pedal, turning and tilting the *Sparrowhawk* as the hunk of magma sailed by.

"What is going on?" I screamed. "We are miles from that island."

The captain grabbed hold of the railing. "The Heart must have amplified the eruption. This is bigger than anything I've ever seen or heard of."

Genevieve ran up onto the bridge. "Captain, we lost one of the cannons when the rope snapped and it crashed out of the gun deck."

"Is everyone all right?" Baldarich asked.

"Yes, so far. Everyone and everything is being tossed around. They tied Heinz to his hammock."

Hot ash and smoke engulfed the aero-dirigible. It poured in through the hole. We coughed and choked as it burned our lungs. I pulled my goggles over my eyes so I could still see, and we burst out from the billowing maelstrom. Ignatius brushed off the dials, and turned to the captain. "Sir, we're overheating, I have to shut down engine three or we'll lose her."

"We need it. Alexander throttle back engine three for now." Baldarich flipped open one of the copper tubes and said, "Gears, I need all my engines or we're not going to survive this."

I pulled the third lever back to one third. I turned the wheel to dodge the ash cloud and found a small pocket of mostly clear air. The airship was still losing altitude and the ocean was getting closer, but I was able to keep our speed up and out run the worst of the eruption. Small pebbles still pelted the hull, some even ripped through and rattled on the deck. Strong winds radiated out from the volcano, pushed us in every direction. I struggled to keep the Sparrowhawk under control, but I knew if I let the gusts dictate our course we'd be torn to pieces.

The aero-dirigible lurched and shook. Those of us on the bridge looked at each other and knew something had struck the Sparrowhawk. The captain flipped open all four tubes and yelled. "Report!"

Mr. Singh's voice echoed back. "We have a burning hunk of rock on the gun deck. We're trying to put it out before it hits the powder."

The captain didn't say anything, but tension built as thick as the ash cloud as we waited for the next minute for a second explosion. Then Mr. Singh's voice called out, "Rock removed. Flames extinguished."

I released a huge sigh of relief as the captain wiped his brow.

Gears voice carried through the copper tube and said, "I've cleaned the ash out of engine three, she's back in business."

"Excellent!" The captain pointed at me. "Full speed ahead, Alexander, get us out of here."

"Aye, aye, Captain." I pushed the lever for engine three back to full and I could feel the speed increasing before the dial in front of me moved.

For the next hour, I dodged hunks of rock hurled into the air, billowing clouds of ash, and winds stronger than I'd ever imagined. Too many times I thought the Sparrowhawk would be torn apart, but she held, and I finally had my chance to fly her. At the one time when it mattered most. I blew the tension through tight lips, sending a slight cloud of grey billowing up from my shirt.

The captain stepped up beside me and squeezed my shoulder. "Starboard turn."

"How far?" I asked.

"I just want to see it and we're far enough away now."

I turned the *Sparrowhawk* and we all stared at the volcano. I couldn't see the island anymore, only a towering maelstrom that reached thousands of feet in the sky, so high it touched the stars. It stretched to the horizon and still spewed chunks of flaming rocks. Lightning arced through the ash clouds. The seas churned, and the winds whipped in every direction.

"Fascinating!"

"Look at that power! Reminds me of something out of the Bible," Genevieve said.

I couldn't believe what I was looking at. I'd never seen anything so destructive.

"I've seen volcanoes before," the captain said turning to Ignatius. "Remember that volcano in Iceland? 1873, I think. We were crossing the Atlantic."

"But we were far to the south, and it was nothing like this," Ignatius said with a shake of his head.

"I don't think there's ever been anything like this," the captain said. "But it's fascinating watching from a safe distance." He turned to me and patted my back. A cloud of dust engulfed me. "You did an excellent job, Alexander. You can be my pilot anytime. You've become a true Sky Raider in these last few months, and I'm proud to call you a crewmember."

My smile grew as my heart soared along in the

clouds. "Thank you, sir. That means a great deal."

"You've been through a lot and it's time for you to take a break. Milady, would you mind replacing our pilot here?"

"My pleasure, Captain." She walked over and I smiled at her grey hair. Everything was covered in ash. I lifted my goggles and stretched, relieving muscles that had been tense for hours. Genevieve laughed. I looked at her and wondered why, but when I turned the captain and Ignatius joined her.

She pointed to my face. "Your face is clean around your eyes."

"You look like a raccoon," the captain said.

I walked over to a window, used my sleeve to wipe away the ash, and saw my reflection: bright skin surrounded by smudged grey. Relieved that we were all still alive, that I'd steered us through a hellish maelstrom, and that Genevieve was here with me, I threw my head back and laughed, too.

"Get the crew up here to start cleaning up this ash." Baldarich sat in his chair. "Take us north, milady."

"Aye, aye Captain," she said and as she took the wheel, she turned to me and winked.

I checked on Heinz who was sound asleep and then made my way down to the gun deck. A large hole lay on the starboard side where the third cannon had smashed through the wall. The rest of the gun deck was covered with ash, though, the wind whipped through the hole, and cleared the dust.

Mr. Singh called me over. "Impressive flying."

"Thanks."

He pointed out the hole. "Check out the wingsail."

I looked and the starboard wingsail had several holes in the fabric. Then he pointed to the winglet, a smaller wingsail toward the back, and I saw a huge chunk was missing. The charred tattered remains flapped in the wind. "Whoa, when did that happen?"

"A flaming hunk of rock slammed into it." Mr. Singh grabbed my shoulder. "You saved us all, my friend."

"It could have been Genevieve or Heinz, I just happened to be the guy in the chair at the time."

"Destiny." Mr. Singh shook his head, "I can't believe one of the Hearts had so much power."

"I can't either."
I sighed. "They have
so many now." I

leaned closer to him. "I'm nervous about what's coming."

"I am as well." Mr. Singh pointed to the hole. "Get some rest and then we'll start patching this bird up."

"Sounds like a plan." I waved and walked over to my room. I brushed the ash off my shirt and poured water into a bowl to wash my face.

Rodin sat in his bed. He watched me clean up, and when I jumped into my hammock he swooped down and settled on my stomach. I rubbed his little head and under his neck. "That was crazy, wasn't it? I wonder when it will stop erupting."

Rodin seemed to like the company, and he laid his head down and slept. I tried to do the same, but I was too wound up. My mind raced over everything I'd seen and done. Rocks as big as houses soared through the air. I'd taken the *Sparrowhawk* on maneuvers I'd never seen her do before. The constant fear that the next flaming rock would be the end. My heart still raced. I tried to breathe regularly to calm myself, but nothing worked. Finally, petting Rodin and having him close eased my pounding heart, and after a while my nerves settled.

I drifted off and woke when Genevieve touched my arm.

"You two look adorable," she said with a smile.

"Who's flying?"

"Hunter for now." She sat in her hammock and ran her fingers through her hair trying to brush out the ash. "You were exceptional today."

"You would have been great, too."

She smiled, but it faded. "Now we have to find my father. Kind of like old times."

"He probably stowed away on the Vimana with the Sikhs he was leading." I hoped it was true.

"On that incredible flying castle."

"Yeah. The Sikh's are tough fighters; I'm sure he's okay."

She nodded. "We will track them down and get him out of there—unless my mother has already captured him."

"Your life has gotten a lot more complicated than mine."

"I suppose it has, and to think I remember when my father brought you home because your father had been kidnapped." She stopped running her fingers through her hair and looked at me. "Now I am the one with the crazy family, and you are the warrior rushing to help me."

"We are different people." I put my hands behind my head. "I didn't have a chance to tell you, but the duel you fought with the pirate queen . . . you were so good. You've gotten better."

"I practiced a lot at the hidden palace." Genevieve stood and came over to my hammock. "There was not much else to do, and I was lonely." She picked up Rodin and climbed in with me. We barely fit, and as she nestled up against me, I wrapped my arm around her as if it was the most natural thing in the world. Rodin snuggled in between us and soon both Genevieve and her little dragon were asleep. I stared down at her. She looked so peaceful with her eyes closed, lashes resting against her cheeks. I pulled her closer and closed my own eyes, happier than I could ever remember being.

After getting a few hours of sleep, I slipped out of the hammock. Finding Mr. Singh, we got to work repairing the *Sparrowhawk*. We started with the hole on the gun deck and then attended to the wingsails. Everyone helped out, and by the time we crossed into China, most of the *Sparrowhawk* had been patched.

Later, after I checked on Genevieve and found her awake, she and I stepped onto the bridge and found the captain working at the map table. Heinz sat in the pilot seat, still bandaged, but the color had returned to his face.

Baldarich called us over. "Let's see what an Armitage and Kensington think." He pointed to the map where he'd drawn several lines from the location of the hidden valley, all of them stopping over the Pacific. "We haven't been gone long enough for them to have crossed the ocean. But would they go north over Mongolia, straight over China, or south along the coast?"

"The Vimana didn't have sails, so wind isn't a factor. I'm guessing they'd choose the shortest route." I pointed at the middle line. "This one, cutting across China."

Genevieve nodded and said, "They have a Chinese nobleman, Shengguan Bo on their side, he might be helping them get through the provinces."

"Smart money says the northern route," Baldarich said. "They'll run into the least number of people. But I'll trust you."

Genevieve pointed to the largest city in China. "Shengguan has contacts in the emperor's court. He might be headed to Peking. They have found three of the Hearts; now they are looking for the fourth," she said. "If we knew where the last Heart was, we would know exactly where they are going."

"I know," I whispered the words. "I know where all four of them are . . . or were."

They both looked at me. "How?" Genevieve asked.

"Since when?" the captain said, his brows furrowed.

"I wanted to tell you, but I knew we had a traitor in our midst, and I didn't know who he was. Besides—" I hesitated.

The captain laughed. "You didn't trust the baron, or Lord Marbury. I knew I liked you! But go on, how do you know where they are?"

"It sounds crazy, but I found a journal written by my ancestor, and when I read it, I had a vision. I saw where he hid the hearts."

Genevieve turned to me. "And? Where is the last Heart?"

"Beyond the American Rocky Mountains." I paused and looked around the room, as if I still had to worry about who was around. But everyone here was my friend. People I trusted with my life. "My ancestor traveled across the sea from China and then journeyed halfway across the continent. He buried it beyond the mountains. In what we now call The Dakotas. He believed it would never be found."

The captain looked at the two of us. "Does the Golden Circle know where the last Heart is located?"

Genevieve shook her head. "I do not think so. The first one they found was in Zululand. That heart, and the Malta hearts led them to the one near the pyramids."

"Wait." I placed my hands on the table, leaning forward. "The Hearts helped them to find each other?"

She nodded. "The two they have helped them find the third one, in an old temple in Tibet."

"Then the three will seek out the fourth." I pointed to South Dakota on the map. "This is where they're going. We need to stop them before they get there."

"That flying palace is too heavily defended. We'd never get close enough to do any real damage. Not without a fleet of airships. We're going to need help." The captain stroked his beard as he stared at the map.

"The baron would know how to contact the Templars. I can send word back to the British in India, but we need someone in front of them to slow them down."

I sighed. "So, what do we do?"

Genevieve shook her head. "We need a Templar or a government official." She gripped the edge of the map table. "We need my father."

Hunter stepped onto the bridge and walked over to check on Heinz. He pointed out toward the horizon. "Captain, I see that flying castle."

My hands went to my hips. "The Vimana?"

I looked, but couldn't see anything. Hunter pointed, and I finally saw a small dot reflecting sunlight.

Captain Baldarich said, "Heinz change our bearings to get behind it."

Heinz changed course, but it would take hours to catch up with them. My stomach twisted into knots and I dropped to the floor. Everyone turned as Genevieve ran to my side.

She locked eyes with me. "Trouble?"

I nodded.

Hunter, Captain Baldarich, and Heinz scanned the sky. Then Hunter said, "What is that?"

Genevieve and I stood up and surveyed the horizon. Finally, I saw the glint of shiny brass or copper breaking out of the trees off our port side. The long shape undulated through the air, like a serpent slithering after its prey. As it came toward us, I could make out four stubby feet with shiny steel claws, and a large head with two long tendrils extending out from the mouth.

"Is that a . . . dragon?" I asked.

The captain squinted into the distance. "Shines like metal."

"So does Rodin," Genevieve said. "I bet it is Shengguan. He mentioned he was working on an airship; he called it his Dragonship." Her expression drained leaving only worry. "In the snake palace, he wanted one of the hearts. He was . . .is . . . willing to kill to get his hands on one."

"That's got to be him!" I turned to the captain. "It's one of the Lords of the Golden Circle in a steam-powered Dragonship."

The captain ran to the copper tubes and yelled, "Battle stations!"

I pulled out my father's telescope and quickly wrapped the leather case around the two lenses. Raising it to my eye, I looked through and saw the dragon's head. The eyes were clear, windows, and I saw men within. Fire shot out of the feet, and on the shoulders were two propellers. I saw two more propellers above the back legs and fire emerged from those feet as well. The body was segmented with overlapping plates almost like scales.

"It's like a flying Milli-train," I said, passing the telescope to Genevieve.

"It really does look like a dragon," she said as Rodin landed on her shoulder. "Not like Rodin, but a Chinese dragon."

"It is probably protecting the flying fortress on its voyage to America." The captain hit the armrest of his chair. "It's fast, climbing hundreds of meters in a matter of moments." He leaned in to the copper tubes. "Get those cannons ready to fire, both sides!"

As the Dragonship flew closer it opened its jaws and I saw three barrels. The center one,shot fireballs that ached toward the Sparrowhawk but Heinz flew above them. The right one spun and was the biggest Gatling gun I'd ever seen. Bullets whipped past us, but as we angled around them the Dragonship twisted away. The left barrel fired cannon shot, and the shells exploded, ripping through the wingsail.

"Fire!" The captain ordered, but our cannon balls bounced off the Dragonship's armored hide.

They'd laid a trap for us and we'd fallen right into it. I worried we'd be destroyed, or at least be knocked out of the sky and unable to follow. While we'd chased Zerelda and the Vimana flew off, the Dragonship laid in wait like a predator. I kicked myself for being so naïve and hoped underestimating the Golden Circle wouldn't cost us our lives.

The Dragonship twisted in the air, rising above the *Sparrowhawk*. I couldn't see it anymore, which meant we were about to be obliterated.

A thunderous roar shook the *Sparrowhawk*, and I waited for us to burst into flames and tumble from the sky. But we kept moving forward. I ran to the window as a dark shadow emerged from the clouds. Dark red scales whipped past the windows, as large dark leathery wings blocked out the sun. *Āgō āmdhī.*

As *Āgō āmdhī* blasted the Dragonship and the *Sparrowhawk* banked to get away, I pressed against the window and watched the Dragonship try to fight back. It opened fire with cannons peeking out from scales along its sides and the Gatling gun in its mouth. *Āgō āmdhī* twisted and arced, dancing in an aerial ballet around the metal Dragonship. The dragon flared out huge wings to hover above its man-made counterpart and then unleashed a blazing torrent of fire that engulfed the head and front sections of the Dragonship.

Still, the Dragonship withstood the onslaught, fleeing at full speed straight toward the Vimana, smoke trailing from its head. Meaning we'd have to get past both of them to find the baron. That was if he was on the Vimana. *Āgō āmdhī* flew up alongside the Sparrowhawk dwarfing the aero-dirigible. We looked like a tiny bird next to this stunning creature of myth. I ran off the bridge to the cargo door. I pulled it open and waved.

"You've saved us once again! Thank you!" I yelled so loudly it made my

throat sore.

The dragon pulled back so its head was right next to me. "My pleasure. I couldn't let a false dragon give us all a bad name." *Āgō āmdhī* laughed, which sounded like rolling thunder.

"You honor us with your help!"

Genevieve came running up next to me, and Rodin leapt off her shoulder and flew out to join the dragon. I turned to her and smiled. "I have an idea, but it's really insane."

"My favorite kind."

"You agree with me that your father is probably on the Vimana?"

She nodded. "As you said, he would have stowed away. The Vimana was the prime target leaving during the battle."

"Then I say we ask *Āgō āmdhī* to take us to the Vimana. They'll think the dragon is chasing them from this attack and we can leap off onto the Vimana."

"That is insane," She smiled and nudged me with her elbow. "Which is why it might work."

I turned to the dragon flying beside us. "*Āgō āmdhī*, I have a favor to ask. Will you carry us once again?"

"Where do you wish to go?"

"See that flying castle up ahead?"

The dragon looked into the distance and then back at me. "Why do you wish this?"

Genevieve yelled, "My father and mother are there, and we need to rescue them."

"All we need is for you to get us to the flying castle." I pointed at the shiny dot on the horizon. "But this airship can't get close enough without a raging battle."

The dragon thought for a moment and Rodin flew

beside it. *Āgō āmdhī* nodded. "Sounds like fun."

"We'll be right back!" I hugged Genevieve and we rushed down to our room. I grabbed whatever I could and shoved it in my leather bag. Genevieve filled the pockets of her coat. Lianhua, who was resting in her hammock with Kō'ilā, watched us for moment, then sat up. "Where are you going? Perhaps I should join you."

I stopped. "You've done more than enough. Besides the crew will need your help. They need to stop and send word to our allies. You can help by staying with Mr. Singh."

"Indihar will want to go with you. He will not like being left behind." The concern on Lianhua caused her to stand. "You will need our help."

"We do need your help," Genevieve said. "To contact the Templars."

I slung my bag over my shoulder and took her hand. "We're going to the Vimana, if they capture us, we'll be fine because Hendrix has some fascination with me and Genevieve's parents are there, but anyone else might get killed. We can't risk it." I squeezed her hand and looked into her eyes. "Please help the crew contact our allies."

She nodded.

Genevieve came over and stood next to me. "And explain to Indihar why we left without him. You are correct, he will not like this."

"I don't like it either," Lianhua said. "But I understand. I will stay with the *Sparrowhawk*."

"Thank you." I turned to Genevieve. "We still have to tell the captain, and he's really not going to like this."

We rushed up to the bridge. Everyone stood by the windows staring at the dragon, except Heinz, but he kept glancing over even as he tried to keep his attention on the controls.

The captain turned as we hurried in. "Oh, no. What do you think you two are doing?"

"We are going after my father," Genevieve said.

"What the hell did you just say?" The captain brushed back his jacket and planted his hands on his hips.

"The dragon agreed to take us to the Vimana," I said. "Once we're gone, you can stop and send word to the Templars, then come after us."

"Are you both—"

"Insane? Maybe. But the dragon can get through their defenses; the *Sparrowhawk* can't."

"It scares me when you two make sense." The captain shook his head. "Get out of here before I come to my senses."

Genevieve and I ran off, once at the cargo door, I waved to the dragon, and *Āgō āmdhī* tipped its wing so it almost touched the *Sparrowhawk*. We jumped on and climbed up onto its back. The dragon craned its neck back toward us and said, "Settle down between my shoulders. And . . . hold on."

We grabbed hold of one of its spiny horns, and the dragon soared off from the *Sparrowhawk*, and within a few beats of its wings, the aero-dirigible was a dot on the horizon behind us. I pulled my goggles down and looked at Genevieve who had grabbed a pair before we left. The wind was too strong to talk so I held up my thumb. She returned the gesture and smiled.

Her hair whipped around her face, and her jacket pressed against her body. My hair danced over my goggles and all I felt was the constant pressure of the wind on every part that faced forward. I'd never traveled so fast. The exhilaration was intense, if my nerves weren't screaming how foolish I was, I'd have been screaming for joy. All I could do was hold on and think about what we'd do once we landed on the Vimana.

Āgō āmdhī checked on us a couple of times. I would raise my hand to let it know we were all right. Then I saw Rodin poke his head out of Genevieve's jacket. He squinted but reveled in the air on his face. Not me. After a while, the biting cold air felt like daggers dragging across every inch of exposed skin.

Soon the Vimana went from a shiny dot to a huge vessel plowing through the sky. The nimble Dragonship circled the lumbering but powerful flying castle. Huge propellers held it aloft, and its impressive fortifications sent fear slicing through me. As we flew closer, I saw soldiers running to the gun installations. They'd spotted us. The Dragonship rounded around the Vimana to cut off our approach.

I glanced at Genevieve and squeezed her hand. She grabbed me and tension firmed her grip. This was it. In moments we'd either be on the Vimana or realizing what a bad idea this was. Seeing the armed response of the Vimana, I really hoped the dragon wouldn't be injured, but so far nothing had come close to hurting this majestic creature.

The Dragonship charged and hurled fireballs from its mouth. *Āgō āmdhī* shook beneath us, and I started to worry it had been hurt. Then I realized the dragon was laughing. I exhaled and held on as a rumble built up deep within the dragon. More intense than the laughter, this felt like rolling thunder and the dragon vibrated as the energy built up inside. As the Dragonship flew closer, the dragon extended its neck and unleashed a column of fire. The entire Dragonship was engulfed in flames and quickly veered off. Hot waves washed over us, and my skin went from freezing to burning. *Āgō āmdhī* dove toward the Vimana.

Cannons and deck guns started firing, filling the air with lead. Shells exploded, and shrapnel rained down around us, bouncing off the dragon's scales. Genevieve and I huddled together hoping one wouldn't strike us. *Āgō āmdhī* banked left and then tilted to the right putting its body between us and most of the attacks.

We were getting closer to the Vimana, but it was still too far to jump safely. As we waited for the perfect moment, I pulled the rope from my bag and tied it around us. Leaning against her I yelled, "When we're ready, we leap on the count of five."

"Wait." She held up a finger. "I have something that will help." She held up the last of the silk parachutes Mr. Singh had made. We secured it to the tether between us. It would never hold us both, but would slow us down enough so we wouldn't break our legs.

I patted the dragon's back. *Āgō āmdhī* glanced back and nodded slightly. With a tip of its wing to shield us from view, we stood up, held each other tight, and jumped.

We fell through the air until Genevieve let the parachute go. It billowed out in a whoosh and kept us feet first, but, slowed us only slightly. With a lurch, we crashed onto the wide ledge of one tier of the pyramid and tumbled across the armor plating. The parachute collapsed, but quickly filled with air again and dragged us toward the edge. If we fell, it would be all the way to the ground, so I pulled out my knife and cut the line. The silk fabric whipped out into the sky, but we remained safely on the ledge.

The dragon spun in the air and roared. *Āgō āmdhī* turned and flew off as the Dragonship hurled fireballs in its wake. The scene looked as though the dragon was giving up its attack and I hoped that's how the Golden Circle would see it. Hopefully they believed our ruse. It would give us a chance to slip in and sneak around.

I ached all over but nothing felt broken. "You okay?" I yelled.

"I think so," Genevieve said.

"Let's go." We ran to nearest hatch. A metal door flush with the wall. I peered through the small round window and saw that the corridor was empty. "Here goes," I said. I yanked up on the handle and we both pulled to pry open a door in the whipping winds. We rushed inside.

Genevieve shut the door and silence enveloped us. The raging wind lay on the other side and I could hear again. She hugged me and whispered in my ear. "We made it!"

I pulled her close and said, "That was unbelievable!"

A muffled squeak escaped between us, and Genevieve pulled back and let the little dragon crawl out of her coat. "Apologies, Rodin." He climbed up onto her shoulder.

"Let's find you father," I said.

She drew her saber and winked. "Agreed, Sky Raider."

We stood in a corridor that arced along the outer wall of the Vimana. Though the wind outside no longer assaulted my ears, the sound of machinery echoed from every direction. Without a clear idea of where to go, we slipped down the hall, stopping at every junction to check for soldiers. Steel arches formed the corridor with sheet metal floors and walls. We found gun decks and machine gun nests on the outer ring and as we moved inward, we passed crew compartments and other rooms like a galley. Everything was empty.

On one of the middle rings of the level we explored, we found a circular staircase that wound around an elevator shaft. The sound of machinery was louder below us, and we heard voices echoing down from above. I stopped and asked, "Which way; up or down?"

"A dungeon or brig would be down, but I can guarantee the Golden Circle is at the top."

"Agreed." I ran my fingers through my hair. "Down there's less chance of getting caught, but up has answers."

"There is one good bit of news."

"What?" I asked.

She pointed to a

bell and striker mounted on the wall. "If they knew we were here, those would be ringing like crazy."

"Good point." I paused. "Let's go down first. Let's see everything we can before we go up and get captured."

"Have faith," she said. "We have to remain positive."

"I am, but they have the Hearts, and I'm worried those demonic relics will tell them right where we are."

"They have not yet revealed us," she said. "But I agree, let us see what this place is all about, and maybe we'll find a way to defeat it."

"An excellent idea." I stepped onto the stairs and we made our way into the depths of the Vimana.

We moved quickly but quietly, trying not to draw any attention. Genevieve moved with her saber at the ready and Rodin clinging to her back with his head peeking over shoulder. I held both Thumpers out ready to smack, or blast, anyone who gave us trouble. When we reached the next level, I saw a series of numbers and letters marking where we were: *Lvl 8 / Ring 4 / West*.

I pointed to the numbers. "There were five main steps on the outside. Those are probably the rings. West could be which side of the Vimana."

"If there is more than one level on a ring then that would explain the levels."

"Now we can navigate," I said. "Should we keep going down?"

Genevieve nodded and we descended lower into the ship. Two levels down, the walls fell away and revealed wide open spaces with huge support beams. The enormous room held giant generators and magnetic coils around the perimeter. I recognized them from the electromagnet they used to pull the comet down to

London. Large cables led to two towers.

I crouched down on the stairs and pointed. "Those must be two of the four towers sticking up out of the pyramid."

Genevieve knelt beside me. "Look there . . . in the center. Those are the armors we saw at the factory."

"There are hundreds of them." My heart sank as I looked at the rows of metal men. "How are we going to fight an army like that?"

From our perch about fifty feet above the floor, Genevieve pointed out several engineers moving about the machinery. "Let's go back up. We're too exposed on the open stairs," she said.

As we moved around the outside ring of this step, we passed gun decks and realized that every hall could be closed off with thick metal doors. This area was meant for battle. We moved closer to the interior and paused several times, ducking into doorways to let small packs of soldiers pass by. When we reached the inner-most section, we found two guards at each door.

"We must get in there. Looks like a brig." I looked around for another way, but saw nothing.

"This way," Genevieve pointed to a door. We slipped into a small room. "My father always says there are two ways into any place. The obvious way, and the obscured way. We need to find a way they have not thought of."

"Like when I used the drain to get in the hidden palace." I looked around the room.

"Exactly; or in this case, a shared wall panel." She felt the inner-most wall and stopped at a seam. "Because the exterior of the palace is armor plated and reinforced to withstand a battle, and they have to carry a heavy payload—all those armors below—the interior cannot be as fortified, otherwise it would be too heavy to fly. Can I borrow your dagger?"

I pulled my bowie knife from its sheath and handed it over. She wedged it into the seam and worked it back and forth. After a few moments, a gap opened in the panel.

"It's working!" She squatted and worked the knife into the seam at the bottom of the panel and soon it popped off. With a quick glance to see if anyone was waiting for us on the other side, she slipped through. I followed right behind her and found myself in a circular corridor with cages equally spaced. Most were empty, but in the center, in a gilded cage obviously meant for special "guests," Baron Kensington hung from golden chains.

"Father!" Genevieve rushed over and tried to forced open the door. It rattled but didn't budge.

He looked up and horror filled his face. "What are you doing here?"

"Shhh," I whispered. I watched for the guards, expecting them to barge in at any moment.

"We came to recue you, of course," Genevieve said. "Are you hurt?"

He shook his head, but we both knew he was lying. His face was bruised and one eye was swollen shut. From the dazed look in his eyes, he looked drugged.

"We need a key," I said. "Maybe we could blast one of the guards and—

"The only keys to this cage," the baron said, "are kept by the Inner Circle. Only one of them can release me."

"I could try to blast it with my Thumper, but the guards will hear."

"Do it," Genevieve said. "I will kill anyone who enters."

"No!" A stern look flashed across the baron's face. "You'll be caught and that won't do anyone any good."

"Then we will steal a key and come back for you!" Genevieve reached through with both arms trying to hug her father, but she couldn't reach him.

"It's too dangerous! You two shouldn't be here," the baron croaked, his voice raspy, parched.

"Zerelda's dead," Genevieve said. "Her Heart is destroyed."

"Good. But that won't stop them." He lifted his head but couldn't keep it up. "I made it a full day running around this place before they caught me."

"Are there any Sikh on board?" I asked. "We'll need to free them, too."

The baron's head dropped. "Four of us made it onto this Vimana ..."

Genevieve gripped the bars. "Are they in another cell block?"

"We were causing some damage to the air fortress when I heard . . . when they discovered us. He killed the Sikhs and captured me. The rest of Shah's army is back in the valley, freeing the workers."

I put my hand on Genevieve's arm. I was sad for those who had died, but relieved more weren't going to be whipped into submission by the Golden Circle.

Rodin climbed through the cage and out one of the baron's arms. He blasted the chains with fire, but only scorched the gold. Rodin tried again, but had to admit defeat and climbed back onto Genevieve.

She tried the cage once again, and it rattled loudly. I pulled her back. "We must go. We are making too much noise, and he is right, we cannot get caught."

She turned and hugged me. Placing her hands against my chest, she pushed back, and stared at me with hate and tears in her eyes. "We are going to get that key!"

I nodded.

She reached back through the bars to touch her father's face. "We will be back soon."

I took her hand and we slipped back through the wall. I put the panel back into place and stood. Genevieve wiped her eyes and stared at me, "Let us find my mother. I want her key!"

42
The Key
to a Heart

Ascending the stairs as quietly as possible, I twitched at every sound in the passageways, and paused with every groan in the metal. Genevieve, however, looked annoyed by my slow pace. She moved with short, quick, harsh movements, and a hardened expression.

We froze as the elevator passed on the other side of the wall. We ascended all the way to the top, but I held us back in the shadows of the staircase. The top level consisted of a round dome with an octagon base. Large curved windows started several feet off the ground and met at the top where a glass covered oculus sat.

The crew worked in a ring about halfway up, while a platform in the center was raised about six feet above the rings. Four sets of stairs, one on each side of the Vimana, led up to the platform. Several chairs were arranged on top, but only Hendrix stood watch over the crew.

"She's not here," I whispered. "We should check out the level below this one."

Genevieve nodded. We slipped down the stairs and exited on the level below. I looked up and saw the same

markings: *Lvl 2 / Ring 2 / South.*

My heart pounded in my chest as we walked down the corridor. The ring was smaller, but the doors were spaced even further apart. One of these doors might be her mother's room; but if that was the case, the rest of these rooms belonged to the other members of the Inner Circle. We had to choose the right one.

"These look like bigger rooms, but how do we know which one is hers?" I kept scanning both ahead and behind us.

"Rodin," Genevieve pulled him off her back and looked at him. "Find my mother."

Rodin flew off down the corridor and we rushed after him. He circled in front of a door, and we slowly approached. Rodin landed on Genevieve's shoulder. I tried the handle, but it was locked. Genevieve knocked and stood with hands on her hips. She had a harsh look in her eye, and I was glad I wasn't the one on the other side of the door.

A soft French voice behind the door said, "What do you want?"

I started to say something, but Genevieve shook her head. She put her finger to her lips. I didn't know what she was planning, but I got my Thumper ready.

"Didn't you hear me? What do you want?" I heard the sound of the door latch and the baroness whipped open the door. Genevieve rushed in, pushing her mother back. They tumbled to the ground, but Genevieve recovered and pointed her saber at her mother. I stepped in and closed the door.

"Hello, *mother*," Genevieve sneered. "I want your key."

"How did you get here?" She looked at me and then

back at Genevieve. We didn't answer her. "You shouldn't have come. Hendrix is angry, very angry, about what happened in the valley. We had to leave early."

"The key. To my father's cage. Now!" Genevieve didn't flinch. "I cannot believe you used me."

"I wanted you at my side." Her mother didn't plead, but spoke in a matter-of-fact tone. "The rest was out of my hands."

"My *father* doesn't deserve to be in a cage." Genevieve's stern voice and firm hand would have made me talk, but her mother remained calm and collected.

"*Genevieve,*" she used the French pronunciation, which didn't help her cause. "He put himself in there. I had nothing to do with it."

"Then he will be grateful when you help free him."

"I can't do that. You don't understand."

"No!" Genevieve stepped closer pressing the blade into her mother's clothes. "I am not leaving without him."

I raised my finger. "Genevieve, I might be a little too much from the school of Diogenes lately, but I don't think she can help us. If she gives us her key, the Inner Circle will know. They'll all turn on her."

Her mother looked up at me and smiled. "I like this one much more than the Duke's son." Her mother smiled. "He has brains, and guts. The other one? *Pah!*"

Genevieve eyed me. "I cannot leave him down there."

"No, we won't, but we have to give your mother an out, it's the only way she'll help us."

"Oh, I *really* like this one." The baroness knocked Genevieve's saber away and flipped onto her feet. She took my arm and led me over to her seating area. There she had an open bottle of wine and several glasses. She poured herself one and offered another to me. I declined. "Tell me…" she took a sip, shifting the stem of the glass with her fingers. "What do you have in mind?"

"Well, I'd take someone else's key, or take yours publicly."

"Hendrix is right about you." She smiled and nudged me with her elbow. "Brains and you're good looking. No wonder she doesn't want her betrothed."

"Please." Genevieve rolled her eyes. "That is not— "

"You are so one of the reasons she left. She knew my husband would make her return to England, make her marry that *boy*." The baroness and I sat down. "I like this plan, and maybe I want to help."

"Can you get us into someone else's room?"

"Maybe, but we are all confined to our rooms, right now. Hendrix doesn't trust anyone."

"Then how can we get off this Vimana, is there a hanger?"

"On Ring Three, there is a bay where the small craft are stored." The baroness leaned in and ran her fingers along the leather strap wound around my chest. "You would actually steal the key from me, in front of Hendrix?"

"If it's the only way, then yes."

Genevieve walked over to us, "No. I'm not going to trade you for my father."

"You won't. I'll get the key. Pass it off to you. You'll get your father, and then we'll meet up at the hanger and fly out of here."

"A bold plan, Alexander," the baroness took a sip of wine. "I like bold plans."

"But are you going to turn on me, tell Hendrix the moment we get on the bridge?"

"She'd better not, or we will match swords again." Genevieve hadn't sheathed her saber and now eyed her mother.

The baroness took a drink, finishing off the glass. She set it down and exhaled. "I . . . I don't like seeing him in there either." She turned away from Genevieve but locked eyes with me. "I know what Hendrix has planned and—"

I could see pain in her eyes. She was truly conflicted about her husband and about Hendrix. Each time I'd seen her before, she was cocky, cool and collected. Now she seemed . . . to care about something. For the first time, she reminded me of Genevieve.

"You two hide in my room. I'll find out the next time Hendrix will let us out of our cages." She turned to Genevieve and waved at a door. "Hide in there. I will be back."

Genevieve nodded.

She went to the door and yelled for a soldier. With only two rooms and a bath, we slipped into the bedroom, each hoping we hadn't just made a big mistake. Genevieve sat down on a chaise lounge, and Rodin stood on the wooden edge. "She could be calling soldiers to arrest us."

I drew in a deep breath. "I don't think so." I looked around at the lavish room. Large circular windows looked out over China slipping silently below us. I walked up to the glass. I stared at the tower with the giant spinning propeller, unable to believe that I stood in a working Vimana. "I think she still cares for your father. And she definitely cares about what happens to you."

"But she's a Horseman." Genevieve took off her jacket and lay back on the chaise. She ran her fingers through the plaits of her braid and shook it out.

I couldn't stop staring at her. She was stunning, and suddenly I felt almost odd about being alone with her. I knew I should wait in the other room, a gentleman would, but I didn't want to leave.

"Come here," she said and patted the chaise lounge.

I sat on the end. She sat up and took my hand. "I don't like this plan. You're risking too much. I'm…"

"It will be okay. They won't hurt me. Hendrix will try and turn me, try to convince me to join him, especially now that he's lost Zerelda. I'll play along and then run. Before they can catch up, we'll be on an airskiff fleeing this place. They'll expect me to go for the baron. You are the reason this is going to work."

She hugged me, pulling me close. "You're the bravest person I know."

"Well, you're the bravest person I know." I ran my hand along her cheek and we put our foreheads together. My hand cradled her neck and the back of her head, and I kissed her. As our lips touched, electricity shot through me like I'd been hit by Baldarich's lightning cannon. I pulled her closer and we didn't stop. I didn't want to stop. Despite the fact that, as gentleman, I knew I most definitely should stop. She didn't pull away, either. Time faded away as we lost ourselves in each other.

* * *

We lay on the chaise intertwined in each other's arms. The baroness appeared in the doorway, and smiled. "I didn't realize you two needed a chaperone."

I sprang up. "Apologies, I . . . I—"

The baroness laughed. "No need to explain. I remember being your age. Besides, I'm the bad one."

Genevieve sat up, "I'm pleased you didn't bring the guards back with you. What were you able to learn?"

"Hendrix will be calling us together about halfway over the ocean." She poured herself a glass of wine. "He is keeping us all caged and guarded in the meantime."

"This is hardly a cage, Mother." Genevieve said. "Not like the one Father is in."

Her mother sighed. "Whatever you want to call this"—she swept her arm through the air—"it feels like a prison to me. He trusts no one and is controlling everything himself."

"Then what is our plan?"

"You'll have to wait until then, my dear. No one suspects you're on board. I would dearly love to hear how you got on and found your father and me without getting caught." She smiled, and looked at her daughter with pride.

"Then we wait," I said. "It will give us a chance to get some rest and go over our plan."

"And time to tell me of your adventures," the baroness said. Then she smiled a wicked smile and chuckled. "Or . . ."—she took a long drink and looked at us over the rim of her glass —". . . I could wait in the other room."

I stammered and didn't know what to say.

She laughed again and shook her head. "How cute you are. You're both blushing."

43
Escape

I sat on a ledge in front of the circular window as we soared over the deep blue ocean. We'd been hiding for a day, and being cooped up was getting to me. *Gulliver's Travels*, one of my favorite books, lay open in my lap, but I couldn't concentrate on it, and reading it in French was getting tiring. Genevieve and her mother were on the chaise lounge talking, and I stared out the window, watching as the Vimana flew above the clouds, as if this castle had come right out of a fairytale—or out of Jonathan Swift's imagination.

A gong echoed throughout the baroness's quarters. A haunting sound emanating from the hall. The baroness stood, took her daughters hands in hers, and held them for a moment before releasing her. She came over to me. "It is time."

I closed the book, set it aside, and stood. "You go ahead. I'll be up in a moment. I need to make a grand entrance."

"God speed to you, Alexander." The baroness touched my cheek lightly, and walked out into the corridor.

Genevieve came over

and wrapped her arms around me. "Please be careful. This is a good plan, but I will be worried about you until we're together again."

I smiled. "You're the one who has to stay out of sight. I just have to walk in and get captured."

"You're risking everything to help my father."

I shrugged, "I'm used to it by now." We laughed. "I'd do it a thousand times, not only do I owe you for rescuing my father, but I owe your father for everything he's done for me."

"You are the most honorable person I know. You are truly a knight." Her fingers ran along my vest and the leather strap.

"Thank you," I said. "But you're the amazing one."

"Let us settle on the fact that we are both amazing," she said and stood on tiptoes to kiss me.

I didn't want to let go of her, but the plan needed to be put into action if we wanted to save her father. "Fifteen minutes. After I slip you the key, you'll have fifteen minutes until I run to the hanger."

"We'll be there."

"Here I go."

"Wait," she kissed me again, this time passionately and I really didn't want to let her go. "For luck," she said finally.

"I feel pretty lucky."

We slipped out of the room and headed up the stairs. I left her to hide in the shadows and I walked right onto the bridge. At first, no one noticed me. General Hendrix was talking to the Inner Circle atop the platform as the crew moved back and forth on their level. I walked up the stairs and reached the top. Hendrix had his back to me, but the baroness sat up and gripped the arms of her chair, an alarmed look on her face. She was an excellent actress. Wilhelm, the Kaiser's liaison jabbed the air, pointing at me, and Antiochus jumped to his feet, nearly tipping his chair over. Lord Marbury's mouth dropped open, and his hand went to his chest. For a weapon or because he thought he'd seen a ghost, I didn't know.

Hendrix turned and stared at me with strange mix of surprise and admiration. "What are you doing here? How the hell did you even get here?"

"I've come to negotiate for the baron's release."

Antiochus turned to the crew, "Search the sky for an armada."

"You won't find one. I'm here alone." I was stoic, standing with a hard but not threatening stance. I made no sudden movements and kept my hands far from my weapons. "As I said, I am here to negotiate."

Hendrix waved his hand and the Inner Circle settled back into their seats. "An armada could never get close to this flying fortress without being seen. For whatever trick he pulled to get here, I think he's earned the right to be heard." He turned back to me. "So what do you want, *Mister* Armitage?"

"I offer a trade. Myself for the baron." I looked at each one of them, trying to see who had their key to the dungeons. The baroness wore hers around her neck, and Hendrix had an identical key on a leather cord around his neck. I didn't see Antiochus' key, but Wilhelm had his around his wrist. Lord Marbury had his tucked into his vest pocket. I could see the same leather cord as Hendrix and the gold tip poking out. If they all had them, they must be used for more than the cages. With so many to choose from, I decided not to take the baroness' key.

"You wish to be my prisoner?" Hendrix clapped his

hands together.

"Prisoner? No." I walked around him, as if addressing each member of the Inner Circle. "I will accept your offer. I will become the Horseman of Death, but only to secure the life of my mentor." I stopped in front of Lord Marbury. "Unlike some, I still owe loyalty to my friends."

"I like your bravado, boy." Hendrix smiled and tipped his Stetson. "You'll make a fine Horseman."

"When we land, I want him released, and until then, I want him treated like a nobleman deserves. If you do not carry through with his safe release, I will not carry through with my promise." I leaned in toward Lord Marbury locking his eyes with mine. He had trouble maintaining eye contact with me. He wanted to turn away, but I held his gaze. I wanted to punch him, to slam my Thumper down on his traitorous head, but instead, I slipped my hand down and snagged his key. I drew it out slowly using my body to block anyone else from seeing my actions. Once I had lifted the key, I bunched it up in my palm.

Hendrix nodded. "He's being well cared for now." His fingers twisted the key around his neck. "But I like your offer. However, if we let him go, he's just gonna come back with an army."

"At that point, I will have fulfilled my duty to him and repaid my debt. After that. . ." I turned back to Hendrix. "After we have the other Heart, no army will stop the Horsemen." I walked back toward the stairs, pacing as if I was impatient and tired of the whole thing, trying to be just as arrogant and confident as Hendrix. Glancing down, I could just see Genevieve's eyes shining in the shadows. I flashed the key in my palm.

Hendrix looked at each of the Inner Circle members around him. "Did you hear that? This kid has more guts than any of you. He's noble, but he ain't a blue blood like you Marbury. He's braver than you've ever been Antiochus. He's got more balls than my assassin, and he's more loyal than the German is to his Kaiser." Hendrix stepped forward, addressing each of them in turn. As they all stared up at him, I did a quick scan of the crew and the Inner Circle, made sure they were focused elsewhere, and then tossed the key toward Genevieve, hoping she'd catch it before it hit the stairwell. When I didn't hear anything, I risked one more glance her way and saw the stairwell was empty. I wanted to jump for joy, but I didn't. Instead, I took a deep breath. I still had a quarter of an hour to stall.

I walked over to one of the chairs and sat as if this seat had been saved for me—which, I realized, it might well have been. They all turned. Antiochus eyed me with a harsh suspicious expression, but Hendrix smirked.

The baroness waved a hand my way. "He's certainly making himself at home. That's a good sign. I can't say I want my husband released, but if that's what it takes for the General to get his prize, then so be it."

Lord Marbury twisted in his chair. "I don't agree. This is a trick."

"No. It's not!" I stared at the traitor with a sneer and spit venom with my words. "It's about loyalty and honor, things you'll never understand. He was your friend and you betrayed him."

Hendrix stomped his bronze clad foot. "I like it! He's right. We have him, because he'll be loyal to ensure the baron is safe. It's perfect!"

"You're being a fool," Antiochus said under his

breath.

"Watch what you say, my friend!" Hendrix growled.

As they continued to argue about whether my offer was some sort of trick, I tried to count the minutes. The only clock I'd seen was down with the crew, and I couldn't tell if it was the right time, or if it was counting down to something. So, I counted in my head. First to sixty several times until I got a feeling for how long a minute was, then at five minutes I tapped my foot. I was getting nervous as the time wound down. No alarms had rung, a good sign, but I had no idea what Genevieve was doing. What if the baron was too weak to walk? Maybe I should have given her more time? I took a deep breath at the ten-minute mark trying to ease my nerves.

Finally, I stood. I watched everyone in the room to see who might try and stop my escape. My biggest concern was Hendrix. He had a grappler on his mechanical arm, as well as a gun. None of the other Inner Circle members looked like they carried weapons. However, there were four soldiers spaced around the room with rifles. I needed a distraction.

The voices in the background rose and fell as I searched for something, *anything*, a valve I could open, a button I could push. Then I saw that the center of the platform was segmented, not a solid disk, but split into four equal parts. It reminded me of the trap door at the Snake Palace. Risking a glance at Hendrix's chair, I saw an upraised button on the right arm. Just a few feet away from where I stood. I knew what I had to do. *58… 59… 14:59.*

As I reached the last few seconds, Hendrix turned to me and declared, "Then it is settled." He retook the center of the room, looking down at the other seated members of the Inner Circle as if he were their lord and master. "Alexander Armitage, I accept your offer, but I will not release the baron until after you have fulfilled your role as Horseman of Death. Kensington has been a thorn in my side for years, and I'd rather not get stuck again." He stood right in the center of the trapdoor. "I pledge to treat him as a guest—no more torture—and when we've conquered the world, you can determine his fate."

"That's not what I offered."

"You said you came to negotiate. So, I'm negotiating. This is my counter-offer."

I stood up and spun around as if considering his offer. I paced around the chair, rubbing my chin. Hendrix turned to Marbury and tipped his Stetson. I took a step closer to his chair. "Well, I reject your counter-offer. The deal's off."

I slammed the palm of my hand down on the button. The floor opened up and Hendrix fell through. Everyone turned toward the trapdoor with stunned expressions. I bolted for the stairs and leapt down them two at a time. As I reached the floor, Hendrix unleashed a blood curdling scream that echoed out of the hole. When I stepped onto the circular staircase, I heard his grappler fire. I didn't look back. I kept running, leaping down as many stairs as I could.

When I reached the third level I rushed toward the hanger. I found Genevieve and her father had already selected an airskiff. A wooden frame like a boat, held a balloon in the front and back of the vessel, with an open section for passengers in the center. A pair of large triangular wingsails sat on each side.

Genevieve stood by the hanger door and the baron

sat in the ship. As I entered, she pulled the lever, causing the gears to turn, raising the large gate.

I jumped into the skiff and cut the anchor lines. Genevieve rushed over and jumped into the craft. She lifted us off and guided us toward the door. Soldiers rushed into the hanger. I aimed my Thumpers and fired. The blast knocked them back and we soared out of the Vimana.

I sat back, but Genevieve lunged forward and hugged me. "You did it!"

My heart was soaring even higher than the skiff. "And I didn't even incriminate your mother." I glanced back at the baron. "I took Lord Marbury's key."

The baron laughed in delight, and Genevieve squeezed me tighter.

44
The Last Heart

The three of us kept looking back at the Vimana. It didn't take long before the guns started to fire, and several Hornets launched from its hangers to pursue us. I took over piloting, as Genevieve tended to the baron who was pale and weak. She wrapped him in a blanket, and sat beside him.

I checked the pressure of the two hydrogen tanks, the one in front of us and the one behind me. I pushed the throttle forward on the burner that turned the propeller. Using what Mr. Singh had taught me, I trimmed the triangular wingsails to optimize our speed. We had a tailwind pushing us, and as cannon balls streaked past, I had an idea to get more speed.

"We need a kitesail!"

"What can we use? I'm not wearing a dress this time."

The baron held up the corner of his blanket. "Use this."

"No!" Genevieve exclaimed. "That's for you, I'm afraid of you getting cold."

"I'd rather be cold here with you than in cellblock by myself."

He looked at her, and pushed off the blanket. Dressed in only a light shirt, he clutched his arms around his chest to shield himself from the air whipping around us.

"Alexander, I need the rope from your bag." Genevieve moved to the center, being careful to keep the blanket from unfurling.

I pulled my leather bag off and handed it to her. Then slipped my jacket off and passed it over to the baron. "Here put this on." The baron took the jacket and covered himself.

Genevieve retrieved the rope from my bag and cut it into four equal lengths. She tied them to the corners of the blanket and threaded the ropes through the mooring clamps. She fed them back to me.

"You'll have to pilot the craft," I said, "and I'll manage the kitesail."

She nodded, passed the blanket bundle to me, and slipped into the seat. I shifted forward, sitting right in front of her. I pressed my feet against the ribbing of the craft and let the blanket go. It billowed in the wind, and my muscles strained as I struggled to keep the blanket under control. The wind pushed against the kitesail and dragged us through the sky. We moved noticeably faster, and I tugged on the ropes to keep it under control.

Together, we guided the craft to the east, pulling out of gun range and putting distance between us and the hornets following us.

The baron pointed toward some clouds on the horizon. "Make for those clouds. Lose them in the fog."

"Of course," Genevieve said, and aimed us for the cloud bank.

As the white mist engulfed us, I continued to strain against the wind, but soon it shifted, the kitesail turned, and I reeled it in. I handed the blanket back to the baron and he wrapped it around his shoulders. We slowed down and Genevieve trimmed the wingsails to keep us moving east at the best possible speed. We continued on until darkness enveloped us. It was difficult to tell time enveloped in a blanket of white and grey mixed with the hues of reds, yellows, and orange that colored the sky. Finally, we broke free of the clouds, and there were no Hornets in sight.

We all sighed in relief and tension slipped off our shoulders like raindrops. Genevieve wrapped her arms around her father, and he grabbed her up in a big bear hug. Rodin circled the two. "I'm so glad to see you," he said.

"I'm sorry I left the way I did, but I had to know the truth." Genevieve's voice was muffled, as she buried her face in his chest.

"Don't worry about that now." The baron kissed her head. "I should have told you everything. Or at least as much as I knew. I'm sorry."

She pulled away but they remained in each other's arms. The baron turned to me with tears glistening in his eyes. "Thank you, Alexander. Your word is your bond. You brought my daughter back to me. I can't thank you enough."

"Of course." I shifted in my seat and smiled at Genevieve.

"You shouldn't have come after me, but I'm glad you did." The baron released Genevieve, but then pulled her back in for one more hug.

She looked at him. "Lord Marbury is the mole."

"I know." His face darkened and he shook his head. "I thought he was on his way back to Lahore for more men, but then I saw him on the Vimana. I couldn't believe it. He'd been one of my greatest friends for many years. In fact, that's why I was discovered. I'd been slinking around, spying and staying in shadows, but then I heard his voice and had to confront him."

"We discovered him at the Serpent Palace," Genevieve said. "He was with Hendrix preparing for your attack." She smiled. "However, I don't think they were expecting the dragon."

"Neither was I," the baron said. "That dragon was real . . . I thought my eyes were deceiving me."

"We met him in the mountains," I said.

Genevieve nodded. "It's what Rodin will look like in many, many years."

The baron laughed and patted the little dragon. "I'm afraid you'll be too big to be a house pet by then." He turned to me and then looked back at his daughter. "You haven't told me how you two got onto the Vimana to rescue me."

"The dragon," she said. "We asked _Āgō āmdhī._"

"The dragon speaks?" the baron said with wide eyes. "I'm truly upset to have missed that."

Father and daughter fell into a comfortable conversation until the baron needed to rest so his body could heal from the beatings. Genevieve and I took turns resting and piloting the skiff, always heading east toward the rising sun. We flew over the widest expanse of ocean I could ever imagine until finally we saw the high cliffs and rocky shores of America's western coast. In the distance, the light broke through the faint outline of mountains on the horizon. I knew we needed to get to the barren land on the other side of the Rockies. Even though I'd only lived on the east coast, the land spreading out below us felt familiar, as if I'd been here before. But it was only because of my visions. I'd seen where Armand Armitage had traveled.

The mountains loomed large across the horizon. I pointed to the northeast, and said, "That way."

I took over the controls from Genevieve and directed the airskiff.

The baron looked at me. "How do you know? We don't have a compass or map."

"I know where the last Heart is… I just have to find it."

His brows furrowed in confusion.

"I had a vision of the Templar Knight, Armand Armitage," I said. "When I read his journal. The places weren't listed, but I saw his journey, like I was following in his footsteps."

"That's astonishing," he said, his eyes widening. But then just as quickly, they narrowed. "Why didn't you tell me while we were on board the *Sparrowhawk*?"

"The mole."

"Did you think it was me?"

"I didn't know who to trust. . ." I paused and then turned back to him. "But no, I didn't think you'd send assassins after yourself?"

"So, where is the last Heart?"

"In a barren, desert place, on the other side of the Rocky Mountains."

"The other side of the Rockies? But that's all plains, a giant sea of prairie grass. Were there any distinguishing features? Anything else you can tell us?"

"Four fingers… I think I'll know it when I see it, though. Or, rather, I think I'll know it when I *feel* it. It's strange, but when I think about this place, I think of it as a 'bad land'."

We flew for hours as we searched the valleys and passes to navigate through the wall of mountains stretched out before us. I'd always wanted to see the West, but I'd expected more deserts, like the penny-dreadful-and-dime novels I used to read. Instead, we passed over thick forests and flew between the snow-capped peaks. Though jagged mountains towered above us, they didn't look as tall as the Himalayas. I thought of all the magnificent sights I'd seen on this journey. I wanted to stop, to touch these mountains and wander among the giant trees, but we had to save the world. I feared the Knights of the Golden Circle would want to destroy this beautiful land.

Later, when we passed over huge herds of big, horned beasts, I pulled out my father's telescope and saw scores of bison dotting the rolling hills below. I locked the controls and leaned against the edge of the craft, propped up on my elbows. "Stunning."

"What do you see?" Genevieve asked.

"Bison… and people!"

I handed her the telescope and her mouth dropped open as she watched them. "There are so many!"

"What are the people doing?" The baron asked.

Genevieve peered through the lenses. "A bunch of men in suits at the rail station."

The baron gestured for the telescope and his daughter passed it over. He put it to his eye and stared down at the gathering. "I know some of them. Alexander, take us down."

I maneuvered the craft and we landed several yards from the train station.

The men, about twenty or so, moseyed over to see

the contraption. The baron stepped out, he rubbed the stubble on his chin and adjusted his tattered clothes. "Mr. Roosevelt, is that you?"

"It is. Baron Kensington, was it? Oh my, you're looking a little worse for wear." A man in dark suit with a bushy mustache tugged at his waistcoat and extended his hand.

"I do apologies for my appearance; I've recently been the forced-guest of the Knights of the Golden Circle." Several of the men grumbled and one spit into the dirt.

"Good to see you've freed yourself of such commitments." His smile peered out from underneath his facial hair. "If I remember right, when last we met you had ventured across the sea to meet *friends* of my father."

"Exactly. I'm traveling again for those same *friends.*"

The man's eyes squinted. "Call me Teddy." He gestured to the other men. "You've caught us on a hunting excursion and when I heard, Mr. Earp was near, a gathering was assembled. Allow me to introduce, legendary law man Mr. Wyatt Earp and his associate, Mr. excuse me, Doctor Holliday. My friend, Mr. Bat Masterson, and then the mountain man Mr. Johnson, the horse trader Mr. Cassidy, with Mr. Britton, Judge Bean, and Mr. Greenbrough on the end. Gentlemen, this is the Baron Maximillian Kensington of England."

The men either nodded or shook hands with the baron. I paused with wide eyes; every American had heard of the shootout at the O.K. Corral. Even at Eton, I read about their exploits.

"This is my daughter and a fellow American, Mr. Armitage. Apologies for dropping in on you like this, but I was wondering if you could assist us."

"Of course."

The baron looked around. "First, where are we?"

The men chuckled. Mr. Earp, who towered over the others, motioned to the rolling hills. "Montana, Hunters Hot Springs to be specific."

The baron shook his head and looked at me, "We're looking for…"

I added. "A large desolate area, like a desert, but without dunes, like a barren area, a bad place."

The men all looked at each other. A couple toward the southeast, and then Mr. Earp tipped his hat. "Sounds like, you're looking for the Badlands."

Genevieve and I snapped a look at each other.

Mr. Roosevelt nodded. "I agree. Only place that fits that description."

I asked. "What are the bad lands?"

Mr. Cassidy chuckled. "A great place to lose a posse… or so I've heard."

A few of the men chuckled.

Mr. Roosevelt leaned back on his heels. "It's a giant scar. A barren land at the edge of the high plateau."

"That's got to be it!" I looked off to the southeast, where they were looking. "I don't suppose you've seen four dirt towers in a row?"

"Why, I think these travelers are referring to the Fingers." The doctor shifted the double-barrel shotgun cradled in his arms.

Mr. Cassidy nodded.

Genevieve snickered. "A bad place for a bad heart." She looked off to the east. "Which way are these Badlands?"

Mr. Earp squinted as he gestured toward the horizon. "Head southeast from Rapid City, once the plateau dips you'll be in the Badlands."

The baron thanked them all, and I waved. He then turned back to the craft. "We have to get going we're kind of on the run… and must make a gathering of our own."

Several of the men nodded, like they understood. He hopped back on the craft and I took off lifting into an orange haze.

Genevieve pointed. "Have you noticed the sky?"

Both the baron and I tilted our heads back and looked up. Everything was tinged with an orange hue, like sunset, but it was midday. As if an artist had painted across the sky with a fiery brush.

"What do you think is wrong?" she asked.

"I don't know, but I fear the Knights of the Golden Circle are behind it."

I worried about what it meant, and used my father's telescope to search the horizon.

Now past the tallest of mountain peaks, we fly over rolling grass-covered hills dotted with thousands of bison. We headed southeast as they suggested. In the distance, I saw a barren, light-colored scar stretching over a huge swath of land. "I see it!" Raising my hand, I pointed. "There, that must be the Badlands." I turned back to Genevieve and her father. "It's huge."

"Now what, Alexander?" the baron asked.

I closed my eyes and tried to put myself back in the vision. Tried to remember what everything smelled and felt like. "Four spires in a row, like the fingers of a hand."

The baron sighed and rubbed his temples as if thinking was a laborious task. I looked over and saw him shiver. He noticed me watching him, glanced furtively at Genevieve, and pointed at the horizon. "Keep searching. Don't worry about me."

I nodded and peered through the telescope. Places started to look familiar, and the bands of light-colored rock that formed the weathered hills looked like places I'd traveled before. I remembered the vision vividly but this was something else. I could hear a sound, like music. Then I knew the Heart was ahead of us, I even knew how far. It was as if it was calling to me, as if it wanted to be found. But why?

After several minutes I called out, "There they are!"

Genevieve set down the airskiff in front of the four spires. She checked on her father as I stepped out and looked over the striped earth. I walked over to the base of the third spire and looked down. Armand had stood right here. But he'd traveling on horseback, and it had taken him months to get from the ocean to this spot. I was relieved flying hadn't taken as long. In my vision, I'd watched him place the Heart here knowing no one would disturb it. I wanted to leave it where it rested, but the sound was louder now. A calling, compelling me to free the Heart. I knew the Vimana and the Dragonship couldn't be too far behind us. The other Hearts would lead Hendrix right here, and if I didn't seize the opportunity to retrieve the Heart now, it would fall into their hands.

I took a few steps back, loaded my Thumpers, and aimed them at the base. I pulled the triggers, and, when the dust cleared, saw that part of the spire had crumbled away. I loaded two more percussion caps and fired again. The spire shook, but remained standing.

I knelt and wiped at the dust. A glint of purple appeared. "I found it!"

Genevieve ran over. "You found the Heart?"

I nodded. "It's buried here in the base of this

finger."

She knelt beside me and cleared more dust and debris away. "I see it," she said. "We don't have much to dig it out."

"I think one or two more blasts will do it."

"How many more do you have?"

I reached in my pouch and pulled out four caps. "I hope it's enough."

"It will be."

I opened the breaches and slipped in two more caps. I placed one to the side of where I thought the Heart was and pressed the button. It blew out the side revealing more of the purple crystal. Then I aimed the other just below the Heart and fired. A huge dust cloud kicked up, Genevieve and I had to turn away. The finger collapsed, crumbling to dust as it toppled over. When I looked again a large cavity stood where the Heart had been and an amethyst crystal wrapped in a coil of silver wire lay at our feet.

I picked up the Heart and a surge of power and exultation—like pure joy—rippled through me. The amethyst and silver coil held a beauty that made it inconceivable this stunning artifact could be so evil. I showed it to Genevieve, but she stepped back. The stone was heavier than I thought and I had to use two hands to cradle the Heart.

"I get the feeling that thing wanted to be found," she said, turning to the airskiff. "We need to get out here."

I nodded and we climbed inside. The baron looked at the Heart and leaned away. He stared at me, with a look in his eyes I'd never seen before. Concern, yes, but something else, too. I hugged the crystal to my chest as

Genevieve lifted the airskiff into the air.

"Apologies Armand," I said softly. "Forgive us for disturbing the place you chose to hide this from the world."

S taring at the facets in the amethyst, I saw only the beautiful purple crystal, and not the deadly power within. So unassuming, this relic could sit in a museum or nobleman's art collection. I held it cradled in my arms. The silver coil wrapped perfectly around the amethyst, looking fused with its six sides.

"Alexander, can you put that Heart away?" The baron pointed to the leather bag I wore slung across my shoulder. "It's too dangerous to hold."

I stared at him for a moment. I didn't want to put it away. I wasn't done admiring it, but I knew of its power over the hearts of men. It hadn't affected me yet, but to be certain it's power wouldn't take hold, I put the Amethyst Heart into my bag. After one last look, I closed the flap, and secured it.

I pulled out my father's telescope, set the lenses in the leather case and peered through. We flew over the Great Plains, an endless sea of prairie grass in every direction. I could see all the way to the Rockies in the west and

almost to the Appalachians in the east. I knew Hendrix had to be following us, and, sure enough, while watching the sky behind us, I saw a speck take shape in the distance that I knew could only be the Vimana. My fears were confirmed when I saw the Dragonship undulating around the Vimana as if guarding its hoard.

"Hendrix is over the mountains," I said, pointing as I continued to look through the telescope.

"Genevieve, take us lower. Hopefully we'll blend in instead of being a dark dot in the sky." The baron pushed off my coat and turned to see our pursuers. "May I see your telescope?"

I handed it over and the baron watched the Vimana and Dragonship for a few minutes.

"Have they spotted us?" Genevieve asked, but her focus remained on avoid the trees.

"I don't think so. They appear to be flying normally."

"I wonder if they'll stop in the Badlands or if the Hearts will tell them to continue?" My hand rested on my bag, and I felt the large crystal through the leather.

"We'll have to wait and see." The baron sat back and handed me the telescope.

Soon, night stretched over the plains like a dark blanket. However, the stars above were obscured by a thick haze making it impossible to navigate, but it was easier to see the Vimana. Huge flood lights illuminated the night's sky above and swept over the ground below.

Eventually I realized they weren't moving forward anymore. They'd grown smaller as we traveled and so I watched through the telescope trying to see what they were doing. We weren't over the Badlands any longer, I wasn't certain where we were, probably Kansas since we hadn't crossed the Mississippi River.

"They've stopped. I think they're searching for something." I kept watching, and saw several Hornets with smaller lights fly out of the Vimana's hangers. "The Dragonship is circling above them."

"Genevieve, turn around. We have to see why they've halted." The baron reached out for my telescope.

I handed it over and said, "Shouldn't we use this opportunity to get further away?"

Genevieve glanced over her shoulder and then turned the wheel causing us to make a sharp turn. "Maybe we will get lucky and they will have broken down."

The baron chuckled. "I doubt it, but stay low and approach from the south."

"Already on it," she said. Genevieve swooped far to the south and when we were less than a mile away, she landed.

We could see that the Vimana was on the ground with the Dragonship curled up beside it. Both vessels sat at the edge of a small canyon or scar dug into the prairie. I peered through my telescope and saw the swinging lanterns and torchlights of several soldiers, plus General Hendrix, walking down into the canyon.

"We need to get closer," the baron said. The baron started to stand, but he was still wobbly. We'd been traveling for a while with little to eat and he was weak.

"I do not think you should be moving through this chilly night air." Genevieve put her hand on her father's shoulder. He looked at her, but she cocked her head. "You still need to regain your strength. Alexander and I will go."

"We'll be back before you know it." I unwrapped the leather case around the telescope, slipped the lenses into the pouch, and put it in my bag.

"Alexander, leave your bag here." The baron pointed at me, and I knew what he meant: leave the Heart behind. I knew I should. I knew there was a chance we could get captured even if we were careful. But maybe the Amethyst Heart would signal to the others. For a moment, I didn't move. I didn't want to leave it. I glanced at Genevieve and then at the baron who held my gaze. Then I pulled the strap off my shoulder, dropped the bag in the airskiff, and Genevieve and I ran off into the night.

Stars tried to twinkle through the haze, but even the Milky Way, which should have arced over us like a river glittering in the heavens, was obscured by the blanket over the sky. The lights from the Vimana illuminated the scar in the ground, burning as bright as day. Beyond this glow, darkness, deeper than any other blackness I'd seen—or felt—surrounded their camp. It allowed us to get very close without being seen. We snuck up to the far side of the small canyon. The edge lay in shadow and peering into this place, we saw the Knights of the Golden Circle.

Hendrix walked from one side to the other looking at odd marks and pictographs on the trees and canyon walls. "Find the double J."

The soldiers fanned out and scoured the entire place. After several minutes two soldiers called out and waved their hands. "General, over here!"

Hendrix strode over and ran his hand along the deep groves of a back-to-back double J. It looked like an anchor with two swooping curls and a single vertical line. Hendrix raised an odd contraption, two disks with holes in them connected by a series of gears. He stood in front of the carving, sighting through the holes as he turned the two disks.

"The heart is over on that tree, and the lightning bolt is on the rock. Check it."

Soldiers moved to the two locations the General pointed out. One at the tree raised his hand, and then the other one at the rock, pointed and lifted his arm. Hendrix walked over to each spot and used the contraption to sight again. He adjusted the disks each time as if dialing in on some location. He had the soldiers pull ropes from the three locations until they all crisscrossed over a center point.

Hendrix pointed at the spot marked by the ropes, and said, "Dig here!"

I looked at Genevieve wondering what they were looking for, but she shrugged and we continued watching as his soldiers dug a hole, several feet deep. Their shovels thumped against something metal. Hendrix ran over, shoving the soldiers out of his way. He jumped into the hole, his mechanical arm switched from the hand to the rifle and he fired several shots. Then he bent over and stood up a minute later with a gold bar glimmering in the flood lights.

The soldiers cheered, and the rest of the Inner Circle walked over. Hendrix climbed out and handed the gold to Antiochus. "I present part of the Confederate States of America's Treasury. Hidden by one of the Knights of the Golden Circle, a Bushwacker from the Confederate Army in Missouri. There's another cache of gold bars just like it in Danville, Virginia. When I said money was no problem, I meant it!"

The soldiers kept digging and pulling metal chests out of the hole. They opened each one to reveal stacks upon stacks of gold bars and coins.

Genevieve turned to me and put her hand on my

shoulder. She motioned for us to retreat, and we slipped away from the edge and back into the shadows."

We moved slowly until we were too far away to heard, and then I said, "There's something familiar about all of this. We need to tell your father."

"Let's go," she said and took off running with me close on her heels. When we got back, he lay quietly in the airskiff. We jumped in and Genevieve sat next to her father, putting her hand to his forehead, "Gold," she said.

"Lots of gold," I added. "Chests full of gold bars and coins. Said it was the Confederate treasury."

"We knew they had caches all over the south." The baron shook his head, "This means they'll be able to double the size of their army for the final battle."

"I remember!" I pushed the hair off my forehead. "Danville. When the Confederacy was ending, Jefferson Davis sent the entire treasury out west so the Union wouldn't get the money. He hoped to rebuild. But in Danville, much of it was stolen, and never recovered. My father's office mate at Princeton was obsessed with the war."

The baron nodded. "The Knights of the Golden Circle probably stole the money so they could resurrect the Confederacy at a later date."

Genevieve said as she bundled her father, "Hendrix talked about resurrecting Emperor Burr's America."

"I heard him say that, too, but America never had an Emperor." I sat behind the controls of the airskiff and we lifted silently into the sky.

"Head east," the baron said as he struggled to keep his eyes open, "we need to make contact with the Knights Templar."

46
The Masons

We flew the rest of the night, and in the morning, passed over the biggest river I'd seen since India, and later over the tops of green-forested mountains, which were barely mountains compared to the Himalayas. It was late the following day when we flew into the nation's capital, Washington D.C.

I'd never been to the capital. I'd seen the crowded streets of New York and Boston, but Washington D.C. perched on the banks of the Potomac River looked spacious, with wide streets dotted with impressive stone buildings that gleamed white against the hazy, still-orange sky.

There hadn't been a blue canopy above us since the volcano exploded, and the ominous burning sky gave me the creeps. I knew a final battle loomed on the horizon. In fact, it soared toward us in a metal castle. With the world on fire, we appeared to be stepping onto a stage, one set for the end game. My only question – *Would we end the Golden Circle once and for all or fail to stop their diabolical plans?*

Looking over at the baron, I was worried. He didn't look good, and

needed a doctor as soon as possible. Hopefully, here in Washington D. C. we could get him one. Genevieve sat beside him, as she'd been doing since we left Hendrix.

"Where do I go?" I asked looking down at the city.

"A temple north of the White House, Scottish . . ." the baron mumbled.

"Just like Athens," I said. "A Templar base lay north of the Acropolis."

I spotted the White House, the gleaming white building in the center of the city. Before it, the towering Washington Monument remained unfinished, the top lying beneath scaffolding. I turned north and used the roads to guide me.

"What am I looking for?" I asked.

I couldn't hear the baron, but Genevieve turned to me and said, "Look for a compass and square." She looked perplexed as her brow scrunched up, but then she lit up. "Masons. Look for a Masonic Lodge."

Looking ahead, I saw a building marked with a compass and square in the brickwork. "Get ready for landing," I said, looking for the perfect spot. But there wasn't one. The street was crowded with people and carriages, and too many trees lined the road. "Maybe a crash landing."

Genevieve snapped a hard look at me, but then held onto her father. As we descended lower, people's faces turned skyward and horses reared and bolted. Apparently, no one had tried landing an airskiff on the streets of the capital before.

"LOOK OUT BELOW!" I bellowed as I clipped a wingsail on an oak tree. The struts crumpled like toothpicks and we spun completely around. I vented the hydrogen and we dropped right in front of the lodge.

Two horses pulling a carriage neighed and reared, bolting around us, causing the carriage to tilt onto two wheels. The passengers inside yelped and the driver cursed as the horses galloped down the street.

Grand Master Sinclair ran out of the lodge and stopped at the top of the steps as several soldiers rushed past him, surrounding us with rifles raised. I lifted my hands in surrender, while Genevieve helped her father up, and called out in a commanding voice, "Baron Kensington needs assistance." She pointed to two soldiers. "Help me get him inside the lodge."

They turned to Sinclair who nodded as he leaned on his cane. Then the two soldiers stepped over to the airship and helped the baron out. Rodin landed on Genevieve's shoulder as she moved alongside her father. I grabbed my bag, slung it across my shoulders, and climbed out.

"Take him to my quarters," Sinclair said to the soldiers as they swept past us.

"What are you doing here?" I asked.

"We got a message from the *Sparrowhawk*, and we've been expecting you. Or at least hoping you'd arrive." Sinclair held out his hand, and I shook it. "Welcome to Washington D.C. though I have to say, we expected the *Sparrowhawk*."

"We were separated back in China." I was about to ask if he'd heard anymore from them, but I remembered the Vimana, and asked, "The Golden Circle is right behind us. They may be here by morning."

"My spies have located them in Danville, Virginia." Sinclair said.

"More treasure." I paused and looked back at the White House. "They're getting the rest of the

Confederate Treasury."

"Come, let's get you inside. The Golden Circle most likely has spies watching our every move."

I nodded and followed him into the lodge as soldiers of the Templar Order grabbed the airskiff and dragged it out of the street.

As the door closed, Sinclair turned to me, "You certainly know how to make an entrance." He patted my back and led me from the foyer into a spacious meeting hall with a long table running down the center of the room. Each side was lined with chairs while paintings and symbols of the Masons decorated the walls. A man with dark hair, chiseled jaw, and a long bushy mustache stood about halfway down the table. He stood under the symbol of an eye in a pyramid, and had the same pin on his lapel. As he extended his hand to me, I saw his watch had the same symbol, and a thirty-three below it.

"Mister Armitage, I've heard a great deal about you."

"Thanks, but who are you?"

"My name is James Revere. I'm a Freemason and in charge of this Lodge."

"Revere, as in the Midnight Ride?"

"Yes, my ancestor was one of the several brave souls who famously warned everyone that the Redcoats were coming."

"Fascinating." I paused, "Can your members be trusted?"

"Of course." He crossed his arms as if annoyed by my question.

"I thought I could trust the Knights Templar, but since we discovered one of them has been a traitor for years, I'm a bit more cautious now."

Shock flashed across Sinclair's face. "You discovered the mole! Who?"

"Lord Marbury," Venom spewed as I said his name.

"Marbury!" Sinclair grabbed his chest as if he was having a heart attack. "I can't believe it!"

"He's with them now and on his way here. He's been working with them since they captured him."

"But that was years ago!" Sinclair leaned on his cane. He forced each breath out. "What is their plan then?"

I paused. I looked at both men, and wasn't certain if I should tell them. I didn't know if I could trust them, but I wouldn't be able to stop the Knights of the Golden Circle if I didn't tell them. A sweet but stern voice from behind me said, "Tell them, Alexander. We do not have much time."

Genevieve came and stood beside me. Sinclair nodded at her, and Mr. Revere stared at her, but mostly at the dragon on her shoulder.

"They're coming in a Vimana, protected by a Dragonship. They've got hundreds of armors and they plan to take over Washington D.C. and resurrect Emperor Burr's grand vision of America."

Sinclair shook his head and sank down into a chair. "But America's never had an Emperor."

"No, but there was a man who tried." Revere stroked his mustache. "Aaron Burr. After the duel when he shot and killed Alexander Hamilton, his political career was over. He would never be considered for the presidency. He fled south, declared himself Emperor of America, and tried to establish a dynasty there. Obviously, that didn't pan out too well for him."

"Gentlemen, the biggest danger is that the Iron

Horsemen are powered by the Hearts of the Horsemen, and the Golden Circle has enough metal to roll over any army we can gather."

"Oh, don't count us out yet, m'boy," Sinclair said in his Scottish drawl. "I brought the Black Knight, and the other Iron Armors with me when I crossed the Atlantic."

"Really?" Genevieve and I said in union.

"More than that, the Tinkerer came too, and he's been working on something new. I think you two will be pleased."

I smiled, turned to Genevieve. "Maybe we have a chance, after all."

A familiar voice caused me to spin around toward the door. "There's more, Alexander. I finished translating all the texts, and I think we have a way defeat them."

My father walked into the room as if we'd just seen each other over breakfast. He pushed his glasses back up onto the bridge of his nose and looked at me with a wide smile on his face. I stood, too stunned to move. He wrapped his arms around me and hugged me close. I paused, but then gripped him tight.

After a few awkward moments, he pushed me back, holding me at arm's length, looking me up and down. "It's good to see you, son." He took his glasses off and wiped his eyes. "I think you've grown. I've been—"

"I've thought a lot about you, too. But we'll have to save reunions for later."

Genevieve stepped up and embraced my father, and Rodin rubbed his head through my father's hair. "It is so good to see you," she said softly. "It is nice to be reunited."

Sinclair stood, leaning on his cane. "Indeed. We've all been very worried."

My father pulled away from Genevieve. "Come, let's go see the Tinkerer, and I'll tell you both what I've learned."

47
The Tinkerer
and Old Friends

My father, Genevieve, Rodin, and I climbed into a carriage and were whisked north to a sprawling house on the outskirts of the city. We didn't go inside but walked around back to a large workshop. I heard a hammer pounding and grinding on metal as we approached. The smell of oil and iron filled the air. The large doors on the side of the shed lay open, and framed within, was a large bellied man wearing half a suit and an apron on top. When he turned to us, I saw goggles with various lenses on the end of articulated brass arms. They enlarged his pupils, which looked like shiny marbles.

His face lit up, even if it was hard to see under his bushy black mustache, still curled and waxed at the ends. Thick stubble covered his face. The ring of hair around his head, as well as the top of his bald head, was covered in metal shavings, wood dust, and smudged grease. He looked like he hadn't left his shop in a week or more.

He exited the shed, his gait pulled to one side by the brace on his right knee. I ran over and hugged him.

"Tinkerer! I have missed you."

He squeezed me in a bear hug, lifting me off the ground, and in a thick Scottish drawl

said, "Alexander! Good to see you! Missed you, too, I did."

He turned to Genevieve and bear hugged her so that only a squeaky "*Hello Tinkerer,*" wheezed out of her.

He set her back down and bowed slightly. "Genevieve, I mean milady, it's so good to know you're safe. This one," he said pointing to me, "promised he'd find you. And he did!"

She smiled and leaned in close to Tinkerer. "Yes, but I actually had to rescue him."

The Tinkerer burst out laughing. "That sounds like our Alexander."

I laughed, too. A warmth swept over me, being around familiar faces, people I'd come to call friends, but hadn't seen in months. However, as much as I wanted to rejoice and hear everyone's stories, I knew we didn't have time. Not with the Vimana and Dragonship heading our way. "So, Tinkerer, is the Black Knight here?"

His smile grew even bigger. "Oh, come my friend." He motioned us into the shed. The center of the Tinkerer's workshop was packed with tools and chunks of metal, but the walls were still covered in the scythes, hoes, plows, and other tools that showed its original purpose.

"I knew we weren't done in Africa. Knew it, I did. So, I went right to work, put my brain to the problem, and came up with some true goodies."

The Tinkerer walked to the back of this shed and whipped off a tarp. The blackened iron armor underneath sent a jolt through me. The Black Knight looked brand new, and I instantly spotted the improvements. More armor plating around the midsection. A reinforced shield. Two cannons lay behind the shield, and more weapons had been attached to the arms. The huge sword was still slung across the back. My heart soared as I reunited with an old friend.

I ran my hand along the machine. "He's . . ." The words choked up in my heart. "I . . . Black Knight . . . we're back."

The Tinkerer clapped his hands. "I'm so glad you like it. I also made several changes inside. No longer a prototype, it's a proper armor now." He turned to Genevieve, "I fixed the Bronze Knight, too, milady. I may have even made a few feminine touches on the inside. No reason you can't have a little comfort in the middle of battle." He whipped the tarp off the Bronze Knight which gleamed in the fading light.

She ran over and touched the arm of her armor. The large, bronze shield was emblazed with her family's crest. Her fingers wound through the intricate design, and she wiped a tear from her eye. "Oh Tinkerer. On behalf of my father, I thank you as well."

"I've been working on a new one, too I just have the body finished. I still need to get it ready, but the Iron Templar, and Iron Zulu are here, too."

"Wait, who's going to pilot the Iron Zulu?" I looked at the Tinkerer and then at my father. "It would be wrong for anyone but Owethu to use it."

"Too true, Alexander," my father said. The Tinkerer's smile grew even bigger.

I heard the door of the house open and I spun on my heel, and a familiar face emerged. Taller than I remember, but still robust and dressed in a fine suit. Owethu ran from the porch. I sprinted toward him and we hugged like brothers.

"Alexander, my friend, my heart swells to see you again."

"Owethu, you came!"

"I told you, whenever you needed me, I would be there."

My vision swam with unshed tears at the sight of my friend. When I'd left Zululand, I wasn't certain if I'd ever see him again. I was overwhelmed and wasn't certain if my heart could take any more surprises.

He gripped my shoulder and said, "My family sends their warmest regards to my American brother."

"Tell them, I think of them often."

"I will."

He saw Genevieve and rushed to her. He stopped and bowed before her. "I am so glad to see you have been freed from that awful Milli-train."

She curtsied and bowed her head. "It is wonderful to see you again, Owethu."

I stepped beside Genevieve. "You'll be pleased to know the Milli-train was destroyed."

"That demonic machine is no more? What wonderful news."

My father looked at me, "How?"

"A dragon named *Āgō āmdhī* melted it with blasts of fire, again and again until it tumbled right off the mountainside."

Everyone fell silent as if I'd damped a fire with a blanket. I wasn't certain if it was the excited way I'd talked about the destruction of the Milli-train or the description of the dragon, but I think they suddenly realized what kind of adventure Genevieve and I had been on. My father might have been locked in his office, the Tinkerer might have spent endless weeks in his workshop, and Owethu might have traveled all the way from southern Africa, but we had been chasing our enemies across the top of the world. Genevieve and I had done so much in the last few months, and I wanted to tell them everything. Well, I might censor a few parts for my father, but we had more important things to do at the moment. The Knights of the Golden Circle were coming. I could feel them looming on the horizon.

I turned to the Tinkerer. "In Tibet we found a hidden valley with a factory that was mass producing armors, smaller than yours, but enough to protect a soldier."

"Mass production," he huffed. "The heart and soul might be the man inside, but the real magic of these machines comes from every hammer strike I make, and every weld I forge." He shook his head. "Your Black Knight won't fall to those knock-offs."

"I don't doubt that, but they have hundreds, and I fear for our forces. Plus, they have a Vimana, or flying castle, and a Dragonship, both armored and equipped with cannons and who knows what else." I pushed the hair out of my eyes again—sure that at any moment my father would tell me I needed a haircut—and said, "I'm afraid they mean to overwhelm us. They even have new Iron Horsemen."

The Tinkerer motioned for us to follow him. "Your father and I . . . well, he told me what he discovered, and I've been working on something that might help."

"One of the texts you sent me talked about how the Crusaders defeated the Horsemen of their time." My father pushed his glasses back onto the bridge of his nose. "The forces of nature can defeat them. They harnessed the earth itself and used landslides, tornados, and volcanoes to defeat the Horsemen. It is possible that we can do the same."

The Tinkerer yanked a tarp off his workbench revealing a long lance with a pronged tip and a large cylinder on the butt end. "I call it a Lightning Lance." It should render any armor or rider incapacitated if employed correctly."

"Fascinating," I said.

"That's not all. I also have a tornado creator and maybe one or two more tricks up my sleeve—if I can get them done in time."

I nodded. "We don't have much time, but we'll make it work." I looked at my father. "It makes sense to use Mother Nature."

A carriage pulled up in front of the house, and we all turned. The footman hopped off the back and opened the door. The Duke and his son, Richard, stepped down. The Duke glanced around with disgust on his face. Richard's eyes locked on me, and Genevieve standing beside me. Anger flashed across his face.

"What is *he* doing here?" The Duke asked.

48
Never

The Tinkerer stepped out of his workshop. "Your Grace, what brings you out today?"

The Duke and Richard walked past him without an answer and stepped over to Genevieve. The Duke eyed her outfit with disdain, but said, "My dear, we are so glad you have returned. Sinclair sent word that you'd arrived safe and sound, and then told me where you were. We've come to pluck you from this mediocrity and take you to a meeting where we will plan our response to the coming attack. Your observations might be needed."

"Thank you, Your Grace," Genevieve said dripping with sarcasm. "I would be happy to attend, but Alexander must as well, he has an even greater knowledge than I."

The Duke gave me a side-eye glance, sighed, and said, "The insolent pup is *not invited*, but if you *insist*, you may bring him along."

My eyes narrowed. I wasn't about to stand for this after all I'd done. "I—"

"See how it speaks without being spoken to?" he said to Richard. "Some lesser men just never learn." The Duke turned his back to me. "My son is positively

thrilled that you are safely returned to us, isn't that right, Richard?" He turned to Richard, who said nothing, but continued to stare daggers at me. "It is our hope to have you two married as soon as possible so we can put all this adventuring nonsense behind us, and you can give Richard an heir. It is, as you well know, of utmost importance that our noble lineage be continued. Now, let us proceed to the meeting. Our carriage is waiting."

Genevieve's mouth dropped open, and for a moment, I thought she might actually slap the ridiculous man. But she regained her composure and said, "It was so good of your son to show his concern while I was kidnapped, Your Grace. Too bad it was another who came after me." She took a deep breath and smoothed out her jacket. "I do thank you for alerting me to the meeting, and I am eager to give my account of the Knights of the Golden Circle. Alexander *will* accompany me, of course, both for his expertise, and as my escort. I thank you also for your offer of transportation, but we will take the carriage that brought us here." She made a delicate wave with her hand toward the front of the house where the carriages were waiting. "Please see that our driver has directions."

The Duke sputtered for a moment, then spun on his heel, and walked off. Richard, who had done nothing but stare at me during the whole exchange, had to run after him to catch up. The footman opened the door to the carriage, and the two stepped in. The Duke leaned out, said something, and closed the door. The footman ran over to the other coachman and then hurried to hop on the back of the Duke's carriage as it rolled off.

Genevieve stomped her foot and let out an exacerbated sigh. "By god, if that man does not just wiggle under my skin like a worm." She turned to me. "I am sorry he treats you in such a contemptible manner, but we should be going before he fills the rest of the Templars' heads with nonsense."

I nodded. "I can't stand him, either. But you're right. We need to get there before they do any damage."

She smiled, turned to my father, and gave him a light kiss on the cheek, which made him blush. "We will see you again soon."

I turned to the Tinkerer. "Before we go, I wanted to tell you that Mr. Singh is on his way on the *Sparrowhawk*, and we have a new friend who will be joining us, too. Do you think you can create an Iron Lotus?"

"An Iron Lotus?" The tinkerer turned his head slightly and twirled his mustache between his fingers. "Hmm . . . yes . . . well . . . right . . . I think I can do that."

"She likes knives and uses an owl like a weapon."

He raised his finger as an idea came to him. He nodded and walked off into his workshop, already deep in thought. I turned to Owethu and my father. "I have to go, but will return soon. Can you help the Tinkerer until I get back?"

Owethu nodded. "It would be my honor."

My father said, "There's something you should know before you walk into this meeting and get blindsided. The Americans and the British have been arguing about how best to defeat the Horsemen. You're stepping into a hornet's nest that's been building for months. Be careful."

"We'll try, but they need to hear what we have to say."

Genevieve took my father's hands, "We will be the

bridge that brings them together, or we will build a bridge of our own." She looked at me and then turned back to my father. "Do not worry. We will return soon."

"I hope your father recovers quickly," my father said as we turned to head to the carriage.

She smiled, but it faded quickly. "Thank you. I do, too."

Genevieve and I climbed into the carriage, and Rodin flew in through the window. After telling the driver to get us to the meeting as quickly as possible, we took opposite seats and waved goodbye as we pulled away from the house. As soon as we were down the lane, she moved next to me. Rodin curled up across from us, and I took her hand, interlocking our fingers.

"I know we were just visited by—"

She turned to me and put her finger to my lips. "I do not want to talk about that right now." She leaned her head against my shoulder and pulled my hand into her lap.

The driver took Genevieve at her word, and we sped toward our destination in Georgetown, nestled on the banks of the Potomac River.

"I know you, and you will not be able to hold your tongue," Genevieve said. "It is something I like about you." She kissed the back of my hand. "Know that I support you, and will be by your side. They need to hear what we—what you—have to say."

"Thank you. Having you at my side means I don't need anyone else. I know what has to happen. They must take on that army of armors, while we take on the Iron Horsemen. They won't like it, but I really do know how to defeat them. At least I think I do."

"We will. I have faith."

"I'm glad you do. Sometimes I fear I'm too much like Diogenes. Too cynical for my own good. I do know if we can defeat the Inner Circle here . . . I think they are too fractured to continue."

Leaning in, Genevieve kissed my cheek. I turned toward her and she kissed me. We didn't stop until the carriage came to a halt. She slid to the door to step out, but I grabbed her hand, slipped my arm around her, and pulled her back to me. With her pressed against me, I smiled. "After this week, everything is going to change."

Her eyes lit up as she stared into mine.

"There's something I've wanted to tell you. I want you by my side, like this, always." I leaned closed and put my forehead against hers. "I never want to be apart again."

She bit her lip, but didn't answer. I knew she couldn't, but I knew what thoughts passed through her mind. Our lives were too complex for idle talk. But I wanted her to know how I felt, how she made me feel. With her beside me, a surge of confidence roared through me like a dragon's call. I felt the leather strap across my chest and shoulders and the weight of the Amethyst Heart in my bag and recognized something else, a deeper, darker feeling. I knew what I wanted, and nothing would stop me from seizing it.

She touched my face, and with a quick kiss I let her go. We slipped out of the carriage and stood before an old wood building. I saw the symbols of the Freemasons on the door and elsewhere on the building. Another lodge.

Inside, light flickered from sconces on the walls in the hallway, and as we entered the great hall with elaborate high-backed chairs arranged in a circle, candle flames danced from the towering candelabras. The Duke, with Richard next to him, Grand Master Sinclair, Eustache de Moley, James Revere, and several other Templar Knights and Freemasons were already seated. They fell silent as we entered and stared at us as we approached. Genevieve curtsied, and I bowed, but without seats, we had to stand on the edge of the circle.

"Welcome," Grand Master Sinclair said. "For those who don't know, allow me to introduce Genevieve Kensington, daughter of Baron Maximillian Kensington, and Alexander Armitage, son of Professor John Armitage of Eton College."

The Duke took a drink from a goblet and said, "They are here because they have accompanied the baron around the world and seen the enemy. Since he is ill and cannot attend, I have asked his daughter to join us."

I swallowed the anger building within me. The Duke would never change. He almost proved Hendrix's point about the Templar being out of touch, but I knew there were others who welcomed me here.

Eustache nodded to me. I smiled at my old friend, but his face held a troubled expression.

Sinclair ignored the Duke and addressed the other men. "Our spies have spotted their airships heading this way. They come in a flying fortress and intend to send an army upon this very city. Alexander and Genevieve, please explain a bit more about their intentions. Tell them what you told me."

Genevieve looked at me, and pointed to herself. I nodded and she began. "They are determined to destroy the Templars and the US Government in one final battle. General Hendrix has already killed anyone who opposed him. The latest was Xerxes, a Persian member of the

Inner Circle. Alexander witnessed this. The Pirate Queen Zerelda is dead as well; she plunged into a volcano. We both witnessed this. The Heart she carried was destroyed, which means they now possess three of the Crusader Hearts and two of the Ancient Hearts, the ones from Malta." She looked at me and at the bag around my shoulder.

I added, "The Vimana, the flying fortress that Grand Master Sinclair spoke of is more heavily armed than any airship in your armada. It carries thousands of soldiers and hundreds of battle armors. They aren't as powerful as the Iron Armors like the Black Knight, but they'll decimate your troops. The Dragonship is heavily armored and more maneuverable than any airship you have—more than anything you can imagine—and together they will wipe your armies away like insects. But worse, if we do defeat them, they know they can use the hearts like a bomb. They'll unleash the power in one act and destroy the city. Either way, they win."

Mr. Revere leaned on his elbow "You make it sound like we are doomed before we even begin the battle."

"On the contrary, I'm trying to make you understand the severity of the situation and what is at stake. But, my father has discovered a power that can defeat the Hearts once and for all."

The Duke waved his hand as if to dismiss me. "We already have a plan. We will face them in combat, defeat their armies, rip the Hearts from the Horsemen, and you won't have to worry about them anymore."

"No. You won't." I said. "You cannot defeat them with traditional armies or traditional weaponry."

The Duke stared at me with narrow, hate-filled eyes. "We're enacting the plan that should have been implemented in London."

"Nothing has changed from London. The baron is not ready for combat, and," Eustache pointed to his chest, "with my clockwork heart, I should not be in battle. Besides, you and the Masons have never piloted these armors."

"And," I said, "Lord Marbury is the mole; he knows that plan. They'll be expecting you, anticipating every move you make."

"They will not be able to defeat us. We are the one with the righteous cause, with God on our side." The Duke took a deep breath, "We've heard enough from this school boy, time to let the men fight. You are dismissed."

"What!" I stared at him as my blood boiled and my hand twitched at my side. "I will *not* be cast aside. This is *my* fight."

"*Your* fight? What a pompous . . ." The Duke could barely speak. "The armors will be piloted by knights, not boys!"

Revere raised his hands, in order to quell our anger. "Gentlemen, please, let's take a moment to calm down. Alexander, you've done great work, but we have warriors and generals who will take it from here." He looked to Sinclair, who held his head in his hands. "We will have a mix of Masonic members and Templar Knights. All of whom have served in the military. We are the best qualified for this task."

I eyed Sinclair, and he nodded, but couldn't look at me. With a furrowed brow Eustache shook his head. Genevieve put her hand on my arm and Richard cringed. The Duke's face contorted with a smug grin. The burning within me, erupted like the volcano. Rage ripped at every inch of my skin as if something were trying to break free.

I turned to Sinclair. "Am I to be made a Templar?"

He looked at me, but before he could answer, the Duke laughed, "You?" He chuckled, the annoying noble laugh that was too constrained to be an expression of joy. No, it was a sign of contempt. "You will never be a Templar Knight, you insolent pup."

I stormed into the center of the chairs, seizing the room like Captain Baldarich would. I stared at each one of them before focusing on the Duke. "First, I don't care what you think or what you've planned. Second, I'm no longer a school boy; I'm a Sky Raider. Third, I'm going to tell you how this battle will unfold and you are going to listen. Indihar Singh will be here soon along with the crew of the *Sparrowhawk*. When they arrive, Genevieve, Indihar, Owethu, Lianhua, and I will take the Iron Armors into battle. Why? Because we have the most experience fighting the Iron Horsemen." I turned to Revere and Sinclair. "Your forces will engage the Knights of Golden Circle's armors and airships. You're going to need all those experienced military men if you want this country to remain whole. I suggest you line up every single soldier and cannon you can find in front of the White House and the Capitol Building. That's where he's going, and that is where I will be. This isn't about your egos or mine. General Hendrix is coming here to become Emperor Hendrix. He killed Kannard and seized control of the Inner Circle to create an American Empire that will spread tyranny across the world. He has claimed the gold hidden by the remnants of the Confederacy— Genevieve and I witnessed this—and he can buy each one of you ten times over. Including you." I turned and stared right at the Duke. "I've spent three years of my life fighting the Golden Circle. My ancestors gave their lives fighting against the Hearts of the Horsemen, and for all Hendrix's, faults he knows one thing to be true, and he made me realize this truth, and now I'm going to explain it to each of you. I, like Alexander the Great before me, will determine the outcome of this battle."

I heard a laugh and turned toward Richard who clamped a hand over his mouth. I met his eyes with a withering stare and continued. "You think this is hubris? You think I'm crazy? Well, let's see what you think once the Vimana gets here. Listen well and know that whichever side I am on will be the winner. I'm going to give everything I have to destroying the Iron Horsemen and preventing their world from emerging. Everyone I care about will be in this fight, my father, my friends, Genevieve. They all might die. But I am going to harness the power of Mother Nature herself to defeat them. You can try and stand in my way, but that would be foolish." I started to walk away but I stopped, and turned to face the Duke again. "I'm going to win this battle, and then I'm coming to find you!" I stormed off as the Duke let out a choked up noise I'd never heard before.

As I reached the hallway, I heard Genevieve. "Don't you get it? This isn't about the Templars and the Golden Circle, this is about freedom and tyranny." I heard the Duke, but couldn't understand him. Genevieve replied, "No. I will be at Alexander's side. I will be in my Bronze Knight, and there is nothing you can do to stop us from saving you all."

She burst out of the room. "We have to get back to the workshop before they try to take the armors."

We stepped outside to find a different carriage waiting. The driver sitting atop the perch was a familiar red-headed Irishman.

Genevieve stopped in her tracks. "Finn? What are you doing here?"

"No time for lovely reunions. Get in! Your father sent me. Had a feeling you wouldn't take kindly to the Templars and Freemasons telling you what to do." As we climbed in, he grumbled. "It's not the steamcarriage, stupid thing has actual horses—*ugh!*—but I'll manage, now let's get you out of here."

He snapped the reins just as I pulled the door closed and saw Revere rushing out of the lodge with several men behind him. He pointed at us and shouted, but we were already on our way.

BOOK III: IRON LOTUS

We arrived back at the Tinkerer's workshop. Finn jumped off and let us out of the carriage. We all ran into the shed and I called out, "Tinkerer, are you in here?"

"In the back," a Scottish drawl called out from behind the armors.

"We need your help," Genevieve said. "They're coming for the Bronze Knight and all the rest of your inventions."

"Who?"

"Sinclair, Revere, and the Duke." I pushed my two front locks off my forehead, "They want to use the Iron Armors instead of us."

"But I customized them for each of you." The Tinkerer looked at the two of us. "They'll probably arrest me for this, but . . . grab those spiky things in the corner and follow me."

In the corner of the shed, we found long iron spikes with coils wrapped around the top. I picked up two, Genevieve grabbed a couple, and she asked Finn to bring the last two. We met the Tinkerer outside the shed.

He turned to us. "Place those at the four corners of the property, an extra one at the road, and the last one by the shed."

"What are they?" I asked.

"A little something I was making to trap the Iron Horsemen. I designed it off the electromagnet they used in London. It will create an electromagnetic barrier that will keep anyone out of here."

"Perfect," Genevieve said.

Once we'd placed the coils around the house, I linked them with a cable, and the Tinkerer threw a large switch. Each coil sparked and arched electricity between them. A low hum surrounded us. I couldn't see anything, but the hair on my arms stood on end as I approached one of the coils. We were surrounded by an electromagnetic field.

I walked over to the Tinkerer. and said, "That is so cool."

"You want to see cool?" He took a wrench and threw it at the coil. About three feet from the spike, the wrench bounced off an invisible wall and fell into the dirt at the Tinkerer's boots. He bent down and picked it up. "We're protected."

"Fascinating," I said, raising my thumbs.

"We're not done yet; I need you to load the Iron Armors while I finish the Iron Lotus."

"Done; we'll all pitch in to get everything ready." I turned to Owethu and Genevieve, "Let's get to work." They nodded in agreement.

My father stepped out of the house. "What is going on? I just tried to step out the front door and was knocked back to the kitchen."

We all laughed, and I said, "Sorry, an

electromagnetic barrier around the house, the Templars and Masons are coming to take the Iron Armors."

"Alexander, what did you do?" He put his hands on his hips.

"The Duke and Richard are not the ones who will defeat the Iron Horsemen. I won't let the world be destroyed because of their egos."

He pushed his glasses up onto the bridge of his nose and nodded. "I agree with that. Anything I can do to help?"

I smiled as my joy burst forth. He was on my side. For the first time, he'd chosen me over the Templars. "The Tinkerer might need some help with the new armor he's creating."

We dove in and did everything the Tinkerer asked. I carried shells to each of the armors, and then loaded some into the Black Knight as Owethu and Genevieve did the same. I opened the chest plate of my armor and stared inside. The Tinkerer wasn't kidding. He'd made it a proper armor. He'd cushioned the bicycle seat, and given me a padded back and headrest. I climbed inside and reached into the arms. The Tinkerer had even wrapped the handles so they didn't bite into my skin anymore. Gauges stacked one on top of the other, told me the steam pressure, the oil pressure, and a split-flap display of how many rounds were left in the guns.

I looked up and saw the Tinkerer standing in front of the Black Knight. His large grin matched mine. He chuckled and I said, "I don't know what to say but thank you! He's great. I love what you did to him."

"You're most welcome. I figured it was time to upgrade 'em. These armors have been through a rough couple of years. They needed some love." He came up and pointed to a chain up by my head. "I added a steam whistle, like a train. I figure, in a noisy battle, you can use it to alert, or call, the other armors."

"Brilliant."

"Thanks. Each of them has one." His eyebrows popped up, "Which reminds me I'd better add that to the new armor." He motioned for me to follow. "There's something else I need to show you how to use… the tornado machine."

"Definitely." I was about to climb out when we heard electricity sparking, and a low thrumming noise from the barrier. "What was that?"

"Someone's trying to break my barrier."

"I've got this." I fired up the Black Knight, and he churned to life. As the heater built up the steam pressure, I closed the hatch and lowered the helmet's visor. Once the steam had brought the armor to life, which took much less time than before, I rolled out of the shed to the end of the driveway.

Two armored steam-carriages, with Gatling guns mounted on top, sat on the other side of the barrier. Several soldiers stood in a line with guns at the ready. Behind them, three carriages had pulled up. Sinclair and a couple of Templar I didn't recognize were in the one with the open top. The next one I recognized as the Duke's closed-top carriage, and Mr. Revere was in a buggy.

The Duke shouted something, and the soldiers raised their rifles. I didn't make a move. They fired. The bullets bounced off the barrier and flew back at the soldiers. Two were hit but one bullet struck the Duke's carriage and he fell back from the window.

"I'm not your enemy!" I rolled the Black Knight to edge of the barrier. "Do not make me one!"

Sinclair stood in his carriage, leaning on his cane. "Let's talk about this, Alexander. We're all on the same side."

"Are we?" As the soldiers formed back into a line, I lowered my cannon. "As the Duke said, I am not a Templar. Nor am I a Mason. You have rejected my help, yet I hold the key to defeating the enemy. If you truly wanted to defeat them, you would use all your resources. You would listen to Genevieve and me. But you refuse. If it's up to us to save the world, we'll do it without you!"

"Alexander," Sinclair said, "we need to talk…"

"Fire!" The Duke yelled from inside his carriage. The soldiers fired and once again their bullets bounced off the barrier. "You idiots, aim at those coils." They fired again and the bullets shot in every direction hitting a soldier in the leg. "Steam-carriages at the ready!"

Sinclair turned toward the Duke. "Calm down, Your Grace! You'll only end up hurting yourself and all our men."

Rage nearly overwhelmed me, I wanted to rip the barrier down and charge the Duke. My cannon was already aimed at his carriage. I could blast him with both barrels and follow through with my sword. This whole mess would be over in a moment. I reaffirmed my grip on the controls, but the Black Knight seemed to hold me back. I wanted to kill him. I wanted to end this.

"I am taking command!" The Duke pointed out the window. "Fire!"

A Gatling gun roared to life and lead rained down on one of the steam-carriages. A shadow cast over the ground, and I pushed the visor up. Leaning forward, I looked up and saw the *Sparrowhawk* hovering above and the soldiers on the ground scattering and took cover.

Sinclair yelled, "Get these men out of here, before something worse happens."

The *Sparrowhawk* fired a grappling line and it struck the ground beside me. Mr. Singh slid down, and Lianhua followed. Kō'ilā swooped down from above. As Mr. Singh landed, he looked at me. "What in the world is going on?"

"I'll explain later, but I am so glad to see you!"

They ran toward Genevieve, who stood with the Tinkerer outside the workshop. I turned back to Sinclair who still stood in his carriage. The soldiers climbed onto the armored carriages and began rolling down the street, but Sinclair didn't move. He stared at me and nodded his head.

"We need to work together," I said. "We can stop them. I know it." I climbed out onto the shoulder of the Black Knight. "Have faith in that."

"I hope you know what you're doing. I promise I'll get every soldier I can to the White House and Capitol Building!" Sinclair saluted with the tip of his cane, and sat back in his carriage as it started down the street.

"We'll be there!"

50
The Battle For
Washington D.C.

The *Sparrowhawk* landed beside the workshop outside the barrier, but I turned off one of the coil-spikes to let them in. I hugged Captain Baldarich. My heart soared seeing the crew again. I was so glad they'd made it safely out of China. Plus, they had contacted the Templars, which was the only reason anyone in Washington D.C. was ready for the Golden Circle at all.

"Great to see you, kid, but we'll have to save the pleasantries for later. The Vimana and Dragonship are right behind us." Captain Baldarich released me and bear-hugged Genevieve.

"We are ready for them," she said, muffled by his embrace.

"I have a plan, but would you be willing to cut some holes in the underside of the *Sparrowhawk*?" He eyed me with a raised eyebrow and I added, "To carry the armors into battle. Two of them."

He stroked his mustache. "This'd better be good." He waved to the *Sparrowhawk* and walked over to the barrier.

I turned to Lianhua. "I told you I didn't think our meeting was coincidence—the girl with the owl from my dreams. The Tinkerer has made you something, and if you want to fight with us, we'd be honored to have you."

Mr. Singh looked at me and then around the workshop. "He made her an armor?"

I nodded. "He did. Customized it for her, too."

She eyed both of us. "I thought I was fighting with you already. And what is this . . . armor?"

"You are," Genevieve said with a smile. "You have been invaluable, but this is something special."

Mr. Singh took her hand. "I know we helped you with The Spice Merchant, but that doesn't make you indebted to our cause. You've helped your people and the people of Tibet, and if you want to sit this part out, no one would think less of you. But we'd be honored to have you on our side against this great evil."

"I would fight for you, but that is not why I will fight this day. I know what a life in chains means. I've lived it. I know what life is like without choice, where others make the decisions for you. Now that I am free, I would not see the whole world fall into chains."

"Then follow me. There is someone I want to introduce you to." We walked into the shed and the Tinkerer pulled the tarp off an armor.

"I call her the Iron Lotus!" the Tinkerer said with a bow.

The outer iron plates, painted red and decorated with a couple of lotus flowers, looked like robes around the dark metallic warrior. A metal spike rose off the helmet and a long plume of red hair spilled down the back. A round shield with a golden lotus flower in the center covered twin cannons. Instead of the large sword like my armor, he'd used the various blades in the shed to make knives. Like the other armors, it stood on two tracked oversized feet, and towered about twice as tall as we were. Similar to the Black Knight, twin smoke stacks extended off the steam tank and engine on the back.

"She's got the cannons mounted underneath the shield," the Tinkerer said. "Grapplers on the hips for stabilizing if the need arises. Two knives on each side and six on the back. Alexander said you liked knives. He also mentioned your owl, so I put a stand in the armor and the arm is padded on the forearm." He opened the chest plate and Lianhua looked inside. Her face lit up and she climbed inside.

"Tiny pedals for my feet!"

"Like I said, the Tinkerer customized it for you."

She locked eyes with me. "Thank you for this new life, Alexander." Kō'ilā landed on her perch inside the armor. "We will be honored to fight at your side."

"Thank you, but it is I who am honored to have all of you at my side." I looked around at the Sikh, my crewmate, who always gave more of himself than he asked of others; the Zulu warrior, who fought for family and honor and showed me what true nobility meant; the Chinese maiden, who guided me through darkness and taught me the truth of freedom—that it was as essential to life as air and water; and lastly, I locked eyes with Genevieve. She'd been by my side since the beginning, in the good times of Paris and bad times of battle. I didn't want to travel through life with anyone else. She'd taught me who I truly was, who I was meant to be. The emotion nearly choked me, but I managed to say, "I couldn't face this tyranny without all of you."

The Tinkerer stepped forward, tears in his eyes that

he kept loudly snuffling back to keep them from falling. "Remember, they might have oil for blood and iron for bones, but it is you, their drivers, that are their souls. Though each of you alone is only a soldier, together, working as one you are a force of nature."

With his words still lingering in the air, we each climbed into our armors. "There isn't enough time for a last meal together," I said. "We'll have to share that after the battle. I hope to see you all." Everyone nodded, the excitement faded from the shed. The tension thickened as each of us thought about what was to come. I worried about each of my friends as they climbed inside their Iron Armors. I prayed, if anyone here couldn't make the meal, to let it be me.

I slipped down onto the seat inside of the Black Knight. The armor still chugged from my run in with the Duke earlier. I took a deep breath and looked over at the Bronze Knight. Genevieve pulled her hair back and tied it in a knot at the nape of her neck, and Rodin sat on her shoulder. I wanted to say something, I wanted to kiss her for luck, but it wasn't the time. As I reached up to close my visor, she looked over and her sweet smile washed over me.

I pulled the five of us together. All the armors in a circle. The sight was intimidating, and I couldn't help but smile. I explained my plan. If they didn't like it, they didn't say anything. Once I was done, I raised my cannons to salute them. They returned the gesture, and, after the Tinkerer shut down the barrier, we raced off. I stopped and opened my visor. "Thank you. For everything."

"Wait, Alexander." The Tinkerer held up two of the coil-spikes. "Here take these, you might need them." He attached them to the back of the Black Knight, and I rushed over to the *Sparrowhawk*.

The crew was hard at work modifying the underside. The Bronze Knight and my Black Knight waited as the other three, the Iron Zulu, Iron Templar, and Iron Lotus rolled off toward the White House.

The *Sparrowhawk* lifted off and hovered above us. Once we were attached by thick chains, the Iron Armors were ratcheted up to their shoulders into slots on the underside of the gun deck. The aero-dirigible struggled to gain altitude but was able to take us up into the clouds. Dangling underneath, we swayed in the wind. Fear rippled through me and bile burned the back of my throat. I held my hand out and pressed my palm against the chest plate. "Let's do this, and let's survive, okay Black Knight?"

Then my hand drifted down to my leather bag. I reached in and felt the sharp angled lines of the amethyst crystal and the cool silver wire coiled around it, and my thoughts drifted to the power I'd seen. I could claim it as my own and defeat these enemies easily. I took a deep breath, opened the bag and looked down at the Horsemen's Heart. I was about to pull it out when Hunter knocked on the Black Knight's helmet. I quickly closed the flap and opened the visor.

"We're almost there," he yelled over the whipping wind. "Get ready to drop!" He held up his thumb and I did the same. I closed the visor.

Turning my attention to the battlefield, I looked down at the national mall. Sinclair had done his part: troops, artillery batteries, the Templar Aircorps, and the cavalry—all forces of the Templars and Freemasons— were lined up in front of, or hovering above the White House and the Capitol Building. All the marble and columned buildings reminded me of the Acropolis

– where this journey had begun. Looking toward the southwest, coming over Alexandria, I saw the Vimana with the Dragonship circling around it.

The sky still burned bright orange. I couldn't tell if it was dawn, dusk, or midday. As if the horror of the sky witch and the power she'd unleashed loomed over the entire world.

The Vimana crossed the Potomac and landed on the riverbank. Huge doors opened and the armors, cannon carriages, and two of the Iron Horsemen charged out. Hundreds of gun ports slid open and large cannons emerged to hurl lead and fire at the troops protecting the capital.

With the Vimana on the ground and the Dragonship flying toward the armies, we had the perfect opportunity to board the Vimana. It might be a fortified base but every castle could be besieged. In the air, it would move about the battlefield raining death, but on the ground it was vulnerable.

The *Sparrowhawk* dove toward the Vimana. I was in front and had the perfect view. I could see the top, the huge propellers atop the towers, and the large windows of the control deck. Hunter pounded twice on my helmet and released the chains. The Black Knight dropped toward the Vimana, barely slowed by the chute I was dragging above me. I braced myself for the impact, uncertain if I'd bounce off the armored shell or punch right through.

I slammed down on the top ring of the Vimana, and rolled forward to get out of the Bronze Knight's landing space. I spun around as Genevieve's armor landed in the same spot I'd just left. I raised my shield to salute her and when she did the same, I knew she was okay.

We lurched as the Vimana lifted off. I gathered myself and aimed my cannons at one of the towers, but before I could fire, the glass windows of the control deck shattered. Two Iron Horsemen burst through and landed in front of us. I recognized the Horseman of War right away, General Hendrix atop his new red-shrouded steed. It was bigger than the last one, with more weapons, but the same inner fire glowed within the iron plates of the steed. The iron horse snorted fire and smoke, and its glowing eyes made we wonder if it was alive or just demonically possessed metal. Hendrix, in his dark, black cloak with the hood drawn far over his face, roared and lifted a huge sword in the air.

The wind whipped the hood off the horseman beside him. Sitting on the back of the green shrouded steed of famine was the baroness, Genevieve's mother.

General Hendrix charged forward and slammed his sword down on me, trying to cleave me in half. I blocked with my shield as I drew the large sword from the Black Knight's back. I thrust the large slab of metal and tried to impale Hendrix. He slashed at my sides and I parried his blade with my shield.

Through the visor of the Black Knight's helmet, I saw Genevieve and her mother locked in combat. My heart raced, the last time they'd faced each other, in the Zulu village, her mother had bested Genevieve with a sword. However, Genevieve had been conflicted. Her mother was saying what she wanted to hear. This time was different. This time she knew better. This time, she wanted to defeat her mother.

I couldn't watch Genevieve, Hendrix pressed his attack, and I defended against each strike. My shield was dented, scratched, and nicked, but I knew it would hold, for now. I had a mission. I wasn't here to keep Hendrix occupied. This Vimana had to be brought down. I rolled back and aimed my cannons at one of the towers. Hendrix charged. I had only

a moment before he reached me. I fired. Smoke and fire exploded from the top barrel and the shell pierced through the armor plating protecting the propeller mechanics.

Hendrix slammed his sword down and I blocked it with my steel plate blade. The Gatling guns on the flanks of his steed roared to life and my chest plate was pelted with bullets. I pushed my shield between us. The bullets bounced off, and I tried to impale Hendrix but the Horseman of War leapt back and avoided my blade. I quickly checked the tower I'd shot, but the propeller still spun at full speed.

An explosion rocked my armor as Genevieve's Bronze Knight blasted one of the towers with both her cannons. The shells ejected and two more rounds slid forward into the breach. Her mother slammed her hooves against the Bronze Knight's shield. Genevieve took the hit and pushed the black shrouded steed off.

We fought atop the Vimana in a desperate attempt to damage it, but from what I was seeing, we wouldn't be enough. I needed part two of my plan. I charged Hendrix's red steed of War as it reared up. The Black Knight's shoulder smashed into the hooves and I used the shield as I'd seen Owethu do at the Zulu village. Coming under the hooves, I lifted the steed up exposing its belly. I pushed forward on the controls and shoved the Iron Horsemen back into the control room of the Vimana.

As Hendrix smashed through the glass, I rolled over to the edge. Opening the visor, I fired off a flare. The bright red ember soared over the battlefield below, drifting on the wind. I searched for my father in the field below. I spotted a carriage by the unfinished Washington Monument. Finn drove the steam-carriage with the

Tinkerer's tornado engine. My father and the baron jumped out to set up the machine. They arranged nine fans in a circle. Each fan had a metal covering to direct the wind. As the fans started to churn, I saw a whirlwind form in the center.

Owethu, in the Iron Zulu, fought the Golden Circle armors. He sped back and forth engaging all their forces with the cannons on his armor and his giant Zulu short spear, the *Iklawa*. He fought with the ferocity of a lion and plowed through his enemies. I raised my sword in salute. The Templars and Freemasons fired from their positions, and the batteries blasted the Golden Circle's forces, but Owethu was in the thick of it, single-handedly keeping the armors away from the White House and Capitol Building.

Then I saw the Dragonship circle to make another pass. A swath of fire had already engulfed some troops. Lianhua and Mr. Singh maneuvered into position under the metallic dragon, and as it blew fire from its gaping jaws, the Iron Lotus and Iron Templar fired the two grapplers on their hips. The hooks sank into the sides of the dragon and both armors were pulled into the air. Retracting the cables, they pulled themselves onto the Dragonship as it undulated back into the sky and tore through a Templar airship sending the flaming wreck crashing to the ground.

Turning to search for Genevieve, I caught a glimpse of Hendrix charging on his Iron Horseman. I pivoted my armor to get my shield in front of his hooves as he slammed them against me. The force was so intense, it knocked the Black Knight off the edge of this ring. I smashed into the tower one level down. The Horseman of War jumped down onto my tier.

Hendrix laughed from atop his steed as I struggled to free myself and stand again. "You cannot hope to win. Look," he gestured to the battlefield. The Vimana's guns were decimating the troops below. Most of the artillery batteries were already destroyed. He appeared to be targeting them first. "Next my machines will destroy the very houses of democracy. I will build my new empire on its ashes just as Emperor Burr wished."

"Never!" I pushed forward on the controls and the armor ripped free. I charged with my sword lowered like a lance. He jumped out of the way, but rounded his horse. The iron plates on the steed's chest opened up and revealed three cannon barrels and a Gatling gun. Hendrix fired. The first slammed into my side, I pivoted the shield intercepting the second and third. Bullets pinged off the armor.

I closed the distance between us and slashed with my sword. Hendrix blocked with his large blade. I pulled on the controls in the arm and pushed on his sword. We struggled against each other, both attempting to assert our dominance. I wanted to send my blade through him, to separate the metal half from the half of flesh. My anger rose and rage burned on the back of my neck.

His wide eye screamed while the other sparked; we both wanted to kill the other.

A tornado whipped up beside the Vimana. The swirling wind arced toward one of the four towers, but missed and struck the side of the Vimana. The tornado ripped a cannon from its port and destroyed several gun installations. The winds churned up the side of the fortress and slammed into Genevieve and her mother on the level above. Genevieve rolled back using her shield to deflect as much of the wind as possible. The Horseman of Famine jumped out of the wind, landing on the far side of the Vimana.

The cyclone ripped through the armored troops below us. I saw a couple of men in Golden Circle armor whipping about in the wind, only to be tossed out. The winds dissipated as the vimana moved off from the generator below.

Hendrix roared. "Do you think a little wind will bring my flying castle from the sky?"

"The forces of nature can stand up to the power of the Hearts." I raised my sword, pulling on the controls of the Black Knight, preparing to strike.

"Nothing is as powerful as the Hearts. You could know this power, but no, you refused me. I offer the world and you raise your sword to me."

"It's my duty to stop the Hearts."

"Duty." Hendrix threw back his head and laughed. "Whose duty? The Templars? The Freemasons? The nobles? You're none of those things."

I charged, swinging the sword, but the Horseman easily leapt over me. But I wasn't trying to hit him, I wanted to give myself an opening. I aimed the two cannons under my shield at one of the towers. I squeezed the triggers and both cannons fired. The rounds slammed into the tower. I saw the explosion before I heard it. Black smoke billowed from the top of the tower, but the propellers continued to spin, and the Vimana remained aloft.

I rolled to the edge and looked over. My father and the baron were setting up to generate another tornado. Owethu in Iron Zulu kept the armored army at bay. I only had to keep Hendrix distracted a little longer and the Vimana would fall.

I spun around and faced the Horseman of War. "Hendrix. I fight because it's what the Armitage do. It's what my friends do. Indihar stands up to tyranny in all its forms. Lianhua stands up to those that would put her in chains. Owethu defends his family and friends. Genevieve fights to redeem her mother. I fight . . . I fight for all them."

Rage flamed in Hendrix's eye, the right one sparking bright white with electricity. He charged, firing the chest cannons, and swinging his sword. I set my shield to take the hits and parried his blade with my own.

My shield buckled under the constant fire. He moved faster than I ever could, and hit my armor in one of the joints. I pulled on a lever inside the armor to eject the shells, and pushed another to load two more rounds. As I did, he dropped the blade under my shield and thrust. It pierced the armor and ran right past me. I looked down, fear rising that I had been stabbed, but no pain overtook me. My vest was cut but not my skin. I moved the arm with the shield and cannons pressed the barrels against the side of his steed. I fired both barrels and knocked the Horseman of War into the tower.

Another tornado ripped up the side of the tower, shearing the armor plating, and ripping the mechanics to bits. I lost Hendrix in the maelstrom. The Vimana lurched and tilted to one side. The Black Knight started to slide and I had to speed up to remain in place. The Vimana twisted as it fell and the tornado shredded the side.

The flying fortress was heading toward the Potomac. I had to get off, but that didn't look possible. The *Sparrowhawk* flew over and Bronze Knight dangled from a grappling line. I saw Hunter manning the second grappling gun, which was usually used to snare airships.

He fired and the line zipped down in front of me. The grappling hook didn't penetrate the thick armor plating of the Vimana's hull, but it didn't need to, I sheathed the sword on the Black Knight's back, and grabbed hold of the line. Pulling back on the controls, I secured the Black Knight's grip and we were yanked off as the Vimana fell out from under me and the *Sparrowhawk* soared off.

52
The Moment

Twisting beneath the *Sparrowhawk*, I saw the Vimana crash into the water. Crunching up like a piece of paper, the flying step-pyramid sent the river cascading over the banks. Smoldering ruins sent smoke and steam into the air, and I pumped my fist in celebration. Then the glint of orange light off the metallic hide of the Dragonship drew my eye to the undulating craft. The large open jaws of the Dragonship tore through another airship, and I realized they were flying toward us.

I was spinning too much to get a clean shot and would never be able to grab my sword while holding onto the line. The Dragonship approached from the side. Baldarich hadn't maneuvered out of the way. He might not have seen them, and I had no way of warning him.

On the back of the Dragonship, I saw the Iron Lotus hooked onto the shoulders, and the Iron Templar secured to the midsection. They were the only hope for the *Sparrowhawk*. The cannons above me fired, but the first shots missed the undulating Dragonship.

Iron Lotus fired her cannons at the port shoulder propeller, and threw one of her large

blades into the other side. The Iron Templar fired at the two propellers on the hips. The rockets in the feet still held the Dragonship aloft, but thick black smoke streamed out of its shoulders and hips.

The Dragonship opened its jaws and maneuvered to get the best shot on the Sparrowhawk. I tried to raise my cannon, but I spun as the wind caught my shield. I felt useless, forced to watch as the Dragonship was about to destroy the *Sparrowhawk* and send us all crashing to the ground. Trailing wisps of shadows and streams of black smoke, the Dragonship positioned itself to strike from underneath the *Sparrowhawk*. The Iron Lotus drew two knives, long, sharp sheet metal, and slammed them into one of the overlapping joints of armor on the dragon's back. She pried open the armor. Shoving her cannons inside the metallic beast, Lianhua fired, then she immediately rolled forward along the back and pierced the Dragonship right behind its head with her knives. She stuck her cannons into the back of the head and fired again. The eyes of the Dragonship exploded out and smoke billowed from the ports. The Dragonship plunged to the ground, as it fell, Lianhua opened her visor and released Kō'ilā. The bird swooped into the head of the plummeting airship and emerged with one of the Hearts, the red urn that we'd found on Malta. The owl spiraled downward in a large circle, following Lianhua as they dropped to the ground.

The Dragonship smashed against the grassy field beside the Washington Monument. The Iron Lotus and the Iron Templar retracted their grappling lines and rolled down the Dragonship's spine. They sprang off and landed on the ground as the Dragonship crumpled into a mangled mess around them.

Kō'ilā swooped down and landed on the Iron Lotus' arm. Mr. Singh yelled something, reaching out from inside his armor. Lianhua collected the heart using the Iron Lotus and raised the urn in the air. As it had in London, time slowed, the wind barely rushed around the Black Knight, and the twisting motion of the cable halted. The Iron Lotus shattered the urn by squeezing its hand and a surge of power exploded out of the Heart in a circle.

There didn't appear to be any damage to the armors, but they didn't move. The Iron Lotus' arm remained in an upright position. The wind resumed rushing around my armor, and I continued to turn around the cable.

Owethu in the Iron Zulu continued to fight the armored Knights of the Golden Circle. I checked on my father and the baron. They worked on the tornado generator, but I couldn't tell what was wrong. As my armor pivoted toward the other two Iron Horsemen, I saw them charging the idle Lianhua and Mr. Singh.

The *Sparrowhawk* continued to descend, lowering Genevieve and I closer to the ground. When close enough to not destroy my armor, I pushed forward on the controls and released the cable. As the Black Knight smashed into the grass, dirt and dust flew up around me, but then a swarm of bugs engulfed me. I rolled forward leaving the swarm behind, but a thought instantly crossed my mind. The Horseman of Famine—Genevieve's mother—her steed had the tuning fork tail. The same one Zerelda used in the Battle of the Thames to summon swarms of bugs. I spun around and saw the black-shrouded Horseman of Famine. Bugs swarmed around the steed like a black cloud.

Genevieve in the Bronze Knight dropped in front of her mother and raised her sword. I knew she had her, a continuation of their duel on the Vimana. I turned toward the two Horsemen: Pestilence, covered in a tattered white cloth, and Death, one covered in a pale-green shroud.

Lianhua and Mr. Singh still didn't move. Smoke no longer poured from the stacks on their backs. The urn's explosion had dampened the flames and cooled their boilers. They couldn't move until the fires were restarted. That would never happen before the Horsemen attacked them. I pressed the pedals all the way forward, forcing as much speed as I could from the Black Knight.

Antiochus on the Horseman of Pestilence, and Lord Marbury on the Horseman of Death, tore up the ground as their steeds' hooves slammed into the ground. I raised my cannon and fired in front of Antiochus. Both Horsemen turned toward me. The Horseman of Pestilence fired the huge bows on the steed's front hips as the Horseman of Death charged.

I raised my shield and one arrow bounced off, but the other pierced through the shield and the chest plate. The point stopped a few inches from my chest. Looking at the large arrow, I breathed a long sigh, but I couldn't rest. Death approached and Pestilence turned back to my friends.

I pushed hard on both pedals and the Black Knight rolled forward. I sped toward Death. At the last moment, as he swung the large scythe, I eased up on the left pedal and the Black Knight veered to the left and raced past Death.

I drew the Black Knight's sword and lowered it like a lance. Charging Pestilence, I heard Death slam its hooves against the ground as it turned around. But, I was focused on Antiochus and the side of Horseman of Pestilence. As the bows were mechanically drawn back by a series of gears, the large black arrows, identical to the one poking through my armor's chest plate, slid out of the steed and loaded into each bow. In a moment he would fire. With the armors unable to move, the arrows would rip right through. I couldn't let that happen.

I leveled my sword and set it in front of me. I pressed both pedals to gain as much speed as I could. I saw the strings pulled back to their furthest point and then release. I slammed into the steed at the same point and my sword ripped through one arrow, tore into the iron plates on the side of the steed, and burst out the other side and cut the bow string. I'd plunged my sword right in front of Antiochus and just behind the steed's two front legs. The Black Knight plowed into the Horseman of Pestilence. Lifting it up, we traveled toward the White House.

I released my sword, and the Horseman tore up the ground as it ground to a halt. Antiochus looked at me and yelled, "You might have tried to kill me but you missed! And my Iron Horseman still moves!"

I still couldn't move. My cannon arm was still pinned by the arrow through my shield and chest plate. My sword remained impaled in Pestilence, and all I had left were two of the coiled spikes, but those weren't really weapons. Behind me, I heard a battle cry followed by, "Death has come for you!" The Horseman of Death, who I'd slipped past and forgotten about, slammed his scythe into the Black Knight's back. The large curved blade ripped through the iron armor and sliced through my shirt nearly cutting my back open.

I rolled forward. I needed a weapon and I needed one fast. What about the electro-lances that the Tinkerer had created? They'd been loaded on the carriage with the tornado machine. I hadn't taken them on the Vimana, because I didn't need them there. Turning, I charged the Washington Monument, knowing my father and the baron were set up near its base.

One good thing, I was drawing the Horsemen away from the Iron Lotus and Iron Templar.

Blood trickled down my back as I glanced back over my shoulder to see both Horsemen charging after me. In the distance, my father, the baron, and Finn stood by the carriage watching the battle. Sticking up out of the back of the carriage, the lances pointed skyward. As I approached, my father pointed at me as he and Finn helped the baron move to the other side of the carriage.

I thought about each action I'd have to take, planning every movement, rehearsing each step in my mind. I'd only have one shot at this.

"First, skid to the back of the carriage." I hit the brakes on the treads and gouged out two ruts in the ground as I stopped. "Don't hit the carriage." I extended the Black Knight's arm and grabbed one electro-lance. "Grab one as a backup." I stuck it into the slot where my sword had gone, and snagged a second lance. "Move quickly to get the Horsemen away from the carriage." I could almost feel the hot fiery demonic breath of the steeds as I spun around. The Horsemen were closing fast. "Prepare the lance." I flipped the switch on the lance, and set it under the Black Knight's arm as if I were jousting in a tournament. "Now, charge!"

I unleashed a battle cry as I rushed toward the Horsemen. I had to choose which one to strike knowing the other would attack me. I focused on Antiochus as his steed was the most damaged.

We collided like boulders smashed together by the hand of God. The electro-lance pierced the chest of the Horseman of Pestilence and sparked. Electricity arced through the metallic steed and the quartz heart blew out from its niche and slammed into the grass, meters away. As Antiochus screamed in rage, I saw my father run over and scoop up the heart for safekeeping. The electro-lance was ripped from my hand as it continued discharging into the Horseman, and within seconds the steed, which had reared up on its hind legs, collapsed as the plates and gears separated and landed in a pile of iron around Antiochus's now limp form. I'd done it! I'd defeated one of the Horsemen.

I wanted to celebrate, but Death was coming for me. Lord Marbury charged from the right, and because my cannon arm was pinned against my chest it only pointed to my right. I pulled the triggers and fired both barrels. The rounds missed but were close enough to force the Horseman of Death to take evasive action, and that gave me the opportunity to grab the other electro-lance off my back. Death pressed forward again, swinging his scythe like a madman. I blocked it with the lance. He raised the scythe to slice me in two, and I had to move. I flipped the switch to prepare the lance, rolled forward, and thrust it up at the rider, not the steed. The scythe slammed down and the Black Knight shuddered as the thick handle thudded on its shoulder. Had the scythe's blade missed me? I didn't have time to wonder as the lance connected with Lord Marbury's chest and sparks exploded all around him, throwing him to the ground.

I suddenly realized the churning and chugging noise

of the Black Knight's engine had fallen silent. I twisted around to look out one of the slits on the back of the helmet and saw the scythe had impaled the engine and boiler tank. I pulled my arms out of the armor's arms and sat there for a moment. The battle wasn't over, but my Black Knight was done.

I heard a high-pitched whine coming closer, and the cannon arm of the Black Knight was ripped off, severed by a cannon blast. I knew more would be coming. With the shield arm gone, and the arrow that had pinned it ripped off, I threw open the chest plate and jumped out, hitting the ground and rolling away. A round slammed into the back of the Black Knight, dead center, leaving a gaping hole the size of my fist.

Where had the shot come from? I turned and saw the Horseman of War charging from the riverbank. I was a dead man if I didn't think fast. Just behind me, stood the Horseman of Death. Marbury's body lay several meters away, but the fire that glowed from deep within the steed still simmered. The tattered green cloth that covered the iron plates fluttered in the breeze as my hand slipped down to the leather pack still slung over my shoulder. My fingers slid over the crystal shaped bulge and the world around me stilled, fading away until all I saw was the steed, the amethyst Heart, and victory.

Alexander the Great looked for the one moment in every battle when the scales of destiny were ready to tip. He would seize that moment and strike, and in doing so, he'd never lost a battle. This was my moment. Two horsemen remained. The army of the Knights of the Golden Circle had destroyed much of the Templar's troops. With this Iron Horseman, I could ensure victory. Not for the Golden Circle, or the Templars, but for

Genevieve and my father and Indihar and Lianhua
and Owethu and Captain Baldarich and everyone who
believed in freedom and rejected slavery. I could win for
me.

Calmly, as if I had all the time in the world, I walked
over and opened the chest of the Horseman of Death.
Inside sat the white urn which should have been in the
Horseman of Pestilence. The amethyst Crusader Heart
was the correct heart for this Iron Horseman. They'd
used the wrong one out of necessity. But holding the
correct crystal in my hand felt like destiny. The traitor
Lord Marbury tried to be Death, but had failed. Hendrix
had tried for years to get me to be an Iron Horseman.
And now, I realized the Templars had feared this
moment. They feared me.

I ripped out the white urn and placed the amethyst
crystal inside. It fit perfectly. Placing my foot on one of
the leg joints I jumped up on the back of the steed and
slipped into the rider's seat, protected by iron plates.

I took the reins of the Horsemen of Death, and
power surged within me. The fire burning inside the steed
exploded out of every joint, but didn't burn me. Dark,
shadowy wisps, whipped off of every edge. The steed
grew, it's power expanding with every moment. The beast
snorted, blowing fire and smoke from its nostrils.

I raised the white urn in the air. The world remained
still, and everything seemed to slow. Except for me. As
the whole world held its breath, I drew my Thumper with
my other hand.

"Hendrix!" My voice resonated like rolling thunder.
"Your power is now my power!" I tossed the white urn
in the air and pushed the trigger on my Thumper. A
concussive blast shattered the urn. A blast of energy

ripped outward like a tsunami and knocked over the Black Knight.

Time sped up to normal. I pulled down my goggles, reloaded the Thumper and slipped it back into the holster. I reached down and my fingers wrapped around the scythe's handle, now sticking straight up out of the back of the Black Knight. Wrenching it free, I held it high and set my sights on the Horseman of War.

"**H**endrix!" I charged the Horseman of War with my scythe raised. The steed's pounding hooves tore up the ground below me, and the hypnotic galloping rhythm, the surging, fiery breath, and the crackle of the fires burning within blocked out all other noise from the battlefield. My vision was clear and focused on the cloaked rider thundering toward me.

General Hendrix swung his large two-handed sword, and I struck with my scythe. Sparks flew like lightning as we clashed. Charging past each other, we spun around to make another run.

"You've joined me boy! Just as I always said you would." Hendrix cackled like the madman he was. He pushed back his hood, pulled out his Stetson, and set it firmly on his brow. "Choose another rider to replace that Roman autocrat, and together we can claim our empire!"

"I'm not here to destroy the world, I'm here to destroy you.!" I screamed so loud my throat felt dry and scratchy.

We clashed again and again, rounding on each other as his sword and my scythe glowed like burning embers against the

eerie orange sky.

Without warning, Hendrix broke away and charged the troops guarding the White House. He attacked the Templar and Freemason troops and the US Army troops behind them. I pressed my attack, forcing him to defend himself against me instead of going after the troops.

Then I saw the Duke's royal seal. I looked up and saw Richard, his father, Sinclair, Eustache, and several other Templar elites on the balcony of the White House. They stood with several men in suits, including Mr. Revere. They hadn't wanted me to fight, and yet now, I was set to save them from Hendrix. I smiled and raised my scythe in salute, but they all recoiled. The Duke had real fear in his eyes.

Hendrix leapt in front of me. The Horseman's hooves shook the ground causing the men on the balcony to grab the railing. He swung his sword, and I defended myself. He locked his blade with mine.

"Strike them, Alexander." Hendrix's steed stood next to mine. I kept the pressure on my blade, and he locked eyes with me. "In one moment, you could end the Templar, remold the Order as you see fit."

I knew he was right. With a swipe of my scythe I could seize the knighthood I'd dreamed about. I could end Genevieve's nightmare. I could destroy the Duke and she could marry me instead of that sniveling Richard. Those around Sinclair had refused my request to become a Templar. They said I wasn't ready, despite saving the Order and the world twice before. They looked down on me because I wasn't noble born. I was descended from Templars, but that hadn't been good enough for them. My ancestor had dedicated his life to hiding the Hearts, but that hadn't mattered. I was an American, and yet

Mr. Revere and the other Freemasons hadn't trusted me. They wanted to fight in the armors, to seize the glory for themselves.

They all disgusted me. None of them were worthy.

I could end the Templar and the Knights of the Golden Circle right now. End the centuries of fighting. They'd been secretly manipulating the world like a game of chess, and now, I had the power to end this destructive cycle, once and for all. To set the world right and remake it as it should be.

I'd traveled further than my namesake, the greatest general in the history of the world. He was my age when he began to conquer the world. I could finish what he started. Hendrix was right.

"Alexander, join me," the Horseman of War said. "Become Alexander the Glorious!"

"I don't need your permission." I pressed on his blade, trying to force my scythe through his defense. "And I don't need you!"

I pulled the reins and my steed reared and pawed the air with its mighty hooves, then slammed down on the Horseman of War, pushing Hendrix back and away from the White House. I turned and from this vantage point finally saw the whole battlefield. Owethu was being overrun by the horde of Armors from the Vimana. I saw a swarm of bugs at the other end of the Mall. A column of flame erupted from its center and I knew Genevieve and Rodin must be within. As I watched, the swarm dissipated, the Horseman of Famine collapsed, and I knew Genevieve had defeated her mother. Looking toward Mr. Singh, I saw him working on the back of the Iron Lotus. He was restarting the boilers on the armors. They would soon be back in the fight.

The Bronze Knight turned toward me; her visor looked like it had been torn off. She saw me, and horror flashed across her face. Genevieve charged toward me and screamed, "Alexander, no!" Her voice pierced through to my soul and the ache in my heart felt like it weighed more than the earth itself.

I sensed danger, but my stomach didn't ache, more like a voice in the back of my mind telling me that Hendrix was about to strike. The future flashed through my mind. I would defeat Hendrix, using my anger to overpower his. Then the four Iron Armors—my friends—would face me, but they wouldn't be able to kill me. I would defeat them one by one. Then I'd face the Duke and force him to flee back to England. Once I had all four Hearts, no one, not the Knights of the Golden Circle or the Knights Templar would ever be able to stop me.

I watched the Bronze Knight crossing the field. If I continued, I'd have to fight her. She reached out toward me and I heard her voice once again call my name.

Then Hendrix struck. I leapt to the side and his blade missed me. I was back next to the fallen Black Knight. I maneuvered around my shattered armor and charged the Horseman of War. Our blades clashed again and again. Then a clang rang out, piercing the thunderous noise of battle. My scythe had cut through his sword, and sank into the neck of his steed.

"I am the Horseman of War! I am the future Emperor. You're just the boy who was supposed to help me!" Hendrix threw his broken sword toward my steed's head, barely missing me. "Victory will be mine!"

"Never!"

Hendrix fired the grappling hook from his sleeve.

The three-clawed hand wrapped around my shoulder and side, then yanked me from the steed as the line retracted. He held me above him as I struggled to get free. "Decide right now, Alexander. Will you stand with me or against me? What is it that you want? I will grant you any wish. All you need do is say the words."

Held aloft, the sun, not the orange fiery sky but the warm rays of that distant ball of fire hit my face. In the distance, Genevieve called my name. She sounded far away, but my sole focus remained on the bright orb above me. My mind drifted to Diogenes. He'd been given the same offer by Alexander the Great. Anything he wished for, and yet all he'd asked was for Alexander to step aside so the philosopher could feel the warmth of the sun again.

Genevieve called my name again.

The Amethyst Heart had offered me a vision of victory, but to get it I'd have to fight my friends. Hendrix offered me anything I wanted, but maybe I was a bit too cynical to think he could offer me what I really wanted. The sun offered me warmth and light and the hope of a brighter tomorrow. Diogenes was a brilliant man. To ask for nothing more than the sun, he'd outwitted Alexander the Great.

"The sun. I want the sun." I said smiling through the pain as the grappling claw cut into my skin.

"What?" Hendrix looked confused. Then his confusion turned to rage. "You fool!" He squeezed his claw and I winced in pain. "Now you die."

"Not yet!" With my hands free, I drew my Thumpers from their holsters and pressed them into the eyes of Hendrix's steed. Pushing both triggers, the head exploded and the concussive blast rippled like a giant wave down through the mechanics of the neck and body. A huge fireball engulfed us, Hendrix was knocked out of the steed, and he released me as we both crashed into the dirt.

I wanted to remain on the ground, not caring what happened next, but then I saw the Jade Crusader Heart glowing below the smoldering husk of the iron steed. My blast had knocked it out of the horse, and if I could get it away from Hendrix, he'd lose his power. I tried to find solid ground to stand, but slipped. My fingers clawed at the churned-up dirt, but I had no traction. Then Hendrix's three-clawed grappled arm snagged the heart and pulled it to him.

Rage burned within his good eye, as the other sparked ever brighter. "I will not lose this day. I will not lose to a brat!" Hendrix spat the words like he was shooting a pistol at me.

I struggled to stand, but I had to face Hendrix like a knight. Gone was my armor. I no longer had the power of the Crusader Heart at my control. All I had for a weapon was the Bowie Knife Captain Baldarich had given me two years ago. I drew the blade from its sheath and took a fighting stance before General Hendrix.

He laughed at me, but I didn't care. Pain racked my body. My back bled, my side and head swam in throbbing pain. But I would not falter before this evil.

Hendrix yanked open the bronze plate over his heart. I saw blood, charred skin, and bone. He shoved the Jade Heart inside and closed the plate. Hendrix fell forward and roared out in agony. He pounded the ground with his real fist, and as he did, the shadowy wisps enveloped him. The metal parts of his body grew and became more menacing, the bronze color blackened, and spikes emerged. His mechanical arm morphed, the gun barrel came out and merged with the blade; sparking with electricity as it formed into a lightning canon. He stood up and raised his arms.

"Power! True power now flows through my veins!"

This wasn't good. He had a lightning cannon for an arm. He looked twice as big as he had, and more menacing than when I'd first met him. All I had was a knife and enough pain that I just wanted to lay down.

Hendrix eyed me. I was too injured to move quickly. Then a bronze flash zipped past me. Rodin, doubling in size, growing from a large bird to a long, thin dog as he flew past, slammed into Hendrix, knocking him over and blasting him with a torrent of fire. But Hendrix just swatted Rodin away.

I dove behind the Horsemen of Death for cover. Hendrix aimed his arm at the steed and a bolt of dark blue light surrounded by arcing electricity shot forth. The Horseman of Death exploded and I was blown back. I sprang up and ran for the still-smoldering Black Knight. Hendrix turned and aimed his arm, but I heard an explosion rip through the air and he was knocked off his feet. Smoke billowed up around him, but I heard laughing from within the cloud and saw him stand.

"I am invincible!" He threw back his head and released a wicked cackle.

"Not good," I turned toward where the shot had come from and saw the Bronze Knight taking aim again.

Hendrix moved as another round flew in and struck the ground near his feet. The shot came from a different direction, and I spun around and saw the Iron Zulu racing this way. Hendrix roared in anger and fired, but Owethu dodged the blast.

Genevieve rolled up beside me. "Grab on and I'll get you out of here."

"I can't leave. We have to stop him."

"I'm out of shells." She looked down at me, pleading as she reached out. "Let's go."

"No! Distract him. I have a plan."

She shook her head, but then her mouth curved up in the smile that made my heart sing. "Will do." The Bronze Knight rolled over to the Iron Lotus and Iron Templar. The three of them charged from one side as Owethu in the Iron Zulu roared in from the opposite direction.

I looked around. Desperate. My mind racing. I *wished* I had a plan, but the plain truth was, I didn't. But I couldn't fail Genevieve. Fail everyone. Then on the back of the Black Knight, I saw the two coil-spikes and remembered the Tinker's barrier and the electromagnetism that pulled the comet down two years ago. I quickly yanked both free and slipped behind the Horsemen of Death as he taunted the Iron Armors.

Lianhua chucked the last of her knives, which Hendrix knocked away like they were annoying flies. Mr. Singh and Genevieve charged with their swords, but Hendrix dodged them easily. Owethu smacked him with his shield, but Hendrix took the hit and remained standing. As my friends circled around him, I flipped the switch to reverse the polarity of the magnet on one of the spikes. Then I ran up and impaled it in Hendrix's back, plunging it in as far as I could.

Hendrix roared in anger, but not pain. As he turned to attack me, I turned the magnet on. He swung his lightning cannon arm around, and I ducked underneath and jumped away. Hendrix tried to push the long spike out of him, but Genevieve rolled by and hit it with her sword, bending the long bar sticking out of his chest so it couldn't be extracted.

Hendrix roared in anger, spinning around until he saw me. He stopped and aimed his lightning cannon. "You fool!" he growled and moved toward me.

I stood my ground and turned on the second coil spike. I held the electromagnet in front of me. With the coil-spike in his back pushing, and the one I held in front pulling, I only had to wait. Staring down the barrel of his lightning cannon, though I only had a moment before he killed me. The bronze plates covering his body, even in their demonic state, weren't magnetic, but the metal permeating the shattered Jade Heart was. The coil-spike tugged on that metal, and I stepped back and pulled on the electromagnet.

Now pain racked Hendrix face. He groaned and waivered as he tried to shoot me. I took another step back and pulled the coil-spike toward me. One more step, and this time I yanked the coil-spike as if it were fishing rod and I had a whopper on the line. Hendrix' face contorted in pain and he clutched at his chest, but the Jade Heart ripped out from behind the bronze plate. Hendrix eyes rolled back into his head and he collapsed in the dirt. I dove for the Jade Heart and flopped onto the ground, clutching it to me just in case he reached for it.

But he didn't. Hendrix was finished.

My friends rolled up in their armors and Genevieve jumped out of the Bronze Knight. I struggled to my feet as she ran up and threw her arms around me. "Are you all right?" She clutched me close, "I can't believe you became a Horseman. What were you thinking?"

I held her tight and buried my face in her hair,

ashamed at how close I'd come to betraying everything I—*we*—believed in. "It doesn't matter. It's over now."

54
The President

I walked over and picked up the Jade Heart, I collected the Amethyst Heart from the Iron Horseman, which collapsed after I did. My father gave me the Quartz Heart he'd retrieved from Antiochus' fallen steed, and Genevieve handed me the Hematite Heart from her mother's Horseman.

I looked at Genevieve, "Is your mother. . . ?"

"She couldn't kill me. She surrendered and handed over her heart."

"I'm so glad." I said softly. My chest heaved in labored breaths and my mind spun. "Thank you, my friends, I have a plan for these. I know how to finish what Armand started."

"You're not going to use them to conquer the world," Genevieve nudged me but I winced and she put her hands on my shoulder. "I'm sorry."

Owethu nodded, "I trust you more than these supposedly wise old men."

Lianhua nodded her head as well. "Agreed."

Mr. Singh looked around. "We'll make certain they never leave your side. You know the Templar will want to store them."

"Exactly, and then they'll just be used again. I just need the *Sparrowhawk's* help. That's all."

Mr. Singh chuckled. "You're a Sky Raider, part of the crew. The captain will listen to you."

"Good." I put all the hearts into my bag and rested against Genevieve.

Finn brought the baron over. I was loaded into the steam-carriage and taken to the White House. The President's personal physician sutured my back and sides and poked and prodded at the rest of me until he was satisfied. I don't remember much of it. My mind remained dazed from the battle and the fading power of the Amethyst Crusader Heart.

My friends never left my side, even when ordered to do so.

Sinclair and Eustache came into the room. I sat in a chair leaning forward. My torn and bloody shirt lay folded on a table. I was just in my dirty, ripped pants and muddy boots. Eustache nodded and said, "Excellent work, *mon'ami*."

The Grand Master of the Knights Templar stood staring at me. I locked eyes with him, unafraid of anything he might say.

"Alexander, you are quite possibly the craziest and bravest man I know." Sinclair had a slight smile as he leaned on his cane.

I chuckled remembering all the times Captain Baldarich had said the exact same thing. "I knew what had to be done, and I still do." I twisted and pulled on the sutures causing pain to ripple through me. "Your people were glory hounds. The Templar and Golden Circle are interested in fighting each other, not saving the world."

"I'd like to think we'd do both."

I looked at Genevieve, then back at Sinclair. "You didn't even know about Marbury. The Duke seeks the same glory as Hendrix. The baron cared only for his wife and daughter. Everyone had another reason, except you and I."

He nodded. "Can't argue with that." He sat down beside me. "What is your plan, lad."

"I'm going to get rid of the hearts once and for all. Finish what Armand started."

"You scared us there for a moment. Several people on that balcony thought you were about to strike us down."

I looked him in the eye. "The scary thing is, I almost did." I ran my fingers through my hair, brushing it off my forehead and thinking about how it felt to be that close to giving in to all that power. "But I couldn't fight my friends. Unlike Marbury, I couldn't betray them. And when Hendrix asked what I wanted, I told him the sun."

My father and the baron stood in the doorway. "Like Diogenes," the baron said with a proud smile.

I nodded.

Genevieve rose and checked on her father, but the baron pushed away her hand as she felt his forehead. "I'm fine," he said and bent to kiss the top of her head.

My father pointed down the hallway.

"The President would like to speak with you."

"I'd prefer to be dressed." I looked down at my muddy boots, but before anyone could answer, the baron and my father stepped in the room and made way for a stout man in a fine suit to enter. Flanked by several other men, I started to stand, but he motioned for me to remain seated. He had a bushy gray mustache just like Captain Baldarich's. He walked up to me and extended a hand.

"Alexander, I'm President Arthur. I believe I owe you and your friends here a great debt of gratitude."

I shook his hand and said, "Thank you sir. It's an honor to meet you. I just wish I was a bit more presentable."

"Nonsense, you just saved our great nation, we should be draping you in the American flag." He turned to one of the men with him. "See that this young man gets a suit."

"Thank you, sir."

"You prevented a great and lasting tragedy here today. Don't worry about what happens here next. I've got the army deployed, and they're cleaning up the mess out there." He turned to my father. "Your son has done a great service for our country, and from what these gentlemen have been telling me, the world as well. We need more civil servants like him."

My father beamed with pride as I struggled to my feet. "I was glad to be of service," I said.

The President turned to the baron and then to his physician. "I have a speech to give trying to explain what happened here today. You all take care of this young man. He's a hero in my book."

The President and his men departed, and the Duke walked in with Richard right on his heels. "I don't know if I'd call you a hero after that little stunt on the Iron Horseman, but . . ." He strained and twisted his neck. "I do have to say, you won the day. The Queen will be happy to hear that this is finally over. I'll be taking the Hearts back to London now."

I reached down to the bag that sat between my feet. "Over my dead body, and not even then." I stared at the Duke. "I will finish the journey my ancestor started. And you, Your Grace will have to explain to everyone how you missed that Lord Marbury was a mole for the Golden Circle. He was one of your dearest friends."

The Duke's eyes narrowed. Genevieve walked over and linked her arm in mine. Rodin flew up beside her and sat on the floor, his head at her side. Mr. Singh and Owethu stepped in front of me, and Kō'ilā ruffled her feathers and screeched on Lianhua's arm, startling the Duke and Richard both.

"The Hearts will be leaving this world for good, and their power will never be used again."

"Can you be certain?" Sinclair leaned on his cane.

"I'll say no more, but yes, I will finish what Armand started."

"Unacceptable." The Duke sneered.

I pointed at the door. "That will be all, your Grace," I said dismissing him from the room.

He smacked his swagger stick against his palm and said, "Come Richard, we are leaving."

They rushed out of the room and a murmur broke out among everyone. Genevieve looked at me and smiled. I nodded and Sinclair said, "That's a sting he'll not soon get over. Nice, lad, but if I may ask what are your plans, for the future?"

"I think I need to go back to Eton and finish my education." My father lit up, and pushed his glasses back on his nose. "After that, I'm not certain, but I have a feeling the *Sparrowhawk* will play a part."

Everyone in the room laughed. Sinclair put his hand on my shoulder, and leaned closer. "Finish your studies, and if you still want to be a Templar, there will be a place in the Order for you. Hell, I'll knight you myself if need be."

"Thank you," I said, and he gave my shoulder one last squeeze and walked out of the room leaning heavily on his cane, and mumbling something about helping the president with his speech.

Eustache stepped up, "If he doesn't, I will." A large smile crossed his face. "It has been a great honor to stand with you. May fortune follow in your footsteps."

"Thank you, Lord de Moley."

"No, no, my friends only use Eustache." He patted my shoulder and followed the Grand Master out the door.

A man walked in with a tailor and said, "We've come to measure, Alexander."

I waved my hand, "Over here, but I just need a shirt."

"I think you'd look good in a proper suit," Genevieve said as she bit her lip.

I locked eyes with her, and said, "If you say so. But I want room for my Thumpers."

55
The Queen

Three days later, I knelt before a chest in the front room of the *Sparrowhawk's* gun deck. I opened the lid and set my sketchbook inside, then stood and walked out of the room. I stopped before the two large holes in the floor. We were flying over the Atlantic Ocean on our way back to England. Captain Baldarich hadn't had a chance to repair the decking yet, which provided me a view of the white tipped water below.

I stood in my new suit, looking more like a man, than when I'd snuck on this aero-dirigible three years ago.

Genevieve, with Rodin walking at her side, slipped her arm around mine. Rodin rubbed against our legs and leaned against us. "How is your back?"

"Good. Feeling stronger."

"What's on your mind?"

I pointed toward the water. "We're almost there."

She cocked her head and said, "England remains days away."

I reached up and flipped open the copper tube. "Captain, can you gather everyone together and

come down to the gun deck?"

Baldarich's voice bellowed back, "We'll be right down."

A few minutes later, my father, the baron, the baroness, Owethu, Lianhua, Mr. Singh, the captain, and the rest of the crew came down and stood on the gun deck.

"Thank you all for joining me here. I want you to bear witness to what I'm about to do, but I also want to have all of you around me at this moment. I wouldn't be here without each of you. From the whole *Sparrowhawk* crew to Hunter, and Ignatius who taught me how to fight. To you, Captain Baldarich, who taught me everything I needed to know about being an honorable warrior. To Baron Kensington, who taught me about seeking what is most important in life, even the baroness who taught me . . . about choices. And Lianhua, Owethu, and Mr. Singh who have stood by me and fought at my side. Rodin, you taught me about loyalty and mysticism. My father, who taught me . . . a lot, but mostly how to live life fully, be engaged, to value learning. And of course, Genevieve." I turned to her and took her hand. "I wanted you all to be here at the end, the end of a journey that started eons ago. The Malta Hearts have been destroyed. Only the Crusader Hearts remain. Unfortunately, they cannot be destroyed. My ancestor tried to bury them, tried to hide them from the world. But still they were found, and it was only with your help that I was able to gather them together. Now, together, we will commit them to the depths of the ocean. We will bury them beneath the waves, and the ocean's depth will ensure no man can ever gather them together again."

I took my leather bag off my shoulder. I hadn't let

them out of my sight since Washington D.C. Opening the flap, I pulled them out one by one and dropped them through the hole. They fell thousands of feet and crashed into the ocean. I pulled the Amethyst heart last. It whispered in my ear one last time, promising me power, but it had no hold over me. I looked at all my friends around me. A power greater than anything this crystal could offer flowed through me. I released the Amethyst Heart, and it plunged down into the watery depths.

"Brilliant," Genevieve said, and kissed my cheek.

* * *

A week later, I stood in Buckingham Palace pacing back and forth. This was it. I would finally be meeting Her Royal Highness, The Queen of England. For some reason, I was more nervous than meeting the President. Maybe then it was because of was the haze I'd been in or the fact that I was injured, but that was all past now.

Genevieve stepped into the room, and I stopped pacing. She was stunning. Dressed in a blue gown, her hair was bound up in curls with a few elegant tendrils trailing down her neck. She reached out a gloved hand and took my hand in hers. My racing heart slowed.

"Don't be nervous. She can be intimidating, I know, but she is very nice."

I tried to smile, but from Genevieve's chuckle, I knew I must look strange. "Am I that obvious? I don't know why I'm so nervous. I think it's because I've wanted to meet her since I met your father, and I don't want to make a bad impression."

She squeezed my hand. "Be yourself and you'll be fine. After all, you're the one who just saved the world."

"Well, if you put it that way." I couldn't help but laugh. "Seriously. Thank you for being here with me."

"Of course, I wouldn't be anywhere else."

There was a soft knock, and I turned toward the door. A man in a fancy suit who looked like he stepped out of a Renaissance novel beckoned us forward. We stepped out into a grand hall, a large set of double doors at the end led to the room where Queen Victoria would be waiting. The man said I was next and that I'd be summoned when Her Majesty was ready.

My heart raced again, and sweat formed on brow. Genevieve reached up and pushed the hair off my forehead. This was worse than facing Hendrix. Genevieve pulled me off to a smaller hallway by a set of stairs and offered me her handkerchief.

"You're cute when you're nervous."

I looked down at her. I knew what she was doing. Taking my mind off the queen and it worked. I pulled her in and wrapped my arms around her corseted waist. "Will you still want to be with me when we're not running around the world on adventures?"

"Are you trying to say you're going to become a boring student?"

"Maybe for a little while. . ."

"I don't know," she said with a coy smile, and a turn of her cheek. "I am a woman of adventure."

"I know and I love that about you." She whipped her head around and looked at me. My heart thundered in my chest, but I wasn't nervous anymore. "I love you, Genevieve Kensington."

She lit up and said, "I love you too, Alexander Armitage."

I pulled her in and kissed her like I never wanted to

stop.

"I do so enjoy seeing young people in love." The voice of an old woman, made both of us stiffen and pull apart, Genevieve patting her hair as I smoothed my suit jacket. We turned and there she was, Queen Victoria. Dressed in black, her face behind a veil, she was descending the stairs followed by a group of attendants. "You must be the young man who saved the world."

I bowed and found my voice. "Yes, Your Highness, Alexander Armitage."

Genevieve's cheeks flushed with bright red hues, she curtsied and said, "Forgive me, Your Highness, I—"

Queen Victoria raised her hand, and Genevieve clamped her mouth shut. "Always a pleasure to see you, my dear." She stopped right in front of us. She looked at me and then at Genevieve. She smiled and said, "Won't my nephew be disappointed." She chuckled and shook her head. "Little twit deserves it."

Genevieve and I turned to each other trying not to laugh out loud. She reached out and took my hand, but we didn't say a word.

The End

The Iron Chronicles

Book I: Iron Horsemen
In a steam-powered Victorian world where secret societies determine the future like a game of chess, and pirates prowl a cloudy sky, Alexander, Genevieve, her little bronze dragon, and the crew of the Sparrowhawk must save London from the four Iron Horsemen.

Book: II Iron Zulu
When a series of murders are blamed on the visiting Zulu delegation, Alexander becomes embroiled in the baron's daughter's dark past as they are captured and taken by armored Milli-train to the hidden city of the sky pirates.

Behind The Iron Door: Steampunk Short Stories
Step through and discover fives tales of fantasy.
The Baroness, the story that inspired the Iron Chronicles
Touch the Stars, inspired by Jules Verne
Doomed Flight of the Majestic, a dieselpunk adventure
A Clockwork Heart, an award-winning story about love
The Legend of Spring-Heeled Jack, a steampunk horror story inspired by the legend.
Plus, a bonus flash fiction, *Man at the Crossroads*

Sparrowhawk
Illustration by Jennifer Stolzer

Milli-train
Illustration by Jennifer Stolzer

Dragonship
Illustration by Jennifer Stolzer

Alexander's Sketchbook

Vimana
Illustration by Jennifer Stolzer

Horseman of War

Illustration by Jennifer Stolzer

Illustrations by Jennifer Stolzer
Visit www.JenniferStolzer.com for more art

Acknowledgements

I want to thank my friends. It is friends who make life worth the journey.

I have to start with my writing friends – they keep me going. Thank you to all the writers I've worked with on the board of St. Louis Writers Guild. Including the current board members: David, Teresa, Peter, Jen, Lauren, and Jamie. Many thanks to the friends I've made through SLWG, some of whom I've known for almost a decade! As always I have to thank my critique partners, I credit all the good words to them – Cole Gibsen, T.W. Fendley, and Jennifer Lynn. Their books are amazing and I cannot recommend them enough.

Thank you as well to the writers I've gotten to know across this country, either from organizations like the Society of Children's Book Writers and Illustrators, from the writer's conferences I've attended, or places like Comic Con, and Archon. It's an amazing community to be a part of. Thanks Joshua, Ryan, Reggie, and Zachary. I have to give a special shout out to the members of the Write Pack, we have too much fun, and you keep me motivated … David, Kathleen, Jen, Melanie, Meredith, Fedora, Matt, Leigh, Jamie, Peter, Teresa, Amy, Michael, George…

To my lifelong friends, like Derrick and Lee, Olivia, and Ashley, thanks for putting up with me, reading for me, and standing by me. It is greatly appreciated if not always stated.

For my furry friends, a special thanks. To my cat and editing partner SamSam, and all the rest of my animal friends, including those at the zoo, you keep me sane when I need it.

Thank you to the artists! Jennifer Stolzer, who creates the illustrations for the Sparrowhawk and the rest of Alexander's Sketchbook. Bringing my visions to life. Georgie Retzer whose work appears on the cover and Kristina Blank Makansi for a third amazing cover.

I love all bookstores, but I have to mention my friends at Main Street Books in historic St. Charles! Thank you, Emily (who named the owl after a real bird named Coal she used to know) and her amazing staff! Drop by and you might find secretly signed copies of my books. Support your bookstores and the libraries; they are the gateways to infinite adventure.

Many thanks to those of you who have read The Iron Chronicles… you are all my friends for coming with me on this amazing journey!

Lastly, all my appreciation to my best friend, my wife Amber.

2022

Not much to add, thank you to all the people above. Life has morphed, and there are a few new people on the board of SLWG, Jessica, Kathy, LaShaunda, and John. However, life is always moving forward, and you simply add to the number of people who affect your life.

Brad R. Cook
BRADRCOOK.COM

About the Author

Brad R. Cook
Author & Historian

I see things that never were and say, "Why not?"

Brad R. Cook is the author of historical fantasy, and award-winning short stories. He began as a playwright, dipped into the corporate writing world, and served as co-publisher and acquisitions editor for Blank Slate Press. He currently serves as Historian of St. Louis Writers Guild after three and half years as President. He learned to fence at thirteen, and never set down his sword, but prefers to curl up with a centuries' old classic.

www.bradrcook.com
@bradrcook on Twitter, Instagram, and tumblr.

www.ingramcontent.com/pod-product-compliance
Lightning Source LLC
Chambersburg PA
CBHW031242310726
48971CB00004B/1129